Wedding

Cressy was born in South-East London surrounded by books and with a cat named after Lawrence of Arabia. She studied English at the University of East Anglia and now lives in Norwich with her husband David. When she isn't writing, Cressy spends her spare time reading, returning to London, or exploring the beautiful Norfolk coastline.

If you'd like to find out more about Cressy, visit her social media channels and website. She'd love to hear from you!

 /CressidaMcLaughlinAuthor
 @CressMcLaughlin
 @cressmclaughlin
cressidamclaughlin.com

Also by Cressida McLaughlin

Primrose Terrace series
Wellies & Westies
Sunshine & Spaniels
Raincoats & Retrievers
Tinsel & Terriers

A Christmas Tail – The Complete Primrose Terrace Story

The Once in a Blue Moon Guesthouse series
Open For Business
Fully Booked
Do Not Disturb
Wish You Were Here

The Canal Boat Café series
All Aboard
Casting Off
Cabin Fever
Land Ahoy!

The Canal Boat Café Christmas – Port Out
The Canal Boat Café Christmas – Starboard Home

The House of Birds and Butterflies series
The Dawn Chorus
The Lovebirds
Twilight Song
Birds of a Feather

The Cornish Cream Tea Bus
Don't Go Baking My Heart
The Éclair Affair
Scones Away!
The Icing on the Cake

The Cornish Cream Tea Summer
All You Knead is Love
Beauty and the Yeast
My Tart Will Go On!
Muffin Compares to You

The Cornish Cream Tea Christmas
Rudolph the Red Velvet Cupcake
Let the Jingle Buns Ring
I'm Dreaming of a Hot Chocolate
All I Want for Christmas is Cake!

The Cornish Cream Tea Wedding

Cressida McLaughlin

FSC
MIX
Paper from
responsible sources
FSC· C007454

This book is produced from independently certified FSC™ paper
to ensure responsible forest management.

For more information visit: www.harpercollins.co.uk/green

HarperCollins*Publishers*

HarperCollins*Publishers* Ltd
The News Building
1 London Bridge Street
London SE1 9GF

www.harpercollins.co.uk

HarperCollins*Publishers*
1st Floor, Watermarque Building, Ringsend Road
Dublin 4, Ireland

This paperback original 2021
1

First published in Great Britain as four separate
eBooks in 2021 by HarperCollins*Publishers*

ISBN: 978-0-00-840878-7

This novel is entirely a work of fiction.
The names, characters and incidents portrayed in it are
the work of the author's imagination. Any resemblance to
actual persons, living or dead, events or localities is
entirely coincidental.

Typeset in Birka by Palimpsest Book Production Ltd, Falkirk, Stirlingshire

Printed and bound in the UK by CPI Group (UK) Ltd, Croydon CR0 4YY

To David, and the perfect day that was
the 10th May 2008

Part One

Down on One Knead

Chapter One

Elowen Moon drove her Mini Countryman, racing green with white go-faster stripes, secretly called Florence after the cat she'd met in the garage where she'd bought it, along Porthgolow's seafront. It was a blustery March day, one of the first that felt as if the year was stepping out of winter and into spring, the sporadic cloud cover performing a shadow and light pantomime over the land. The Cornish village was busy, as if, at the first sign of a warmer sun, everyone had decided to make the most of it.

The quaint seafront was bright and welcoming, hanging baskets outside the Pop-In shop the pastel blues, pinks and whites of hyacinths and snowdrops, the Seven Stars pub sign swinging gently in the wind. The beach, the elegant curve of a typical Cornish cove, was busy with dog-walkers, couples and families, most in lighter spring jackets, hats and scarves discarded.

And then there was the Cornish Cream Tea Bus, the vintage Routemaster, taking pride of place on the edge of the sand. It glowed pillar-box red, and Ellie, having had many a cream tea on it, could almost smell the warm, buttery scones as she drove past. It was closed for the time being, something Ellie was directly responsible for. She drove up the hill, turning neatly between the brick posts that signified the entrance of Crystal Waters.

The spa hotel, with its glass front and honeyed stone, looked starring-role beautiful. Still, Ellie thought the building would look impressive in the thickest sea fog; its warm, glowing interior would be welcoming on the darkest night. She felt a rush of nerves, stronger than any she'd had since getting a phone call from a bright, quick-talking woman called Delilah Forest who wanted to hire her to plan her cousin's wedding.

When Ellie had found out the wedding was between Charlie Quilter, owner of the Cornish Cream Tea Bus, and Daniel Harper, proprietor of Crystal Waters, she thought all her dreams were being realized. It would be the boost she needed for her business, New Moon Weddings, which, despite Ellie's dedication never wavering, hadn't been succeeding as well as she'd wanted – no, *needed* – it to. This wedding would be high-profile; it could get her back on track. Ever since she'd agreed to meet with the couple, however, the doubts had been creeping in. But doubts wouldn't turn a profit, so she was just going to have to suck it up.

She ran her hand over the steering wheel and wondered, as she often did, if the original Florence was still alive; stalking through the garage with her tortoiseshell tail flicking; prowling over bonnets, overseeing her kingdom. Ellie had had her car almost ten years and felt that, as long as the cat was still thriving, then her Mini would, too.

She took her worn leather handbag from the passenger seat, heavy with her chunky planning notebook, and stepped out into the sea breeze. At the hotel's glass entrance, complete with lollipop bay trees, she stopped, smoothed her rose-gold hair over her shoulders and her hands down her blouse and skirt to free them of wrinkles, and walked into the foyer.

She had been here for dinner a few times, and the space, with its stone floor and natural hues, a glass wall on the far side proudly displaying their unbeatable coastline views, always brought a sense of calm along with it. And right now, calm was exactly what she needed.

She approached the reception desk, where a young woman with a spray of freckles on her nose smiled at her. 'Good morning, welcome to Crystal Waters. How can I help?'

'I'm Ellie Moon,' she said, 'from New Moon Weddings. I've got an appointment with Mr Harper and Ms Quilter.'

The woman's face brightened further. 'You're the wedding planner! Oh, isn't it exciting? I can't wait to see them get married. The whole village is in a spin about it. I don't think a day goes by when someone – other than Charlie or Daniel, I mean – mentions it!'

Ellie smiled, trying not to feel the added weight of a whole village's expectations on her shoulders. 'I'm glad it's not just the bride and groom looking forward to it,' she said. 'Weddings are guaranteed to bring happiness. Not always in the planning, of course – the pressure of getting it right can cause all kinds of frustrations – but that's what I'm here for. To take that stress away.'

'It must be the best job,' the woman said indulgently. Her name-tag read *Chloe*. 'So much fun.'

'It can be,' Ellie agreed. 'But working here must be similar. People checking in for holidays or to visit the spa. It's a beautiful hotel.'

'It's Daniel's pride and joy,' Chloe said. 'Other than Charlie, of course. And then there's Jasper, too. And I suppose Marmite, now he and Charlie are . . .' Her words trailed off and she gave a sheepish grin. 'Sorry. I'll get them for you. Would you like to take a seat?' She gestured to a cosy-looking sofa over by the glass wall. Ellie thanked Chloe and went to sit down.

She took out her notebook and turned to the next blank page, then wrote Charlie and Daniel's names at the top, along with the date. The space was quiet around her, most of the guests already finished breakfast and off sightseeing or exploring the village, and Chloe's voice was low as she spoke to somebody on the telephone. Ellie took a couple of subtle, deep breaths. She was planning the wedding of two of the most successful businesspeople in this part of Cornwall. Talk about added scrutiny.

'Elowen, is it?' She looked up from her doodle of a spiralling trail of vines to find a couple smiling down at her. She stood, smoothed down her pale blue skirt and held out her hand.

'Ellie,' she said. 'Please call me Ellie.' She shook Charlie's hand first. She was tall, with dyed red hair and an instant warmth in her twinkling eyes, and Ellie recognized her from visits to the Cornish Cream Tea Bus. Then she shook Daniel's hand, the confidence almost radiating off him, his features classically handsome. No wonder they were so successful: their combination of friendliness and self-assurance was dynamite. 'It's lovely to meet you,' she said.

'You too,' Charlie replied.

'Thank you for coming,' Daniel added, and then gestured to a door behind him. 'We thought we'd sit outside, as it's a nice day. What can I get you to drink?'

'A cappuccino, please,' Ellie said.

'Coming right up.' Daniel went to speak to Chloe, while Charlie led the way into gardens that were gently manicured; winding pathways through shrubs and herbs that looked tended but not aggressively pruned. The rosemary and thyme were flourishing, the leaves of the purple sage especially colourful, and Ellie wondered how they were able to stay so healthy in such an exposed environment. She wondered if Daniel would let her speak to his gardening team, but that was off-topic and she needed to stay focused.

'Are you close to here?' Charlie asked, turning back to her.

'I'm in St Eval now, so not too far, but I have a cottage on the outskirts of Porthgolow. My sister and I love coming to your bus for a cream tea.'

'Oh, really? That's lovely to hear.' Charlie gestured to a round table that was part of the outside dining area, one level up from the covered, outdoor swimming pool. 'I'm sorry I don't recognize you.'

Ellie took a seat. 'There's no reason why you should. You must serve hundreds of customers every week.'

'Yes.' Charlie gave an indulgent smile. 'Gertie's firmly established in Porthgolow now, and with the food markets and tours I run, she's getting to be well known all over Cornwall, too.'

'Gertie?'

'That's the name of the bus; my uncle Hal named her when he was touring her round the Cotswolds.'

'Ah,' Ellie said, nodding. 'I've been to the food market. It's hard to stay away when I know there are so many delicious things just waiting to be sampled. Sometimes I fancy I can smell all the tantalizing smells from my cottage. I mean, I could. I used to.' She gave a brisk smile.

'Whereabouts is it?' Charlie took the seat opposite her.

'A bit further along the road, beyond Crumbling Cliff. It's on the outskirts, pretty much on its own. Cornflower Cottage.'

'What a beautiful name,' Charlie said, tucking her hair behind her ear as the breeze turned mischievous.

'I think so,' Ellie agreed. 'I renamed it when I moved in a couple of years ago. There's a persistent crop of wild cornflowers which bloom in the summer months right outside the front door, and that was part of the reason I fell in love with it to begin with.' Even thinking about her quaint, white-walled cottage, so traditional it was almost a cliché, made her ache with pride and longing.

'But you're not living there right now?' Charlie pressed. Ellie could see she was genuinely interested, and thought that was part of the secret to her success; she wouldn't give any of her customers only cursory attention.

'I'm renting it out for the time being,' Ellie explained. 'I've moved in with my sister, Rose, in St Eval. It's different of course, but we get along, so it's going to be fun.' At least, she hoped it would be. 'But I know Porthgolow well,' she went on, trying to get the meeting back on track and away from the fact that she was struggling so much she had had to rent out her beloved home to raise some extra income. 'So I think I can do you and Daniel proud.'

'I'm sure you can,' said Daniel, putting a tray with coffees and a plate of mini sausage rolls on the table. 'I've had a look at your website, and the photos and testimonials are impressive.' He sat next to Charlie, and Ellie saw him take her hand under the table. 'Please, help yourself.'

'Your sausage rolls?' she asked Charlie, and the other woman nodded. Ellie took one and nibbled a corner, the buttery, flaky pastry and well-seasoned sausage meat like a culinary hug. 'Wow.'

Charlie seemed pleased, but not surprised. 'It's taken a while to perfect the recipe, but I think I'm there now.'

Ellie nodded, her nerves returning. This couple oozed competency, and Ellie was about to ask the one question that had been on her mind ever since she'd found out the details from Delilah Forest, but Charlie was ahead of her.

'To be honest, Ellie,' she said, 'we probably could have done this ourselves. The wedding, I mean.'

Ellie nodded but didn't reply, waiting for her to go on.

'But this year, well – the last couple, really – have been so busy. The bus is growing in popularity, and Daniel's making some changes to the hotel, too. There's so much to think through and we just thought—'

'Charlie's cousin thought,' Daniel interjected, 'that we should have it taken off our hands. I think we need to admit that we're both worn out.'

'We *could* do it,' Charlie said, and Daniel looked at her.

'It's OK to admit you're human, Charlie,' he said softly, his dark gaze meeting hers. Affection radiated between them, stronger than the sun on an August day, and Ellie swallowed. Her nerves felt slightly different all of a sudden; slightly less panic-ridden.

'And do *you* ever do that?' Charlie asked Daniel with a cheeky smile.

'I'm going to now, for the sake of our wedding – the sake of us. Let Ellie take charge of it all. Pass the responsibility over to a professional.'

'That's very kind of you,' Ellie said. 'But shall we have a chat about what you'd like, first? We need to see if we're a good fit, if I can do everything you're hoping for. But,' she added when Daniel raised an eyebrow, 'I would *love* to plan the perfect wedding for you. Something uniquely tailored to the two of you, that you will remember for ever – for all the right reasons. Something that speaks to both your hearts, and kicks off the next stage of your lives, like a football pro scoring the most outlandish penalty in a World Cup final; never to be forgotten by anyone who witnessed it.'

Charlie and Daniel both laughed.

'Great speech,' Daniel said.

Ellie returned his smile. 'It wasn't my usual one, but I feel inspired. By both of you; by your attitude. The fact that you could do this yourselves, could squeeze it in alongside everything else, but want to give it the attention it deserves.' It was true, too. She had started off with her usual spiel, but she suddenly felt more fired-up than she had done in a long time. She had made a resolution at the start of this year to make New Moon Weddings not just good but great, but her confidence had been dealt a blow by the need to rent out Cornflower Cottage to a total stranger; temporarily give up her beautiful home and the garden that was her sanctuary. She was meeting her new tenant after this, but she wouldn't think about that now, because here was a loving couple who were putting their trust in her to plan the best day of their lives, and it might well be the event she needed to turn her fortunes around.

'Do you want to tell me your wedding hopes and dreams, and we can start thinking about how to make them a reality?' She took another sausage roll from the plate, and Charlie's smile widened.

'Sounds good,' she said, with a laugh. 'Where to start, though?'

'Ready to admit you're human, Charlie?' Daniel asked.

'For now,' she said. 'But on my wedding day, I want to be a princess.' She said it with a gleam in her eye, as if such a statement couldn't be said entirely seriously.

Daniel laughed, and Ellie quietly marvelled at how they switched easily from calm professionals to doe-eyed lovers. 'Wedding-day princesses I can definitely do,' she said, opening her notebook and tucking a few stray bits of paper inside. 'Now, tell me exactly what type of princess you want to be.'

When Ellie got back to Florence, the wind was whipping the sea into a frenzy, and she could hear the waves breaking against the rocks far below. Charlie and Daniel had been enthusiastic and receptive to her ideas and so, despite the suggestion that they could have been organizing the whole thing themselves, she was encouraged.

She unlocked her car and climbed in, found a radio station that was playing hits from the Noughties – was it possible to listen to 'Rule the World' by Take That and not want to sing along? – and started the engine. She patted the dashboard when Florence gave a little groan before puttering fully into life, then drove out of the car park.

The moment she left the confines of Crystal Waters, her confidence began to fizzle and die. That meeting wasn't ever going to be the most difficult item on today's to-do list; this next bit was – officially handing Cornflower Cottage over to the new tenant.

Even the sunshine making the sea sparkle, and the huge bunch of scarlet roses in the window of the B&B on Porthgolow's seafront couldn't stop her feeling apprehensive, and the roses reminded her that, along with her house, she would be giving up her garden.

The generous patio outside the back door where she loved to sit and watch the sun come up with a cup of coffee; the formal flower beds with a swathe of daffodils, crocuses and snowdrops in spring; lupins, delphiniums and gladioli as the summer months came in, the few trees – silver birch and hawthorn, a flourishing laburnum – that provided architectural detail all year round. It was a much larger garden than the small cottage deserved, but Ellie had been overjoyed with the amount of land it came with. Two years later, there was still a large, wild area beyond the flower beds that she hadn't had a chance to tame, and which she referred to, somewhat optimistically, as 'the meadow'. But last summer it *had* been rich with the yellow and white of yarrow and oxeye daisies. She'd been planning to tackle it this spring, but now that would have to wait.

She'd almost put 'must be good at gardening' on the list of rental requirements, along with a commitment from whoever moved in to keep an eye on all her flower beds, but Rose had told her that was far too specific and nobody would be interested. Now she wished she'd listened to herself instead of her sister.

She drove up the hill on the other side of the village, automatically slowing to a near crawl as she reached Crumbling Cliff. It was much safer now, with sturdy barriers at the edge, but she was always careful. Florence made a wheezing noise as if she couldn't cope with the incline – or maybe she was sensing Ellie's reluctance. Ellie put her foot down and kept going.

Cornflower Cottage was outside the built-up area of the village, ostensibly in the middle of the countryside, though it had a Porthgolow postcode. It was halfway up the hill, the sea visible from the front-facing windows, beyond a patchwork of rolling fields. A care home called Seascape House was the first and only other obvious building on her road – aptly called Wilderness Lane – though a couple of muddy tracks led off it, which she assumed went to farm buildings nestled deep in the rural landscape. Whenever she passed the slightly weatherworn sign, with *Seascape House* written in sky blue on a cream background, her spirits lifted, because it meant she was nearly home. Now, that pleasure would go to someone else.

As she neared the turning to Wilderness Lane, she slowed the car and then felt the unevenness of the road beneath her as the Mini bump-bump-bumped, and then let out a sound equivalent to what Ellie imagined a dying monster would emit.

'Shit,' she muttered, as she came to an unplanned halt. After fruitlessly trying the engine a few times, she leaned over to the passenger door, pressed the button that released the bonnet catch, and got out. This road wasn't quite as narrow as Wilderness Lane, but her blocking it would still make life difficult for other drivers. At the moment, though, Ellie didn't have a choice.

She yanked open the bonnet, glanced hopelessly at her cream silk shirt, and leaned over to get a better look. Parts of the engine were steaming. Unfortunately, she wasn't sure which parts those were, whether they were meant to do it and, if not, what that signified. She prided herself on being an excellent trouble-shooter – it was one of the most important skills of a wedding planner – but the innards of cars were not her strong point.

She heard another vehicle approaching and stepped towards the hedge. The silver Golf looked twice as old as Florence, and she waited for it to pass so she could go back to her puzzling, but instead the car slowed and pulled in behind her Mini. Ellie felt simultaneously grateful and irritated. She had no idea how to fix her car, but she was conscious of what she must look like, standing there in her smart blouse and skirt with a bemused expression on her face. She turned back to the engine, trying to arrange her expression into something less clueless.

'Are you OK there?' The voice was low and soft, and Ellie looked up and saw a man who, on first glance, was as scruffy as his car. His hair was the colour of Cadbury's Dairy Milk, but it looked like either he'd let a toddler give him a haircut, or he'd recently been tasered: it stuck up in all directions, the strands rebelling against any kind of cohesion. He was about her age, she thought, with a jaw she could only call chiselled, and as he got closer, she noticed crinkles around eyes that were the colour of sea glass when the light shone through it. She hadn't realized eyes could be that green. He was wearing a grey shirt and dark jeans, straddling the border between smart and casual.

The man cleared his throat as he walked round the car. 'Sorry,' he said. 'You can't have heard me.'

'I . . . what?'

'Are you OK?' he repeated. 'You look shell-shocked. Can I take a look for you?' He gestured at the engine. It was still steaming which, while good on frothy cappuccinos, was less desirable when it came to cars. The man was glancing between her and the open bonnet, and his expression turned wary. 'Did you crash?' His voice was sharper, concerned, and Ellie noticed that he had a Cornish accent, his deep tone making it seem stronger than her own. It was warm and lyrical, comforting.

'No,' she said, finally. 'No, I didn't crash. She just gave out . . . one little moan and that was it.'

'She?' The man came to stand alongside her, but kept a bit of distance between them. Despite that, Ellie could smell his aftershave: lime and nutmeg, sharp and spicy all at once.

'My car,' Ellie explained. 'She's called Florence.' She had no idea why she'd admitted that.

The man nodded and tapped the bumper. 'She's a beauty. It looks like she's overheated.'

'Overheated?' Ellie repeated. 'It's only March – the sun's not that hot. And I've only been driving for ten minutes. Half an hour, earlier in the day. I'm not pushing her to the limit, or anything.'

'It doesn't always matter how much you've been driving her, or how hot the weather is,' he said. 'Usually, it's something wrong with the cooling system. A leak, maybe.' He rolled up his sleeves, treating Ellie to a view of tanned forearms. He leaned towards the engine without another word, and she stood back against the hedge, giving him space.

'You seem quite comfortable under the bonnet,' she commented, glancing at her watch. She hated being late for things. She'd left herself plenty of time between her meeting at Crystal Waters and welcoming her new tenant to Cornflower Cottage, but she had no idea how long this was going to take, and she still felt on edge.

He gave a low chuckle. 'You could say that.' She waited for him to elaborate but he didn't, so Ellie turned away, examining the hedgerow behind her instead of the man leaning over her car.

'You've got a leak in the cooling system,' he said, standing up straight and turning to face her. He didn't seem remotely smug that he'd diagnosed her problem before even looking at the engine.

'Is that bad?' she asked.

He tipped his head on one side. 'It'll keep overheating until it's fixed, but it's a fairly simple job.'

'And can I drive it to the garage? Or do I need a tow?' She smoothed a hand over her hair. This day was not getting better. 'I need to be somewhere in twenty minutes, and I really don't want to be late.'

'She'll cool down in about half an hour,' the man said, giving Florence another pat, as if the car was a much-loved Labrador. 'But I could mend her for you, if you like? I'm moving into my new place today, and it's not far from here. As long as there's room to park her up once I can get her going again, I'll have her sorted for you in no time.'

'You'd do that?' Ellie asked, his words flashing warning bells in her mind.

The man nodded and wiped his – now grease-covered – hands down his jeans. 'Sure.'

'And you're moving today? To a new house?' She supposed it wasn't that much of a coincidence, considering he would need to go down this road to get to Cornflower Cottage.

'A rented place,' he said. 'I've fallen on my feet, really. It's ideal. Though I've not actually seen it in person yet, which I suppose isn't the usual way of doing things.'

Ellie nodded, wondering how often he rubbed his dirty hands on his clothes. She thought of the biscuit-coloured sofas in the front room of Cornflower Cottage; the light, neutral furnishings that always inspired a sense of calm, except when they got marks on them.

'You didn't have time, and were happy to take it on spec,' she said, remembering his words from their email exchange. 'And I had your references, I knew that you were a mechanic with regular work, and was prepared to accept on those terms.' She exhaled. 'So you're Jago Carne, then.' *This* was her new tenant: Twinkly green eyes, the epitome of laid-back scruffiness.

For the first time since he'd approached her car, he looked alarmed, his brows shooting up towards his hairline. He was cartoon-character startled, and Ellie would have laughed if this whole situation, her entire morning, hadn't been so emotionally stressful.

'I'm Elowen Moon,' she said, holding out her hand. 'Ellie. I own Cornflower Cottage.'

His brows lowered and creased, and then he grinned at her, and she got the full effect of the smile lines round his eyes. 'You're my landlady,' he said. 'Great.' He clasped her hand with his own. It was large and warm and strong and, despite his attempt to clear the engine grease off, not entirely clean.

Ellie nodded in the affirmative, but she wasn't sure 'great' was the word she would have chosen.

Chapter Two

Jago's Golf didn't smell of lime and nutmeg, it smelt of mustiness and engine oil, and the back seat was full of boxes with things spilling out of them haphazardly. Even if the boot was equally crammed, it didn't seem like a lot for one person moving their life somewhere new. Perhaps he had a van coming later.

Ellie slid into the passenger seat and, while she couldn't fault his kindness – he'd helped her instantly, even before he'd known who she was – she felt on the back foot. Poor Florence was going to stay on the side of the road and then, Jago said, he'd walk down and get her when her engine had cooled, bring her up to the cottage and set her right again before Ellie left.

'This is going to be a bit of a change from Plymouth,' he said, gesturing to the hedges, the fields beyond, then starting the Golf and checking the road before edging out past Ellie's Mini. 'But Cornflower Cottage was exactly what I was after.'

'Are you moving back for good?' She assumed it was "back" because of his accent, and she hoped it came across as small talk rather than an interrogation. Obviously, it was up to her how long she rented her cottage out for, and as long as she gave him a generous notice period it shouldn't be a problem. But, she reminded herself, she needed to do this. She couldn't think of the cottage as hers any more.

He shrugged, his eyes on the road as he indicated left and turned onto Wilderness Lane, beginning the incline that started gently and then got steeper. 'I'll see how it goes.'

Ellie smiled. She wished she could have that laissez-faire attitude sometimes. With her, *see how it goes* included a ten-point plan at the very least. 'Which garage will you be working at?'

'I've got a part-time slot at a garage close to the airport,' he said. 'And I'm hoping to pick up some other odd jobs around the place – DIY, decorating, that sort of thing. I still have a few contacts in the area, so I'm sure I'll get work.' He glanced at the sign to Seascape House as they passed, his brow furrowing. 'What do you do – other than being a landlady?' His eyes flicked to her shirt and skirt. The fabrics were silky smooth, the skirt a bright blue. She took a lot of care with her appearance; she enjoyed wearing clothes – and having hair – that made her stand out. The rose gold had worked better than she'd expected; her hairdresser nodding with appreciation and quiet pride when it was done.

'I'm a wedding planner,' Ellie explained. 'And landlady makes me sound like I'm old and frumpy, with those special stockings that help your circulation, and rollers in my hair.

Definitely a floral housecoat. Baking my own bread or clotting my own cream.'

'You're talking about Nora Batty from *Last of the Summer Wine*,' Jago said. 'I can picture her perfectly from your description.'

Ellie snorted. That was *exactly* who she was imagining.

'Firstly,' Jago went on, 'she was never a landlady. And secondly, you're as far from Nora B as it's possible to be. You could launch a whole new category of landlady. Is this your only property?'

'Right here,' she said, gesturing, and Jago made the turn. 'It's my only property. It's . . .' She paused. She was supposed to be being professional, but there was something about this man that encouraged complete honesty. It was both reassuring and irritating. 'I've moved in with my sister for a bit.'

'Oh?' Jago brought the car to a halt on the gravel driveway. 'So this is your place. Bloody hell.'

'Bloody hell?' Ellie echoed. She was gazing at the front garden, its rose bushes perfectly pruned and ready to burst into colour in only a few weeks' time; the low privet hedge; the stone birdbath next to the iron chandelier sporting bird feeders for each food-type – peanuts, mixed seed and fat balls. The cottage stood behind, with its white walls and rustic, tiled roof, a bench nestled below the living-room window.

'It's like one of those jigsaw puzzles,' Jago said as he got out. 'I saw the photos on your ad, but they never do it proper justice, do they?' He put his hands on his hips and gave a loud huff.

Ellie got out of the car. She had the sense that he wasn't

entirely happy with this revelation. 'I usually leave the photographs up to experts,' she said. 'But I took the ones for the advert.' She didn't know why she was making excuses.

Jago turned to her with a wide grin. 'You know how I said I'd fallen on my feet? It was an understatement. This is a country-cottage show home.'

Ellie flushed with pride. It did look good. In the two years she'd lived there, she'd turned it into a *real* home. 'Shall I show you around?'

'Sure,' he said. 'And there was something in your ad about a cat?'

'Oh, Lord Montague – yes! I only moved out of here two days ago, and I've been coming back to feed him—'

'*Two days* ago?'

'Just in time for you to move in,' she said hurriedly. 'My sister, Rose, is allergic to cats, so he couldn't come with me. Lord Montague, uhm, Monty, is very affectionate. He doesn't want just to be fed twice a day; he wants love, too.'

Jago nodded distractedly. 'Sounds like a sensible cat. But I feel like I'm stepping into your shadow – I thought this was just a rental place.'

Ellie gave him what she hoped was a professional smile; she needed to rein it in. 'This is going to work out for both of us, Mr Carne. Please don't worry. I wouldn't be renting out Cornflower Cottage if I didn't want to. And for my first foray into the world of non-Nora Batty landladying, I believe I've fallen on my feet too, having you as my tenant.'

His shoulders dropped. 'Please call me Jago,' he said.

'Jago. Let me show you where everything is and then I can help bring your things in.'

'You don't need to . . .' he started, but she shook her head.

'You're going to fix my car for free. It's really the least I can do.'

Ellie showed Jago around the neat two-bedroom cottage, its rooms small but perfectly formed, with beams and slightly uneven floors, and all the other period features she loved so much. Jago's enthusiasm didn't dampen, and she was pleased that he appreciated it, because it meant that he would look after it.

At the weekend, she and Rose had cleared out all of Ellie's personal things, including photos and the few ornaments that had dotted the surfaces, and then they'd put on new pillows and duvet, new linen in a smart white-and-navy print. It wasn't a cottage that could be devoid of character, but there was no longer any of Ellie's character left. It was as simple and as appealing as a holiday home. Her heart was still here, but it didn't show.

Even so, it felt strange showing Jago where she had, until recently, slept every night. 'This is the bedroom,' she said, gesturing at the king-sized bed, as if clarification was needed. The early afternoon sun spilled in through the window, bathing the room in a warm glow.

'Great.' Jago rubbed his hand across the back of his neck, and Ellie felt a twist of guilt. She shouldn't have told him she'd moved out so recently; it was too weird. She should have found a landlady class to go to – if such a thing existed. Or hired a company to manage the whole process.

She was trying to think of something to lighten the mood, when Lord Montague came out from under the bed, stretching his back legs out one by one, as if he was shaking off uncomfortable slippers. He had been such a dainty kitten, but now, at two years old, he was a huge hulking tabby, his fiercely green eyes not that dissimilar to Jago's. And he definitely lived up to the 'Lord' moniker. But right now Ellie could have kissed him for breaking the weird tension that had settled around them like dust.

'Monty!' she said, as the cat hopped onto the bed and strolled over, lifting his head for a stroke. Ellie obliged, and his purr resonated around the bedroom. 'Monty, this is Jago.'

As if understanding, Monty padded over the duvet to where Jago stood, but instead of raising his head, he lifted his front paws and clawed into Jago's shirt.

'No, Monty!' Ellie shouted, but before she could take him away, Jago lifted the cat under the front legs and, with a slight groan, hauled him against his chest. Monty's purring got louder as he butted his head against Jago's chin.

Her new tenant was laid-back about giant cats too, apparently. 'You can keep him out of the bedroom, of course,' she said. 'I just haven't shut any of the doors over the last couple of days, because I felt bad about leaving him.'

'And you think he'll be happy if I try and ban him now? He's big enough to terrorize me.'

Ellie shrugged. 'He might kick up a fuss. But with a bit of coaxing—'

'It's fine. Lord Montague and I are going to rub along well together.' He gave her one of his crinkly-eyed grins, and Ellie relaxed. 'Your car's probably cooled down by now.'

'Don't you want to bring in your things?'

'I can do that later,' he said. 'Please don't feel like you have to help. But maybe a cup of tea when I get back?'

'Done,' Ellie said. 'It really is very kind of you.'

'If I hadn't come along and helped, I would have been waiting here for you and wouldn't have been able to get into my new place.' He put Monty gently on the floor. The cat gave a miaow of protest, then led the way down the stairs.

'Right,' Jago said at the front door. 'See you in a few.'

Ellie nodded, and then said, 'Keys!' She rootled in her handbag and gave him her car keys. Then she added another set, this time of house keys. It felt like an afterthought, and she wondered if she should have handed them over in some sort of grand ceremony.

But Jago was already strolling through the neat front garden towards the driveway. Ellie watched him, disconcerted by how easily he'd taken everything in his stride. Strangely, the fact that he was so relaxed made her mildly suspicious, as if it was a front for something. Or else she had unwittingly rented her cottage to the friendliest person in the world. Maybe she *should* ask him to tend to the garden – she couldn't imagine him saying no, now.

She went into the kitchen, where she and Rose had stocked the fridge with a few essentials for his arrival: butter and cheese, milk and eggs, some vegetables and salad, along with slices of cold ham and chicken. She'd bought a loaf from the baker's just yesterday, knowing it would stay fresh in the bread bin. She was also pleased that she'd put a few beers in the fridge door, as Jago seemed like a beer man. Except that was an assumption, and she tried her best not to go in for those. She'd gleaned the barest details about him from their email exchange – though not enough to realize who he was when he'd rescued her on the side of the road – but now, having met him, she had a million other questions.

Why had he moved back from Plymouth now, and why had he moved away in the first place? Who were these contacts he spoke of, and why did he feel he'd fallen on his feet with Ellie's cottage which, she was happy to admit, was not masculine at all? And what was an attractive man like him, early forties and with such a warm manner, doing moving in, solo, to this remote part of Cornwall? Did he have a girlfriend he was moving back for? Kids nearby? A wife tucked away in Porthgolow?

Ellie got mugs out of the cupboard – the smart Denby she'd bought instead of her *World's Best Gardener* and *Wedding Planners Need More Coffee* mugs, which had gone with her to Rose's – and pottered about. The kitchen was at the back of the house, looking over the garden, the meadow's long grass framing the formal plants and flowers in front. She sighed. She could have done a lot worse, and she'd known he was a mechanic when she agreed his tenancy. She should have considered the possibility of oil and grease stains long before they sealed the deal, but it was too late now.

'It's for the best, Monty,' she said, retrieving a packet of treats from the cat food cupboard. 'You'll look after each other, won't you?'

Monty put his head on one side and pawed at her leg. She stepped backwards, saving her bare skin. 'Uh-uh. No claws.'

The cat chirruped, which didn't fit with his arrogant bruiser attitude.

'Go on, then,' she said, and crouched to give him a treat.

He put his paw on her wrist while he nibbled it off her palm. She was going to miss Monty almost as much as she would miss her garden.

When Jago puttered back into the driveway in Florence, Ellie was pulling up weeds from around her lupins. This was the year they would fully come into their own, their first flowers appearing in May. There were purples and whites, a couple of mixed plants and a lemon yellow variety that always made her want a gin and tonic. She loved lupins because their leaves were almost as beautiful as the statuesque flowers; it was only in the colder months when they seemed diminished. She knew she shouldn't be out here, that this wasn't her garden right now, but it was hard not to think about what would happen to everything she'd so lovingly nurtured if they were to suffer months, perhaps years, of inattention.

'Hello?' Jago called from the hallway, and Ellie hurried back to the kitchen, flicking on the kettle as she went.

'Florence started, then?' she asked.

'Yup, no problem.' He strolled into the kitchen, his eyes dancing over the light, airy room; the cream cupboard doors and pine worktop. 'I bet people always gravitate to this room during parties,' he said.

Ellie tucked a strand of hair behind her ear. 'I'm quite proud of how it's turned out,' she replied, not wanting to admit that she hadn't ever had a party here. 'It gets the best light in the mornings, though. Now, onto the most important question. How do you take your tea?'

'Strong and milky, but no sugar.'

'Because you're sweet enough?' The words were out before

she had a chance to vet them. She resisted the urge to cover her mouth with her hand.

Jago chuckled. 'Not close,' he said, and there was something in the tone of his voice that Ellie felt low in her stomach. 'Thanks, though. I'd better get changed; can't wear my "meet the landlady" get-up for this next part.'

Ellie glanced at his grey shirt and jeans. 'No, of course. Do you have a special "fix the landlady's car" get-up as well?'

'I'm a mechanic,' he said. 'That's basically what I live in.' He grinned and sauntered out again, whistling.

Ellie shook her head. '*Because you're sweet enough?*' she muttered to herself. 'Seriously?' Even Monty was looking at her disdainfully. Or maybe he was just angling for another treat.

By the time she took the tea out to the driveway, Jago had Florence's bonnet open and a toolbox at his feet. He was wearing a black T-shirt and jeans that made his last pair look almost black-tie appropriate. They were ripped at one knee, and not in a fashionable way.

Ellie put his mug on the bench outside the front door. She and Rose had painted it white one afternoon soon after she'd moved in, with the radio playing and Prosecco flowing. The paintwork was patchy, there were several visible splodges where it had dried unevenly, but because of that the memories remained strong: the two sisters celebrating Ellie's newly found single status, free from a marriage that had gone stale long before she'd chosen to do something about it.

'Tea for you,' she said, and Jago looked up, his forearms already streaked with grime.

'Thanks.' He turned his attention back to the engine.

Ellie didn't know what to do with herself. She couldn't leave until her car was fixed. She shouldn't go and tend to her – *the* – garden again.

'What weddings have you got on right now?' Jago called, and Ellie sat on the bench, relieved.

'I've got three at the moment, and I had my first meeting with one couple this morning. They're in Porthgolow, so it's very local, and it should be lots of fun.'

'Is it a nice village?'

'The best. Quaint and seaside-y, with a vintage bus that sells cakes and a pub that's upped its food game over the last few months. You didn't live round here before, then?'

'No, I was in Falmouth. I grew up there, then ended up travelling for most of my twenties, and settled in Plymouth after that.'

'So you've not been back for a while?'

'Not to live. I've been back to see my folks, but after being in some pretty remote places, I was craving somewhere busier, which is why I settled on Plymouth. More work, more interest.' He selected a new tool, then returned to the car.

Ellie tried to look everywhere other than his jean-clad backside and the flash of those forearms. 'Where did you travel?'

'All over, really. Australia and New Zealand, where it was easy to pick up work. Asia. I spent some time in Africa; helped to build a school in Ghana.'

'Wow,' Ellie said. 'That's . . . it sounds amazing. Challenging, but so worthwhile.' He didn't reply, and she wondered if he'd heard. She raised her voice. 'So why the

29

change now? Why are you back here, if you don't mind me asking?'

'Oh, family stuff,' he said, his voice slightly muffled. 'What about you? You must get on with your sister if you're living with her?'

'We do get on well,' Ellie admitted, aware that he'd side-stepped her question. 'She's a couple of years older than me, and definitely bossier, but she has a big heart. She's a district nurse, which is a much more worthy occupation than wedding planner.'

Jago turned, leaning on the car and crossing his legs at the ankles. 'People want to get married, and they want to do it properly. For a lot of them, it's the most important day of their lives. You shouldn't belittle what you do. If everyone was a nurse, the economy would collapse.'

Ellie laughed. 'True. It just doesn't seem to measure up to helping people heal.'

'What about fixing cars? Where would that go on your scale?'

'Up there with nurse,' she said. 'I wouldn't be able to get anywhere without Florence. Especially not in Cornwall.'

'I'd better get back to it then,' he said. Instead, he picked up his tea and took a sip.

Ellie was happy to sit and chat to him while he worked. It was enforced, because until her car was better, she was stuck. But the view from Cornflower Cottage – over rolling hills and down to the sea – was one she could gaze at for hours, and had done, frequently. Today, the sun and wind were competing to produce a not-unpleasant afternoon, and her new tenant was easy company.

She couldn't remember the last time she'd met anyone

this horizontal. He had moved house today – one of the most stressful life-changes you can make – and instead of settling in, unpacking and then sitting down with a beer, or going to catch up with old friends, he was fixing her car. And he seemed completely fine with it. He was the polar opposite to Ellie, who had started to flap the moment her carefully scheduled day showed the first signs of unravelling. *Except*, a little voice in her head said, *for right now*. But this was different, she told it, because she was trapped.

She felt a glimmer of disappointment when Jago stood and stretched his arms up to the sky, then gave her his wide, warm smile and said, 'All done. The leak is fixed. Florence should be as good as new.'

'Thank you *so* much.'

'No problem. Just call me if you have any more issues, but she shouldn't overheat any more. I've also topped up the oil and the washer bottle, as they were both running low.'

'You didn't have to.'

He laughed. 'I sort of did.'

She nodded. 'I'll just go and wash these up.'

'No need,' Jago said. 'I'll do that.'

'Of course.' He'd said it easily, but she felt slightly chided. She had to let him get used to his new territory. 'Thank you again, Jago. And the same goes for the house – if you have any issues or questions, please give me a call. I'm close by.'

'Thanks, I'll do that.' He rubbed his forearm over his hair, flattening some of the strands. He had a sheen of sweat on his brow.

'See you soon, then,' Ellie said as she got into her newly mended Mini. She reversed expertly down the driveway and, just before she turned the car around, gave him one final glance. He was smiling at her. With a quick wave, she drove away, leaving Jago Carne, Lord Montague and her treasured cottage behind. She prayed that they would get along well together.

'It was so weird,' Ellie said, as she laid the table in the dining room of Rose's end-of-terrace house. 'It would almost have been better if he *wasn't* so friendly. Or maybe I shouldn't have been,' she went on, wafting an empty wine glass around before Rose glared at her through the hatch between the kitchen and the dining room, and she put it on a coaster. 'It felt like I was showing him *my* house and then leaving him to squat in it.'

'That is basically what you're doing though,' Rose observed. 'Except that he's paying you for the privilege.' Ellie turned to look at her sister. She was slightly taller, slightly broader, her hair kept to its natural dark brown and always tied back neatly on a work day, even once she'd changed out of her tunic. 'You've not let go of Cornflower Cottage.'

'I don't want to let go of it,' Ellie said. 'This is temporary.'

'Of course it is,' Rose said soothingly, 'but you don't want to give him that impression, do you? How would you feel if you were moving to a new place, excited about your fresh start, and the owner was breathing down your neck, constantly pointing out that you were on borrowed time?' She lifted a saucepan off the hob and drained spaghetti in a colander.

'I should have put in a clause about the garden,' Ellie said. 'It's going to go to rack and ruin without any attention.'

'He's a mechanic, good with his hands, practical. He might be a better gardener than you.'

Ellie gave her a look, which Rose parried with a sweet smile. 'I didn't mention it,' Ellie said.

'You could,' Rose replied. 'Give him a few weeks to get settled in, then go back with a bottle of wine and bring it up in conversation, see how he feels about it. And what I'm *not* talking about,' she added, ladling the pasta into bowls, 'is turning up on his doorstep with a list of all the things he needs to do and when he needs to have done them by. He's not house-sitting, even if he is cat-sitting.'

Ellie tipped her head up to the ceiling. 'I should never have rented it out,' she groaned. 'I didn't think it through properly.'

'All you needed to think about was how to get your business and your life back on track, and this was the best way. You and me, baby. We'll change the world together.' She said the last words in a fake American accent and Ellie couldn't help grinning. 'Anyway, tell me about this new wedding you've picked up. Is it really the woman who owns the Cornish Cream Tea Bus? God, I love her scones. Are you going to have them as part of the wedding breakfast?'

'I doubt it,' Ellie said, coming into the kitchen to fill a jug with water. 'Her cousin brought me in so that Charlie and Daniel wouldn't organize the whole thing themselves, so I can't schedule in Cornish Cream Tea Bus cream teas, and if I do cream teas that *haven't* come from there, then either they won't be as good, which would be disappointing, or they will, which would be embarrassing.'

'She must have other chefs,' Rose scoffed, ladling a delicious-smelling bolognese sauce on top of the pasta.

'I don't think so,' Ellie said. 'I get the impression that she's a one-woman whirlwind.'

'Just like you, then,' Rose replied.

Ellie smiled. Her sister might be bossy and intrusive and sometimes altogether too much, but she could always be counted on to back Ellie up, and boost her ego when she needed it. That character trait forgave all the other ones a thousand times over.

'Oh,' Rose said, as Ellie walked past her with the jug and a couple of tumblers, 'don't think that this is the end of the conversation about your new tenant. I didn't miss the way you talked about him, and I need to know everything. Has he got a chapter in the Elowen Moon young, fun and single chronicles? He sounds like ideal spring-fling material.'

'He's my tenant,' Ellie said stiffly, 'so no way. I am not mixing pleasure with landladying. I've already made it far more awkward than it needs to be.'

'You're not denying you think he's cute, then?'

Ellie rolled her eyes. 'I'm forty years old, and he's about the same. Cute is not a word I should be using, unless it's about babies or puppies.'

'All this protesting,' Rose said gleefully. 'We are *definitely* continuing this over dinner.'

Ellie looked at the bowls of spaghetti bolognese, which her sister was sprinkling with parmesan. Even a conversation she really didn't want would be worth it for Rose's home-cooked food. She waited until she was in the dining room before letting out a sigh. She loved her sister, and she was beyond grateful that she could stay with her, but she hoped that this new wedding, and renting out her cottage, would help her set a new course for success. She needed to get on top of her life.

Chapter Three

Ellie had not expected a committee for her next discussion about Charlie and Daniel's wedding, but it seemed that was what she was getting. There were two other women at the table in the cosy snug of Crystal Waters; the lounge-cum-bar area that was so plush Ellie wanted to adopt it as her new office. Charlie stood up when she walked in, and Ellie could see that she was nervous, her usually calm demeanour replaced with bristling agitation.

'Ellie, hi,' she said, keeping her voice quiet as she approached. 'I am so sorry about this. I mentioned to Lila that you were coming, and she said she wanted to meet you. And,' she glanced at the table, 'I was already meeting Hannah for a coffee this morning and she's . . . decided to stay on and say hello.'

'Hannah?' Ellie looked at the young blonde woman.

'She's a good friend, and the chef at the Seven Stars.'

'Really? I love the food there. It's got even more delicious over the last few months.'

'Well, that's all down to Hannah. But if you'd rather I shooed them away, please just say. It might be a struggle with Lila, but she'll understand eventually.'

'Honestly it's fine,' Ellie said. 'I've dealt with bigger wedding committees than this in my time.'

'Oh, it's not—' Charlie started, but Ellie put a hand on her arm.

'It's *fine*, Charlie. If they're important to you, and *you* don't mind them hearing about the wedding plans, then I don't either. I once had both the bride and groom's entire families insist on coming to every meeting. There were over thirty of them, and every suggestion took about three hours to discuss. In the end they went with a church wedding and a reception at a boutique hotel: I don't think there were more than ten guests who hadn't been involved from the very start.'

'That sounds very stressful,' Charlie said. She wasn't laughing like Ellie had hoped she would.

'Please don't worry about anything,' Ellie went on, leading her back to the table. There was a plate of pastries in the middle of it, and her stomach growled in anticipation. Since living with Rose, she'd developed a greater appreciation of hearty food, and quite possibly a couple of extra inches around her waist. Still, she wasn't about to turn down one of Charlie's cakes.

'Everyone,' Charlie said, 'this is Ellie, our wedding planner. This is my cousin Delilah. Lila.'

The slim, dark-haired and undeniably beautiful young woman stood up and, rather than holding out her hand, stepped forward and gave Ellie a hug. 'We've spoken on the phone. It's so lovely to meet you! I love your hair.'

'Oh. Thank you.' Ellie stroked a hand over it self-consciously. Charlie gave her an apologetic look over Lila's shoulder.

'And I'm Hannah,' the blonde woman said, shaking Ellie's hand. 'I hope you don't mine me – us – being here. When Charlie told me you were coming, I really wanted to meet you. We're all so excited about Charlie and Daniel's wedding.'

'Yes,' Daniel said dryly, 'but we thought you were going to be guests, rather than our little helpers.'

'Oh, shush.' Lila waved a dismissive hand at him. 'If it was up to you, you and Charlie would be in charge of the whole thing. You'd probably forget to come and stand at the end of the aisle, because you'd be checking on the food while Charlie went round talking to all the guests, making sure they had everything they needed.'

Daniel pursed his lips, then shrugged. 'That's not an entirely unfair assessment.'

'Please ignore their bickering, Ellie,' Charlie said. 'I promise we're not totally dysfunctional.'

Ellie laughed and sat down. 'I didn't think that for a moment. What are these?' She pointed to the plate of fluffy, golden pastries.

'They're chocolate custard Danishes,' Charlie said, slumping into her chair with relief. Daniel ran his hand along her shoulders, stopping to rub her neck. 'Please have as many as you like.'

'Thank you.' She put one on her plate, and waited for Daniel to pour her a mug of coffee from the large cafetière. Then she got out her notebook and put it purposefully on the table. She took a subtle breath and raised her eyes, looking at each of them in turn, smiling warmly, getting their full attention. 'Now,' she said, glancing at the notes she'd written up. 'These are the thoughts I've had so far.'

'The most important thing is the venue,' Charlie said, when Ellie had run through all her ideas – which at this point were fairly general. She wanted to make sure she got the feel of the wedding right before homing in on specifics.

'It has to be in Porthgolow,' Lila said. 'But *not* here.'

All eyes swivelled in Daniel's direction.

'I completely agree,' he said. 'I will get involved if we have it here – I won't be able to help myself.'

'Wow,' Lila said. 'Amazing that you're happy to admit it.'

'What can I say? I'm a modern man.' He spread his arms wide and grinned at Lila. Ellie was reminded of Jago's kind smile, and pushed it firmly to the back of her mind. Or at least, she tried to. She wondered what he was doing in her cottage – *his* cottage – right now. Was Lord Montague harassing him, or had they found some common ground? What did his tanned skin look like against the white linen? She cleared her throat, mortified at the direction her mind had wandered, and realized everyone was looking at her.

'There are a couple of hotels along the coast I've been looking into,' she said. 'They have availability for the June weekend you're after, and I've brought some brochures along. But I wondered if you'd prefer somewhere a little less straightforward.'

'What kind of thing were you thinking?' Charlie asked.

'As you're after something a bit more rustic, less polished, then neither of these hotels are ideal. There's a barn, a couple of small stately homes and an old lighthouse, all of which have potential. Let me show you.' She gestured to the iPad on the table. She really should get one of her own, rather than having to commandeer guests'. Her ancient laptop was on its last legs and not something she wanted to cart around with her, but now that she was serious about resurrecting her flagging business, she needed to step up her game. 'Is it OK if I use this?'

'Sure,' Hannah said. 'I didn't really need to bring it, but it's a habit now; something I learned in a previous job.'

'Do you use it for your recipes?' Ellie asked. 'I love your fish pie.'

Hannah blushed. 'Thank you, I didn't realize you knew the pub.'

'I live just over the hill,' she said, realizing as she said it that it wasn't the truth any more, but deciding nobody would care. 'I've spent some lovely evenings in there.'

'I've only been working here a few months,' Hannah explained. 'But it's the best job I've had. And I use my iPad all the time, especially when I'm creating recipes.'

Ellie nodded. 'I need to get one, but I'm reluctant to part with my trusty notebook.' She tapped it and then, with four eager pairs of eyes on her, opened up the iPad and typed in a web address.

She'd built up relationships with the owners of most prominent wedding locations in Cornwall, and was able to negotiate good rates. But from what Charlie and Daniel had said about their hopes for their big day, the standard corporate hotel offerings weren't suited to them. Crystal Waters was achingly elegant, but it had character, too. When Daniel was a happily married man and no longer her customer, she wanted to talk to him about adding it to her list. But Daniel and Charlie both had flair, and were charming in very different ways, and their wedding needed to reflect that: no conference rooms or bland set menus for them.

Hannah loved the lighthouse, and Lila went a bit misty-eyed over one of the stately homes which had a beautiful stained-glass window, even though that was by far the standout feature, and the rest was a little bit *too* shabby-chic for Ellie's liking. She nodded and added to her notes, but it didn't escape her attention that the two people who mattered had stayed quiet throughout the discussion.

'Do you like the look of any of these?' Ellie asked them gently.

Charlie and Daniel exchanged a glance.

'I like the barn,' Daniel said.

Charlie gave him a sharp look. 'Really?'

'Really.'

'You're not just saying that because you know I like it?'

'How would I even know that?'

Charlie's expression softened. 'This wedding is as much about you as it is me. If you don't like the barn, we'll find somewhere else.'

'I liked the barn. The only problem I have with all these places is their distance from Porthgolow.' He turned to Ellie. 'I know that probably sounds ridiculous, but we want to make the day easy for our friends and family. And Porthgolow . . .' he sighed. 'This is our home; the place we love. It seems counterintuitive to have it somewhere further afield. I know people get married in Las Vegas or Italian castles, but—'

'I agree,' Charlie said, taking his hand. 'It seems strange to put all our effort into our businesses here, to live here and take our dogs to this beach every day, and then go somewhere else for the wedding.'

Ellie nodded. She would just have to be creative.

Lila huffed. 'So you're restricting yourselves to here, or the Seven Stars, which is lovely but a bit small, or the beach, like Juliette and Lawrence. And that was a wonderful wedding, don't get me wrong, but do you want to do the same thing as them?'

'It's not a competition,' Charlie said, shrugging.

'Let me have a think,' Ellie interjected. 'I know the area well, and this is the kind of challenge I'm good at.'

'It sounds like a tall order to me,' Hannah said.

'It's what I do,' Ellie replied. 'Weddings are all about matching the event to the bride and groom; making it everything they want it to be. No two couples are the same, so it's not something that follows any kind of rules – other than the legal part, obviously, and the common aspects like vows, cake cutting, the first dance. But not everyone wants all those elements: it depends on culture, religious beliefs, personal desires. Flexibility is my middle name.'

'Ellie flexie Moon,' Lila said, laughing.

'Exactly.' She turned her attention to Charlie and Daniel. 'Porthgolow is important to you, so I'll do some research and see what I can come up with. If you have any ideas, or a sudden brainwave, in the meantime, then just get in touch.'

Charlie smiled. 'I'm so sorry we didn't say this last time.'

Ellie shook her head. 'Often you don't realize what you want until you're presented with the wrong options. We'll keep going, narrow things down until the perfect solution presents itself. We've got time to get this right, and that's what we'll do.'

'Thank you,' Charlie said.

'Yes, thanks Ellie,' Daniel added. 'It's good to have you on board.' He looked as cool as ever, but Ellie thought she heard relief in his voice. Her role was as much about keeping her clients happy and stress-free as it was about creating the perfect wedding. There was no point in getting the right fabric for the chair coverings or hitting on a cake flavour that everyone would enjoy if, by the time the big day arrived, the bride and groom were so overwhelmed that they couldn't appreciate a single moment.

'Once we've got the venue, we can start to imagine how it will look. And of course looks aren't everything, but with the right aesthetics, other things start falling into place.'

Taking the iPad again, Ellie navigated to her own website, which was the one area she'd invested in recently. She had photo galleries of previous weddings she'd organized, and while Charlie and Daniel had already seen them – Lila, too, as she'd tracked Ellie down – it would help visualize her point.

'This one had a nautical theme because the groom was a fisherman, and they lived as close to the sea as you do.' She showed them photos of fishing nets strung with fairy lights; table centrepieces of pebbles, sea glass and bunches of campion; the oyster bar. Everything in the seafront hotel was decorated to look like a luxury version of a fisherman's hut, but without the slippery floors or the smell.

There were murmurs of appreciation, as Ellie knew there would be, because she only used photographers she was confident would capture every key moment, every design element, beautifully.

'Noah would love this,' Hannah said, pointing at a photograph of guests sitting round driftwood tables. The smoothed sea-glass pebbles were striking, their frosted greens and blues beautifully complementing the pink campion flowers.

'Noah is Hannah's boyfriend,' Lila explained to Ellie. 'He's an eco-consultant. He's all about recycling and repurposing, *and* his dad's a fisherman.'

'I always factor in sustainability,' Ellie said. 'A wedding is just one day, and I think of it as a marker, a starting point, for how you want to live the rest of your lives.'

There were nods around the table.

'Look at this one,' she continued, finding a wedding that had a rustic, intimate feel similar to what Daniel and Charlie had said they wanted.

She let them scroll through the photos, making notes of their comments, paying particular attention to Charlie and Daniel's thoughts. After their initial reluctance to get involved, they were warming up, becoming animated as they discussed guest numbers and the order of the day, what type of wedding breakfast they wanted and the merits of having a live band versus a DJ or sound-system. Ellie knew that was partly because they'd voiced their desire to have the wedding in Porthgolow. It was important to them, and she would do all she could to fulfil that dream even if, right now, it seemed near enough impossible.

When her sister got home from work that evening, Ellie was looking up iPads on her decrepit laptop.

'What are you so engrossed in?' Rose asked, hanging up her coat.

'I need an iPad. I can't keep using my clients'; it makes me look completely hopeless. But then again—'

'It's an investment,' Rose said, standing in the doorway. 'If you're going to bring your business kicking and screaming – or rather dancing and singing, let's be positive about it – into the present, then you need to modernize. I love a chunky notebook as much as the next person, but you're a professional, organized person, and having an iPad would reflect that.'

Ellie nodded. 'So wise.'

'So stop biting your lip and get it.'

'I will,' Ellie said. 'And I've made a cauliflower cheese, and some chicken saltimbocca, and the oven's on so you just need to have a shower and get changed while I get everything ready.' She flicked through to the payment plan page, wondering whether to buy it in instalments or up front. When she looked up, Rose had her mouth open and her hand pressed to her chest. 'What?'

'You've cooked? From scratch? Are you feeling OK?'

'I can't take over half your home *and* let you do all the cooking. I looked up the recipes online. They might be a complete disaster.'

'I don't care if they're a disaster,' Rose said. 'You cooked! Ellie, this is wonderful!'

'You're making it sound like I've just performed a miracle.'

'That is basically what you've done. I can't remember the last time you cooked.'

'I'm over that part of my rebellion,' Ellie said. 'I need to start being more of an adult in other areas of my life, not just New Moon Weddings.' She had given up cooking elaborate meals after her divorce, throwing herself into the free

44

and single life, preferring simple salads, things on toast, takeaways and eating out with Rose.

It wasn't that she didn't like cooking, just that it reminded her of the neat lines of her marriage, the stereotypical division of duties that her husband had taken far too seriously. Her: cooking and cleaning. Him: mending and fixing. Their house had had a tiny garden, and while Ellie had lovingly tended the plants in the meagre flower beds, he had spent hours tinkering with his road bike on the patio. As their relationship deteriorated she hadn't wanted to be out there with him, the space so small they inevitably got in each other's way.

'There is a difference between being an adult and being grown-up,' Rose said, 'and I don't want you to lose your fun side. I feel it slipping, now you're focusing on the business again. Don't lose that balance, or you'll wear yourself into the ground. Now I'll go and get in the shower before you tell me off for interfering.'

She disappeared, leaving Ellie to ponder her sister's words, her failed marriage and how she was supposed to fit fun in alongside giving her business the boost it so badly needed. She looked at the jaunty images of iPads, the way Apple advertisers made it seem as if this one device would solve every problem she'd ever had, and clicked through to the 'buy' page. It wasn't going to work, of course, but it might be a start.

Ellie was as proud of the meal she'd cooked as she had been of anything in a long time. She watched her sister's reaction, the way her eyes widened and then closed, as if her other senses needed to hibernate so she could put all her energy into tasting the food.

'Right, that's it,' Rose said when she'd finished, placing her knife and fork together on a plate that looked as though it had been licked clean. 'You can cook from now on.'

'Hang on,' Ellie laughed, 'I'm not a natural. That took me *hours*.'

'And look at the result. The crispy pancetta round the outside of the chicken, the sage butter inside. And your cauliflower cheese was just right – not too cheesy, the veg still crunchy. It was exactly what I needed after today.'

'Was it particularly tough?' Rose's job as a district nurse was demanding, but she tended to brush over the difficult parts, as if Ellie was a delicate flower that needed to be sheltered from harsh conditions.

'Nothing I haven't coped with a thousand times before,' Rose said, 'except I have this new patient; an older gentleman I'm finding it hard to get through to. His troubles are emotional as much as physical, as they so often are, and I'd like to help him with more than his broken hip. He just seems so lost; so shut off from the world.'

'And he's immune to the Rose Moon charms?'

'Sadly so,' Rose said. She sounded genuinely worried. 'I come across loneliness all the time, and often it's something that can't be helped: a patient lives somewhere rural, or they've become less mobile. As they've got older, friends and family have moved away or died, and they have no idea how to combat it; how to find new people to be with. But this gentleman . . .' She sighed. 'He's in a care home. I've spoken to Mo about him.'

'Mo?'

'The home manager. We get on.'

'You get on with most people,' Ellie said.

'Not this older gentleman. But that's down to him, rather than anything I'm doing. Mo says he's the same with everyone. He won't join in any of the group activities, and spends a lot of his time in his room. He's an upright sort of man, very regimented. Unbendable. You get what I'm saying? God, of course you do.' She gave Ellie a warm smile. There was no pity in it, but Ellie still felt a shiver of discomfort.

Mark had been unbendable. He knew exactly how he wanted things to be and wouldn't waver. At the beginning, Ellie had loved his certainty about everything, the way he approached every situation with a calm authority. As time went on, and especially once they were married, she realized he wouldn't compromise even when he knew it mattered to her. She'd given up trying in the end, and they'd drifted further and further apart. He refused to see what was wrong, and after Ellie had realized how little happiness her life was giving her, she had challenged him on it.

Then divorce, a new life she loved, a cottage she saw as home. She'd never once regretted ending her marriage, and it meant she was fully attuned to people like the old man Rose was talking about.

'Some people are perfectly happy being like that,' she said now. 'Not everyone wants help.'

'My patient does,' Rose assured her. 'He just doesn't realize it yet. I need to open his eyes.'

Ellie shrugged. 'It doesn't always work.'

'Oh hush,' Rose chided gently. 'We're not talking about Mark, here. He was a lost cause. This man . . .' Her expression turned thoughtful, and Ellie was intrigued. Her no-nonsense sister was going soft. 'I can see it in him,' she continued. 'He's alone, he's grieving for his wife who died a couple of years ago, and there's a part of him, deep down, that wants someone to recognize it. Like when a young child finds a perfect hiding place, but they make a lot of noise getting there, so even though you have to close your eyes and count to one-hundred while they're hiding, it's easy to find them.'

'What noises is your old man making?'

'Fuss,' Rose said. 'He fusses about everything. Complains. Nothing is right, nobody is the right person to spend time with or understands what he needs. If he was really intent on being alone, he'd be quiet as a mouse so everyone would forget he existed.'

Ellie laughed. 'Is this a professional medical diagnosis?'

'It's a professional Rose diagnosis. I'm meeting Mo for coffee tomorrow to talk about what we can do.'

Ellie didn't miss the way her sister's eyes slid to the side. And in the cosy lamplight of the dining room, she thought she saw the slightest tinge of pink on her cheekbones. Could it be that, as well as showing a particular interest in one of her patients – even more than the usual commitment – her sister, confirmed single woman because it-was-just-too-much-trouble-trying-to-keep-yourself-*and*-a-man-happy, was attracted to the manager of one of the care homes on her rounds?

Ellie wanted to find out more, but decided that now wasn't the time. She would take her to the pub on Friday night, buy a bottle of rosé, and catch her off guard when she was in weekend mode.

Right now, she had wedding venues to investigate. She had to find the perfect place, in Porthgolow, for Charlie and

Daniel to get married. Because she knew the village well, she was almost entirely certain that the only eligible options were Daniel's hotel, the beach and the seafront pub. None of those would give the couple the atmosphere and space they wanted.

Ellie never shied away from a challenge, and this one had a lot resting on it. She thought of her cottage, currently occupied by a scruffy, green-eyed mechanic and her cat, and knew – if she wanted to reclaim it in the foreseeable future – she had to make this the best wedding she had ever planned. Both for Daniel and Charlie's sake, and for her own.

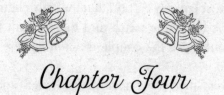

Chapter Four

Ellie woke with the larks. She had been tossing and turning for hours, with so many things running restlessly through her mind: Charlie's pensive face at their last meeting; lighthouses and stately homes; olive-coloured chair coverings that she didn't think were right for anybody's wedding, and doves fluttering over rose-twined arbours; Mark and his road bike, his handsome face all smooth lines and symmetry, so like the man himself.

The duvet was twisted around her legs, and she was too hot. The first, milky hues of sunrise were visible through the gaps in the blinds, and she knew there was only one thing that would sort her head out. She shouldn't do it, but it was all she could think of right now.

The air still had a night-time chill to it as she climbed into Florence, the engine starting with a gentle purr. She felt a flash of guilt: Jago had been so kind to her, was this really fair? But then she glanced at her gardening gloves on the passenger seat. They looked forlorn, as if they couldn't understand why she hadn't wriggled her fingers into them recently. It was so early, it was likely he wouldn't even realize.

Cornwall was always striking, whether in bright sun or being battered by a howling gale, but Ellie thought it was particularly beautiful at the bookends of the day. Sunrise and sunset; the golden hour, when everything was tinged in a light so pure it was as if something otherworldly was at work.

Florence drove like a dream, and soon she found herself turning into Wilderness Lane, driving past Seascape House, and to the watering can full of begonias that marked the turning into Cornflower Cottage. She slowed to a crawl, hoping Jago slept too deeply for the crunch of gravel to wake him, and parked far enough back on the driveway that he wouldn't see the Mini if he looked out of the window. His Golf was in front of the cottage, and both were bathed in the ethereal, early morning glow.

Despite her subterfuge, the moment Ellie heard a robin singing, she relaxed. She took her gloves and her gardening pouch, complete with trowel, secateurs, and a bottle of fungicide for the roses, and unlatched the wooden gate at the side of the cottage that led to the back garden. Her inappropriate but quiet ballet pumps soaked up the early morning moisture.

She went straight to her hydrangeas, which ran down either edge of her garden, providing a glossy green border for the flower beds between. They had been one of her favourites for as long as she could remember, the plant in her childhood garden bearing delicate pink petals in large pompom clusters through the end of the summer and into autumn. When so many other flowers had finished blooming, her hydrangeas brought a much-needed burst of colour, but they wouldn't do that nearly so well if she couldn't prune them now.

Taking out her secateurs, she crouched and got to work, snipping back the old stems, leaving the new, healthy shoots exposed. A blackbird joined in with the robin's chorus as the sun rose ahead of her, the scent of rich, loamy soil filling her nose.

She soon forgot herself and was kneeling on the damp ground, all her attention on the task at hand, so when something brushed against her bottom she let out a strangled scream and almost cut off a finger instead of a stem. She turned to find Lord Montague gazing up at her. He narrowed his green eyes in pleasure, his purring competing with the birdsong, which was still going despite her cat's presence.

'Monty,' she whispered, 'how are you?' She gave him a thorough stroke, noting how silky his fur was, how content he appeared. He nuzzled against her leg and tried to climb onto her lap.

'Has he been looking after you?' she asked. 'Is he more chilled out than I am? Silly question: of course he is.'

Monty chirruped, and after she'd finished petting him, he settled on the grass at her side while she carried on snipping and trimming.

She had almost finished the hydrangeas along the left-hand border when she heard the unmistakable sound of the back door unlocking. She whipped round, then scuttled sideways and hid as much as possible behind the nearest bush. The door swung open to reveal Jago, and Ellie's breath deserted her.

He was wearing nothing but a white, fluffy towel. It was wrapped around his hips, leaving his top half exposed. Ellie tried to swallow, but her throat was dry. She hadn't been a nun since her divorce. She'd had a few flings, had gone out with men and, for the most part, enjoyed the sex, but she couldn't remember any of those encounters causing quite this reaction. Heat rushed over her as she took in Jago's honed torso, the brush of brown hair on his chest. She supposed wrestling with carburettors and hefty tyres on a daily basis would keep him trim. Or maybe he worked out? Whatever the cause, the results were impressive.

'Monty?' He ran a hand through his hair which, Ellie noticed, was darker, damp from the shower. 'Monty?'

The cat looked up at her. 'Don't you dare,' she whispered, crouching lower. If he found her, not only would it show her as being wholly unprofessional, he would think she was spying on him. And admittedly, at this moment she was, but—

'Lord Montague!' he shouted sternly, and Ellie couldn't help it: she laughed. It was more of a snort, really, but it cut through the quiet morning air and Jago's head shot up, his eyes homing in on her general area. She bent lower. Monty miaowed loudly, and Jago stepped onto the patio. His feet were bare, Ellie noticed in the seconds before his expression changed. Their gazes locked, and surprise flashed in his eyes.

'Ellie,' he said, clearly baffled. 'Is everything OK?'

Monty strolled forward, entirely unperturbed.

'Everything's fine,' Ellie managed, standing up slowly, her embarrassment deepening when she realized how muddy her jeans were. 'I'm really sorry, Jago—'

'Do you want tea?' he asked, then cleared his throat. 'Is that the kind of thing a tenant does during an unscheduled inspection?' Monty wound himself around Jago's ankles.

'Oh, no!' Ellie said, mortified. 'I'm not here to spy on you.' Shit. That had come out wrong. Why were her eyes travelling over his chest again? She could feel her cheeks turning scarlet.

She expected Jago's mortification to mirror her own. She expected to see the moment when he realized he was only wearing – barely wearing – a towel in front of her. Instead, his mouth lifted into a lopsided smile. 'I'll make tea,' he said again, then turned around and went inside. Monty trotted happily after him.

Ellie addressed her hydrangeas. 'That couldn't have gone any worse, could it?' she said, stroking a shiny leaf. 'Time to face the music, eh?' She took a moment to gather herself, then walked to the back door, which Jago had left open. Still, she knocked, then peeped her head into the kitchen.

It wasn't as polished as she usually kept it, but it wasn't a mess, either. It simply looked lived in. There were empty beer bottles rinsed on the draining board, ready to go in the recycling; a fresh box of Cornish Tea bags next to the kettle; a notepad open by the toaster with a biro lying on top and then, she noticed with a twist of some unnameable emotion, a white fabric mouse on a string, looped over a cupboard handle.

Jago's smile kicked up a gear. 'Don't stand there like a vampire waiting for an invite. Come in.'

Ellie did. 'I'm so sorry Jago, I shouldn't have done this.'

'Done what, exactly?' He folded his arms, raising his voice over the blur of the kettle. 'The not-spying?'

'I was pruning my hydrangeas.'

His brows knitted in confusion. Ellie had to work hard to focus on his face, because he hadn't tried to cover himself up, and the rest of him was calling to her, daring her to look.

'The bushes along the borders,' she went on. 'If you cut away the older stems now, you get better flowers later in the year.'

He nodded, but she got the impression he still had no idea what she was going on about. Not a gardener, then. She sighed. 'I love my garden. I'm finding it . . . hard, to let it go.'

He turned back to the kettle and made the tea. The quiet ticked on, the only sound Monty eating his breakfast, oblivious to the tension in the room. Finally Jago faced her again, handing her a mug.

'So what you're saying,' he started in his low voice, 'is that you snuck back to your cottage, the one you're renting out to me, at some crazy-ass time of the morning, purely so you could look after a few plants?'

Ellie bit down on a gasp. 'They're not just a *few plants*. They're beautiful. And they need looking after. Everything does, if it's going to thrive.' She knew she sounded indignant, but she couldn't help it. Then indignant turned to embarrassed as Jago's smile widened.

'I'm kidding,' he said softly. 'I don't have a clue about gardening myself, but I understand why people are passionate about it. Why didn't you say anything before?'

Ellie gripped her mug, feeling the burn of the hot porcelain against her palms. 'This is your place now. I can't keep haunting it.'

Jago gave a one-shouldered shrug. 'If the garden needs looking after, and you want to do it, then I don't see why you can't. I have to admit that I had noticed how nice it was, and not given a second thought to the fact that meant someone had put a lot of work in. It's not the kind of thing I focus on.'

'There's no reason why you should,' Ellie said, hope flickering inside her. 'But you'd really be happy for me to come and tend to the garden? You wouldn't think I was stepping on your toes?'

'My toes are decidedly un-green, and it's better than it becoming neglected. I'll still get to enjoy it, so really it's selfish on my part.'

Ellie bit her lip. 'Not at all. It's very kind of you.'

Jago chuckled. 'Doesn't seem that way to me.'

Was there nothing that fazed this man? Ellie's face had returned to a normal temperature and, she hoped, a normal colour, but she couldn't get used to the site of him in a towel. Could any heterosexual woman? She was much closer, now, and he was even more distracting. She realized she was staring, and raised her gaze to his face. For a second she thought she saw something in his eyes, a flash of heat, and then his lazy smile was back.

'How are you settling in?' It came out as a scratch, and she swallowed a mouthful of too-hot tea.

'Good,' he said. 'I've caught up with a few old friends, and I'm all sorted at the garage. And I'm comfortable here, as I'm sure you can imagine. It's working out well.'

'Monty's not giving you too much hassle?'

Jago gave the cat an affectionate look. 'No, we're getting on OK. I bought him a gift to placate him, just in case.' He gestured to the mouse.

'That was very sweet of you.'

'Sometimes he's up for a game of mousing, sometimes he looks at me as if I'm the most stupid human on the planet.'

Ellie laughed. 'That doesn't surprise me. He's definitely in charge.'

'Yup,' Jago said. 'But in some ways that's good; it takes the responsibility off me.'

It was a throwaway comment, but Ellie thought there might be something more to it. He was her age, seemingly on his own and living in a rented cottage. Even his job was fairly flexible. Was that why he was so laid-back, because he shied away from responsibility? Still, she could talk. Forty years old, living with her sister, running a business that wasn't exactly flourishing. No man, no children, her cat left behind with the property. And she was so wound up she needed to come back to her old garden just to feel remotely normal.

The quiet settled again, but it was a warm, comfortable quiet. She still felt jangled by the proximity of his naked flesh, but his calm demeanour somehow overrode even that.

'Do you want to sit down?' he said. 'I've been rude, not even offering you a seat.'

'Rude? To the woman who sneaked into your garden uninvited? You made me tea.'

'Go through to the living room and I'll chuck some clothes on.'

Ellie was so tempted to stay in his soothing orbit. She could hide in her cottage with its new occupant and her cat, forget about her own responsibilities, her challenges with this latest wedding.

'I need to get going,' she said instead. 'It's very kind of you, considering this wasn't the wake-up you were expecting.'

'Not an unpleasant one, all the same.' Their eyes held for a moment longer.

'Right then,' Ellie stuttered. 'Thanks for the tea, Jago. And for the permission. I'll let you know when I'm planning on dropping by next time.'

'Great. That would allow me to be more presentable.'

She put her mug down and stepped outside, into a day that was almost fully dawned, the cooling chill caressing her face. *I really didn't mind the way you presented yourself to me*, she thought, and then, when she glanced back, saw that he was staring at her from the open doorway, his smile transformed into a grin.

'Thanks,' he said, his eyes bright with amusement, and Ellie realized she had said it out loud. Heat rushed through her, from the top of her head to her toes. Before her mortification could swallow her up, she gave him a quick wave and fled to the side gate, picking up her gardening pouch as she went.

Not only was the Flying Caterpillar in St Eval the most randomly named pub Ellie had ever frequented, it was also one of the nicest. More modern than the Seven Stars, it bridged the gap between pub and wine bar, with pristine white walls and dark walnut tables and bar-top, the soft furnishings lime green and neon pink, the bar taps brushed copper. It was a smidgen pretentious, but the mostly local clientele helped soften the edges, and it did a good selection of local wines.

Rose and Ellie were in their favourite booth in the corner

furthest from the door. It had an excellent view of the whole bar and was close to a log burner. Their wine bottle was half-empty, the bar snacks were ordered, and Ellie was about to pluck up the courage to ask Rose about Mo, the care-home manager, when her sister surprised her.

'I need your help with something,' she said.

Ellie sat back. 'OK.' It was unusual for Rose to request help; she was the care-giver, both in work and out.

'It's about my older gentleman,' she continued. 'The one I mentioned to you the other day. I take patient confidentiality seriously, but I've spoken to Mo about it and I think there's something we can do to help him. That thing involves you.'

'Me?' Ellie asked. 'Why? And how was Mo?' she added, raising an eyebrow.

'Mo's great,' Rose said, unmoved. 'We're on the same page about most things, and he agrees this particular situation could do with outside assistance.'

'Your gentleman doesn't want to get married, does he?' Ellie took a sip of her wine. 'It would be nice to have an older couple on my books.'

Rose sighed instead of laughed, which was unlike her. 'He's still grieving the loss of his wife,' she explained. 'I expect the last thing he wants to do is get married. The one thing that does give him pleasure is tending to a small garden in the care-home grounds. He's created it himself and it looks as pretty as a picture, with those mini daffodil things and some tall white flowers that look like corn-on-the-cob, and then there are these purple ones, crocuses I think, and—' she stopped when she saw Ellie's expression. 'Mo showed it to me. We tried to get Arthur – that's my older gentleman – to give me a proper tour, but he said it wasn't worth seeing, which is absurd but perfectly demonstrates the situation we're dealing with. If he'd shown me, he could have told me the names of everything.'

'I want to know what the corn-on-the-cob flowers are.' Ellie narrowed her eyes. Hyacinths? It was towards the end of the season for them.

Rose shook her head. 'This isn't a joking matter.'

Ellie's smile fell. 'If he's got this lovely garden, then why do you need me?'

'That's the thing,' Rose said. 'He won't have it for much longer. They're extending the home, starting work in the next couple of months, and his garden is right where they're building. Mo said they've had to change the original renovation plans, move the extension from one side of the site to the other, because the survey found some issues with subsidence to the south of the existing property. He wouldn't have let Arthur have that patch of garden if he'd known it would only be temporary; he realizes how damaging that can be.'

'That's awful,' Ellie said. She tried to imagine being told her garden, so carefully planned and lovingly looked after, was going to disappear under concrete and steel foundations. It brought a lump to her throat. It had been bad enough when she moved out, and it made her realize what a gift Jago had given her, not only by allowing her to go back there, but by making it so easy. She gave him a mental hug, and wasn't surprised when that image included his half-bare, towel-clad form. 'How can I help?' she asked Rose.

Her sister filled up their glasses, then waved at Pitch, the inky-black dog that was a constant presence in the bar. Ellie had never worked out whether he belonged to Jimmy, the pub's owner, or one of the permanently installed regulars. Pitch flapped an ear then went back to snoozing in front of the fire.

'Before we tell Arthur about the extension, we want to find him another garden,' Rose said. 'Somewhere he can move the existing plants, and grow new ones to his heart's content. We want it to be as painless as possible. Mo and I are both clueless when it comes to gardening, but we thought you could have a look round the grounds, find somewhere suitable with the right soil and outlook and . . . whatever else you need to consider.'

Ellie chewed her lip. 'He's going to be devastated, if he cares about his garden as much as you think he does.'

'Yes,' Rose huffed. 'We know that. But Mo can't stall the development. This is our best bet.'

'Then of course I'll help,' she said. 'Just let me know when you want me to have a look.'

Rose's shoulders sagged. 'Thank you, Ellie. That's such a relief. And if you could help him move the flowers, too. He needs to gradually increase his mobility to help his hip heal, but he stiffens up quickly, so . . .'

Ellie rolled her eyes. 'Of course there's more to it.'

Rose grinned. 'You'll help, though?'

'You know I will.'

'Excellent. So, how was your day?'

Ellie groaned and leaned back against the cushions. 'I drove round Porthgolow, hoping the perfect wedding venue would magically spring up out of the rocks.'

'For this couple, Charlie and Daniel?'

61

Ellie nodded. 'They want to get married in Porthgolow, but Daniel's hotel is out of the question. I want somewhere with rustic charm and character, preferably already set up for weddings. Other than the pub, I'm not sure it exists, and the Seven Stars isn't ideal for so many reasons.'

'Can you go further afield?'

'Why? What are you thinking?'

'I don't have anywhere specific in mind, I just think you'd make it easier for yourself if you widened your scope.'

'But the Porthgolow element is really important to them. The catering is already sorted, but that's been the easiest part so far.'

'Who are you going with?'

'Hannah Swan,' Ellie said, feeling a burst of satisfaction. It was such an obvious solution, and Hannah was only too happy to accept, both from a professional and personal point of view. 'She's the chef at the Seven Stars, and she's good friends with Charlie and Daniel. She hasn't done any event catering, but I'm confident she's more than capable, and I'm going to bring in Lizzie, from Falmouth Feasts, to support her. I just need to sit down with Hannah, Charlie and Daniel to plan the menu.'

'So at the very least they can have a luxurious beach picnic,' Rose said.

'At the *very* least. And I'm not giving up on finding somewhere, I just need to get creative.'

'OK, but get creative over this first,' Rose said, as their sharing platter appeared. There were onion rings and buffalo cauliflower wings with spicy mayo; a tomato and pepper salad; local sausages and seasoned fries with a trio of different dips. Ellie's mouth was watering before it was put on the table. They shared out the food and ate contentedly for several minutes.

Ellie felt a rush of affection for her sister. They might be two spinsterly sisters living together, but they got on like best friends. Not everyone would want to spend Friday night in the pub with one of their relatives. The thought of their spinsterhood tripped her back to Jago, to him leaning in the doorway in that frankly indecent towel, the golden hour casting its magic on his skin. She took a deep breath, a forkful of fries hovering inches from her lips.

'OK?' Rose asked. 'You've got a strange look on your face.'

'I went to see my garden this morning,' Ellie blurted.

Rose rolled her eyes. 'I knew you wouldn't be able to stay away. I *knew*. This is why you can help Arthur: you and green things growing from the ground – honestly! I sometimes wonder if that's the real reason you divorced Mark, because you didn't love him as much as you love your Cyclanthrocops, or whatever they are.'

'I have no idea what plant you're referring to, but it sounds dangerous. And prehistoric.'

'You do know that it's illegal to visit tenants without giving twenty-four hours' notice, don't you?' Rose went on. 'Of course you do, you were the one who told me that when you were looking into renting out Cornflower Cottage. Is that something you've conveniently forgotten?'

Ellie shifted on her seat. 'I wasn't planning on seeing my tenant, just the garden.'

'But from the way you're avoiding meeting my eye, I'm

assuming it didn't work out like that. So how did young Jago enjoy your impromptu visit?'

'He was rather . . . caught off guard by it.'

Rose sat back, her dinner temporarily forgotten. 'In what way? Did he have a friend over? For God's sake, Ellie! For someone who prides themselves on being professional.' She shook her head.

'Oh, no! What if he *did* have someone over?' There had been no other car, no sign of anyone else, and he hadn't acted like he needed to get back to someone who was waiting for him upstairs. But the thought hadn't even crossed her mind as she'd been driving from St Eval to Porthgolow at stupid o'clock in the morning.

'That's not how he was caught off guard?'

'He'd just come out of the shower,' Ellie explained.

'Oh, really?' Rose waggled her eyebrows. 'Do tell.'

So Ellie told her, all the time waiting anxiously for her sister's response. She'd always cared what Rose thought, always wanted the respect and approval of her big sister. It was something she would never grow out of, not even when she was ninety.

'So,' she said when she'd spilled every detail. 'Am I the biggest idiot ever?'

Rose took her sweet time to pick a couple of onion rings off the platter and put them on her plate, cut one in half and dip it in the homemade ketchup, deliberately letting Ellie stew.

'You're not an idiot,' she said eventually. 'But, next time, you should do exactly the same thing.'

'What?'

'Turn up unannounced, the same time of day, and then

64

when he comes outside in very few clothes you can enjoy it all over again, and also take a photo so I get to enjoy it, too.'

'Rose!' Ellie tried to sound outraged. 'That is a disgraceful suggestion. A few minutes ago you were admonishing me for being unprofessional.'

'I was, but that ship sailed a long time ago, which means you need to make the most of it.' Rose speared a sausage with her fork, gave Ellie a familiar, wicked grin and popped it in her mouth. Ellie wanted to be cross with her, but the thought of returning to Cornflower Cottage and getting another eyeful of a scantily clad Jago Carne wasn't exactly horrifying, even though she'd inadvertently admitted it to him as she left. What was happening to her?

Helping Rose with Arthur and his garden was exactly what she needed. With that alongside her weddings, Charlie and Daniel's venue conundrum, she wouldn't have any brain space, or energy, left to use up on thoughts of her far-too-attractive tenant.

Chapter Five

It was Monday morning and Ellie was putting off wedding duties so she could go with Rose to Seascape House, because that was where her older gentleman, Arthur, was. Her iPad had arrived on Saturday, and she had spent much of the weekend organizing it, downloading apps and setting up folders, turning it into a digital version of her hefty notebook.

'It won't plan weddings for you,' Rose had said, emerging at lunchtime on Sunday still wearing her pyjamas. 'But perhaps you could ask Siri to find you the perfect Porthgolow venue?'

'I thought you were all for me getting one of these?'

'I am, and I'm glad you have. But when have you known me to pass up an opportunity to tease you?'

'Never,' Ellie had said darkly, reminded of how many times Jago had come up in the conversation since the pub. She never should have told Rose about her visit to Cornflower Cottage.

And, she thought now, as she followed her sister to the care home that was only a stone's throw from her cottage and the man in question, she needed to put him out of her mind. Out of all the care homes Rose visited on her rounds, trust Arthur to be a resident *here*.

She had never been beyond the weathered sign on Wilderness Lane before, and what she found was a bland but inoffensive building, in grounds of easy-to-maintain lawns. No wonder someone with a bit of knowledge and enthusiasm had taken it upon themselves to create something better. And now it was going to be destroyed to extend the space at the home which, while good for those extra residents – and no doubt the home's profits – would do little for the wellbeing of the current patients.

She followed Rose's car to the side of the building, parked next to her and got out.

'Ready for this?' Rose asked, smoothing down her tunic.

'Of course.' Ellie had put her gardening tools in the boot, in case Mo and Arthur wanted her to start moving the plants straight away. She had this morning free, and a meeting with Charlie and Daniel that afternoon. She felt nervous about turning up without a venue in mind, but she had found a couple of options just outside Porthgolow and hoped to scout them out beforehand.

Ellie followed Rose into the home's spacious reception. It had a clean, slightly floral scent, and she was cheered by the bright welcome from the receptionist and the comfortable-looking visitor chairs, the colourful artwork adorning the walls. It gave a much better impression than the outside of the building and the bland grounds.

'Hello, Rose,' the receptionist said. 'I'll just get Mo for

you.' She disappeared through a door and Ellie glanced at her sister, registering the moment her expression warmed, and realized it was because the care-home manager had appeared.

He was tall, had a wide, friendly smile and was wearing smart jeans and a cosy-looking green jumper; he radiated friendliness and brisk efficiency.

'Rose, great to see you. And you must be Ellie?' He grasped her hand in his. 'I'm Morris Césaire, but everyone calls me Mo. Thank you for agreeing to this. Rose hasn't stopped singing your praises, and if you can help Arthur keep his garden, then I'll be in your debt.'

'I'll certainly do what I can,' Ellie said, taken aback by his openness. She could see why her sister might be holding a candle for this man. 'Do you want to show me the garden, or shall we talk to Arthur first?'

'I'd like to see if we can re-home his plants before we have to tell him, if possible, but I admit to being clueless when it comes to anything botanical. We have a young woman come in to mow the lawns, but without anything more complex than grass on site, I haven't needed to call on an expert so far.'

'Gardening is wonderful for mental and physical health,' Ellie said. 'I'm surprised that you don't have any beds on site. Even a simple herb garden, or a few shrubs, would make a difference.'

Mo gave her a rueful smile. 'I've only been here four months; I'm still getting my head around the place. The redesign for the additional wing is going to include some landscaping work, and I fully agree with you about the importance of the outdoor environment, but I don't believe that lessens the need for Arthur to have his own space. That's what we want to protect.'

'Understood,' Ellie said. 'Do you want to show me, then?'

'Sure. Della, you'll be OK if I head out, won't you? I've got my mobile, and I'll be on site.'

'Of course, Mo.' The woman behind reception nodded.

Rose and Ellie fell into step alongside him as he took them to the west side of the building, where the hill sloped gently downwards. Ellie noticed how much moss was mixed in with the grass, and winced as she imagined the job ahead for the landscapers tasked with creating a space that the residents could take pleasure in.

'How did Arthur start the garden?' she asked Mo. 'Did he tell you that was what he wanted to do?'

Mo gave a deep chuckle. 'Not at all. One of our other residents, April, was sent a huge bouquet by her daughter. She's been working on an intense project for the last couple of months and hasn't been able to visit. As soon as it arrived, Arthur was there, examining the flowers, telling April what to do with each of them, how far up the stem to cut, the water and plant food they would need to last. I wouldn't describe him as a tender person, but he treated those flowers with such care.' Mo shook his head. 'He's ex-Navy. He was a commander, so fairly senior. The phrase "stiff upper lip" could have been invented for him.'

'Apart from when it comes to gardening,' Ellie said softly. They had turned a corner and there, in a sheltered section between the wall of the building and a brick and glass conservatory, was a riot of colour.

'Apart from when it comes to gardening,' Mo echoed.

'Isn't it beautiful?' Rose said.

'He told me that he took it up when he retired,' Mo went on. 'He'd spent so long away from home, away from his family, and he'd never had a chance to look after something long-term, to see it grow and flourish.'

The patch of ground couldn't have been more than ten foot square, but it was crammed with shades of pink and yellow, blue and cream, as daffodils nestled alongside the upturned cups of crocuses, and little, fried-egg anemones cosied up to pink pearl hyacinths, the blooms still glowing despite being close to the end of their flowering season. He had rosemary and lavender, sage and lemon verbena plants in terracotta pots, and there was even a young magnolia tree, its boughs shaped into a pleasing orb. The space would get full sun in the afternoon, and the whole area was thriving.

'This is stunning.' Ellie crouched and gently rubbed an anemone petal between her cold fingers. 'Does he come out here every day?'

'Without fail, regardless of the weather,' Mo said. 'Rose will be the first to tell you his mobility isn't at its best, but it doesn't stop him. He treats the plants like children; more important than he is.'

'Gentle movement is a big part of his recovery plan,' Rose added, 'and we've got him a gardening mat so he can kneel without too much strain. It's the only time I've seen him close to content. His wife, Hetty, died just over two years ago, and he had to move here six months ago, after the operation on his hip. This has been a lifeline for him.'

'Does he have visitors? Any children who come to see him?' Ellie asked. She couldn't bear the thought that this pocket of life and colour would have to be dismantled, and that it was the only thing keeping Arthur going.

'He's got a son,' Mo said. 'But they're not close. I haven't seen him here since I started working at Seascape, and getting any information out of Arthur is difficult, to say the least.'

'It's shocking,' Rose said vehemently. 'Abandoning your grieving father like that.'

'We don't know the circumstances,' Mo replied. He was just the right amount of placatory towards Rose, without being patronizing. They may not have been working together long, but Ellie could see Mo knew how to get the best out of her. She stifled a smile, which faded on its own when her gaze returned to Arthur's garden. From what Mo and Rose had said, he would internalize his sadness at losing it, which would only make things worse.

'So we need to find somewhere to move the garden to,' she said.

'If you could.' Mo rocked back on his heels. 'I have the plans for the new extension, so we can avoid anywhere that's going to be built on.'

Ellie nodded. 'Let's go, then.'

They walked round the site, Ellie checking the soil conditions and how the light would fall, shade cover and shelter from the wind, the proximity to the existing building and the mature trees around the edge of the plot. There were a couple of sites she thought might work, but none as suitable as the one Arthur had already found.

'There's no chance of the extension plans being changed to accommodate the garden?' she asked eventually.

Mo sighed, his hands on his hips. They had returned to

the home's entrance, the earlier sun obliterated by thick cloud cover as a shower headed their way. 'I've already had a meeting with the chief executive, and he says we can't change the plans for one resident. The good of the many outweighs the good of the few, was his argument. And I'm just the manager: I did everything in my power without getting aggressive.'

'You should have got aggressive,' Rose said with a glint in her eye.

Mo's mouth lifted at the corners. 'That would have made things worse.'

'It would have been fun to watch, though,' Rose countered.

Mo chuckled and then, catching Ellie's gaze, his serious-ness returned. 'Time to talk to Arthur?'

'I'm sorry,' she said. 'I don't think I've found the perfect solution.'

'You didn't need to come at all. I'm grateful that you're here.'

'Even her presence is calming,' Rose said. 'It's because she breathes order amongst chaos. Things never feel hope-less around Ellie because she's always got a plan.'

'Not this time,' Ellie said. 'Or at least, not one I'm entirely happy with.'

'But that's more reassuring than you could know,' Rose replied, 'because you're a perfectionist. And whatever you've got is more than we've come up with so far.'

'Let's go and find our resident gardener,' Mo said.

They found him in a day room on the first floor, sitting with his chair facing the window, set apart from the other residents. Some were playing chess or cards, a few were settled on sofas around the fireplace, books forgotten while they talked animatedly. The telly was switched on, the volume low and the subtitles playing on a buy-a-house-in-the-country programme.

It was a light, airy space, the furniture modern and well-kept, the thick carpet with stripes from a recent hoovering. Bold landscapes adorned the walls; Cornish scenes of boats on stormy waters or swathes of wildflowers on sweeping cliff tops, the blue of the Atlantic behind them. It was a cheerful room, one that wouldn't be out of place in a seaside hotel.

'We try and keep it spruced up,' Mo said, clearly noticing her assessing gaze. 'The nature of the organization and the costs involved mean we can't quite manage five-star opulence, but we look after our residents.'

'I can see that,' Ellie said. 'And that's Arthur?' She nudged her head in the direction of the man Rose had pointed out.

He had a large hardback on his knees, but his gaze was trained on the window. He looked to be in his late seventies, with thinning hair that was more grey than brown. He had a strong jaw and salt-and-pepper brows, and his eyes were steely and full of intelligence. He was wearing dark trousers and a green fisherman's jumper, and was sitting perfectly upright, a model of composure and restraint. Ellie felt a quiver of panic; he wasn't going to like what they had to tell him.

Mo pulled a chair close to Arthur's armchair.

Arthur turned his head, his eyes narrowing. 'Mo,' he said in a deep voice.

'Arthur, how are you doing today?'

'As well as always,' he said. 'I have no idea why today

should be different from any other: not in this place. Rose,' he added, a glimmer of something – affection? – in his eyes when she and Ellie joined them, bringing over chairs that had been resting against the wall. 'And who's this? It looks very much like it could be your sister, despite the hair.'

Ellie tried not to show her surprise. 'We are,' she said. 'I mean – I am. I'm Ellie. It's nice to meet you.' She held out her hand and Arthur clasped it firmly. Ellie couldn't help feeling cowed under his gaze. Would she have felt the same if Mo hadn't told her he'd been a naval officer? She wasn't sure.

'And you,' he said. 'What are you doing here?'

'I, uhm—'

'We have a proposition for you, Arthur,' Rose cut in.

'It's a long time since I've been propositioned about anything.'

'Then hopefully you'll find this interesting.' Rose smiled, but Arthur's expression didn't change.

Mo took up the baton. 'We know you're aware of the impending improvements to Seascape House, because we had that meeting a couple of weeks ago—'

'You mean the company's decision to increase profits by building a minuscule extension and cramming more of us in here, so we're battery rather than free range?'

'I hope that wasn't the angle we put across,' Mo said smoothly, 'because that is not the intention.'

'That's always the intention,' Arthur replied. 'The only thing that changes is how much effort the powers that be put into denying it. As this is a home for people with physical, rather than mental, deficiencies, I can see it's more effort than most.'

'Arthur,' Rose chided softly, 'doesn't your cynical outlook get boring?'

'It's all I have to keep me entertained,' Arthur said shortly.

The old man was a practised curmudgeon, but Ellie could see a spark of humour in his green eyes. She could tell he enjoyed tying Mo and Rose in conversational knots, and had a feeling she wouldn't escape unscathed either.

'Why have you brought reinforcements?' Arthur gestured to Ellie. 'Don't tell me, she's—'

'Arthur, my love.' A woman had appeared next to their cluster of chairs; Ellie hadn't noticed her approach. Her hair was a cloud of white curls, and she had soft blue eyes and pearl studs in her ears. She was wearing a fuchsia skirt and a pale pink cardigan over a white shirt, and Ellie got the sense that she was tougher than her appearance suggested. 'What's this?' she asked. 'A party we're missing out on? Hello, Mo. And Rose, always lovely to see you.'

'It's nothing to concern yourself with, Iris,' Arthur said, waving a dismissive hand.

'Something interesting's going on.' Iris's gaze intensified. 'I'd like to stay.'

'Actually, Iris—' Mo started, but Arthur interrupted him. 'They're here to tell me that the extension to Seascape House is going to destroy my garden, and they've got some half-cocked plan to re-home the plants elsewhere. If they'd asked me earlier, I could have told them that there is no other suitable place. Is that why you're here, Ellie? Are you a gardener? If so, then you must have already come to that conclusion.'

For a moment, Ellie couldn't speak. When she glanced

at the others, she saw Mo was as surprised as she was, and Rose was fighting back a grin.

'There's a spot on the north lawn that *might* work,' she said, eventually.

'You're going to bulldoze over his garden?' Iris asked sharply. 'What on earth are you thinking? Arthur loves that place, and we all enjoy going out there. A few of the others, Kay and Edith in particular, would barely move from this room if they didn't have the garden to visit. We were just talking about which species of butterfly we might see this summer. You were going to add a buddleia, weren't you, Arthur?'

'I was,' he said. 'But not now. Seascape House is determined to crush any joy we might find, any initiative we unearth. They want us hovering somewhere between pensioner and vegetable.'

'Now hang on, Arthur,' Mo said, 'that's not true and you know it.'

'What other conclusion would you like me to draw? I'm sorry for your wasted journey, Ellie. And we don't have a visit scheduled until tomorrow, Rose. This proposition isn't one I'm going to be taking you up on.'

'You haven't heard all of Ellie's suggestions,' Rose said softly.

'She knows there's nowhere else, not even her spot on the north side. Not without digging up that scrub and rock you call a lawn, bringing in richer soil, cutting down the overlooking ash trees. Otherwise hardly anything will flourish. That's an awful lot of work to placate one old man.'

'It's not about placation,' Mo said. 'We care about you, and we know how much you treasure the garden.'

Arthur glanced out of the window, and Ellie saw a muscle working in his jaw. When he turned back, his gaze was fixed firmly on Mo. 'When you get to my age, you will come to realize that nothing good can last. Not gardens or marriages, families or contentment. I know you've done what you can, but you should accept, as I have, that it's over. I will put the pots outside my bedroom window – I might be able to keep them going there – and that will have to be enough.'

'We can move your garden,' Ellie said firmly. 'Why not try it, at least, instead of giving up at the first hurdle? We can set up the new area as best we can; get compost to mix with the current soil, and I don't mind pollarding the ash trees even if we're not allowed to remove them completely. A few hours of our time, doing something we both love, and more might survive than you think.' She was leaning forwards, her hand inches from Arthur's knee. 'What have you got to lose?'

Ellie waited for his reply, for the reasons her plan wouldn't work, but nothing came.

'Listen to the woman, Arthur,' Iris said gently. 'It seems like she might know a thing or two about perseverance.'

'Iris, you know full well that I am beyond—'

'Ellie is the strongest person I know,' Rose cut in. 'She's been through a lot over the last few years, and she's met all her challenges head on. I don't tell her enough, but she's inspiring.' Rose placed a hand on the older man's arm. 'Let her inspire you, too.'

Ellie couldn't speak past the lump in her throat. Her sister often paid her compliments, but this – in front of so many other people – was new. And Ellie had been feeling so uninspiring, so down about giving up her cottage, and being unable to solve Charlie and Daniel's first important wedding quandary, that her sister's words cut straight through her. Which meant she was doubly unprepared for the next person who walked through the door; so out of place in the current scenario as to be laughable.

She watched, her thoughts off kilter as Arthur started in his chair, dislodging Rose's hand from his arm almost as if he'd been given an electric shock.

'Hello,' Mo said pleasantly to the man standing just inside the room. 'How can I help you? I trust Della on reception authorized you to come up here?'

'She did,' he replied, his gaze flitting between Mo and Arthur, and then landing on Ellie. She watched the moment recognition, and shock, hit him too. 'I . . . uh, I didn't mean to interrupt anything.' He gave Ellie a questioning look, and she saw a sudden nervousness in the man who, until that moment, had been nothing but easy charm.

'You're not interrupting anything, son,' Arthur said, his words clipped, his eyes unfriendly. 'Kind of you to grace us with your presence. How long has it been?'

Quiet descended on the room, the sound of the television like an annoying fly in the background, as everyone waited for Jago Carne's answer.

Chapter Six

Jago and Arthur stared at each other. The older man's stance was defiant, Jago's much more hesitant, and there was a building tension in the room.

'We should leave you to it,' Ellie said, grabbing Rose's arm. 'We'll discuss the garden another time.'

Jago frowned, opened his mouth and then shut it again. Arthur grunted, which Ellie took as agreement. She pulled her sister towards the door.

'Nice to see you,' she said as she passed Jago, and got a waft of his lime and nutmeg scent. He was wearing a black shirt over navy jeans. It was similar to his "meet the land-lady" get-up, though included many more clothes than he'd been wearing the last time he'd encountered his landlady. Ellie's cheeks warmed as she led a reluctant Rose through the door and down the stairs, past Della on reception and out into the fresh air.

'What was that about?' Rose put her hands on her hips.

'He was starting to soften around the edges; we were close to convincing him.'

Ellie felt a sudden burst of frustration. 'There's nowhere else on this site for his garden! If they're really going to bring in an expert to landscape the lawns as part of the renovation, then that's great. Right now, I can't see anywhere with the right balance of light and shade, the right type of ground. And isn't it going to be worse if I help him move it all, give him that little bit of hope, only for everything to die anyway?'

'All right, keep your hair on.' Rose folded her arms, her gaze turning curious. 'That's not why you're in a fluster, is it? You seemed as surprised to see Arthur's son as he was.'

Ellie exhaled roughly. 'That's Jago, my tenant. It turns out the family issues he mentioned, the reason he's come back to Cornwall, might well involve Arthur.'

'Well, well, wonders never cease.' Her sister sounded amused.

'It's a small world, isn't it?'

'He's more handsome than you implied,' Rose said. Then her expression sobered. 'Arthur doesn't like talking about him, and he's not visited before as far as I know. Clearly, they're lacking a loving father-and-son bond. I wonder what's happened?' She shook her head. 'Still, I think on our next visit we can get through to Arthur. We have to do something for him.'

'Hmmm.' Ellie bit her lip. It seemed pointless to tell her sister, again, that she didn't think there was a hope of making Arthur happy about his doomed garden.

'I'll see you at home later,' Rose said. 'Thanks for this.'

'No problem.' Ellie wished there was a way she could

help. She walked to the edge of the car park and looked again at the grounds, trying to see something new in the lawns stretching around the building, or get a sudden spark of inspiration, but her thoughts had been derailed by Jago turning up, and Arthur's reaction to him. Ellie and Rose had had a happy childhood. Their parents were still very much in love and enjoying retirement in the north of the county. The two sisters saw them regularly, neither of them ever having a desire to move too far from where they grew up.

From what little she knew of Jago, and now Arthur, they seemed like opposite ends of the scale: upright naval officer who didn't suffer fools at all, let alone gladly, and a laid-back mechanic and odd-job man who'd spent years travelling and was happy adopting someone else's cat.

By the time Ellie's thoughts had drifted back to her to-do list, Rose had gone. She still had a couple of hours until her meeting with Charlie and Daniel. She heard a door slam, and turned to see Jago walk a few steps from the care home's entrance and then stop. He rubbed his hands over his face, and when he dropped them, Ellie saw that his features were tight, his jaw clenched.

'Hey,' she called.

He looked up and his expression softened. 'Hi.' He walked over to her. 'I didn't expect to see you here.'

'Likewise. Arthur's your father?'

'Yes. He's . . . It's the first time I've seen him in a few months. The manager, Mo, said you were here to help Dad move a garden?'

'My sister, Rose, is his community nurse,' Ellie explained. 'She asked for my help. Did Mo explain what's happened?'

'No,' Jago said. 'Not really. He wanted to give the two of us some space, but Dad wasn't exactly welcoming, which I suppose I deserve.'

Ellie resisted the urge to ask what he meant. 'Let me show you what he's created.'

'I've got to get to the garage.'

'This will take five minutes.' She touched his arm lightly, and he seemed to come back from whichever dark place his mind had taken him.

'OK,' he sighed.

As they walked, she explained the situation. The proposed extension, how demoralizing it would be for Arthur to lose something he'd put so much time and effort into. When they rounded the corner and the small garden came into view, Jago stopped in his tracks.

'Beautiful, isn't it?' she said.

He made a sound in his throat, as if he couldn't find the words.

'It will be hard for him to give it up,' she went on. 'I know if I was going to lose my garden . . .'

'It must be bad enough that you can't spend time in it every day,' Jago said softly. 'You can come back whenever you want; I'd never stop you.'

'That means a lot, thank you.' She glanced at him; his throat was working, an unreadable look on his face.

'It's hard to think of him like this,' he said eventually. 'As a man who spends time creating . . . this. All the attention to detail, the delicacy. After Mum died, we . . .' He breathed out. 'It didn't bring us closer. I had hoped it would, but I'm as much to blame as he is for failing to put our differences aside. I came back for a couple of months, to help with the funeral and the arrangements, and again when he had the operation. I helped him move here, helped clear the old house, but I kept the visits short and focused on what needed to be done. We aren't very easy around each other.'

'You're here now, though,' Ellie said quietly.

Jago gave a humourless chuckle. 'And already it feels like a mistake.'

'He didn't want to talk to you?'

He shook his head, but didn't elaborate. Instead, he walked away from the garden, to where the rolling hills and the sea were visible through the trees' budding branches. Ellie followed him.

'How's Monty?' she asked.

Jago grinned. 'That cat is an idiot,' he said affectionately. 'A lumbering, canny idiot. In the evenings he always comes to sit on my lap, and then whenever I want to get up, for a tea or a beer or a cheese sandwich, he's worked it so that he won't release me unless I give him a treat, too. If I go into the kitchen and he doesn't get one of his biscuits or, more usually, a bit of meat, he yowls and yowls until I give in.'

Ellie laughed. 'He's got the measure of you.'

'And I'm fine with that. It's good to have some company.' It was such a simple statement, but it made Ellie's chest ache. Both for Jago, and for herself. She was lucky that she had Rose, and she had enjoyed her freedom over the last couple of years, but the thought of companionable evenings, of sharing details of her day and listening in turn with someone other than her sister, of not going to bed alone, suddenly seemed like heaven.

She cleared her throat. 'He's a good cat, on the whole.'

When Jago didn't reply, she cast around for another subject. 'You know, the cottage is only a little way up the hill, but you get a completely different perspective from down here.' She pointed to the countryside ahead of them, a couple of roofs visible, then the thin strip of blue-grey sea. 'I had no idea about those other buildings between here and the coast. I've noticed the tracks leading off Wilderness Lane, but I've never seen any farm vehicles. I thought they must be abandoned, but see that roof, there?' She pointed. 'It looks anything but dilapidated.'

'It's a big swanky barn,' Jago said.

Ellie's heart missed a beat. 'What?'

'I got the turning wrong a couple of days after I moved in, thought the cottage was before the care home, not after, and ended up in a cobbled yard with an old wagon and chickens, like something out of a historical drama.' He laughed. 'But the buildings look newly refurbished. All polished wooden frames and triple-glazing.'

'Do you think it's a house, or something else?' The words came out slightly strangled, and he shot her a curious look.

'Too big to be a house, I think. I fancied taking a proper look, but this old woman with mad grey hair came rushing out with a broom, so I did a quick reverse and left her to it. Why are you so interested?'

'If it's a commercial venue, it might be good for weddings.' For Charlie and Daniel's wedding, specifically. 'But the old woman doesn't sound ideal, so maybe it's a no-go.'

'It wouldn't hurt to check it out,' Jago said. 'It looked impressive from the little I saw of it. But take some kind of weapon with you – she had a strange glint in her eye that put me on edge.' He grinned.

'I'll do that, thanks.' Jago was back to his amenable self, his green eyes bright, his hands shoved in the pockets of his jeans. Knowing he was here for his dad, even though their relationship was obviously strained, filled in some of the gaps and made her warm to him even more. But that was something she didn't have time for – cosy fantasies of snuggling with him and Monty in the living room of Cornflower Cottage aside – and certainly wasn't appropriate in her role as his landlady.

'I'd better get back,' he said.

'Need a lift?'

'No thanks, it's only a ten-minute walk. See you soon?'

She nodded. 'If that's OK?'

'Always.'

When Ellie got back to Florence, her mood had lifted. She might be on the way to solving her venue issue, thanks to Jago; she could visit her garden as often as she wanted, thanks to Jago; and she had been warmed from the inside out by their brief conversation. She scouted around for a reason to be happy that didn't involve her new tenant, and realized she didn't have one. Discomfort mingling with her happiness, she drove away from Seascape House.

It had been a while since Ellie had been on board the Cornish Cream Tea Bus. She had happy memories of eating its decadent, delicious cream teas, of whiling away a couple of hours with Rose or one of her friends, Porthgolow's beach sparkling outside the window, the bus full of chatter. Now, as she stepped on board, even though Charlie had shut it slightly early for their meeting and it was without its usual buzz, she was reminded why it was such a special place to come.

The sea was more grey than blue this afternoon, but the cheerful interior instantly perked Ellie up, and it still smelled of rich, fruity scones that must have been warming in the oven not that long ago. Charlie beckoned her to one of the downstairs tables and turned to the coffee machine. Ellie could see a stack of washing-up on one of the tiny kitchen counters, the gentle hum revealing the dishwasher was already at work.

'Jonah's been helping me this afternoon,' Charlie said, noticing Ellie's gaze lingering on the piles of crockery. 'He's a teenager in the village; he hasn't reached that sullen stage yet and he's always willing to pick up a few shifts after school and at weekends. Quite often, those shifts are eighty per cent entertaining the customers and twenty per cent actual work, but he's so popular with the regulars, I can't begrudge him his slight lack of focus.'

'He sounds brilliant,' Ellie said, laughing. 'It's been far too long since Rose and I came here.'

'You should come this weekend,' Charlie said, perching on the table opposite where Ellie sat. 'I'm sorry Daniel isn't here; he's been held up with one of the building companies he's seeing, but he'll join us if he can.'

'That's fine,' Ellie assured her. 'This was always going to be a quick meeting, but I'm hoping, now, it will be a positive one. I might have found a venue for you.'

Charlie's face lit up. 'Really? In Porthgolow?'

'On the edge of the village, just south of Crumbling Cliff.'

'Where?' Charlie asked. 'I thought we'd given you an impossible task. I've been itching to contact you to ask you to start looking further afield, but Daniel told me to have faith.' She shrugged. 'It's not that I didn't – please don't think that. Also, Daniel's *so* keen to get married here. He's been in Porthgolow longer than I have, and his heart is even more firmly rooted here than mine. He'll claim nonchalance, but I think he'd be really disappointed if we ended up somewhere else for the wedding.'

'I understand, and I hope I've found a solution for you. Although, quick disclaimer, I haven't been able to find out all the details yet.' She sipped the cappuccino Charlie had handed her, the top perfectly frothy and dusted with chocolate.

'Tell me everything,' Charlie said, her eyes wide with anticipation.

Ellie settled into her seat. With the bus otherwise empty, it felt as if they were having a clandestine meeting; two friends huddling in the bike shed to talk about boys.

'I had to visit the care home near my cottage this morning, and while I was there I noticed a building further down the hill. I'd never seen it before, and it looked like a farm site, but I always thought the farms were no longer in use. A friend told me he'd been there by accident, and that it looked newly renovated.' She didn't add the bit about the old woman with the broom, which was a detail she didn't think Charlie would appreciate right now. 'I went to have a look myself, and it's a barn with a cobbled yard, chickens, an old-fashioned wagon and a brickwork wall surrounding the whole thing. The barn was laid out with long tables, as if it's set up for events. From what I've seen, it's a good blend of rustic and polished; exactly what you're looking for.'

'Do you have any photos?'

Ellie took out her phone and handed it to Charlie. 'I

couldn't find anyone to speak to right then, and it's not been on my radar as a venue, but it could be new. The updates to the barn look recent. I know it's a risk telling you this when I haven't been able to confirm any details, but I have a really good feeling about it.'

She had felt a surge of adrenaline the moment she'd driven into the courtyard. It was the venue Charlie and Daniel were searching for; more perfect than anything Ellie had seen on Pinterest. She would track down the owner and, even if it wasn't a commercial space, even if she had to deal with the old lady with the broom Jago had encountered, she would negotiate. Her instincts were telling her that this was their venue, and in the past she'd been right to trust her instincts – most of the time, anyway.

'It looks beautiful,' Charlie said, zooming in on a photo. 'I'd love to see some pictures of the inside, too, and show them to Daniel.'

Ellie nodded. 'Give me a couple of days, and I'll be back with details of the hire costs, more photos and, hopefully, a date for you to visit it yourselves.'

Charlie looked up. 'I know it's not a definite, but I really appreciate you showing me this.'

Ellie finished her drink and stood up. 'I didn't want you to think we were out of options. And if we can find this place nestled away in deepest Cornwall, then it proves that, even if this isn't the one, we just need to keep looking. But I can't claim any of the credit for this discovery.'

'That doesn't matter – you know about it now. And just down the hill from your cottage, too!'

Ellie laughed. 'It's *very* close to my cottage; and I had no idea it was there. I should have been looking closer to home.'

Something flickered in her mind, just out of reach, and she gave Charlie a distracted goodbye and stepped off the bus, turning to wave as she reached the edge of the sand. A couple strolled past her, a pair of yellow Labradors running ahead of them, intent on the slate-coloured waves and all that sea spray.

But even if the water had looked inviting rather than inhospitable, Ellie didn't have time for a dip. She was heading back to the barn, only a couple of hours after her first visit, in the hopes that someone might be inside the adjoining cottage when she got there. She had searched on the internet, but had found no trace of the venue; not a website or Facebook page or tag on Google Maps. It was all but invisible, and Ellie hoped that, if it was a fledgling business, she could contribute to its early success by booking it for a beautiful summer wedding. If it turned out to be private, then she was prepared to barter, bribe or go into full-on battle, because *this*, she was sure, was the perfect venue for her bride and groom.

The thick cloud cover began to dissolve, letting out a gauzy, late-afternoon sun, and as she drove it streamed in through the windscreen. She winced as she thought of the way she'd tried to bring Jago into the conversation. *I can't claim any of the credit for this discovery.* She'd been waiting for Charlie to say, 'Oh? Your friend, did you say? Who's that, then?' And then she would have been able to talk about the man who had come into her life so unexpectedly, but who she already felt grateful to know. She kept replaying their meeting in the garden of Cornflower Cottage, the way she'd behaved like a giddy eighteen year old.

Still, now she had a possible venue that, despite some

promising signs, was likely to be a challenge. She might have to negotiate hard to get it and then, if she was successful, there might be yet more work to do to make it meet Charlie and Daniel's expectations. Far from being daunted by the prospect, she was filled with a fire that had recently seemed absent. Old woman with a broom or not, Ellie had a job to do, and she was going to make damn sure she succeeded.

She drove up the hill, leaving behind Porthgolow's quaint seafront, the jetty with the speedboats moored up and the Seven Stars, where Hannah would be prepping for the day's covers or planning new recipes for the summer season. The sea sparkled like cut glass on a deep blue carpet, and Ellie felt a burst of exhilaration. She could make this wedding her best yet, and it would be the start of getting her life back to where she wanted it to be.

And then she thought of Arthur sitting in his chair by the window, the resignation in his voice, as if he'd known all along that his garden was too good to be true. She pictured Jago's tight jaw, the tension radiating off him when he spoke about his dad. He'd made the effort to move back to within shouting distance of him – his claims that Cornflower Cottage were ideal made a lot more sense now. It was hard, but he was trying to close the gap between them.

As Ellie turned onto Wilderness Lane, now the artery leading to three buildings which were, all of a sudden, fairly significant to her, that earlier flicker in her mind solidified into a firm, shining thought. *Closer to home.*

She knew exactly how she could help Arthur. How she could help Arthur *and* Jago and also – though this was by no means the main motivation – herself. It was an idea so glaringly obvious, so perfect, she was cross with herself for taking so long to think of it.

She imagined the glee on Rose's face when she told her; pictured Arthur losing his cool disinterest as she explained her plan. And Jago – he'd be pleased, wouldn't he? Surely this would make things easier for him? And if he could see his dad being happy, doing something he loved instead of isolating himself, then that could only be a good thing, couldn't it?

Ellie turned onto the uneven track she had believed, until today, led to deserted farm buildings, keeping her hands firmly on the wheel until she reached the yard that was, as Jago had said, like something out of a period drama. She smoothed down her shirt and glanced in the mirror to check she had no mascara flecks under her eyes. When she returned her gaze to the windscreen, she saw a woman wearing a long brown overcoat and fingerless gloves, her short grey hair standing up in all directions, a broom outstretched in her left hand.

Ellie took a deep breath, then opened the door and stepped onto the cobbles. However hard this was going to be, it would be worth it. You got out of life what you put in, and from now on, Ellie was going to put in a hundred per cent. She was holding other people's dreams in her hands, and she had to do everything in her power to make them come true.

Part Two

Two Tarts Beat As One

Chapter Seven

'I am so, *so* sorry.' The woman was petite, with glossy, dark brown hair cut in a neat bob. She looked about Ellie's age, or maybe a few years older. 'My mum is rather averse to unexpected visitors, and we do seem to have had a few over the last couple of days.' She frowned, and Ellie felt a stab of guilt.

'I shouldn't have turned up unannounced,' she said, 'but a friend told me about this place – he found it after he took a wrong turn. He's probably the other person who unsettled your mum.'

The two of them were standing in the courtyard of the impressive-looking barn, with brassy chickens pecking around their feet. Elowen Moon had been keen to speak to someone about the venue, hoping it would be the solution to her current pressing problem; she needed to find a place where Charlie Quilter and Daniel Harper could get married, either in – or very close to – Porthgolow. She had been approached, or rather accosted, by an older lady with a broom, but before she could become truly alarmed, the dark-haired woman had coaxed her mother – as Ellie now knew – back to the small cottage on the other side of the yard.

'Ever since we moved in we've had builders on the site,' the woman went on. 'It was always going to be the case, with so much work to do here, but Mum hasn't settled down yet. She will do in time, I'm sure.' She shook her head quickly. 'Sorry, I'm Jane. Jane McTavish. Have you come about the barn?'

'I have,' Ellie said. 'I couldn't find any references to it online. As I said, I only discovered it because a friend of mine took a wrong turn.'

Jane rubbed her forehead. 'That's next on my never-ending to-do list. We've only just finished the conversion, and as you can see the exterior is still a bit rough and ready. I've started putting feelers out, but I need to sort out a proper marketing plan.'

Excitement tingled through Ellie's limbs. This was perfect: they were going to help each other out. 'I'd love to have a look around, if that's OK?' she said. 'If it meets all the requirements of my clients, I might want to book it for a wedding.'

'Clients?' Jane looked surprised. 'It's not your wedding?'

'I'm a wedding planner,' Ellie explained. 'I've got a couple in Porthgolow who want to get married in June, and I'm still searching for the right location. Your barn could well be near the top of the list.'

Jane smiled. 'In that case, let me give you a tour.' She gestured to the wooden doors halfway along the building. Ellie glanced through the windows as they passed, but in the late afternoon sun, the glass reflected the yard back at her.

'Have you owned the farm long?' she asked, swerving a couple of chickens that were intent on their task.

'It was my uncle's,' Jane explained. 'He died last summer, and left it to Mum. She's long wanted to move back to Cornwall, and I was looking for a change of scene, too. We came up with the plan to convert the barn into a commercial property. It's been a lot harder than I anticipated.' She gave a gentle laugh, and Ellie couldn't help probing.

'And is your mum happy . . . with how it's turned out?'

Jane paused, her hand on the door. 'The part of Bristol she was living in was fairly rough. There was a lot of social disorder, regular burglaries, and Mum was on her own, and getting increasingly frightened. She didn't want to move to Oxford, where I was, but when I suggested we come back here, make a go of the barn, she jumped at it. She's happier here, but it's also been a lot of work to get as far as we've got, and with builders on site all the time, she's struggled. I'd like to think now it's nearly done, she'll be more content. We'll obviously be holding events, but she'll throw herself into them, I know it, and wedding parties aren't the same as the dusty disruption of building work. Sorry,' she went on, pushing open the barn door and flicking on the lights, 'this isn't the most professional sales pitch, is it? Here's our brand-spanking-new event venue, complete with irate old woman.'

Ellie shook her head. 'Moving house and starting a new business are both impossibly stressful, and you've done them together. People deal with things in different ways, and I . . . goodness, Jane. This place is beautiful.' And it was; breathtakingly so.

It was a rectangular space, with a high, vaulted ceiling, criss-crossed with wooden beams. Three delicate chandeliers were evenly spaced along the building, their teardrop glass beads shimmering with soft gold light. Wall lanterns like old-fashioned gas lamps helped illuminate the room, and the walls themselves were exposed brick which, Ellie could see, had been treated to give an almost glossy finish. Wooden tables were laid out banquet style, the spare chairs stacked against a wall. There was a bar at one end of the room, with gleaming brass beer pumps, and a raised stage at the other. Tall windows looked out either on the courtyard, or offered views down to the sea.

'It was a dark space even when we updated the lighting,' Jane explained, 'so I embarked on the epic feat of adding windows. The builders weren't sure the barn would survive it, but they brought in an architect and . . . well, it was worth it, I think.' Ellie could hear the pride in her voice.

'It's magnificent,' she said. 'Truly. You get the original features and the floor space of the barn, and all these extra details. The windows give it so much natural light, but then, at night . . .' She gestured to the chandeliers. 'And what's it like when there's a good sunset?'

Jane's grin made her look several years younger, and Ellie had the sense that, despite the hardships she'd faced, she was happy with her decision to move back to Cornwall and convert the barn. Ellie didn't blame her; this venue would be a shining light on the wedding and events circuit. She felt a sudden, pressing urgency to book it up for the entire summer, or come to an arrangement with Jane where she at least got first dibs on bank holidays. The only issue was the bumpy farm track leading up to it, but maybe that was next on Jane's list of things to tackle.

'Sunsets make this place glow,' Jane admitted. 'You should come back one evening to see it. Which reminds me that I need to hire a photographer to take some photos for the website.'

'I can give you some names if you like?' Ellie said. 'But right now, I'd like to see if you're free for the wedding I'm planning.' She took her iPad out of her bag.

'Let me get the diary,' Jane said. 'In fact, why not come through to the house? I'll make us some tea. I'm only just starting on the event packages, but I've got a few different options we can discuss.'

'Could I have a list? I'll need to talk through the possi-bilities with my clients. Would I be able to bring them here in the next couple of days?'

'Of course!' Jane led her out of the barn, and Ellie felt some of the tension seeping from her neck and shoulders. This place had the potential to be the wedding venue of Charlie and Daniel's dreams, and Ellie loved nothing more than turning potential into certainty.

After her meeting with Jane, which included finding out that there was another, more substantial road that led to Porthgolow Barn courtyard, and that the track leading off Wilderness Lane was a back route to the site, Ellie arranged to take Charlie and Daniel there that Friday.

Jane had assured Ellie that her mum was getting better, that a broom-wielding woman wasn't one of the added extras, and Ellie wasn't worried. She could see so much promise in their venue, and she had a fierce urge to help them with it; to share her contacts and the knowledge she'd gained from years of working in the events business. She could imagine Porthgolow Barn being suitable for so many happy couples in her future – perhaps even one of the others she had on her books right this moment, Philip and Samira, who wanted an autumn wedding in a rural setting.

As for Charlie and Daniel, it was everything they had hoped for. They wanted a happy day with their friends and family in beautiful Porthgolow surroundings, and Jane's barn would give them that.

Ellie spent the following day at home, going through wedding magazines and marking pages of dresses and morning suits, phoning the cake companies she worked with to request samples, and perusing the local florists' websites for their new-season blooms and bouquets, everything geared towards the approaching summer season. All the while she had one ear on the door, waiting for the key in the lock.

Her sister, Rose, got home just after four, bustling in in her usual, loud way. 'Yoohoo, I'm back! All ready to put your plan into action?' She appeared in the doorway. 'You look nice,' she added, and Ellie tamped down a groan.

'It's just jeans and a jumper.'

'Your favourite cashmere jumper. And eyeliner. I approve.'

'Go and get changed,' Ellie said, and Rose did as she was told, a gleeful look on her face.

The day before, Jago Carne, Ellie's tenant, had turned up at Seascape House care-home, revealing himself to be the son of Arthur, one of Rose's patients, in whom she had taken a particular interest. In the small amount of time that had passed since then, Rose had dropped endless hints about him – most of them as subtle as a ten-ton truck. Comments about his eligibility and handsomeness, and about how he had appeared in Ellie's life in more than one context, and how that had to mean something.

When Ellie had told Rose her idea about how to help Arthur, Rose had declared her a genius. Ellie wondered if that was because it would solve her patient's problem, or because it meant more contact with Jago Carne.

'All right, then,' Rose said, coming down the stairs. 'Let's go and see lover boy.'

'If you call him that once more,' Ellie replied, 'then I will not be held accountable for my actions.'

Once they were in Rose's car, Ellie began to wonder if what they were doing was really wise. For one thing, she was spending more of her time travelling back and forth to Cornflower Cottage than she had done when she was living there, before she'd been forced to rent it out to boost her income. However relaxed Jago was, her frequent appearances in his life might start to annoy him.

A light drizzle was falling and, as they got closer to the coast, became a fine mist that made the sea invisible, the cliffs looming out of the grey as if they marked the end of the world. But her cottage looked pretty even in the mist; the rosebuds were jewelled with raindrops, and the white walls seemed bright in the gloom. The lights were on in the living room and bedroom, and Ellie pictured Jago moving between them, navigating the stairs with his long gait, jumping over Monty the cat who liked to lie, stretched out, on the bottom step.

'Ready for this?' Rose asked softly. She was the queen of

teasing, but she was more sensitive to Ellie's moods than she liked to let on.

'Is this even a good idea?' Ellie said. 'I feel like, once again, we're going behind Arthur's back; trying to fix his problem without consulting him first.'

'But we can't offer Arthur the chance to spend time in your garden if Jago isn't happy about it,' Rose said. 'He's OK with you coming here, but this is his home now, and the laser beams that passed between him and Arthur the other day suggest there's some difficulty there. We need to do it this way round.'

'Should we be doing it at all?' Ellie pressed. 'I've already asked so much of Jago, and this feels like treading on too many toes. I've got ahead of myself, thought up a solution that *seemed* ideal but is probably a step too far for everyone involved.'

'Or,' Rose countered, 'it could work out just as you hope. If Jago's genuinely trying to build bridges with Arthur but doesn't know how to go about it, bringing him here for gardening rather than reconciliation reasons could be the baby-step he needs. Not too far at all.'

Ellie chewed her lip.

'And here's the crux of it, Elowen,' Rose went on. 'You'll never know if you don't ask. Do you think Jago will mind us asking?'

Ellie shrugged. 'Probably not, but . . .' She thought of how he'd looked when he'd emerged from Seascape House; angry and forlorn and nowhere close to relaxed.

'Come on, then.' Rose patted Ellie on the shoulder and then, before she could say anything else, got out of the car. Ellie followed, trying not to drag her heels.

Rose rapped on the front door. She never pressed bells, preferring the more direct approach of a solid knock, even though, for Cornflower Cottage, Ellie had spent a long time finding just the right one, with a pretty, inoffensive chime. They stood side by side, the thick door masking the sound of footsteps beyond it, so that Ellie jumped slightly when it swung open to reveal Jago, his expression welcoming.

'Hi, Jago,' Ellie said. 'This is my sister, Rose, who I mentioned on the phone earlier. You met her briefly at Seascape House.'

'Very briefly,' Rose added, holding out her hand. 'Hello.'

'Hi.' Jago shook it, then stepped back and ushered them inside. Ellie's body prickled with familiarity. A quick glance at the carpet showed her he hadn't tracked in any dirt, and she felt overwhelmingly grateful. 'Can I get you both a drink? Tea, coffee, beer?'

'A tea would be great,' Rose said. 'How are you finding it here?'

'Oh, it's grand,' Jago replied. 'Ellie, would you like tea?'

'Yes, please.'

'Give me two minutes. Go through to the front room.' He gave them a quick smile and disappeared into the kitchen.

'I don't think we should have come,' Ellie hiss-whispered to Rose. 'I should have just asked him over the phone.'

'He obviously doesn't mind us being here,' Rose said. 'And this way, you can use your not inconsiderable charms to persuade him. Eyeliner, remember.'

'He doesn't strike me as the kind of man to be swayed by a bit of eyeliner.'

'Well, what *would* sway him, then?'

'Are you both OK?' Jago asked from the doorway. 'You can go and sit down, you know.'

Ellie felt her cheeks redden. 'We're fine,' she said. 'Sorry. We're just—'

'We were just going,' Rose finished brightly. She pushed Ellie into the living room and dragged her onto a sofa. Monty looked up from the armchair he was dozing on, eyed them beadily and then jumped down and began to make his way over.

'Oh, no, you don't,' Rose said, and sneezed. 'Bugger. I forgot about your cat.' She moved to the opposite sofa and watched warily as Monty jumped onto Ellie's lap, raising his head in a quest for affection. Rose sneezed three times in quick succession, and got a tissue out of her bag.

'Here we go.' Jago set three mugs down on the coffee table. 'I wasn't sure how you took it, Rose, so I've brought sugar. Help yourselves.' He settled into the armchair Monty had vacated. He was wearing a navy T-shirt that clung to his torso, inevitably taking Ellie's thoughts back to the other day.

'It's kind of you to see us like this,' she blurted.

'No problem. I wasn't particularly busy. What was it you wanted to ask me?'

'It's about the garden,' Ellie said. 'How you said it was fine for me to come here whenever I wanted.'

Jago rubbed his cheek. 'And I'm still fine with that. Nothing's changed over the last couple of days.'

Ellie nodded. 'How's work going? Are you getting on OK at the garage?'

He looked bemused, and Ellie heard Rose hiss air out through her teeth.

'It's a good place to work,' he said. 'It was always going to be slow to start with, but I'm picking up a fair few jobs. How's the Porthgolow wedding coming along?'

'Oh!' Ellie sat forward, almost dislodging Lord Montague. 'I have to thank you – that barn is looking like a real possibility.'

His eyebrows shot up. 'It's for hire? Even with the disconcerting welcoming party?'

Ellie nodded. 'That's the owner's mother. She's quite fragile, apparently; taking a while to adjust to their new surroundings. But you should see inside the barn, Jago. It's beautiful. There are these lamps—'

Rose cleared her throat loudly, and Ellie pushed down her irritation. The more she thought about what they were asking, the more it seemed like too big a favour. She couldn't back out now without confusing Jago completely, but she didn't want to go in like a bulldozer.

'Sounds great,' Jago said, glancing at Rose.

Ellie sighed. 'Jago, you know I showed you your dad's garden at the care home yesterday?' The change was instant; his whole body tensed, and his green eyes seemed to darken, like storm clouds gathering over the sea.

'What about it?' he asked.

She swallowed. 'I explained that they're going to destroy it as part of the home's renovation.'

He nodded.

'Well, I . . .' She glanced at Rose, who gave her an encouraging smile. 'What I thought was that, uhm, maybe . . . maybe he could come here? He could help to look after this garden.'

Ellie's suggestion was met with quiet; the ticking of the

Thomas Kent wall clock and Monty's loud purring filling the void. She watched Jago's lips part as he tried to take in the request.

'Actually,' she said quickly, 'it's not a great idea. It's too—'

'You want to bring Dad here?' His voice sounded strangled, and Ellie wished she could rewind the last ten minutes.

'He'd always be accompanied by me or Mo, the care-home manager,' Rose said, either unaware of or ignoring the tension in the room. 'It would be me, more often than not. It would give him the freedom to work on a garden close by, to do what he loves, and it might give you two a chance to talk outside the care-home setting. Somewhere a bit less formal.'

Jago stared at his knees, his brows knitted together.

'But if it's too much . . .' Ellie started.

'I don't know,' he said, looking up. 'I can see why it makes sense. But this . . .' He gestured around him.

'It's your home,' Ellie finished. 'Your sanctuary.' That was exactly what Cornflower Cottage had become to her after her divorce. Somewhere she could hide and deal with her feelings, where she could find comfort and safety and start to piece her heart back together.

Jago nodded. 'It already feels like that, and I'm not sure . . .' He glanced at Rose, then turned his attention back to Ellie. 'You know I've not had the easiest relationship with Dad, and I *am* here to fix that. I'm as close as I can be to the care home, and of course I want him to be happy.' He sighed. 'But having him here? How often were you thinking?'

Ellie exchanged a glance with Rose. 'I see him twice a

week,' Rose said. 'For treatment on his hip. I was thinking that, to begin with, one of those visits could be here. Recovery is quicker when you feel positive about it, and being in the garden would be therapeutic for his soul, as well as his body.'

Jago gave Rose a wry grin, and Ellie's heart gave a little jolt. 'You're pretty persuasive, aren't you?' he said.

'You're telling me.' Ellie rolled her eyes. 'Imagine what it's like living with her.'

'Does that mean it's a yes?' Rose asked.

Jago stirred his tea absently. 'Can I think about it? The last thing I want is to hurt Dad, but I need a while to get used to the idea.'

Rose nodded. 'Thank you for even considering it,' she said, with more gentleness than Ellie would have expected. 'We realize that what we're asking isn't straightforward. Shall I go and check on your lupins?' She turned to Ellie, then stood abruptly.

'Oh. OK. Thanks, Rose.' Ellie tried to hide her confusion. Rose didn't have a clue what a lupin flower looked like, let alone the plant when it wasn't close to blooming. Her sister bustled out of the room, leaving her alone with Jago and the dozing cat. He smiled at her and she returned it, the air between them thickening.

'Please don't feel like you have to agree to this,' Ellie said. 'I won't put your rent up or anything.'

Jago's smile became a grin. 'I didn't think you would.'

'And you know,' she went on, 'if you ever fancied getting together for a drink at the Seven Stars – whether you want your dad to come here or not – I'm often about. Doing wedding things, you know. Venues and meetings, planning bits and pieces. In Porthgolow.' She was gabbling, flustered. Was she asking him *out?*

Jago looked surprised. 'Sure. I mean, that would be great.'

Ellie chewed her lip. 'And that barn really is ideal,' she continued. 'I had no idea it was there, just down the hill, and I thought I knew the area so well.'

'Cornwall's full of hidden corners,' he said. 'That's one of the things I love about it; that you can change direction or take a different route and discover a new bay or country house or incredible view of the coastline. I could be here until I was a hundred and never discover all its secrets.'

'That's a lovely way of describing it,' Ellie said. 'Have you had a chance to explore Porthgolow yet?'

'Not really. I've been focusing on getting comfortable here, establishing myself at the garage. A trip to the pub would be very welcome.'

Her stomach fluttered. He was bringing the conversation back to her invitation, holding her to it. Did that mean he wanted to spend more time with her? 'Right then!' She leaned forward to put her mug on the table and watched as Monty slid off her lap. He woke abruptly, finding his feet with ease, and gave an indignant yowl.

'Sorry Monty,' Ellie said, as Jago burst out laughing. He got a feline stare for his trouble, which made Ellie laugh, too.

With the tension broken, she was reluctant to leave. But Rose was possibly standing outside getting drenched, staring at plants she couldn't name and didn't understand the appeal of, and she felt bad.

'I'd better get back.'

'And I'd better get on.' Jago gestured vaguely in the

direction of the kitchen, and Ellie wondered what he was having for dinner. Was he a good cook or chaotic in the kitchen, limited to beans on toast? 'I'll think about your suggestion, and I won't leave it too long to let you know the answer.'

'There's no pressure,' she said hurriedly. 'You need to be completely comfortable.'

The side of his mouth kicked up in an embarrassed smile, and Ellie wondered what it would be like to kiss that smile, to feel his stubble against her skin.

'Let me know about the pub,' he said, as she walked to the front door.

'Will do.' Ellie put her hand on the handle and turned to say goodbye, only to find that he had walked up behind her. He was standing so close, she could see slivers of gold in his green eyes. 'Bye Jago,' she said. 'Thanks for the tea.'

'See you soon, Ellie.'

Rose was in the car, looking at something on her phone, and Ellie would hazard a guess that she hadn't been in the back garden at all. She didn't know whether to throttle her sister for manipulating the situation, or hug her. She pictured Jago's warm smile and his unkempt hair, just crying out for Ellie to run her hands through it, and thought, for the millionth time, that it was impossible to be annoyed with Rose Moon for longer than five minutes.

Chapter Eight

It had rained heavily the night before, but still, Ellie was unprepared for the sight that met her when she drove down the main approach to Porthgolow Barn. She had imagined the cobbles gleaming with rainwater, small puddles reflecting the silky blue, early morning sky, everything smelling fresh and promising. But instead . . . her mouth fell open in dismay.

She was meeting Charlie and Daniel here in five minutes, and it looked like a scene from a disaster film.

There *were* puddles, but they were of the murky, muddy variety. The cobbles were barely visible beneath the thick brown sludge, the chickens picking up their feet as they stalked across the yard. The barn itself looked impressive, rising defiantly out of the mire, but it also seemed unreachable. Ellie pictured dainty silk wedding shoes, the long hem of a pearl-encrusted dress sliding through the mud, and winced.

And on top of all that, just to complete the effect, there

was a large pig standing in the middle of the courtyard. Its pink skin was mottled with patches of dirt, and it was eating something that looked very much like a cabbage.

Slowly, Ellie got out of the car. She didn't check her watch, because she didn't want to have to accept that this was the scene with which Charlie and Daniel would be presented.

'Hello,' Jane said breezily, emerging from the cottage with wellies on over her jeans. 'It's so lovely that the sun's decided to make an appearance. I was worried your couple would see the place under dark clouds and go away with the wrong impression.'

Ellie balked, unsure how to respond.

Jane's smile faded slightly, her shoulders dropping in a sigh. 'This is Millicent,' she said, gesturing towards the pig. 'She belongs to the next farm along, but she has an adventurous spirit I haven't been able to curb.'

'Right,' Ellie replied. 'So what shall we do?'

'We'll work around her!' Jane clapped her hands and Millicent looked up briefly, before returning to her brassica.

Ellie took a deep breath to try and quell the panic rising up inside her, and counted to five. 'Will you have someone who can come and clean the courtyard if it's like this on the day of the wedding?' she asked.

Jane looked surprised. 'Well, yes. Of course. If you think it needs it.' She turned in a circle, her face pinched in concentration. 'Yes, I suppose it does, really, doesn't it? OK.' She took a notepad out of her jeans pocket and scribbled something down, and Ellie felt slightly, only *slightly*, happier.

The sound of a car cut through the quiet, and she watched as a BMW drove into the yard, Charlie and Daniel in the front. Charlie's face was eager, and Ellie hoped she would see something good in the place, even in its current state.

'There's a pig,' Charlie said as she got out, laughter in her voice.

'The pig isn't part of the package,' Ellie assured her. 'Hi Charlie, hi Daniel. This is Jane, the owner of Porthgolow Barn.'

'Hello.' Jane strode over and shook their hands. Greetings were made and then Charlie and Daniel appraised the space. Daniel glanced down, his brows furrowing, as a chicken pecked at his boot.

'So this is the courtyard,' Jane explained. 'It will be gleaming on the day of your wedding, the stones like polished gems! None of this mud malarkey.' Ellie was relieved she'd finally realized it was a problem.

'And the pig?' Charlie stepped towards Millicent. Millicent grunted and trotted to the other side of the yard.

'Millicent will be back with her owner,' Jane confirmed. 'She's come for a holiday, which she does occasionally, but *not* on wedding days. And I'm going to get an arbour just here, where you step into the garden.' She led Charlie and Daniel round the side of the barn, to a gap in the brick wall at the edge of the courtyard. Through the gap, Ellie could see a patch of waterlogged grass. There was a small, unintentional lake separating the yard from the grass, and she was put in mind of Dame Judi Dench in *Shakespeare in Love*, trampling on someone's cloak to avoid getting her feet wet. Would she need to make sure there were cloaks on hand on their wedding day? Or arrange for wooden boards to be laid down over the impromptu pond?

'It's got great views,' Charlie said, and Ellie was grateful to her for focusing on the positives. The garden faced west, so a swathe of sea was visible beyond the last few fields between the barn and the coast. Right now it was a deep blue, churning with the previous night's rain, the saltiness reaching them on the breeze.

'It will be tidied up,' Jane assured them. 'Plant pots round the edges, a wooden bench just over to the side. It'll be a beautiful spot for photographs.'

Daniel and Charlie exchanged a glance, but Ellie couldn't read it. What were they silently communicating to each other; hope, or horror?

'Shall we look at the barn itself?' Ellie said. 'Obviously, this is a new venue, and not completely finished, but I hope you'll like the main space.'

'Of course.' Jane patted her pockets and gave them a winning smile. 'I'll just go and get the keys.'

She hurried back to the cottage, leaving Charlie, Daniel and Ellie with Millicent's gentle snuffles and the quiet scrabbling of the chickens. The sound of another car made Ellie turn, in time to see a gleaming Land Rover park behind Daniel's BMW. Lila and Hannah spilled out, along with two young men. One was dark blonde, with high cheekbones and kind eyes, and Ellie thought there was something familiar about him. The other had dark curls, glasses and a slightly remote expression.

Lila's laugh burst into the morning air. 'Oh, my God, there's a pig!'

It was Charlie's turn to look contrite. 'They wanted to come and see it, too.'

'That's fine,' Ellie said, aiming for cheerful. 'The more the merrier.'

'I don't think you've met Sam or Noah,' she added. 'Sam is Lila's boyfriend, Noah is Hannah's. Noah, Sam, this is Ellie, our wedding planner.'

Ellie said hello to them both, and she realized where she knew Sam from: he was an actor, one of the main stars of *Estelle*, the BBC's latest Cornish-set period drama. Charlie had told her about Sam and Lila, how they'd met, and that Lila was part of the show now, too. Ellie tried not to be too star-struck, but Sam seemed perfectly at ease, no hint of celebrity about him as he shook her hand and gave her a friendly smile.

There was a gleam of amusement in Noah's eyes as he surveyed their surroundings. Lila was tiptoeing daintily around the mud puddles, and Hannah was peering through one of the barn's big windows. 'It looks amazing inside,' she said, turning to Charlie with a broad smile. Ellie could have kissed her.

'Jane's just starting out,' Ellie explained. 'There are some things still to do, and I know this doesn't look as picturesque as it could, but as Hannah says, the barn itself is magnificent. And I can work with Jane to get the approach and courtyard up to scratch.' As she said it, she realized that she really wanted to make it work. She wanted Jane and her mum to fulfil the dream they'd had coming back here. It was such a beautiful place; it just needed some extra work and enthusiasm to make it truly special.

'There are always teething problems at the start of a business,' Daniel said kindly.

Charlie nodded. 'I had some proper disasters when I was starting out with the Cornish Cream Tea Bus.' She winced.

'That's how you grow. You make mistakes and learn from them.'

'Yes,' Ellie said, smiling brightly, 'but I want to make sure your wedding is not one of those growing opportunities. Once you see inside, you'll see why I was so keen to bring you here.'

'Here we are,' Jane said, jangling a large set of keys.

'Ooof.' Sam bent forwards as Millicent nudged her snout into his crotch.

'Oh, look, Sam,' Lila said, barely containing her laughter, 'you've made a friend.'

Ellie's relief was palpable when Jane unlocked the barn and switched on all the lights, and everyone stepped inside. The chandeliers glittered and the wall lamps glowed, and the pure spring light washed the brick walls with gold. Daniel ran his palm over the bar-top and peered behind it, while Charlie strolled the length of the building, trailing her fingers along the walls. Noah and Hannah stood at one of the sea-facing windows, their figures silhouetted against the glass, and Sam and Lila hovered near the doors, gazing into each corner in turn, their fingers entwined.

Ellie's heart stopped thudding quite so hard. The court-yard might inspire horror, but the barn was leaving them awestruck for all the right reasons, just as she had hoped it would.

'We can have whatever layout you want, depending on your plans for the reception and your number of guests,' Jane said. 'And this area is a dance floor.' She walked to the middle of the space and pointed down, and Ellie saw polished, inlaid panels in the stone floor, forming a large square. They were subtle enough that she hadn't noticed them on her last visit.

'They light up.' Jane went over to a box on the wall. 'You can have them all one colour.' She flicked a switch and the panels glowed a translucent white, then glossy black, then gold. 'Or you can have a disco effect.' She pressed another button and the panels started changing colour, pulsing through red and pink, yellow, blue, purple and green, the pattern seemingly random. 'Any combination you like, really.'

'Holy shit,' Lila murmured. 'That is the coolest thing I've ever seen.'

'Barn meets nightclub,' Sam added, his eyes wide.

Jane pressed another switch and the lights faded. 'There are hooks along the walls for any floral or lighting arrangements you want,' she continued, 'and there are speakers embedded throughout. The stage can be set up for a DJ or live band, and there's a screen that comes down if you want to play a video or photo montage.' She strode towards the stage, her footsteps echoing, and everyone followed. When she pressed another switch on the wall a screen began sliding down from the ceiling.

Daniel folded his arms. 'I hope you're not going to have a PowerPoint as part of your speech, Sam.'

There was a moment's silence, then Sam took a couple of steps forward. '*My* speech? Why am I doing a speech?' The confusion on his face quickly turned to understanding. 'You want me to be your best man?' he asked quietly.

'Only if you'd like to be.' Daniel said it casually, but Ellie could see a muscle flickering in his jaw.

116

Sam ran a hand through his hair. 'Seriously? I'd be honoured. Thank you.' He shook Daniel's hand and then came in for a manly embrace, patting him on the back.

Lila's eyes were bright when she said, 'You're going to be the best man, and Juliette and I are the maids of honour.'

'No bridesmaids?' Noah asked.

Charlie shook her head. 'No, I don't think so. I'm not really a bridesmaid sort of person.'

Lila laughed. 'I'm half expecting you to find some kind of jeans-and-jumper version of a dress, something practical so you can go and help with the catering if you need to. Short sleeves, definitely not floor-length. Ellie,' she said, turning to her, 'do you think you can find a wedding dress that has a built-in apron?'

'Hey,' Charlie said, laughing. 'I'm not *that* bad, and actually, the dress is one area where I'd like to go all in.' Her cheeks had gone slightly pink, and she shot a glance at Daniel. 'I don't mean I want to spend thousands of pounds or have a huge puffball of a dress, but I do want it to be feminine. Lacy, even. I love the idea of vintage lace, and I definitely don't want an apron.' She shrugged.

'We can find you the perfect dress,' Ellie said. 'Don't worry about that. Vintage lace would suit you, too. Let's discuss it more next time we meet.'

Charlie nodded, her smile small but relieved.

Hannah let out a squeal of glee. 'I am *so* excited about this wedding!'

'Have you thought about what the dogs are going to do?' Lila asked.

Charlie laughed. 'What do you mean?'

'Marmite, Jasper and Spirit *have* to be involved. We could

give them all little bows! Or hats – or their own vintage lace dresses.'

'Don't get too carried away,' Charlie said. 'Marmite might not fancy wearing anything, and there's a good chance he'll protest by wrecking the whole place.'

'Looks like our wedding's going to have its own menagerie,' Daniel added, grinning.

At first, Ellie thought he was talking about the dogs, and she'd let her mind stray, wondering whether Lord Montague would be happy wearing a little cat-jacket if the occasion ever called for it. Then she saw why Daniel had made the comment; Millicent had wandered through the open door and was rootling around one of the tables.

'Oh bum,' Jane said, and tried to shoo the pig out. Noah, Sam and Hannah went to help her, and Millicent proved how quick she could be by evading them all and trotting into a corner.

Ellie had felt on the verge of victory, but could see it slipping from her grasp. She wouldn't blame Charlie and Daniel for turning this place down, with its over-friendly chickens, mud-tracking pig and waterlogged courtyard. She wasn't usually one for counting her chickens – she almost laughed at the irony – but despite Porthgolow Barn being rough around the edges, she had thought she'd found the perfect solution.

Rousing herself, she went to help move Millicent back into the courtyard, which they achieved only by Noah going outside and finding the remains of the cabbage, then coaxing her out that way while Sam, Hannah and Ellie walked behind, ensuring she couldn't change direction at the last minute.

Once Millicent was back in the sunshine, Jane cleared her throat and clapped her hands together. 'We've got the kitchen and cloakroom, and the gents and ladies in an extension at this end.' She gestured to a door at the end of the barn, and led them through.

She spent time showing them round the kitchen, which Hannah was especially interested in, asking questions about the cooking and storage options, the size of the fridges, and then they moved onto the cloakroom. There were two spacious, carpeted rooms at the end of the barn's annexe, which Jane explained could be used as changing rooms. 'If you've got a dress change or need some time out,' she said. 'They're sort of like green rooms. We can furnish them however you want.'

As the tour continued, Ellie's confidence grew. Jane and her mum had thought of everything except the exterior; maybe they'd run out of money, or perhaps outdoor spaces just weren't Jane's thing. But Ellie could help with that, because they were definitely hers.

Jane took them back to the main barn. 'I'll leave you to have a talk,' she said. 'Would you like coffees? Tea? Fruit juice?' She found out what everyone wanted then disappeared, leaving Ellie in charge.

'Shall we sit down?' She took chairs from a stack against the wall and put them round the closest table. Noah and Daniel helped her, and soon they were all seated, the chandeliers shimmering high above them.

She felt like a politician at a scrutiny hearing. Part of her wanted to rush in and make excuses, but she didn't want to do Jane a disservice. If this venue wasn't right for them, then she would find something else. If it needed work to meet their expectations, then she would help to make that happen.

'What are your initial impressions?' she asked.

There was a moment of silence, and she had the sense that Lila, especially, was trying desperately not to say anything. Ellie kept her attention on Charlie and Daniel.

'It's an impressive venue,' Daniel said. 'The way the modern elements are subtle, so they don't detract from the charm of the place.' He shook his head. 'Some of it puts Crystal Waters to shame.'

'I love the windows, the combination of artificial and natural light,' Charlie said. 'And it has a nice feel to it. It's big, but even though it's not particularly warm today, it doesn't seem too cavernous.'

'Can you imagine yourself getting married here?' Ellie asked. 'And you have to be honest. There's no point in telling me you love the view and are impressed by the facilities, if the muddy courtyard and Millicent make it totally unsuitable for you. But we have time to improve the outside space, especially, if you're seriously considering it.'

To her relief, Charlie grinned. 'I quite like Millicent,' she said. 'Especially when she trod on Noah's foot.'

'Hey,' Noah said, laughing. 'She's bloody heavy, OK? I was planning on doing a ten-miler tomorrow.'

'You were going to run for *ten miles*?' Ellie asked. When Noah nodded, she added, 'Why?'

Lila and Hannah descended into laughter, and Sam said, 'Good question.'

'Seriously, though,' Ellie went on, 'having Millicent as one of your flower girls aside, you have to really consider whether you want to get married here. And I don't want your final decision now; you should go away and think about it. Ask Jane any questions you have, and if you think of any more over the next few days, come to me and I can liaise with her. Some people know instantly, in their gut, if a venue is right for them; others like to mull it over, weigh up the pros and cons. And if you want to come back and see it on a day when it's less . . . swampish, that can definitely be arranged.'

Charlie nodded. 'Thank you, Ellie. I like that it's not a hundred per cent polished. I just . . . I'm wondering if it's too big for us? Our wedding's going to be quite small, with only close friends and family, and this place could fit hundreds of people.'

'We can close off the bottom third of the barn if you want a smaller space,' said a voice, and a woman walked through the doors and put a tray of mugs on the table. Ellie took in her grey bob, kind blue eyes and willowy frame. She almost fell over in shock when she realized it was the woman who had accosted her with a broom. She handed out mugs, matching up drinks to their owners. 'I'm Pauline,' she explained. 'Jane's mum.'

Jane followed with a plate of homemade chocolates. 'And she's made these. Please, help yourselves.'

There was contented mumbling as everyone took one and tried them. They were delicious, the chocolate dark and bitter, Ellie's flavoured with praline.

'You can really close off part of the barn?' Charlie asked.

'With these doors.' Pauline walked over and tapped a ceiling-height door which, on first glance, had looked like a feature piece of rustic wooden panelling. 'They slide across, and we can store any unneeded furniture in the unused part.'

'Any more tricks?' Daniel asked, grinning.

'We want to give our customers an authentic countryside experience,' Pauline said, 'but without any compromise. I'm aware that the courtyard and gardens aren't meeting your expectations right now, but we've been focusing on getting the interior right, and we've got plans for a landscaper to come and look at the surroundings.'

Charlie rested her elbows on the table. 'That's really good to know, thank you Pauline.'

'And pigs are not part of the offer,' she added, 'unless you book the hog roast option, of course.'

'We have the catering arranged already,' Ellie said, exchanging a glance with Hannah. 'Thank you, though.'

She sipped her coffee and tried to take in Pauline's changed demeanour. The older woman had been honest and shrewd, proving to Ellie – as if she needed a reminder – that it was always better to be upfront, rather than fudge your way into your clients' good books. Jane had tried to put a positive spin on everything, which of course was important, but you needed to gain people's trust, and Pauline had done that by admitting they weren't quite where they wanted to be, but were working hard to get there.

The group asked Pauline and Jane questions while Ellie made notes. Despite the shambles when they'd arrived, it was looking as though Porthgolow Barn could be the venue Charlie and Daniel were looking for, after all.

When they'd finished their drinks, Lila, Sam, Hannah and Noah said goodbye, and Jane and Pauline went back into the cottage. The sun was warmer, the chickens seemed less frantic, and as Ellie strolled with Charlie and Daniel back to their car, there was no sign of Millicent.

'Thank you for finding this place, Ellie,' Charlie said. 'We'll have a proper talk about it and get back to you.'

'Only when you're ready.'

'I still can't believe that dance floor,' Daniel added, taking a final look around the courtyard. With the few remaining raindrops glistening on the cobbles – Ellie was convinced that either Jane or Pauline had washed away some of the mud while they'd been in the barn – it looked much more inviting.

It was funny, she thought, as she waved goodbye to the couple, the difference a bit of sunshine or polish could make. And she would have to tell Jago about Pauline's transformation. She had her phone in her hand before she realized they weren't on texting terms yet.

Yet. She had invited him for a drink, but she hadn't followed up on it. Before she could talk herself out of it, she dialled his number.

It took a while for him to answer, and when he did, he sounded out of breath. 'Hello?'

'Jago? It's Ellie.'

'Ellie, hi. How are you?'

'Am I interrupting?' She strolled to the gap in the wall and, careful to avoid the small lake, watched the sea shifting from grey to blue, as if huge sea monsters were moving under the surface rather than clouds casting shadows overhead.

'I'm on a job, but I could do with a breather. You're phoning to see what I think about Arthur coming to Cornflower Cottage?'

123

'I wasn't actually,' she said. 'I was wondering about that drink. How about tomorrow evening?'

He didn't reply immediately, and she heard the rustle of fabric. 'Sounds good. And that'll work as my deadline too. I'll have an answer for you by then.'

'Thank you. And I've got something to tell you about Porthgolow Barn.'

'Oh?' He sounded intrigued, and Ellie smiled to herself; she had his attention, and she was going to make him wait.

'I can't talk now. I'll tell you everything tomorrow night.'

'OK,' he said slowly. 'But I want it to be acknowledged that I don't appreciate you keeping me dangling like this.'

Ellie laughed. 'I had to give you an incentive, so you wouldn't forget about our drink.'

'I wouldn't have forgotten,' he told her.

'Good to know.' She tried for nonchalance. 'I'll see you there at seven?'

'Seven. I'm writing it on my hand in permanent marker, just to make sure.'

Ellie grinned. 'Bye then, Jago.'

'Bye Ellie.'

As she hung up, she saw that Millicent had reappeared, and was watching her as if she might have a cabbage hidden in her handbag. She edged round the animal and went back to her car, thinking that, despite how chaotically the morning had started, things were beginning to look up, both for New Moon Weddings and Elowen Moon.

Chapter Nine

Ellie was grateful to the powers that be that Rose was working late.

Her sister knew that Ellie was meeting Jago at the Seven Stars, and although Ellie had tried to sell it as part of her attempt to get him to agree to Arthur spending time in Cornflower Cottage's garden, the glint in Rose's eye suggested she was having none of it. But at least she was being left to get ready on her own, with soothing acoustic music and a cup of camomile tea.

She looked in the mirror, at her dark jeans and the floaty red top that complemented her rose-gold hair, and pressed a hand against her stomach, trying to settle the jitters that had set up home there. She was annoyed with herself for being nervous. She hadn't wallowed in self-pity since her divorce, but after the tumult of feelings it had produced – the guilt at her failed marriage, the confusing mix of anger and an echo of affection she had felt for Mark in those last months, the regret, heartache, then relief – she had been avoiding anything that might prick her deeper emotions. Which was why she had stuck to fun, flirting and lust, and nothing stronger.

This felt different, and she tried to work out why. She had only known Jago for a few weeks, but it already felt as if they had a friendship, albeit quite tentative still. Was it because he was her tenant, or because he was now, through Arthur, connected to Rose as well as her? She turned her attention to her make-up, wishing she had Monty to talk it over with. He was a good listener, and definitely less probing than her sister.

She was ready with forty minutes to spare – the curse of the over-organized – and spent the time researching barn aesthetics, getting some concrete ideas about how Charlie and Daniel's wedding could look if they chose Jane's venue. When she left, the evening air was crisp, the darkening sky clear of clouds and heady with a blackbird's joyful song. It was a perfect spring evening.

Florence had purred like a well-behaved feline ever since Jago had fixed her leak, and soon Ellie was in Porthgolow, on the seafront with its pretty streetlights flickering on, the beach a hazy golden crescent in the dusk, and the pub sign – a painting of seven, different-sized stars illuminated from above – drawing her closer. She pulled into a car-park space and looked for Jago's Golf. She wasn't sure whether he would drive or walk. She had done it several times from Cornflower Cottage and, while it was nice on a summer's evening, it took close to an hour, and the walk home was uphill all the way.

'Stop dallying,' she told herself, and got out of the car.

The pub was warm and welcoming, and even half-full

the chatter was upbeat, laughter rippling between tables like a Mexican wave. There were two old men, who looked like they had grown into their stools, drinking in silent companionship at the bar, and the smells wafting from the kitchen replaced Ellie's nervous anticipation with a growl of hunger.

'Good evenin'.' Hugh, the pub's landlord, greeted her from behind the bar.

'Hi,' Ellie said. 'I was wondering if I could have a table for two?'

'Pick any you like, but there's one left over by the window.' Hugh gestured to a table snug in the corner, with a view that looked out over the beach. 'Get yourself settled, and just order when you're ready.'

'Thank you. I'll wait for my friend to arrive, if that's OK?'

'No problem.'

Ellie settled herself at the table and fussed with the beer mats. She imagined all the things Rose would say to both irritate and reassure her in her typically contrary way, and what she would say in response. It was one evening in the local pub, and she was mostly doing it for Arthur; she wouldn't even be here if it hadn't been for Rose asking for her help. She didn't realize she was silently mouthing the words until she raised her head to find Jago looking down at her, a curious smile on his lips.

She jolted in her seat. 'Hello.'

'Hi, Ellie. OK if I join you? You seem a bit preoccupied.'

She forced a laugh. 'Sorry. I was working through my to-do list while I waited.'

He shrugged off his jacket and slid into the chair opposite her. 'It takes longer than you think, that walk.'

'I should have warned you,' Ellie said. 'It seems so close when you do the journey in the car, but that hill's a challenge, even on the way down.'

'My knees are protesting. Can I get you a drink?'

'I'll get them. What do you want?'

'A local ale, please. Dark, if they've got it.'

'I'll see what I can do.' She went to the bar, ordering a ginger ale for herself and a dark ale that Hugh assured her was brewed locally.

'Thanks,' Jago said, when she brought the drinks back to the table. He was wearing a blue and white checked shirt, his jaw clean-shaven, his hair as messy as ever. He looked particularly lovely, and Ellie's stomach went back to its nervous flip-flops.

'This is a lot better than my local back home,' Jago said, resting his elbows on the table. 'It's a novelty not to stick to the carpet when you walk in.' He rubbed a palm over the varnished wood of the table, and Ellie wondered if he was aware that he'd referred to Plymouth as home. 'It's good of you to meet me tonight,' he added. 'Over and above the remit of a landlady. Not that we're calling you that, of course. There's no Nora Batty insinuating going on.'

Ellie laughed. 'I should hope not. But things have got a little more complicated, now. With Arthur. With the garden.'

Jago raised an eyebrow. 'You don't waste time, do you?'

'Oh, no!' Ellie reached a hand out, almost knocking her glass over. 'I didn't mean to—'

'Ellie.' Jago squeezed her fingers, then let go just as quickly. 'I'm joking. I know what you mean. It isn't as straightforward as it was.' He ran a hand through his hair, re-energizing the wayward strands. 'The easy answer, the *right* answer, would be to say yes. Dad's the reason I'm back in Cornwall, after all. It would be churlish *and* counterproductive to say no.'

'But you're not loving the idea?' She could still feel the tingle of Jago's touch, as if her memory was determined to hold on to the sensation.

'I wanted to be close to him, which was why your cottage was perfect. But now it's tipped the other way; it turns out it's a little *too* perfect.' He laughed gently. 'The thought of Dad being there . . . It means I go from being miles away and seeing him once every six months, to him being in my personal space; where I wind down after work, or after visiting him.' He shrugged. 'Man up, right? That's what I need to do.'

'Not at all,' Ellie said. 'So many families have tensions, and sometimes relationships are downright impossible. Just because you came back to build bridges, doesn't mean you're ready for your dad to be so close. I still feel bad about asking, but Rose got this idea in her head to help Arthur, and once there's a problem to solve, my brain can't help making leaps—'

'It's an obvious leap, though. The cottage has a huge garden. It needs looking after, and Dad's down the road, with green fingers and nowhere to use them. It couldn't tick any more boxes. I'll say yes, just give me to the end of the evening.'

Ellie laughed. 'That makes no sense.'

'I know.' Jago grinned. 'Let's talk about something else.' He took a long sip of beer and leaned back in his chair. 'Tell me about you, Ellie. What got you into wedding planning? What's this big secret with Porthgolow Barn? How come you're living with your sister and, before that, were in Cornflower Cottage by yourself? I want to know it all.'

'Oh you do, do you? That is a lot of questions, Jago Carne.'

'I'm a curious guy.' He raised a solitary eyebrow, the gesture making Ellie's heart thrum.

He was so different to Mark; all soft edges and shrugs, a smile his go-to expression. She wanted to answer everything he'd asked and more, to lean close and whisper it conspiratorially, if only to see the depth of his green eyes and smell his citrusy, spicy scent. Instead, she sipped her ginger ale and told him why she'd become a wedding planner; her love of organizing combined with her early delight in all things romantic driving her towards it. She had been looking at wedding magazines, drinking in the dresses and cakes, the lace and flowers and sheer perfection of it all, while her school friends yearned for riding lessons or joined the school football team.

'The organization bit I get,' Jago said, toying with the corner of the menu. 'All the frills and fancies of weddings, I don't really see that in you. Not so far, anyway.'

Ellie sighed. 'Is it strange to say that getting married made me grow out of it?'

'Not strange,' Jago said. 'A little sad, though. So the fairytale ending, the "happy ever after", you don't believe in that any more?'

'Oh, I do,' she said quickly, 'for other people. Obviously I know that relationships fail and divorces happen all the time, and that's no reason to go into a marriage with anything but the utmost conviction that it'll work out, but I suppose I had my parents as a role model. They're still together, almost fifty years after getting married, and I wanted – had hoped – I could have that as well.'

'My folks were together a long time, too.'

'I'm sorry about your mum,' Ellie said softly.

'Thanks,' Jago replied, not quite meeting her gaze. 'How long have you been divorced, if you don't mind me asking?'

'Just over two years. Mark and I were very happy for about the first six months of our marriage. And we didn't have a huge blow-up; there was no cheating or anything like that. I just got to a point where I *wasn't* happy any more, and I knew, from the way Mark was behaving, that he wasn't either. We'd reached the end of the road with a whimper, not a bang. What about you? Are you single, or have you got someone hiding away in one of those secret corners of Cornwall we were talking about?'

Jago took another sip of beer. 'I was with my last partner, Sarah, for eight years. We met soon after I settled in Plymouth, after I'd finally satisfied my travelling bug. We'd agreed that we didn't want to get married, that neither of us wanted children, that we were happy just being together. She's an engineer, a lot more ambitious than me. We both love hiking, getting outdoors, simple things. But she *did* cheat on me, with a colleague, and I realized that, despite all our years together, she just hadn't wanted to do any of those things – marriage, kids – with me.' He shook his head.

'I'm so sorry,' Ellie said. 'That sounds horrible.'

'It was. But it hasn't stopped me believing I can find someone I want to be with until all my hair falls out.

131

Everyone hits speed bumps; Sarah was just a particularly big one.' He shrugged and picked up the menu. 'What's good here?'

'The fish pie,' Ellie said. 'It's the best I've tasted. Are you really not angry with her?'

Jago frowned. 'Sarah? Not any more. I was to begin with, of course. But what would be the point of her staying with me if she wasn't happy? It's like you and Mark; your relationship had run its course, so the best thing was to go your separate ways, as painful as it was at the time. Aren't you happier now?'

'I am,' Ellie said. 'Much. Would I be able to use that line in my opening pitch to clients?'

'What line?'

'You have found the person you want to be with until all your hair falls out,' she said in a dramatic voice. 'My role is to plan the perfect wedding so you can celebrate it.'

Jago laughed. 'That's a great opening gambit. You should try it on the Porthgolow couple next time you see them.'

'Charlie and Daniel? I don't think they'd mind, actually.'

'What did they think of the barn?' He leaned towards her, one elbow on the table. Ellie could see the shape of his forearm through his shirt. She knew from previous encounters how nice it was.

'It's not perfect,' Ellie said, 'but then no venue ever is. It's got potential, and I think Charlie and Daniel saw that.'

'I can't believe that was what you were going to tell me, though; the thing you dangled in front of me to make me come here tonight. That the barn has potential.' There was a glimmer in his eyes that Ellie was mesmerized by.

'That's the only reason you came, isn't it?'

'Of course. And honestly? It's been a wrench. Monty wasn't happy with me leaving. He clawed my leg.'

'Really? God, I'm sorry.'

He waved it away. 'All I'm saying is that I put up with a lot to come tonight. It's a big deal, Ellie.'

She knew he was joking, but those words – *it's a big deal, Ellie* – taken in isolation, could have meant something else entirely. She was glad Hugh appeared to take their order at that moment. When he'd gone again, she felt on firmer ground.

'So firstly,' she said, 'there's a giant pig.'

Jago spluttered, only just holding in his mouthful of beer. 'A *pig?*'

'A giant pig,' Ellie repeated. 'Millicent is—'

'Hang on,' Jago interrupted. 'The pig is called Millicent?'

Ellie nodded, and told him the rest: about Jane and Pauline, the homemade chocolates, the dance floor and the screen and all the technological wizardry nestled amongst the building's rustic charm; about how Pauline seemed like a completely different person, no inkling that she was anything other than completely in control. Jago leaned closer while she spoke, and Ellie was barely conscious of the chatter around them, the clink of cutlery, the sound of the waves hitting the beach beyond the glass. Jago was captivated by her story, and she was captivated by him. It was only when two steaming bowls of fish pie were brought to their table that they sat back, the spell broken.

They tucked in, going from intense conversation to satisfied silence, Jago declaring it the best fish pie he'd ever eaten, once his plate was scraped clean. They ordered another round of drinks.

'You know,' he said, as Ellie speared her last few peas with her fork. 'My dad grew up around pigs. My grandparents had a farm over near St Keyne. You wouldn't think it, would you? I've always thought of him as a Navy man, but he probably spent a lot of time outside when he was little. His mum and dad had an impressive kitchen garden, from what I remember.'

Ellie nodded, not wanting to interrupt him.

'Millicent, Pauline . . .' he shook his head. 'It's like they're some kind of sign. Jane's taking care of her mum; they're living together, running a business together. I can't even spend ten minutes in the same room as my dad.'

'You're different—' Ellie started, but Jago shook his head.

'I need to put my selfish reasons for not wanting Dad to come to the cottage aside.' He rubbed a hand over his eyes. 'It would be so good for him, I know that, and it might be good for me, too. At the very least, I'm not going to fix things between us by living a few hundred yards away but never actually seeing him. Osmosis is not a strategy.' He chuckled.

'You're sure?'

'Yup. It's the right thing to do.'

'But not the easy thing?'

'The most worthwhile actions are rarely the easy ones, isn't that what they say?' He gave her a tired smile, and Ellie wanted to put her arms around him. She wondered if he was lonely, with just him and Monty in the cottage. Was he still getting used to being single?

She considered what she would have done if she'd been out for an evening with Rose, and spotted him across the pub. She wouldn't have thought too hard about it, she realized, because the attraction was there; he was handsome and friendly, he radiated kindness and invited confidences. She wondered how he would have reacted. Was he up for a bit of harmless fun? The thought of seeing his bare chest again in even more intimate circumstances than last time bought a flush to her cheeks, and she realized he was looking at her intently.

'OK?' he asked. It came out slightly rough, as if he knew what she'd been thinking about. His Adam's apple bobbed, Ellie struggled for a response, and that's how Hannah found them; in the middle of the first uncomfortable silence of the evening.

'Ellie? I thought that was you. How are you?' Hannah was wearing chefs' whites, her blonde hair in a netted bun beneath her hat, her cheeks prettily pink.

'Hannah, hello! We're good thanks – just here to sample your fish pie. This is Jago. Jago, this is Hannah.'

'Hi Jago.'

'Hey.'

They shook hands, and Hannah grinned. 'How was the pie?'

'Delicious as always,' Ellie said.

'The best I've ever tasted,' Jago added. 'Is it your recipe?'

'Hugh's,' Hannah confirmed. 'Though I've given it a few of my own twists.' She tapped the side of her nose. 'Ellie, I've already got loads of ideas for Charlie and Daniel's wedding breakfast, and I've been testing them out at home. Noah, my guinea pig – and my boyfriend,' she added, turning to Jago to explain, 'is loving them, though, as he keeps on telling me, he's had to up his running distances because of all the extra calories. Are we meeting next week?'

Ellie tamped down her laughter. Hannah had seemed reserved the first couple of times they'd met. 'That sounds great. Shall we get together on Monday? I could come here, before your shift starts.'

'Great.' Hannah nodded. 'And I'm sorry I interrupted date night. It's easy to get tied up with work, isn't it? So important to get out and do something different.'

'Oh, we're not—' Ellie started, but when she glanced at Jago he was watching her with a grin on his face. 'You're right,' she said instead. 'It's so easy to stay at home, do the same old things. Going out for food once a week should be obligatory, even if it's just coffee and cake at a café.'

Hannah nodded. 'Like the Cornish Cream Tea Bus. There's no better cake in the whole of Cornwall – but don't tell Daniel I said that, or his chef, Levi, will hunt me down. I'll leave you to it. Lovely to meet you, Jago. Have a good evening.'

'You too,' Jago called as Hannah hurried back to the kitchen. 'She seems excited,' he observed.

'Weddings will do that to people,' Ellie said, sighing. 'I'm lucky to do what I do. My sole purpose is to bring people happiness, to take the stress out of what should be one of the most joyful days of their lives. I know what I said earlier, but I do love it.'

'A good thing too,' Jago said wryly, 'considering you can't seem to escape it, even on a night out.'

Ellie laughed. 'Charlie and Daniel live in Porthgolow, and in case you haven't noticed already, it's quite a small place.'

Jago's mouth lifted at the corners. 'Oh, I've noticed.'

By the time they left the pub, the sky was a dark quilt with pinprick stars, the moon hanging lazily above the silvery sea. The streetlights lit up the buildings along the seafront, but away from it, towards the hill and Crumbling Cliff, only moonlight showed the way. It was breathtakingly beautiful, one of those moments Ellie wished she could hold on to. A photo wouldn't do it justice, and anyway, she wanted the sounds, smells and sensations, too. If she could capture the memory, she would title it: *A moonlit night in Porthgolow, following a perfect evening.*

'Let me drive you back,' she said to Jago.

'I should walk off some of the beer and pie.'

'Do you even have a torch?'

'I've got my phone.'

Ellie gave an exasperated sigh. 'I'm giving you a lift. I'd never forgive myself if I let you walk off into pitch darkness next to a sheer cliff drop, and something happened to you. And don't forget you've got to pass the entrance to Porthgolow Barn. Who knows what Millicent is like after dark? Have you seen *Hannibal*?'

Jago laughed. 'Weren't those people already dead when the pigs ate them?'

'I don't think so,' Ellie said ominously, as she unlocked Florence.

'Your persuasive tactics are on the dark side, you know that Elowen?' Jago shook his head, and Ellie considered how much she liked the sound of her full name spoken in his deep voice.

The journey seemed to take seconds, and soon she was pulling up in front of Cornflower Cottage, its outside light welcoming Jago home, the garden shimmering eerily in the moonlight and a pair of familiar green eyes peering through the living-room window.

Jago shifted to face her, and she did the same.

'Thanks for a great evening,' he said. 'My social batteries are fully recharged.'

'I had a good time too,' Ellie replied. They were so close, only the gear stick stopping their knees from brushing. 'That fish pie is a secret that needs to be spilled as widely as possible, and it's your local now, so you should make the most of it.'

'I'm going to. Will you, or your sister, be in touch about Dad coming here?'

'Oh. Of course. I'll ask Rose when she's seeing him next, what the plan is.'

'Great. And thanks again – for tonight. I'm enjoying these added perks of being your tenant.'

'Perks, eh?'

'That's how I'm thinking of them.' He leaned towards her, his hand skimming her shoulder. She had time to register his delicious smell, the way his touch seemed to burn through the fabric of her top, straight to her skin, before he brushed his lips gently against her cheek, lingering there for a second longer than was polite. 'Night, Ellie.'

'Goodnight, Jago.'

He shut the car door with a gentle click and walked to the porch, pulling his key out of his pocket. He turned, gave her a wave and then went inside, leaving her alone on the driveway. Even Monty, she realized, had gone from the window – gone to greet Jago with enthusiasm and, no doubt, the suggestion that he might enjoy a late-night snack.

Ellie felt a pang of longing, but she didn't know if it was for her cottage and her cat, or if the man she'd just had dinner with was part of it too. She did a neat three-point turn and drove slowly down the driveway. When she glanced in the rear-view mirror, she saw that a different pair of green eyes, looking at her from a higher viewpoint, had replaced Monty's at the living-room window.

Chapter Ten

The following day, Ellie was standing in the middle of one of her favourite florists in Truro when Charlie called. She apologized quickly to Freya, who had been running through the wedding catalogue, showing her designs for bouquets and table sprays, and strolled to the far corner of the shop, next to a display of Tête-à-tête miniature daffodils.

'Hi, Charlie,' she said. 'How are you?'

'Good thanks – great, in fact. How about you?'

'I'm really well. How can I help?'

She heard Charlie exhale, and then, 'Daniel and I would love to get married at Porthgolow Barn.' The excitement and certainty in Charlie's voice made a few of the knots in Ellie's shoulders loosen.

'That's such wonderful news!' she said. 'I'm so glad, and I'm certain we can make it everything you want it to be.'

'We actually loved the chickens and the pig,' Charlie

admitted with a laugh. 'I'm not saying we want a farm-themed reception, but we liked how genuinely rustic it was. And the barn's got more than we were expecting in terms of facilities, so we're happy for the surroundings to be a little on the chaotic side.'

Ellie raised a fist to the ceiling in silent celebration. 'OK, I'll sit down with Jane and Pauline, get an idea of the different packages and do some calculations. Shall we meet in a few days and get some things ticked off the list?'

'Sounds brilliant,' Charlie said. 'I have to go and take some scones out of the oven, but I'll speak to you soon.'

'What kind of scones?' Ellie asked, reaching out to stroke a silky yellow petal.

'Bacon and rosemary,' Charlie said, almost apologetically.

'Wow. They sound delicious.'

'Come to the bus if you're free. Bring your sister.'

'I'll see if I can fit it in,' Ellie said. 'Bye Charlie, speak soon.'

She would love to swing by on her way home, but she didn't think she'd be able to spare the time. She had so much to do, with three weddings on her books and this one, with the tightest time-frame, stepping up a gear. Now they had the venue, it opened up a whole new layer of planning. A visit to the Cornish Cream Tea Bus would have been a nice treat, but the truth was she *wanted* to keep busy. She wanted her thoughts to stop returning to the previous evening, to Jago and the feel of his lips on her cheek before he'd said goodbye.

'How did it go last night?' Rose asked when she walked through the door at lunchtime, flower and cake catalogues weighing her bag down. Her sister had still been in bed when she'd left the house that morning. 'How was Jago Carne in all his delicious scruffiness?'

'Not that scruffy,' Ellie said. 'And he's agreed to let Arthur come to Cornflower Cottage. I'm going to make a list of the jobs I had lined up for the next month, but I get the feeling that once Arthur sees the garden, he'll know what to do.'

Rose, wearing navy jogging bottoms and a T-shirt with a heart motif on, sank onto a sofa, and Ellie took the one opposite. She had expected glee, but her sister only looked relieved. 'That's wonderful news,' she said.

'Do you think Arthur will go for it?' Ellie asked. 'It's all well and good getting Jago's agreement, but Arthur might flat-out refuse. He might not be ready to spend time with his son, and he's not the type to be mollycoddled.'

Rose waved a hand. 'I'm going armed with photos of your garden, and that place even inspires me. When Arthur sees what's waiting for him, he won't be able to resist, and when he gets there, he'll be so in his element he won't worry about Jago – which will make it easier for them to talk.' Rose nodded. 'I'm not wasting any time over this. I'm going to go and see Mo, and then hopefully Arthur, later on today.' She got up. 'Coffee?'

'I'd love one, thanks,' Ellie said. And then, because it was still baffling her, 'Why do you care so much about Arthur?' She followed Rose into the kitchen. 'You see so many older people in your job. What is it about him?'

Rose heaped coffee into the cafetière. 'Because he's stuck inside himself,' she said eventually. 'Lots of lonely people are desperate not to be: they keep me in their homes or rooms, telling me long-winded stories, asking me to do unnecessary jobs. They're reaching out for help, and it's easy for me to give it. It means longer hours, but if I know Kathleen in St Austell has had a couple of hours of company, I go away happy. Arthur is resisting any kind of companionship. He thinks he can be self-sufficient, deal with his grief and sadness on his own, but he's lost inside it. The garden was his only release.'

'What about that other woman, Iris? They seemed friendly.'

Rose shook her head. 'He doesn't let her get close. You've been there once; if you knew the number of times I've turned up and he's just been sitting there, alone, staring out of the window.' She got the cream out of the fridge. 'Or in his room. Some rule or boundary he's set himself won't allow him to reach out. He internalizes everything, which is probably part of the reason he and Jago don't get on. I just keep thinking, what if something happened to Mum? How would Dad cope?'

Ellie thought about their parents, still so much in love after decades together. It was almost as if they didn't need anybody else, and Rose was right; she didn't think her dad would reach out for help if he was suddenly on his own, desolate and alone after so many years of close companionship.

'Anyway,' Rose went on, 'I didn't expect it to become this big *thing*. I thought you'd help us find somewhere we could move his flowers to, and that would be that. But now there's your garden – which is the most wonderful idea, by the way, don't think it isn't – and the added complication of Jago. Layers upon layers. *But*,' she added, using a spoon to point at Ellie, 'that's a good thing. We're giving Arthur the most spectacular garden to work in, to bring him happiness and, potentially, help him reconnect with his son. It'll be worth the effort.'

'It might not work,' Ellie said.

'But it might,' Rose countered. 'It's better than us doing nothing, letting them destroy Arthur's garden and leaving him to sit for endless, lonely days, in his chair by the window. And even if Arthur's reluctant to take the first step with Jago, Jago looks as if he's prepared to make the effort.'

Ellie thought back to his reticence the previous night, but she didn't want to dampen her sister's spirits, so she just smiled and nodded and gratefully accepted a coffee rich with cream. Rose had always believed that positive thinking was more important than planning. Ellie would argue against that, because being organized was one of the main rules she lived by, but she had to concede that, when it came to family relationships, planning wasn't always helpful: you couldn't predict how another person would behave, you just had to see how things panned out and hope for the best.

Over the next few days, Ellie was elbow-deep in wedding paraphernalia, which was one of her favourite places to be. She met with Hannah to discuss the catering, and she arranged to go back to Porthgolow Barn to talk through packages with Jane and Pauline. She went through the cake and flower brochures she'd picked up, selecting the ones she thought would be most suitable for the couples she was working with, and checked the availability of photographers she frequently worked with.

She was feeling increasingly positive about Charlie and Daniel's wedding. With Porthgolow Barn confirmed, she could almost picture it; the space full of glinting lights and wicker candlesticks, wildflowers and lace, everything faded and natural with a few pops of bright colour to bring it all together.

While she was living in a cloud of romantic possibility, Rose had showed Arthur the photos of Cornflower Cottage's garden and convinced him to visit it, with a view to spending time there in the spring and summer months. Ellie had been flabbergasted that he'd agreed, and then proud of her sister for convincing him, and then thrown into turmoil at the thought of telling Jago.

She wondered if he'd only agreed to the plan because he thought his dad would say no, but when she called him to arrange Arthur's first visit, he seemed his usual relaxed self, and said it was fine. She hadn't seen him since their night out, and she couldn't help wondering if he thought about it as much as she did. But there had been no follow-up from either of them. *Because it wasn't a date*, Ellie kept reminding herself.

And yet that didn't stop her dallying on the morning of Arthur's introduction to Cornflower Cottage. Being late was one of her biggest bugbears, but she found it surprisingly easy to keep her bum on the sofa until she only had ten minutes to get there for the prearranged time.

There was a hint of spring warmth in the air, the sky a watery blue without a cloud in sight, and Ellie breathed it all in as she walked down Rose's front path. She decided that today would go well. There would be no awkwardness between Jago and Arthur, none between Jago and her, and

Rose wouldn't be at all overbearing. If Ellie was both organized *and* positive, what could possibly go wrong?

Rose's car was parked next to Jago's in the driveway of Cornflower Cottage, so she left her Mini further towards the road. She knocked on the door and Rose opened it, giving her a wide smile that wasn't entirely genuine.

'Ellie! So brilliant that you're here! Come in.' She bustled her into the living room. Jago was sitting on one sofa holding a mug of tea, and Arthur was on the one opposite. The atmosphere was about as friendly as a dentist's waiting room. Arthur looked smart in dark cords, a pea-green jumper over a shirt, and a navy wool coat. He glanced up when Rose brought Ellie into the room.

'Here she is!' Rose said, overly brightly.

'Hi Jago, Arthur.'

'Good morning, Elowen,' Arthur said. 'You have a wonderful garden, from what I've seen of it.'

'Would you like a tour?' Ellie asked.

Arthur gave her a tight smile. 'That would be grand, thank you.'

'Ellie, hi.' Jago stood up. His gaze held hers and her nerves jangled. He'd made an effort too, wearing a grey shirt, the sleeves rolled up to the elbows, and black jeans. She could see that he was more nervous than she was.

Rose helped Arthur to his feet, though he scoffed and tried to bat her attention away, and Ellie led them through the kitchen, to the back garden.

'This is where I've been focusing my attention,' she said, flourishing a hand towards the flower beds beyond the patio, the blooms brightening the April day with a variety of spring yellows and pinks, delicate blues. The hydrangeas added some height down either side, and with a gusty breeze blowing, the meadow seemed especially unkempt.

Arthur took in the view, a muscle moving in his jaw. 'Am I able to walk through it?' he asked eventually.

'Of course! You can go wherever you want,' Ellie said. 'I've got a list of the jobs that are coming up, but I'd love to get your ideas, too.'

She waited for him to step across the patio and onto the grassy pathway between the beds. She felt a stabbing pain in her lower back and turned to see Rose glaring at her. Understanding dawned.

'Shall I take your arm?' she asked, and Arthur nodded.

They walked slowly through the garden together. A robin sang from a branch in the hawthorn tree, the sun made emeralds out of emerging shoots, and Ellie felt her tension start to lift. When she next glanced at Arthur, she thought he looked slightly less severe. As she showed him the beds, the established and fledgling plants and flowers, and explained her reasoning behind each section, Arthur began to unfurl, as if he was a flower himself. He asked insightful questions and gave Ellie tips, some of which she hadn't heard before.

'You should get some more ornamental grasses,' he said, as they reached a bed with a gap Ellie wasn't sure how to fill. 'You'd get good sound and movement from them in the sea breeze, and they'll add some structure to this low section.'

Ellie prodded the bare soil with her trainer. It was still damp from yesterday's rain. 'We had a huge pampas grass in the garden where Rose and I grew up. My dad hated it because it blocked out the light, so we dug it up together.'

Arthur chuckled. It was the first time she'd heard him laugh, and it sounded dusty through lack of use. 'How long did that take? A week?'

'It felt like it,' Ellie said, groaning at the memory. 'I've never seen my dad so incensed. The roots just kept going, and he attacked it like it was personally insulting him. After half a day we were both exhausted and sweaty, and we'd made hardly any progress. To me it felt like we were bonding – and I didn't mind the mud – but to him it was torture.'

'Once a pampas grass has taken up home, it's there to stay. Could we?' Arthur gestured to the wrought-iron bench halfway down the garden. Ellie had painted it white, the same as the wooden one outside the front door, but this more delicate structure had been a trickier job.

'Of course.' They walked over to it and sat down.

'Once I start gardening, this does loosen up,' he said, slapping his right hip. 'It's just slow to get going.'

'Is it painful all the time?' Ellie asked. She glanced at the house, and saw Rose and Jago sitting at the patio table, chatting animatedly. She wondered what they were talking about.

'Only about eighty-five per cent of the time,' Arthur said. His words had no levity to them, but there was a glint in his eye that reminded her of Jago. 'But it will be worth it to be here. If you're sure you don't mind, and your sister hasn't chivvied you into it.'

Ellie laughed. 'It was actually my idea. I couldn't see anywhere else suitable at Seascape House, and then, when

I thought about it, this seemed obvious. I can't be here as often as I'd like to.'

'Because you've rented it out to my son,' Arthur confirmed. 'Don't worry, Rose told me everything.'

'Everything?' Ellie echoed, her voice squeaky.

'She does seem to appreciate a good story.'

Ellie didn't know what that meant, so she changed the subject. 'Have you been a gardener all your life?'

'Not at all,' Arthur said. 'I was often away for months at a time, and Hetty, my wife, had enough to do without me asking her to take care of the garden in my absence. But my parents were farmers with a lot of land, and when I was little, I was fascinated by the miraculous things that could grow out of a seed or a bulb, or by simply burying a potato in the ground. But, as I grew up I had other interests, other priorities. I didn't have the time or inclination to explore gardening until I retired.'

'You had a garden back home, before moving here?'

Arthur sniffed, and pulled a handkerchief out of his coat pocket, wiping his nose. Everything he did was efficient, Ellie noticed, which probably stemmed from his time in the Navy. 'Hetty and I lived in Falmouth,' he explained. 'It's where Jago grew up, and once he'd left home, we had no reason to move. Our garden was small but it was south-facing, exposed to a lot of sun. I spent hours out there.'

Ellie waited for him to go on, to wax lyrical about his garden, but he had gone quiet, as if he only had a set number of words a day and he'd used up his quota.

'Well,' she said, 'I'd be happy for you to go to town here. Do whatever you think will work.'

Arthur chuckled again. 'You'd trust an old man like me with this?'

'Of course. You clearly know what you're talking about, and I'm excited to see what you do with it.'

Silence settled again, and Ellie realized she was going to have to go slowly, to tease Arthur out of himself, just as Rose had said. She watched a pair of dunnocks chase each other out of one hydrangea bush and into another, their sharp calls filling the quiet air before they disappeared from sight.

'Why don't we go and see the meadow?' she said eventually. 'It's the one bit of the garden that's uncharted territory. You can tackle it with me.' She stood and held out her hand, and Arthur let Ellie help him to his feet and lead him towards the back of the garden.

They walked past her cultivated beds, the few trees she had framing the space; the cherry and the hawthorn, her laburnum, a beautiful silver birch with pure white bark, and then came to a stop at the edge of the long grass. Amongst it, she could see the tangled brambles, nettles dotted about, a trail of ivy that she hadn't yet tried to vanquish.

'You call this the meadow, do you?' Arthur said.

'Bloody hell!' Ellie's body tingled with awareness as Jago came to stand on her other side. 'What's this bit?'

'This, my boy,' Arthur said, a hint of amusement in his voice, 'is the meadow.'

'Meadow?' Jago echoed.

'This garden is a physical representation of Ellie's mind,' Rose explained. She was standing on Jago's other side, the four of them in a line, as if they were a quartet of intrepid explorers staring out over an uncrossable canyon.

150

'Think carefully about your next words,' Ellie warned her sister, and to her surprise, felt Jago gently nudge his shoulder against hers. Except, as he was a few inches taller than her, it was his firm bicep that connected with her. She swallowed.

'The front garden,' Rose went on, 'with its rose bushes and its cheerful bench, is like her warm smile and her shiny hair, welcoming and beautiful. And then you come out to the back here, with its neat beds and big . . . bushy things. That's how she comes across: organized and enthusiastic, friendly, with a wealth of good ideas and passion, and just the occasional gap in her positivity.'

'We're going to fill those gaps with ornamental grasses,' Arthur cut in.

Ellie rubbed her forehead. 'How does that—'

'And then *this* bit,' Rose continued, ignoring her, 'is all the stuff under the surface. Her confidence wobbles and her fear of being alone, her general insecurities and the way she sometimes goes down a planning rabbit hole, and forgets the point of what she was doing in the first place.'

'That's not—'

'What do you mean, a planning rabbit hole?' Jago asked.

'She can spend hours creating lists and mood boards,' Rose explained. 'And then it's too late for her to actually book anything or call back a client. Everything is perfectly organized, but no progress has been made.'

'That happens very, *very* rarely,' Ellie protested. 'And what does it have to do with my meadow?'

'Meadow,' Jago repeated, laughing.

'Hey!' Ellie said.

'I would be hard-pressed to call it a meadow,' Arthur added.

'See?' Rose sounded smug. 'It's all Ellie's hidden bits. She may seem fully sorted on the outside, but she needs untangling. And I think we're the team to help her, aren't we boys?' She turned to them, her expression one of gleeful triumph.

Ellie shot her sister a look.

'It would certainly be a challenge,' Arthur said, 'but just think what you could do with all this space when it's cleared. You could have a wildlife pond or an extensive vegetable patch, a small orchard, perhaps. The possibilities are endless.'

'I hate to think of your mind being tangled like this, Ellie,' Jago added, clearly amused.

'Then we're all agreed,' Rose said. 'This summer our challenge is to get the *meadow* cleared, and help Cornflower Cottage garden, and Ellie, fulfil their promise. The four of us would make a formidable team if we put our minds to it.'

Ellie felt something brush against her ankle, and Lord Montague let out a loud meow.

'OK, then,' Rose said, sighing dramatically, 'five of us. As long as you stay away from me, Monty. It'll be bad enough with all the grass pollen as it is.'

Arthur chuckled. 'Good lord, this will be tricky.' But he was rubbing his bony hands together, and his severe mouth was curved into what could, almost, be considered a smile.

Jago must have noticed too, because he gave Ellie a look of surprised delight. Ellie felt warmth rush through her at the thought of them all out here, drinking glasses of lemonade as they pulled up weeds, chopped down grass and added compost to the earth, preparing it for something new and vital. She imagined Jago and Arthur thawing as they worked, helping each other pull up the ivy, gradually loosening their own knots.

Ellie was going to take Rose for dinner at the Flying Caterpillar. Her sister might have done it at Ellie's expense, something she would much rather hadn't happened – especially in front of Jago, who might now be worried that Ellie's inner tangles were unstable or psychopathic – but even so. This might actually work.

'Tricky for sure,' Jago said, turning to Arthur. 'But do you think we can do it?'

'Of course,' Arthur replied. 'A bit of planning, some elbow grease. We'll have this meadow looking respectable in no time. I might be able to teach you a thing or two about gardening along the way, if you're prepared to listen.'

Ellie winced. 'This might backfire spectacularly,' she whispered to her sister.

'Oh, it might well be carnage,' Rose agreed happily. 'But no truces were ever made with stony silence. Sometimes you need to have the fight before you can have the reconciliation. And if these boys need that, then Cornflower Cottage's garden is the place to do it.'

'I thought it was my tangled mind?'

'It's whatever we need it to be, Elowen Moon. I thought you prided yourself on your creativity?' She patted Ellie on the shoulder, then went to help Arthur back to the house. Jago followed, running his hand through his hair and looking pensive, and Monty trotted at his heels, probably hoping for a treat.

Ellie stared at the sea of grass and weeds, every conceivable shade of green below a cloudless sky. It was potential, she realized, however you looked at it. A big patch of potential, waiting, at the bottom of her garden, to be unlocked.

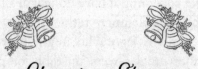

Chapter Eleven

Everything was slowly coming together. She had found Charlie and Daniel's venue, Hannah's wedding breakfast ideas were mouth-wateringly good, and Rose had arranged to bring Arthur to Cornflower Cottage a couple of times a week. Jago had readily agreed, even though it was more than her initial suggestion of just once a week, and Ellie wondered if he'd been encouraged by the way Arthur had softened when they'd been staring at the meadow. Rose said Ellie didn't need to be there because it was clear Arthur knew what he was doing, and while Ellie knew that her garden was in safe hands, she had added the dates they'd settled on to her calendar. She wanted to be a part of it.

Crystal Waters looked handsome in the April sunshine, and the place was buzzing with activity. Four people were queuing patiently at reception, a couple were sitting on the cosy sofa in front of the glass wall, the sunlight falling onto them, and there was laughter coming from the snug.

Ellie joined the back of the queue, but Charlie appeared and waved her over.

'Ellie, hi,' she said. 'Come out to the gardens.' She was wearing a long red skirt and thin black jumper, her hair pulled away from her face. She had a radiance about her it was hard to ignore.

'How are you?' Ellie asked. 'You're looking really well.'

'Thank you,' Charlie said. 'Things are good. Daniel's had a glut of spring bookings, and although I'm not quite back to full summer opening hours on Gertie, when I *am* open, I'm usually busy.'

'That's great,' Ellie said. They stood against a wall to let a family of five pass them in the corridor; twin girls were in front, their ponytails flying behind them. 'I've had a few new enquiries this week, too. I thought it was because I've revamped the website, but maybe everyone's emerging from the winter doldrums; it really feels like summer's just around the corner.'

'I'm sure that's it.' Charlie grinned as they stepped outside. 'I think this year's going to be a good one, all things considered.'

'Not least because you're marrying the love of your life.'

Charlie laughed. 'Very true. And here he is now.' She kissed Daniel on the cheek.

He narrowed his eyes at her, then said hello to Ellie. 'Should my ears be burning?'

'Definitely,' Charlie said, gesturing for Ellie to sit down. There was a cappuccino and a plate of mini tarts already on the table. 'Chocolate and hazelnut, lemon, and the red one's raspberry. I'm trying out some new recipes for the bus. They're bitesize so you can have one of each without feeling guilty.'

'I'm not sure that's true,' Ellie said. 'But I'm willing to defer to the expert.'

'If you can stop at one of each, then you've got more willpower than I have.' Daniel pinched a lemon tart off the plate.

Ellie chose raspberry: her conversation with Charlie about the approaching summer somehow demanded it. The vivid pink colour, the slightly gooey filling that was sweet and sharp all at once, and then the crunch of short, buttery pastry. She would have closed her eyes if the view hadn't been part of what made this moment so magical. But beyond the gentle sweep of the hotel's gardens – the herbs, low shrubs and meandering paved walkways – the cliff ended and the sea began. Today it was a bright, azure blue, channelling the Mediterranean. The breeze was brisk but not cold, and Ellie could easily have sat there for ever, drinking it all in, eating Charlie's baked creations. She had a flash of inspiration: this was where she would bring Jago next. *Next?*

'These are sublime,' she said, holding up the pastry crust that was all that remained of her tart. 'I see what you mean, Daniel; they do not inspire willpower. But it'll be your turn to be tasters next. Hannah's come up with some great ideas for your hot buffet, and we need to arrange a session at the Seven Stars so you can narrow it down. I also want to talk to you about the cake, and what you're thinking of in terms of flowers.' She took her iPad out of her bag. 'Alongside that, we have the other options for the barn to decide on.'

'A glitter ball?' Charlie asked, scooting her chair round so she could see the screen. 'Could you get hold of one?'

'Of course,' Ellie said. It wasn't the first time she'd been asked for a glitter ball. If Porthgolow Barn hadn't already got a fitting for one, she was sure Jane would be happy to accommodate them.

'You really want a glitter ball?' Daniel said.

'You *don't*?' Charlie laughed. 'Come on Daniel, this is our chance to party with our friends and family, to celebrate all the good things: to celebrate us. We will never have this day again. Never have you and I standing up there, saying our vows, telling each other "I do." This is the one occasion where we can do whatever we want; where we can – and should – go all in. For me, that includes a glitter ball.'

'If you say so.'

'I do.' She handed him a chocolate and hazelnut tart.

'Is this bribery?' He smiled, but Ellie noticed it didn't quite reach his eyes.

'Maybe,' she said lightly, then turned back to Ellie. 'What else do we need to decide on?'

'The dress,' Ellie suggested. 'After what you said at the barn, I've been looking at vintage lace styles, and I wondered if you'd had a chance to see what's out there for yourself?'

Charlie wrinkled her nose. 'I've been to a couple of places in Truro with my friend Juliette, and I'm going again with her and Lila on Saturday, but nothing so far has grabbed my attention.'

'You don't necessarily need to buy off the peg. With your budget, we could do something a bit more bespoke. Have a look at some of these.' She navigated to the dress images she'd saved.

Charlie scrolled through the photos, emotions playing across her face.

'Do I need to head off for this bit?' Daniel said.

'Could you refresh our coffees?' Charlie asked.

'Good plan.' He took the empty mugs with him.

Charlie watched him go, then turned to Ellie. 'I have a really specific idea about my dress, but I just . . . I haven't *found* it, and it feels like one of those things where I'll know, with absolute certainty, when it's right. Is that ridiculous?'

'Not at all,' Ellie said. 'If you've got an idea in mind, then we can create it. There's a designer I know called Gina. She's based in Devon, but she has a lot of clients in Cornwall and a boutique in Truro she works out of when she's here. You could meet with her, discuss what you want, and I guarantee she will be able to come up with something you love.'

'And it wouldn't cost thousands?' Charlie asked.

'She's very reasonable,' Ellie said. 'Shall I set up a consultation with her?'

'I would love that. Thank you, Ellie.' She browsed through the images on Ellie's iPad, a thoughtful look on her face, until Daniel returned with a tray of fresh coffees, and wordlessly put them down on the table.

'We've done the dress chat,' Charlie said. 'Ellie and I have got a plan.'

'Great.' Daniel sat down and rubbed a hand over his jaw.

Charlie's eyes narrowed. 'I've found a peach and lime coloured gown that looks like it's made out of Italian meringue. It's absolutely perfect; you're going to love it.'

Daniel nodded, his gaze fixed on his coffee. 'Sounds good.'

'Hey . . .' Charlie put a hand on his arm. 'What's wrong? You haven't been listening to a word I've said. Even if it was what I wanted, I think you'd be hard-pressed to get married to a summer fruits meringue.'

'What?' He looked at Charlie, then Ellie, and Ellie was surprised by how worried he seemed. 'What are you talking about?'

'What's happened?' Charlie pressed.

'What do you mean?' He sat up straighter. 'Nothing's happened.'

'You expect me to believe that?' she said softly.

Daniel shook his head, clearing his anxious expression. 'A couple of guests complained about the hot tub,' he admitted. 'They were quite aggressive with Chloe, and I'm wondering what to do. Sorry. Where are we up to?'

'The fact that I am *not* going to wear a peach and lime meringue pie dress,' Charlie said, laughing when Daniel looked horrified.

'That sounds hideous.'

'I knew you weren't listening. But we do have a plan, and I'm excited about it.'

Ellie grinned. 'It's a good start. And now—'

'Oh, God, my croissants!' Charlie stood up. 'They've been proving, and I need to check on them.'

'Go for it,' Ellie said. 'I was just about to say that Daniel and I need to talk morning suits.'

Charlie hurried inside, and Ellie smiled at Daniel. The one he offered her was weak in comparison. There was a burst of laughter from one of the other tables, people enjoying the spring sunshine.

'Why is Charlie baking in your kitchen?' Ellie asked.

'She's opening the bus this afternoon,' Daniel said. 'She decided, a while ago, that the kitchen here is much better equipped for her baking than the one at home, so she's commandeered a corner of it. My chef, Levi, doesn't seem to mind, and I would protest, except I love having her here.' He shrugged. He still looked less than happy, so Ellie persevered.

'Were you really distracted by an unsatisfied guest?'

'What?' Daniel met her gaze. 'Oh. Yeah. That did happen, but . . .' He ran a hand through his hair, his jaw clenching.

'But what?' Ellie said softly. 'I am here to de-stress your wedding, to take all the hard bits away from you. If there's something you're worried about, something you don't feel you can discuss with Charlie, that is *exactly* what I'm here for.'

Daniel blew out a long stream of air. 'It's what she said earlier. About this being our one opportunity. She's so excited, about the dress and the glitter ball, about the barn – even the pig! I feel like I'm not stepping up.'

Ellie frowned. 'In what way?'

'I should be doing more, for Charlie. I want her to have the glitter ball and her perfect dress; I want her to have fireworks and a pod of dolphins swimming past when she walks on the beach that morning – anything she has ever imagined, in her wildest dreams. I know that sounds Disney-level ridiculous.' He laughed. 'But I want our wedding to be perfect.'

'It will be to you and Charlie,' Ellie said. 'And I can guarantee that mostly what she's been dreaming about is having you slide a ring on her finger, kissing you in front of everyone you both love, and knowing she gets to spend every day being with you.'

He shook his head. 'I know all that but I . . . I want to do something really special for her; something she'll never, ever forget.'

'Daniel, she won't forget getting married to you. But if you wanted to do something extra, on top of the plans we've got, then . . .' Ellie pursed her lips and gazed around her, at the garden and the sea beyond, the sky still mostly clear, but with a few puffs of cloud towards the horizon. They had the barn and Hannah's wonderful food, plans for a glitter ball and Charlie's dress, a cobbled courtyard complete with Millicent the pig, and Gertie. Ellie was sure they could get the Routemaster to the barn, so that wasn't an issue, and while Charlie was *definitely* not allowed to do any baking, Lila had suggested using it as an additional bar: she had offered to create a special menu of coffee-based drinks and cocktails. What could they do on top of that?

'Sorry Ellie,' Daniel said. 'Maybe I need to think about this myself. A gift I could get her, or—'

'What about Gertie?'

'What *about* Gertie?'

'We could give her a wedding makeover.'

Daniel's shoulders straightened. 'You mean a repaint?'

Ellie smiled. 'A full redesign, just for the wedding. You could be outlandish and paint her silver or gold, get a message written on her, redo the interior. It wouldn't be cheap, I expect, but it would be memorable – and it would add another element to your big day; something really glossy and glitzy. I'm just thinking aloud, and it might be too much, but—'

'It's genius,' Daniel said. 'Charlie transformed Gertie when she came to Cornwall and started the Cornish Cream Tea

161

Bus. Her red paint is iconic, so it would have to be temporary, but I think she'd love it.'

'She'll have to know about it, though. We can't make her bus disappear for a week without any kind of explanation.'

Daniel shook his head. 'We're almost half-way through April, and the Cornish Cream Tea Bus had its grand opening on the May bank holiday – I've still got the ticket.' He grinned. 'Charlie's spending the week before getting ready, creating a new menu for the start of the summer season.' He gestured to the tarts. 'What if I convince her Gertie needs a check-over too? Like an additional MOT before the tours and festivals get going. If I get in touch with Pete, who did the first redesign, and explain, I'm sure he'll be able to do it. He can call Charlie and tell her he's found something which means Gertie needs to stay for a few more days than expected – something with the water tank or the oven.' He shrugged. 'She's also shutting a fortnight before the wedding, so she has some proper time off, but I don't know if we should leave it that late.'

'I think it would be better to do it now,' Ellie said. 'Although that means Gertie will be wedding-themed for about six weeks. Do you think Charlie will mind?'

Daniel grinned, his anxiety all but gone. 'I think she'll love being extra noticeable on the beach. Charlie isn't the type to shy away from any kind of celebration.' He slapped the table. 'This is why we pay you the big bucks, Ellie. Actually, we should probably be paying you more.'

Ellie laughed. 'Not at all. I'm just glad I could come up with a solution.'

'A solution to what?' Charlie asked as she sat back down, a smear of chocolate across her cheek.

Daniel leaned forward and wiped it off, the infectious sparkle back in his eyes. 'A niggle I had about my wedding outfit.' Ellie marvelled at his ability to switch from concerned to confident in a heartbeat. 'I can't tell you, though, because it has to be a surprise.'

'I don't think it works the same way with your suit,' Charlie said.

'Well, I'm not telling you about it. You'll have to wait and see. But I think,' he mused, giving Ellie a quick wink, 'you'll be pretty impressed.'

'Oh, will I? Don't tell me *you're* going for peach meringue because I refused to?'

'No clues Charlie,' Daniel said smoothly, holding out his hand. Charlie entwined her fingers with his, the movement almost unconscious.

Ellie's heart gave a little leap. This, right here, was what true love looked like. Spending time with Charlie and Daniel, seeing how committed they were to each other, lifted her spirits. It made her feel passionate about her business, and it made her think of Jago, and the way he'd held her gaze over the table in the Seven Stars.

She left Crystal Waters with Charlie and Daniel grinning, with Daniel's whispered assurance that he'd set the foundations for getting Gertie whisked away, and with ideas of how to turn a bus that sold Cornish Cream Teas into the ultimate wedding vehicle swirling around in her head.

Over the next week, she liaised with Daniel about their secret Gertie makeover. He told her he'd convinced Charlie to let Pete spruce up the bus, and the pick-up was arranged. They also had a tasting session at the Seven Stars, Hannah producing hot buffet food that had them all delirious with deliciousness – and Daniel seriously worried that his hotel restaurant was no longer the prime eating establishment in Porthgolow – and Ellie spent time at Cornflower Cottage with Rose, Arthur and Jago.

They made an unlikely foursome, she mused, as she drove there early one morning, the sea sparkling and the sun shimmering higher in the sky: the two spinster sisters, and the not-quite-estranged father and son. All of them partnerless, whether by design or circumstance, and all of them, in their own way, a little bit lost.

They didn't spend the whole time working in the garden together, Rose and Jago often leaving her and Arthur to the weeding and cutting back while they supplied refreshments and talked each other's ears off on the patio. On those occasions, Ellie was torn between tending to her plants and being in Jago's presence. But she got on well with Arthur, and while he was undoubtedly a proud, private man who lived by a certain code, she saw hints of the warmth and humour that were so readily there in his son. But Jago was the one subject the older man wouldn't address, and whenever Ellie tried to turn the conversation in that direction, he would go quiet, or pointedly return them to a discussion about the garden.

Sometimes, all four of them would work on the patch of land that Ellie insisted was called the meadow, and which Jago had rechristened the wilderness. He said it was after the lane Cornflower Cottage resided on, but she knew he was teasing her. And those times, with all of them sifting carefully through the grass – because she and Arthur had insisted there might be plants worth saving in amongst the mess – were Ellie's favourites. She felt part of a team, doing hard graft that made her sweaty and put dirt under her fingernails, with her sister and two men who, in very different ways, she was coming to care about.

Her life was busy and fulfilling. She was working harder as wedding season approached; she enjoyed spending time with her sister, and she hadn't entirely had to give up her beautiful cottage. In fact, the situation came with a couple of additional perks – as Jago might say – that she was coming to rely on for her happiness. She started each day with a spring in her step, looking forward to whatever lay ahead, whether it was arranging for a floral bouquet to be delivered to Charlie for her inspection, or turning over the soil in an empty patch of land, ready for new plants to be bedded in.

Ellie was seeing all her plans, slowly but surely, coming to fruition. She just hoped nothing unexpected was waiting in the wings, preparing to knock her off course.

Chapter Twelve

Today, Ellie decided, was going to be another good day. The sun was making everything sparkle and the air smelt crisp and fresh, with a hint of the summer warmth to come. She was standing on the beach alongside Daniel and Charlie, because Gertie was about to be picked up by Pete to be taken to his garage in Newquay, so he could begin her transformation into full-on wedding bus. Of course, Charlie didn't know that this was what was happening, and Ellie had turned up on the pretence of bringing her some dress brochures at just the right time, because this was her idea, and she wanted to see that it all happened the way it should.

Daniel had his arms folded as a bright blue VW van drove into the beach car park, Charlie standing next to him. Ellie could feel the nerves radiating off the future groom as if, now it had come to it, he wasn't entirely sure about their plan. But he had told Ellie that Charlie trusted Pete completely, that he had done such a good job on the

Routemaster's original transformation, so there was nothing to be worried about.

Two men got out of the van, one tall and wide and wearing a too-tight T-shirt, the other his physical opposite, short and slender, with a curtain of brown hair falling over his eyes. The second one, Ellie thought, looked about twelve. They began making their way across the sand.

'What's going on?' she asked, hoping she sounded relaxed and curious.

'Gertie's getting a check-up,' Charlie explained. 'Before the summer season starts. She's going to Pete's garage for a couple of days.'

'Right.' Ellie nodded. 'Which one's Pete?'

'Neither of these are Pete, but I recognize the bigger one from his garage. Hello,' she said, as they approached. 'Have you come to take my bus?'

'That's right,' the tall man said. 'Your Cornish Cream Tea Bus. Lovely scones.' He patted his stomach. 'Liam here's going to drive her over.'

'Hey,' the skinny one said. 'Have you got the keys?'

Charlie handed them to him.

'Do you have a licence to drive double-deckers?' Ellie blurted. Charlie gave her a curious look.

'Oh, yeah,' Liam said. 'Had it four years now. Do you want to see?' He shoved his hand in his jeans pocket.

'No, that's OK,' Ellie said quickly, giving what she hoped was a placatory smile. At least he didn't seem offended that she'd asked.

Liam jangled the keys, then climbed on board the bus.

'You OK?' Charlie asked Ellie.

'Of course,' Ellie said. 'Fine. Absolutely. Why wouldn't I

be?' She could feel Daniel's gaze burning into the side of her face. She didn't want to mess up the surprise. 'He just looks so young, that's all.'

Charlie grinned. 'They all do. It's one of the perks of getting old.'

'Hey, Liam,' Daniel called. 'Give us a call when you reach Pete's, OK?'

'No problem!' Liam shouted back. 'Three rings, eh?' He held his hand up by his ear and waggled it in the universal gesture of the telephone, then disappeared inside the cab, while the bigger man trudged back across the sand to the VW. Gertie puttered to life, and Liam turned her slowly and drove her towards the road, the VW waiting and then following behind. Ellie watched the mini procession until it was out of sight.

'Bye-bye, Gertie,' Charlie murmured, once the three of them were alone on the sand. She turned to Daniel. 'I still don't know why you wanted to come and see her off.'

He shrugged. 'I wanted to give you a lift up to the hotel afterwards.'

Charlie smiled. 'Your chivalry knows no bounds, but I could have walked.'

'I didn't want you to.' He leaned in and kissed her, then stood back. 'Good to see you Ellie.'

'You too,' she said, crossing her fingers behind her back. She was relieved that Daniel, at least, didn't seem remotely worried by their subterfuge.

'What are you doing with the rest of your Saturday, Ellie?' Charlie asked. 'Do you want to come with us and have a cream tea? It's a beautiful day for sitting outside.'

Ellie frowned. 'But your bus has gone.'

Charlie grinned. 'I can put one together for you up at the hotel. I'm going to be doing some planning there anyway, while Gertie's out of commission, and I've already baked the scones.'

Daniel rolled his eyes good-naturedly, and then strolled over to where his BMW was parked in the car park. Ellie remembered him telling her Charlie had taken over a corner of his hotel kitchen.

'I'm very tempted,' Ellie said, 'but I have a date with a man and my garden.'

'Oh?' Charlie raised an eyebrow. 'Ooh, is this the man Hannah saw you in the pub with? Jago, isn't it? How long have you been together?'

Ellie's heart gave a little kick. 'We're not together. He's renting my cottage, and his dad is a keen gardener. He lives in a care home, and it's all a bit complicated, but basically Jago's dad has been helping out in my garden.'

'As a sort of therapy?' Charlie asked.

'It's a multi-pronged attack,' she explained. 'Arthur gets to do what he loves, and it helps me out because while I'm not living there the garden still needs work, and then also . . .' she chewed her lip, 'Jago and his dad could do with spending time together. It's worked out better than I hoped. So that's where I'm off to. Cornwall Cottage, to meet Arthur and Rose, my sister.'

'And Jago?'

'I don't know if Jago will be there,' Ellie said, giving a nonchalant shrug.

'But you'd quite like it if he was?'

Ellie laughed. 'I wouldn't mind. But it's already a complicated situation, so I shouldn't be adding more complications.'

'Fair enough,' Charlie said. 'I suppose I'm just in a romantic mood.'

'As well you should be, Mrs Bride-to-Be. How are you feeling? Looking forward to meeting Gina?'

'Yes!' Charlie clasped her hands together. 'I was so worried about the dress, because I want to look good, but I don't want to spend a fortune on a few bits of material.'

'I remember you telling me at our first meeting that you wanted to be a princess, and you should be – whatever kind of wedding-day princess is right for you. I love the dress fittings; you'll feel sky high in the right outfit.'

Charlie laughed. 'I've got summer bus plans to focus on, so I can't spend the whole day dreaming about our upcoming nuptials. Sure I can't tempt you to make a quick detour to the hotel for a scone?'

Ellie thought for a moment. 'You wouldn't let me buy some to take away, would you?'

'I won't let you *buy* any, but you can have some! You can decide whether you want fruit or cheese, or a selection of both.'

Ellie walked with Charlie to the car park where Daniel, and Florence, were waiting. The stop would only add ten minutes on to her journey, and surely they would be extra pleased to see her if she turned up with some freshly baked scones.

Cornflower Cottage looked pretty and inviting, the roses in front beginning to bud, the white bench gleaming in the sunshine. She gave a little sigh of happiness as she thought of Rose, Arthur and Jago beavering away in the back, and imagined their faces when she appeared with Charlie's wonderful scones.

As she went round the side of the house, she heard loud voices. Were they *singing?* But it didn't sound like singing, it sounded like . . . shouting. Ellie felt a jolt of alarm. There were male voices, raised, and her sister cutting in, trying to be heard over the top.

'Look, it doesn't matter,' she heard Rose say as she pushed open the side gate.

'He has *no* understanding of what kind of care is needed,' Arthur said, his voice ragged with fury. 'He never does! He never considers anything properly.'

Ellie took in the scene in front of her. Arthur was on the patio, clad in his green wellies, dark trousers and a warm-looking jumper, his eyes blazing. Jago stood on the grass next to Ellie's lawnmower, the cord trailing to the kitchen doorway. His T-shirt and jeans were muddy, and his face was pale. Rose stood between them, like a buffer.

'I had to get out of the way of Monty,' Jago said. 'I don't think Ellie would have been happy if I'd mown over her cat.' Ellie surveyed the garden, but could see no sign of Monty.

'It's a whole crop of delphiniums, Jago. If you'd been paying more attention—'

'I'm sure we can get some more,' Rose said, her voice edged with desperation. She caught Ellie's eye. 'Don't you think, Ellie?'

'That's hardly the point,' Arthur spat. 'The boy has no concept of what it takes to do a good job. He shrugs and makes a half-hearted attempt with everything, does what-ever he feels like, frankly, and thinks that's an admirable way to live his life.'

Arthur didn't look in Ellie's direction, but Jago did: his eyes found hers and Ellie was shocked at the hurt in them.

'I'm fairly sure I'm a man now, rather than a boy,' Jago said calmly, 'but if that's what you think, then I'll leave you to it.' He turned and walked inside the house, and a moment later the lawnmower plug was flung onto the patio, followed by the kitchen door slamming shut.

'We can plant some new del-whatsits, can't we?' Rose said again. 'And I'm assuming they're less important than your cat.'

Ellie nodded. 'It's honestly fine. We can get some new flowers. Arthur, what happened?' She was sure the delphiniums had taken on the unhappy job of being symbolic of something deeper.

'He doesn't care about anything,' Arthur said. 'Nothing important, anyway. He's forty-one years old and he has no sense of responsibility; no wife or children, no home of his own. I had thought that I'd raised him right, but he's a waste of space!'

Ellie was taken aback. 'It looks like he was trying to help, and I have made those strips of grass quite narrow. Monty loves getting under people's feet, and somehow he's lost all fear of the mower, despite the terrible noise it makes.' She smiled, but Arthur didn't return it.

'He barrelled in there with no thought of the consequences.'

'It was an accident,' Rose said, gently rubbing Arthur's arm. 'Come and sit down. I'll put the kettle on.'

'No.' Arthur shook his head. 'I need to go back to Seascape House. I shouldn't be here.'

Ellie and Rose exchanged startled looks. 'Come and take

a load off, Arthur,' Rose said confidently. 'You've been working hard all morning.'

'I've got scones,' Ellie said lamely. 'I'll put them in the kitchen, and maybe we can talk about that bed and what we could plant in there instead. I'm just going to see if . . .'

'Go,' Rose murmured. 'I'll stay here.'

Ellie hurried inside, through the empty kitchen and to the living room. Jago was staring out of the window, his hands in fists at his sides. Monty was sitting on the arm of the sofa, staring up at him and miaowing softly, almost as if he realized he was partly responsible.

'Jago,' she said quietly. 'Are you OK?'

'What do you think?' he asked, not turning to face her. 'This was a bloody stupid idea, having Dad here. I never should have agreed to it.'

Ellie took another step into the room. 'It's just one argument,' she said. 'And don't you think – if there's been tension between you for years – then it's not unexpected? You're not likely to find common ground immediately, I mean.'

Jago shook his head, his gaze still trained on the view outside. 'Did you hear what he called me? I heard it from here.'

Ellie winced. 'I'm sure he didn't mean it, he—'

'Oh, he meant it!' Jago spun to face her, and she saw the fire in his green eyes. 'He meant it all right. That's what he's always thought of me; that I'm a waste of space, a poor excuse for a man. The funny thing is, he's probably more pissed off with himself than he is with me, because he's let his standards slip, allowing me to grow up to be so useless.'

Ellie couldn't hide her shock. It was as though he was a

completely different person; she could almost see the years of tension and hurt burning, like coal, under the surface.

'Jago, don't.'

'Don't what? Don't let him get to me? He's my dad. How am I meant to just let it go?'

'You need to find a way of meeting in the middle,' she said, holding a hand out. 'He needs to accept that you live a very different life to him, and you—' she sighed. 'I think you're doing what you can. By having him here, I mean. But then I don't know any of the details—'

'No, you don't.' His voice was quieter, but it still had an edge. 'You have no idea. You asked me to let him come here, and I knew it was a mistake, but I thought it might not be as bad as I was imagining. I thought maybe I'd got it wrong, that he wasn't ashamed of me, that he wouldn't treat me as if I was still five years old.'

'Is he really ashamed of you?' Ellie asked softly.

'Disappointed, at the very least. He always fucking has been.'

Ellie clasped her hands together, the silence stretching between them. 'It's Monty who's to blame here, and look at him, acting all innocent. My cat's at fault, not you.' She took another step towards him.

Jago gave her a weary half-smile. 'Monty has even less idea about what's going on than you do. I can't point the finger at your cat.'

'I shouldn't have suggested this arrangement,' Ellie said. 'I went into it without the facts.'

Jago shook his head. 'I could have told you. Or, better yet, I could have said no. Blaming you – or Monty – for this is exactly what my dad would expect of me; passing the buck, refusing to take responsibility. Where he's concerned, I *do* feel like a bloody five year old.'

Ellie stepped closer. She wanted to tell him that, from her point of view, he was very much all man. But that would be corny, and inappropriate, and she was currently using up most of her energy deciding whether empathy or lust was winning her emotional tug of war. He looked like a wounded puppy; a dishevelled, muddy, wounded puppy, with sweat darkening his hairline, his muscles defined under his thin T-shirt, his chest rising and falling rapidly.

'I'm so sorry Jago,' she said.

His eyes met hers, and there was a new kind of fire there. One that made her heart pound. 'I think I can forgive you,' he murmured, 'even though you really are to blame for all this.'

'How come?'

'Because it's difficult to say no to you.'

'It is?'

'You know,' he went on as if she hadn't spoken, 'coming back here has been confusing. I feel like a child when I'm with my dad, and then when I'm with you . . . I feel like a bloody teenager again.'

At first she didn't think she'd heard him right. But then he brought his hand up to her face, and she was consumed his scent, the touch of his hot skin against hers. 'Jago,' she whispered.

'Hmm?' His eyes were drinking her in, roaming over her face, and it made every cell prickle to life in pleasure and anticipation.

She swayed towards him, her body taking charge. She parted her lips, watched as he bent his head towards her and then . . . her phone rang. She had it set to loud; a jaunty ringtone that she would always notice. Even if she'd wanted to ignore it, the moment had shattered like a terracotta pot kicked across concrete.

Jago smiled and stepped back, but his hand dropped to her shoulder and stayed there, warming her through her thin cotton jumper. She took her phone out of her pocket and saw Daniel's name on the screen.

'Hi Daniel,' she said, wondering how long it would take her pulse to settle.

'Ellie, hi. Look, I know this isn't your issue directly, but I just . . . I needed to tell you.' He sounded out of breath, and his voice was shaking slightly.

Ellie stiffened, all her thoughts now on her client. 'What's wrong? What's happened?' She was vaguely aware of Jago's hand tightening around her shoulder.

'It's . . . fuck. Sorry, I shouldn't have—'

'It's OK,' Ellie said hurriedly. 'Just tell me.'

She heard him exhale. 'It's Gertie. It turns out that skinny kid, Liam? You were right to question his credentials. He's crashed her, on the way to Pete's garage. He's OK, nobody's hurt, but apparently the bus isn't in a good way. Charlie and I are about to go there now, and I know you wanted to be fully clued in on the makeover, so—'

'You were right to call me,' Ellie said, her stomach plummeting. 'Can you tell me where the crash happened? I'll meet you there.'

'Ellie,' Daniel said, 'I'm taking full responsibility for this. I thought it was a great idea. I—'

'It was my idea, Daniel, and accidents happen.' She sounded a lot calmer than she felt. 'Please don't blame yourself. The important thing is to check everyone, and then Gertie, are OK.'

There was a pause and then, 'You think we should tell her?'

'I'm going to come and meet you, and she'll wonder why I've turned up. But even if I wasn't going to, I think we should tell her the truth. I'm not sure you could live with yourself if you didn't.'

'OK.' She heard him swear under his breath. 'You're right. Got a pen?'

Ellie glanced around the room and Jago, clearly understanding, hurried out and came back with a notepad and pen. Ellie smiled her thanks and, with her phone tucked under her ear, took down the details Daniel gave her. She assured him she'd leave straight away, then hung up.

'That sounded bad,' Jago said quietly. 'Are you OK?'

Ellie nodded, but she didn't feel OK. 'Charlie's Routemaster has crashed on the way to the garage. We were going to give it a wedding makeover as a surprise. Nobody's hurt but the damage is bad, apparently, and . . .' She swallowed, forcing herself to meet Jago's gaze. 'It's my fault. It was my suggestion, and I had reservations about the driver who came to pick the bus up, but it was only gut instinct. He was from the garage, this is just a horrible accident, but if I hadn't—'

'No, Ellie. You can't start blaming yourself. You said you were going to the crash site?'

She nodded, clutching the piece of paper with Gertie's destination on it.

'I'll drive you,' he said. 'Let me go and tell the others. Wait there.' He squeezed her arm and left the room, and

Ellie sank onto the sofa. Lord Montague climbed onto her lap and bumped the top of his head against her chin.

She stared out of the window at the rolling hills, and thought about how much promise the day had started with, and how it had fallen, so quickly, to ruins. The Cornish Cream Tea Bus, Charlie's livelihood, her pride and joy, was damaged. She didn't know how badly yet, but it didn't sound good. And Jago and Arthur were at war; father calling son a waste of space, Jago wishing he'd never agreed to her plan. *Her* plan. Just like the bus makeover. Both of them had failed in ways that, if she'd been thinking properly, she could have avoided.

Ellie thought she had been doing so well, excelling professionally and making good choices in her personal life. But, she realized, as Jago came back into the room with his car keys, and she put Monty on the sofa and followed her tenant, the man she had, only a few moments before, been about to kiss in another astounding lapse of judgement, she was utterly fooling herself.

Part Three

You May Now Eat the Cake

Chapter Thirteen

The reality is always less extreme than what you're imagining, Elowen Moon told herself as she sat in the passenger seat of Jago Carne's Golf and they wended their way south of Porthgolow and Cornflower Cottage, towards the place where the Cornish Cream Tea Bus had crashed.

And so Ellie imagined all the terrible things that could have happened to the bus. She imagined it falling off a cliff and plunging into the sea; she pictured it catching fire and going up in flames, all those pretty teapots and fairy lights nothing more than melted blobs welded to metal. Then she imagined less dramatic scenarios: a minor scratch on the bumper, a cracked windscreen, a burst tyre; things that would take mere hours to fix. If she pictured those things, then maybe it would be even *less* horrible? It made no logical sense, but it was the only way to quell her feelings of utter hopelessness.

'Doing OK, Ellie?' Jago asked as he confidently took a turn in the road. He hadn't changed out of his gardening clothes, but Ellie was used to him looking dishevelled and, while she hadn't been overjoyed when she'd first considered the combination of him and the cream carpets at Cornflower Cottage, she now found his scruffiness comforting. Besides, she had also seen him much smarter than this and, on one unforgettable occasion, wearing only a towel.

'I will be, as soon as I see Gertie and we know what we're up against.'

'Do you know how it crashed?'

She shook her head. 'Daniel didn't give much away. All I got was that Liam, the driver from Pete's garage, had crashed her. He assured me he was qualified, even though he looked far too young, and I—'

'It was an accident,' Jago said. He reached over to squeeze Ellie's hands, which were knotted together in her lap. 'You couldn't have predicted it or stopped it.'

'I should have. I'm the wedding planner.'

'The wedding planner,' he repeated. 'Not God. No amount of list-making would have predicted that Liam would crash the bus. The road could have been slippery, the gear lever slightly dodgy, a deer or dog running out in front of him. Anything.'

Ellie sighed. 'I thought this was such a good idea. But I should have made a proper plan before suggesting—'

'Stop,' Jago said firmly. 'Stop, now.' He squeezed her fingers again and then put his hand back on the wheel. Ellie wished he could drive one-handed the whole way, but at the same time she didn't want *them* to crash on the way to the first crash.

It was easy to spot the location, even without Daniel's precise directions, because there was a police car, its blue lights flashing, parked horizontally across the road. A policeman was directing cars to turn off before they reached the blockage.

'We're here to see the bus,' Jago said, once he'd rolled down his window. 'I'm a mechanic.'

The policeman frowned, but waved them through. Jago pulled up on the side of the road, and Ellie got out. From where she was standing, Gertie looked fine; her back end was unmarked, her hazard lights flashing. But the bus was angled into the side of the road, too close to a sheer rock face that rose at least fifty feet above them.

She followed Jago, who had hurried on ahead. She was relieved that he was with her, and that he would be able to help. She walked calmly down the road, glancing in Gertie's windows at all the tables that, by next week, should be full of happy customers eating cream teas and sausage rolls. She hoped nothing would change that.

She found Charlie, Daniel and Jago near the front of the bus, with another man. He was slender, with close-cropped hair and tanned skin. He and Jago were crouching at the place where Gertie had connected with the cliff, Daniel and Charlie standing a little way back.

Charlie, for the most part, was looking composed, but Ellie could see unshed tears in her eyes. Daniel had his arms folded tightly over his chest, a stricken look on his face.

'Are you both OK?' she asked softly as she joined them. 'How's Liam?'

'Ellie!' Charlie went from upset to startled. 'What are you doing here? Why are you—'

'Liam's fine,' Daniel cut in. 'He's been checked out by paramedics and he's suffering from mild shock, but has no physical injuries.' He glanced at Ellie. 'But we do have something to tell you, Charlie. *I* have something to tell you.'

Ellie stepped forward. 'It's such a relief about Liam,' she said. 'But Charlie, this is my fault.'

'What?' She frowned and wiped at her cheek as a tear fell. 'Why?'

'Because this was my suggestion. Sending Gertie for a check-up, when really we wanted to give her a full transformation, in time for the wedding.'

Charlie stared at her, lips slightly parted.

'I wanted to do something for you,' Daniel added. 'Something special – unforgettable – for the wedding. I wanted to come up with some grand surprise.'

The words hung in the air. It was both surprising and unforgettable, Ellie thought with a wince.

'So you suggested that Gertie could do with a once-over in Pete's garage,' Charlie said slowly, 'but you were really taking her away to . . . what? Cover her in glitter?'

'It would have been a bit more stylish than that,' Daniel said, a hint of defensiveness in his voice.

'Why not tell me, then?' Charlie folded her arms, looking from Daniel to Ellie and back again. 'Why keep me in the dark about this? It's my *bus*,' she said, her voice rising. 'My entire business!'

'We know that,' Ellie said gently. 'We had no idea that this would happen.'

'You cooked up this scheme together,' Charlie went on, 'and got Pete involved too? How long have you been planning it? Did you even check he had the time to do it? Maybe he was stretched and had to use Liam because you'd put him under pressure!'

'Charlie,' Daniel said, 'I am so, so sorry. I thought this would be a good thing; I thought you'd be over the moon.' He looked so upset, and Ellie's guilt increased tenfold.

Charlie huffed and turned to Ellie. 'You're supposed to be taking the stress out of our wedding, not adding to it.' She sounded more hurt than angry, and Ellie had to resist the urge to hug her, though she knew it might not be welcome. It was Daniel who did that, pulling Charlie against him, stroking her hair. He mouthed 'sorry' to Ellie over her shoulder, but Ellie shook her head and pointed a finger at herself.

Charlie was right. She was supposed to be removing – or at least absorbing – their wedding stress, and this was not part of the plan. But it had happened now, so all she could do was put things right; oversee Gertie getting back to her former glory.

'I'm sure it looks worse than it is,' she said. 'We'll have Gertie back to you, as good as new, long before the wedding.' From where she stood, she could see that the windscreen was shattered and the bumper was crushed, the solid red metal looking like a crumpled piece of cardboard. Still, now was not the time to be negative. 'It's going to be fine,' she added. A group of seagulls flew overhead, their cries like unfriendly laughter. 'I know this is so far from ideal, but all these things are fixable, right?' She glanced at Jago and the other man, who she assumed was Pete.

He ran a hand over his head. 'We won't know the full extent of the problems until we get her back to the garage. Obviously, there's some cosmetic damage that needs repairing, but I'll have to take a look underneath before I can give you a prognosis.'

'But the cosmetic stuff can sometimes make it look hopeless,' Jago added, 'even when what's under the bonnet is fairly sound.' Ellie felt a rush of gratitude for his positivity in front of Charlie and Daniel. 'I'm going to go with Pete and help out.'

'You are?' Ellie managed.

'All hands to the pump.' He stood and wiped his hands down the back of his jeans. 'My workload's fairly light at the moment, so I can fit it in.'

'My insurance will cover the repairs and Jago's time,' Pete said, 'and I could do with the extra help so I can prioritise getting Gertie back to you.' He gave Charlie a warm smile.

'Don't lose faith,' Jago added. 'She's in good hands.'

Charlie managed a smile. 'Thank you.'

'I didn't realize you had an in-house mechanic, Ellie,' Daniel said.

'I'm a recent add-on,' Jago replied, holding out his hand and introducing himself. 'But this is right up my street. With Pete and I working together, Gertie's got the best possible chance.'

Charlie glanced at Ellie, then looked away.

'I'll be in touch later on today,' Ellie said.

Charlie nodded, but didn't meet her gaze.

'Thank you, Ellie,' Daniel said firmly, and Ellie managed a wobbly smile, relieved that at least he hadn't lost faith in her. 'Speak soon.'

Once they'd gone, walking slowly back to Daniel's car, Ellie tried to tamp down her frustration. Gertie crashing wasn't just a practical problem, it also seemed symbolic. The bus was Charlie's livelihood, the thing she was most proud of, and, on a whim, Ellie had suggested taking it away to be spruced up – and look what had happened. She remembered being horrified at a bit of mud and an overly friendly pig, and fervently wished that was still their biggest worry.

'Do you really think it's going to be OK?' she asked Jago and Pete, who were peering underneath the cracked bumper.

They both looked at her, the silence dragging on in a way that Ellie found more than a little disconcerting. 'We're going to do all we can,' Pete said, eventually. 'These old Routemasters are pretty solid. It just depends how far the damage goes.'

Three pairs of eyes travelled up the height of the bus, to where the second deck was nestled against the rock face, a hairline crack running the full width of the windscreen. Despite the sun beating down on them, Ellie felt chilled. 'I really appreciate everything you're doing,' she said. Then she walked away from the broken bus and covered her face with her hands. 'Fuckity fuckity fuck,' she said. When she glanced behind her, Jago was watching her with undisguised sympathy, which only made her feel worse.

'Back home and then to the pub?' Rose asked, as Ellie got into her car. 'I expect you need a whole vat of wine after today.'

'I'm not sure that would be enough,' Ellie admitted. She had watched Gertie being winched away, listened to the crunching, ripping sounds as it had been detached from the cliff. She had been so relieved that Daniel and Charlie had gone by then, because it might have destroyed any hope they might still have.

'Let's start with a vat and see how we go,' Rose said.

Ellie shook her head. 'I want to go back to the cottage.' It was the only place she could imagine feeling remotely calm; amongst her plants and flowers, with blackbirds singing and the rustle of wind through the trees. And she knew Jago wouldn't be there, so she wouldn't be getting in his way.

'You sure?' Rose asked softly.

'I need to tidy up, put the mower away,' she said. 'Unless you and Arthur did it?'

Rose tutted. 'No, I couldn't get him to do anything after their fight. Stubborn as a mule, that one. But I hope once he's had a chance to mull everything over, he'll come round. As awful as they are, I think these arguments might be necessary for him and Jago to work through their past.'

Ellie just nodded. She couldn't help thinking that Jago and Arthur's bust-up had been her fault too, for interfering when it wasn't her place.

'Where's Jago now?' Rose asked, when Ellie didn't say anything. 'I assumed he'd be bringing you home.'

'He's gone with Pete to help out with the bus,' Ellie said. 'You should have seen it, Rose; how crushed it was. I haven't just messed up their wedding, I've actually ruined Charlie's business. Gertie wasn't a prop to play about with; chuck a bit of sparkly paint on and have her brightening up the courtyard.' Ellie rubbed her forehead, trying to soothe away the headache that was building.

Rose huffed. 'I could spend hours telling you why this isn't your fault, that it's simply a cruel twist of fate, and I will if I have to. At least nobody was hurt; that's all that really matters. Every other problem can be solved, one way or another. I'll take you to potter in your garden, but don't stay there too long. I want you home for dinner, OK?'

'I'm not a child,' Ellie said, but she smiled at her sister.

'No, but you need to listen to me. I'll have a bottle of cold rosé waiting. God though,' she added after a moment, 'life's a funny old thing, isn't it?'

'What do you mean?'

'Your clients, Charlie and Daniel, about to take that pivotal step into marriage. Poor old Arthur, grieving his wife's death and Jago, confirmed bachelor, trying to do what's right and finding it harder than he imagined. It doesn't matter what stage you're at, or how positive you're trying to be. Life can still kick you where it hurts, and does so repeatedly, in my experience.'

Ellie stared at her sister, incredulous. 'If that's the sort of positive pep talk I'm going to get with my bottle of rosé, then I'll go to the pub on my own.'

As soon as Ellie was in the garden of Cornflower Cottage, her tension began to ease. The sun was hovering, like a golden ball, just above the roof, beaming intense amber rays onto the patio.

Ellie put the mower away and inspected the bed where her delphiniums had been. She cleared up what was left of the ruined plants, then refreshed the soil, turning it over so that there was no sign anything had gone wrong, preparing it for something new. She lost herself in the task, relishing the sensation of mud under her nails and her lower back burning with the effort. And then, because she didn't want to think about poor Gertie, or how distraught Charlie must be, she went to the meadow.

They had made a good start on clearing it of brambles and bindweed, shortening the grass, looking out for solitary-bee holes and skylark nests as they went, but there was still a lot to do. Ellie got out her secateurs and began snipping, collecting the grass for the compost heap. She still didn't know what to do with the space once it was cleared. What would Arthur suggest? What would Jago like to have here? They could turn it into a proper meadow, complete with a host of colourful wildflowers that attracted all kinds of wildlife, or turn it into a more structured nature garden, maybe with a pond. They could plant some more trees; apple and pear trees, a nice plum to shield her garden from the open fields beyond. She loved the idea of a vegetable plot, too. There were so many choices.

The sun slipped behind the cottage, the air noticeably cooling as Ellie immersed herself in the sights, sounds and smells of the garden. She watched a pair of blue tits collecting bugs from the hydrangeas as she tugged up brambles, their sharp thorns threatening to pierce her thick gloves. Sweat pooled in the waistband of her jeans and gathered at her temple.

While she worked, her unconscious brain tackled other issues: what to say to Arthur when she saw him next; how to lift Charlie and Daniel's spirits while they were waiting to hear about Gertie; whether she needed to back off completely with Jago. She let it all happen in the background while concentrating on her garden, on all its potential and possibilities.

'Hello?' The voice barely registered at first. But then it came again, louder and closer. 'Ellie, is that you?'

She turned, her knees protesting at kneeling for so long, and saw Jago. He looked exhausted, but when she pushed herself up and brushed at her muddy knees, he smiled.

'Sorry, I—'

'Don't apologize,' he cut in. 'Do you want a beer?'

She licked her lips. The house had been locked up when she'd returned; she hadn't had anything to drink since a coffee at home that morning. She could have one beer and still drive home. 'OK,' she said. 'Thanks.'

She collected her tools and pulled off her gloves. The sun was almost gone now, replaced by the still, blue-grey of dusk, the shadows creeping closer so that Ellie was surprised, now she was near the house, that she'd been able to see what she was doing.

'Here you go.' Jago put two beers on the table and flopped into a seat.

Ellie sat next to him. 'You look worn out.'

He rubbed a hand over his chest, as if trying to relieve some ache there. 'It was a challenging afternoon,' he said quietly, and Ellie felt all the hope that she'd been keeping locked inside her slip out like air from a balloon.

'Is it a lost cause?'

Jago sighed. 'The impact was worse than we initially thought. She'll likely need a new engine, but the cracked chassis is the most worrying part. I mean – it can be done. It *will* be done. It's just going to take a lot of work.'

Ellie pressed her lips together and nodded. She felt bone tired. She'd been waiting all afternoon to hear better news than this.

'But,' Jago added, sitting up straighter, 'she's not a write-off. That's the main thing. And if Pete and I are tackling it together, the job'll be easier.'

'You're going to keep working on her?'

'He's offered to hire me for the duration of the repair

work,' Jago said. 'And I can split my time between my scheduled jobs and Pete's garage. He's a great mechanic, and with his bus and van expertise, and my stubbornness, Gertie will be back to her best in no time.'

'Do you mean that, or are you just trying to make me feel better?'

Jago's eyes held hers. 'I'm not going to lie and say it'll be straightforward, but we're both determined to return Gertie to Charlie as good as new.'

'God,' Ellie said, 'thank you so much, Jago. Do you know if he's spoken to Charlie and Daniel?'

'He called them as I was leaving. They know the score, and he was tactful and optimistic, but realistic too. He explained it better than I've done.'

'You must be so tired,' Ellie said. She wanted to make him dinner, to thank him in some way that was more meaningful than words, but she was conscious about being here, again. About being in his space.

She was about to get up when he said, 'It's been a strange day, all things considered. But I could be coming back to worse than this.'

Ellie decided he was talking about the cottage. 'I've made some progress in the meadow.' She emphasized the last word, and Jago chuckled.

'I'll clink to that.' He held his bottle out and she touched hers against it, then they drank in silence as the light faded. Ellie closed her eyes, trying to slow her spinning thoughts, and realized that actually, after having no lunch or water, she shouldn't have agreed to a beer.

'Hey,' he said softly.

She opened her eyes.

'I could make us a couple of sandwiches. Cheese, bacon or fried egg. It's not exactly fine dining, but—'

'You've been working all day,' she protested. 'Basically on *my* wedding.'

His brows knitted together. 'And you've been sunbathing, have you?' He gestured to her muddy jeans. She didn't want to think about how much of a mess she looked.

'This was my choice,' she said. 'I really needed to come back here after what happened.'

'And now you need sustenance. What are you having?'

'I should get home to Rose.'

'Tell her you've had too much to drink to drive safely, that you have to stay here until you're OK to get behind the wheel. Or just tell her that I've offered you dinner.' He shrugged. 'Bacon, cheese or egg? Or a combination of all three? Actually, that sounds great. Right. You call Rose, I'm going to play chef.' He picked up his drink and went inside before she had a chance to stop him.

Ellie messaged Rose: *Things have got a bit late here. Jago's making me a sandwich. I'm sorry about dinner. E. Xx*

Her sister's reply was almost instant: *This is such a surprising turn of events that I haven't even bothered to cook. Don't forget to use protection, and HAVE FUN! ;) x*

Ellie was too outraged to reply with more than an eye-roll emoji, and she was glad Jago was inside and couldn't see her furious blush.

They ate sandwiches of crispy bacon, fried eggs and grated cheddar, under the soft glow of the cottage's outdoor light. It was motion-activated, so every now and then one of them had to wave their arms to get it to switch back on. Ellie really needed some proper lighting out here.

After her beer, she switched to water, while Jago opened another bottle of lager. The evening slipped away and night took over as they talked about everything and nothing; about Ellie's plans for the garden and Jago's travels; about their favourite memories of growing up in Cornwall, and the places they still loved to visit. It felt easy and natural, especially as they stayed firmly away from the hard subjects: Arthur and the earlier argument, the sorry state of the Cornish Cream Tea Bus and what that meant for Charlie and Daniel's wedding.

It was exactly what Ellie needed: to think about nothing except the next mouthful of sandwich and being carefree on Cornish beaches, and what type of bats were flitting about in the dusk, their movements so distinctive. Lord Montague had joined them soon after Jago arrived, had claimed bacon from them both, and was now lazily chasing a moth that was dancing under the light's beam. Ellie didn't think he'd catch it.

'Ellie?' Jago said after a lull in the conversation, his voice thick with exhaustion.

'Yes, Jago?'

'I hope you didn't think I was pissed off with you, earlier.'

She frowned, then realized what he was talking about. 'You mean about Arthur, the delphiniums?'

He nodded. 'What I said to you before – it was my decision to let Dad come here. And you're right, I shouldn't have expected it to be easy. I had *hoped*, but perhaps that's just another example of my apathy.'

'You can't think like that,' Ellie said. 'Nobody agrees to

something and hopes that it'll be hard work. It's human nature to imagine the best-case scenario.'

He looked at her for a moment, as if weighing up his answer. 'I don't think *you* do,' he said eventually.

'What?' She slid her finger into a smear of ketchup on her plate.

'I think you're always expecting the worst: setting yourself up to deal with disappointment. It's why you're so intent on organizing everything down to the very last detail. You go through every possible, terrible scenario, and make sure you have a game plan.'

'I don't—'

'I understand why,' he went on. 'It's a coping mechanism. Picturing everything that could go wrong so that you feel prepared for any eventuality. But Ellie,' he leaned forward, his empty bottle dangling between his fingers, 'you have to leave some room for things to just . . . happen.'

'What do you mean?' She thought of all the ways she'd imagined Gertie had been broken while they were on their way to the accident site.

'I would put money on you having arranged that bus pick-up as thoroughly as you could. You made sure you were there when it happened, even though Daniel had pitched it as a quick check-up for Gertie before she was open again full time.' He held up a hand when she went to protest. 'Pete told me what the plan was, and he also told me that Liam is really experienced. His dad's been a bus driver all his life, he got his licence as soon as he was old enough, and he keeps his refresher training bang up to date. You were as organized as you could be, Pete was professional, Liam took it seriously, and the bus still crashed.

'You can never plan for every possible chain of events; you can't always stop the bad stuff happening. I know you need to be on top of your job, but you have to leave some room for spontaneity, too. You can't control everything, you'll drive yourself mad trying to, and you'll feel like a failure every time something goes wrong. It's a vicious circle.'

She let out a hollow laugh. 'I don't try and control *everything*,' she said, but she realized Jago's words were unnervingly close to speeches she'd given Mark during the last months of their marriage. The way she'd questioned his insistence that everything should be in its place, should happen exactly as he wanted it to. Was that her life, now?

'I'm not trying to pull you apart,' Jago said softly. 'God knows, after today, we could both do with focusing on the positives. So I hope . . .' his breath caught, and Ellie forced herself to look at him, her nerve-endings tingling at his expression. 'I hope that you can see what a good person you are, how much you do for other people. I'm not saying any of this for my sake, but for yours.' He leaned closer, brushing his hand against her arm. She had the sense that he was restraining himself, that there were other places he wanted to put his hands – or maybe that was just wishful thinking. 'You do a great job, always,' he went on. 'You just need to relax more, to give yourself space to breathe. You should be happy with what you achieve, and not beat yourself up when it doesn't go exactly according to plan.'

Ellie didn't know what to say. She felt the weight of his words, unasked for, settling on her chest. She also felt the weight of his stare, and the tension that had bubbled between them earlier that day, fire back to life. He must have felt it too, must have been as unsure what to do with it as she was, because he pushed his chair back abruptly and took their plates inside, where the light in the kitchen showed off the strong lines of his silhouette just to taunt her.

Jago was her tenant, he was Arthur's son, and now he was helping Pete out with Gertie; he was involved, albeit inadvertently, in her wedding business. The one man who, Ellie was coming to realize, she would love to see without an agenda, and yet he was mixed up in every aspect of her life that had a business label attached to it.

And wasn't his speech just now, even unconsciously, warning her off trying to organize him and his dad? After what had happened that morning, Ellie knew she'd already overstepped the mark, and now things were even worse between father and son.

Jago might want her to leave things to chance, but surely it was just that she'd been putting her efforts into the wrong things. She needed to get Charlie and Daniel to trust her again, focus on New Moon Weddings, and let Jago and Arthur find their own way.

Besides, if she threw caution to the wind, if she let life simply *happen*, then it was bound to happen in all the wrong directions. Ellie still needed to be in charge, she just had to do a better job of it.

Chapter Fourteen

Jago's words were still going round Ellie's head as she drove to Truro three days later, to meet Charlie and the wedding dress designer. She found herself double-checking everything, seeing how closely she'd planned every stage, which was ridiculous because it meant she was adding *more* layers of scrutiny, not less.

The sun was hiding behind clouds that looked like mountains, white and harmless at their peak, grey and foreboding lower down. She hoped that nothing would put a dampener on today, for Charlie's sake. Pete was giving them daily updates on Gertie, and while Ellie was sure he was focusing on the positives, it did sound as if there was hope for the stricken Routemaster. They had stripped her down to get full access to the damaged chassis, and a new engine was on order.

The news was reassuring, and when Ellie had spoken to Charlie to confirm today's meet-up, she had seemed friendlier; perhaps not back to her old enthusiastic self, but that was understandable. But Ellie needed Charlie to trust her again, so today really mattered.

She parked behind Truro's impressive cathedral, and made her way through the smaller streets of the city to the boutique where Gina worked when she was in Cornwall. There was a mannequin in the window wearing a black dress with a print of peony-style blooms in red and purple. The cut was asymmetrical, and the hem of the skirt was ruched. If Ellie described it to Rose it would sound awful, but on this slender silver model, it looked stunning.

'Ellie, hi,' Lila said, hurrying up to her. 'How are you?'

'Good thanks, how about you?'

'Great. Good. We've started filming, so—' she paused to take a deep breath. 'I thought I was late.'

'Is this for the second series of *Estelle?*' Ellie asked. 'I *loved* the first series.' It still blew her mind a tiny bit that Lila and her boyfriend were bona fide actors, working on a starry BBC drama set that was filmed along Cornwall's stunning coastline.

'Thanks! Well, I was really a caterer for that one. On board Gertie, with her cakes and mini quiches and . . .' Her smile fell. 'I still can't believe that Gertie's broken. All those trips around Cornwall, to Penzance and Tintagel and Mousehole, and she even went down to the beach in the middle of the night once, and didn't even get a flat tyre. And then, on the way to getting dolled up for the wedding – *bam.*' Lila smacked her hands together.

'I am so sorry it happened,' Ellie said, the guilt threatening to overwhelm her all over again.

Lila looked surprised. 'Why are you sorry? It was a great idea, giving Gertie her own wedding makeover, and Pete's totally trustworthy, according to Charlie. It was just a horrible accident. And anyway, it's clearly fate.'

'Fate?' Ellie pushed a strand of hair behind her ear.

'This has happened for a reason.' Lila leaned against the wall. Her dark hair was tied back, and there was a smudge of thick concealer on her cheek that stood out on her freckled skin. 'Maybe Gertie had some other, hidden problems, and the only way of finding out about them was for her to be in that crash. You know, like that story where the old man got mugged, and when they took him to hospital they discovered he had cancer. And he actually *thanked* his muggers because it meant they'd caught the cancer in time and he could be treated.'

'Seriously?'

'Things happen for a reason.' Lila said again, as if it was the most obvious thing in the world. 'This is horrible and devastating, and Charlie's been really shaken by it, but I have faith that it will all turn out OK. Charlie and Daniel are meant to be together; their wedding will be exactly how it's supposed to be. Oh look, here she is now.' Lila waved and Ellie turned to see Charlie approaching, her long legs clad in loose jeans, a maroon jacket over her T-shirt.

'Hi, Charlie,' Ellie said, annoyed that her palms were sweating.

'Hello.' She gave Ellie a quick smile. Lila got a hug. 'I'm so looking forward to this.'

'It's princess time!' Lila punched her cousin gently on the arm.

'Shall we go in?' Ellie opened the door and let the others go ahead of her. Usually, she would have introduced Gina and the bride and then left them to it, but she wanted

Charlie to know she was committed to making up for Gertie's accident, and so planned to stay for as long – or as little – as Charlie wanted.

Behind the small but immaculate shop floor, there was a larger, thickly carpeted room that had a fitting area cordoned off with a cream curtain, and a beige leather sofa next to a table piled high with wedding magazines.

'Elowen Moon.' Gina was slender, with dyed-black hair cut into a pixie crop that accentuated her angular features. 'It has been far too long. And which one of you is Charlie? Who's our beautiful bride?'

'That's me,' Charlie said, raising her hand. 'And this is my cousin Lila; she's one of my maids of honour.'

'Congratulations,' Gina said, her expression softening. 'I understand from Ellie you want something with a vintage feel?'

Charlie nodded. 'I'd love to look at that sort of thing. Though I won't know for sure, I guess, until I try a few of them on.'

Gina gave her an assessing look, tapping a pen against her red lips. 'Vintage style would suit you. You have strong features and a good figure. Let's focus on finding the right silhouette first. Once we've got that fixed we can move on to the detail. Please take a seat, and we'll get started. Bubbles?'

'Yes please,' Charlie said. 'Daniel dropped me off, and Sam's picking us up later, isn't he?'

Lila nodded. 'Once he's finished having clandestine meetings with ghosts on Cornish cliff tops.' She grinned.

'Let me,' Ellie said, when Gina came back with a cold bottle of champagne, condensation beading on the outside

201

of the glass, and three flutes. Ellie poured Charlie and Lila generous glasses.

'What's the most expensive dress one of your clients has ever bought?' Lila asked Ellie.

She poured herself a glass of sparkling water while she considered the question. 'The range is pretty big. There was one, a long time ago now, that was close to three thousand pounds.'

'Three *thousand?*' Charlie repeated with wide eyes.

'Wow.' Lila shook her head. 'I bet it was beautiful, though.'

'It had crystals individually sewn all over the bodice,' Ellie said. 'It was a work of art.' She didn't add that it was, in her opinion, a little too extravagant. But it had fitted her client perfectly, matched her extroverted personality and her long blonde hair. 'But I've also had brides who buy their dresses from high-street shops, and a couple who've made their own. One woman found her dress in a second-hand shop and altered it, and it was beautiful. Everyone wants something different.'

'That they do,' Gina said, returning with her arms full of ivory silk. 'And today, Charlie, we are going to create the perfect dress for *you*. I have a few different shapes to start off with, and we'll see which one best suits.'

Ellie loved this part of the process, when all the hours of admiring dresses in magazines paled into insignificance in the face of trying them on. She loved the moment when the bride-to-be came out of the changing room in a dress they loved; the recognition in their eyes that this was something they could wear when they married the person they wanted to be with for ever. There was anxiety associated with *getting it right,* but Gina's confidence in her creations was infectious, and Charlie and Lila were soon giggling with the thrill of it.

'Look at this one,' Charlie said, stepping out of the curtained-off area wearing a slim-fitting Empire-line dress with the thinnest of spaghetti straps. It suited her body shape, and even without embellishments, she looked stunning.

'Oh, Charlie!' Lila gasped. 'Oh. Wow.'

'This is promising.' Gina stood back to assess her. 'We could add some lace or floral detail along here.' She indicated the high-waisted bodice. 'Perhaps a trail of detail on the skirt, coming down in this direction.' She gestured with her arm, making a diagonal swoop down the skirt of the dress. She tapped her pen against her lip again, then scribbled something in her notepad.

'You look amazing, Charlie,' Lila said.

'I feel good.' Charlie turned to the mirror and smoothed the dress over her hips.

'Just good?' Lila asked. 'Because good isn't good enough.'

'I'm just . . . considering. Do you think Daniel will like it?'

Lila laughed. 'Daniel would love it if you turned up in a bit of old carpet. He worships you.'

Charlie didn't reply, and Gina glanced at Ellie then slipped back into the stockroom.

'Are you OK, Charlie?' Ellie asked.

She looked up, her eyes bright. For a second Ellie felt the resistance between them, Charlie battling with her anger, or reluctance, to open up to her again. And then she sagged slightly. 'I just don't want Daniel to be forgotten,' she said. 'There's always so much focus on the bride, isn't there? With the dress and the flowers, it's all a bit . . .' she sighed. 'He planned Gertie's makeover for me, and I know that the last thing he – or you – wanted was for it to go wrong the way it did. And now he feels terrible, and I'm worried he'll step even more into the background.' She came over and perched on the arm of the sofa.

'That's what he likes doing,' she went on. 'It's what he does with the hotel; makes sure everything runs smoothly, watches it play out from behind the scenes. But I don't want him to feel that way about this. It's as much his day as it is mine.'

'Get some expensive new underwear for the wedding night,' Lila said. 'That'll make him feel truly cherished.'

'Lila!' Charlie laughed. Lila gave her an impish grin.

'We'll make sure Daniel isn't forgotten,' Ellie said. 'I know he feels guilty about Gertie, but he really shouldn't. I suggested it, and I was in charge of making it happen. Please let me make it up to you.'

Charlie stared at the floor. She really did look beautiful, sitting there in the simple dress, her expression a mix of concern and contemplation. Eventually, she looked up. 'I know the crash was an accident, that you couldn't have prevented it, I was just so shocked. But Pete seems pleased with how the repairs are going, and I . . . I want to do something for Daniel. Something special. Will you help me?'

'Of course,' Ellie said. 'Do you know what kind of thing?' It was exactly what Daniel had asked for, and that had resulted in Gertie being crashed into a rock. Ellie would have to consider this much more carefully; to weigh up the pros and cons of whatever suggestions emerged.

Charlie shook her head. 'I'm not sure yet. Some kind of surprise, or gift, for the wedding day.'

Ellie nodded. 'I'll come up with a few ideas. How are you feeling about that dress?'

Charlie glanced down. 'It's beautiful.'

'But is it the *one*, Charlie?' Lila leaned forward. 'Is this what you want to get married in? Is this how you want to look in photos that will be pored over thousands of times, by you and Daniel and your children and grand-children? Your great-grandchildren? How you want Daniel to picture you when he closes his eyes—'

'Steady on!' Charlie's laugh was nervous.

'I'm sure Gina has a few more designs,' Ellie said brightly. She loved Lila's passion, but it wasn't always helpful to pile the pressure on the bride. Charlie needed to feel relaxed enough to try on dresses until she found the one, however long that took.

'Ellie's right,' Gina said, waltzing back into the room right on cue. 'I have a lot more to show you. And if you think those were good, Charlie my dear, then be prepared for a whole new level of spectacular.'

Ellie was relieved to see Charlie's smile flicker back into place. Charlie and Daniel deserved their happy-ever-after, and it was up to Ellie to see that it got off to the best possible start.

Ellie left Charlie and Lila in Gina's capable hands, with assurances from Charlie that she would call her later with an update, and a definite thawing between them. Ellie had an appointment at a dance hall close-by where she was, hopefully, going to secure the loan of a glitter ball. Jane had assured her they would be able to fix one to the vaulted ceiling above the dance floor at Porthgolow Barn, so Ellie had started ringing round her contacts and struck lucky.

While they'd been inside the dress shop it had rained, leaving the pavements slick with water, everything gleaming as the sun returned. She walked to her car, then drove to the outskirts of Truro to meet Orwell, who held everything from dinner dances to auctions to the occasional hamster race in his art-deco hall, Guinevere House. If she could come to an agreement with him about the glitter ball, then it would be one of Charlie's most desired items ticked firmly off the list without any disasters at all, and Ellie would start to feel slightly better about how things were going.

An hour later, she had her glitter ball loan confirmed, some very generous terms from Orwell, and a deep-seated sadness that a venue that had once thrived, and had some of the most beautiful features Ellie had ever seen, had fallen into disrepair. The place had been musty and dark, with a thread-bare green carpet in the foyer and paint peeling from the walls. At one time, Ellie had had Guinevere House on her books, but she hadn't used it for several years. The glitter ball had seemed wildly out of place, gleaming with promise in the gloom.

She drove out of Truro with her mind on Porthgolow Barn. In some ways, it wasn't that dissimilar to Guinevere House, though Jane and Pauline had kept the shabby-chic look on purpose. It was a beautiful venue, and while the mother-and-daughter team had done so much already, and certainly had the enthusiasm to make it a success, Ellie still thought they needed a push to get it over the finish line.

Half an hour later, she had driven straight past the turning to St Eval, and was on her way to Porthgolow.

The seafront was busy with tourists. One of the bright yellow Seaking Safaris boats was just leaving the jetty, packed with intrepid explorers in colourful waterproofs, and a dog-walker was strolling across the beach, an eclectic mix of pooches on leads around her, spread out like a canine maypole. Ellie kept going, driving out to Wilderness Lane, and then took the turning to Porthgolow Barn.

'*Ellie!*' Jane found her gazing at the cobbles and the chickens and the empty, old-fashioned wagon that was just crying out to be decorated. 'How lovely to see you. What can I help you with?'

'I've sorted out the glitter ball,' she said. 'I was hoping to arrange a date with you for delivery.'

'Excellent,' Jane replied. 'Let me know what works for you.'

Ellie nodded. 'I also have a couple of other weddings I'd like to talk to you about. And I wondered if you wanted any help with your marketing plan, with building up a list of local suppliers you can use in the future?'

'Ellie, I . . .' Jane paused, a smile bunching her cheeks. 'Are you OK?'

'I've just been thinking,' Ellie said. 'About how much potential this place has, how you solved my sticky venue issue. I want to help you – but only if you and Pauline would like me to. I don't want to step on your toes, or . . .' she faltered, thinking of what Jago had said. 'Or interfere, or over-organize you in any way. But the truth is I *do* have lots of contacts in the events business, and with all this . . .' she gestured at the courtyard, the wagon, the patch of lawn that was still slightly waterlogged. 'I have a bit of gardening experience, too.'

'You really want to help us?' Jane looked slightly shocked. 'I'm not too proud to say that we could do with some guidance. We spent so much more on the interior than we'd planned, adding the windows, especially, and I know we're not there yet. Do you want to come and have a cup of tea? Mum's inside, so we could talk it through.'

Ellie nodded. 'I'd love that. Thank you.'

Jane laughed. 'I don't know what you're thanking me for, when you're the one offering all the help.'

Ellie hid her smile. 'It would be my pleasure,' she said, and followed Jane inside.

When she left the cottage an hour later, her to-do list was significantly longer. Jane and Pauline had seemed both thrilled and relieved when Ellie had gone through the types of people she could put them in touch with, and explained that she'd be happy to assist with their garden and courtyard herself.

It would be a lot of work, but it would also be good for her to have an outdoor space she could turn her attention to without disturbing Jago. Arthur would be at Cornflower Cottage, and she would be here. It was like a game of musical gardens; everyone moving round one. All she needed was for Pauline to pop up to Seascape House and work on *their* lawns, and the circle would be complete.

Jane's mum had seemed as confident and on the ball as she'd been during Charlie and Daniel's visit, and Ellie wondered if she was fully recovered; feeling settled and completely safe in Cornwall. Ellie wouldn't be surprised.

Cornwall had a calming effect on most people – unless you got stuck in one of the summer's legendary traffic queues; they weren't calming *at all*.

She was about to start her drive home when her phone rang. Her stomach performed a quick somersault when she saw it was Jago.

'Hello,' she said. 'How are you? How's Gertie?'

'Gertie is being rebuilt as we speak.' She heard him walking, the background sounds of metal against metal fading as the seaside took its place, seagulls and shouts and waves crashing in the distance. 'She's fully on the road to recovery.'

'She is?' Ellie sagged against her seat, barely noticing as raindrops started falling on the cobbles outside. 'That's brilliant news. Charlie and Daniel will be over the moon.'

'We should make good progress this afternoon, then Pete'll be in touch with his usual update. That's not what I'm doing now, by the way.'

'I feel like you're my spy,' she said, then bit her lip. She hadn't meant to say it out loud.

Jago laughed. 'We're all on the same side. But it's going really well.'

'That is *so* great,' Ellie said. 'Honestly, I can't tell you how relieved I am. But if you weren't phoning to give me a secret update . . .?'

There was a long, drawn-out silence, and she thought the connection had cut out. 'I felt I was a bit heavy-handed.' He cleared his throat. 'The other day.'

'What do you mean?'

'At the cottage. I was knackered, and I shouldn't have said what I did. Your outlook is yours alone and, God knows, I can't talk, the way things are going with Dad. I guess I just . . . Shit. Look, I'm doing it again. It's none of my business.'

'But you're right,' Ellie said, laughing. 'I do plan everything to the very last detail. I have to take charge, and I . . .' She thought of the meeting she'd just had with Pauline and Jane. 'I don't know if I can just stop doing it. I feel so much better when I'm in control.

'But I also appreciate your point of view, about leaving space for things to play out naturally. Charlie's cousin told me that Gertie's crash was fate, which I don't believe for a minute, but I'm also trying to accept that there was nothing I could have done, *despite* all my planning.'

There was another pause, and then Jago said, 'Well, that's good. Because it *wasn't* your fault.'

'It wasn't my fault,' she repeated, trying to believe it. At least Charlie was starting to warm to her again. It might take more for Ellie to completely regain her trust, but she would do whatever it took. 'How are you, anyway?' she asked. 'Other than working stupidly hard on Gertie?'

'I'm OK,' he said. 'Dad's coming round tomorrow, with Rose.'

Ellie's heart leapt. 'Really?'

'I'm going to try and stop being so stubborn, see if we can move past what happened at the weekend.' He sighed. 'If Dad has stuff to say to me, I'm going to let him say it. Perhaps if we get it all out there, it'll make things easier in the long term. I'm going to give it a go, anyway. The fridge is fully stocked with beer, which feels important.'

'That's brilliant, Jago.'

'I'd love to see you, if you've got any time? I know Arthur

likes being in the garden with you; you're kindred spirits in that respect.'

'If you're sure,' Ellie said, conscious of not wanting to get in their way. 'I have a few jobs to do first thing, but I should be able to make it after those. What time is he arriving?'

'Eleven, I think.'

'I'll try my best to be there.'

'Great. And I'm glad what I said didn't offend you. I was worried I'd upset you.'

'It'd be very hard for you to offend me,' Ellie assured him. She'd meant it to be light-hearted, but she wasn't certain she'd managed it.

'See you tomorrow, Ellie,' he said quietly.

Once they'd hung up, Ellie headed for home, with butterflies flapping low in her belly. If she kept her focus on her weddings and Porthgolow Barn, and away from Arthur and Jago, then perhaps she could do what Jago had suggested; she could allow her visits to Cornflower Cottage to be about nothing more than spending time with people she cared about. Maybe Ellie *could* give up control in some areas of her life. It was a scary thought, but also, if she was honest, a little bit exhilarating.

Chapter Fifteen

Ellie did see Jago, Arthur and Rose the next day, and quite frequently over the next few weeks as they continued to work on the meadow at Cornflower Cottage. The weather was heating up the further into May they got, the wind was non-existent and being outside was stifling and sweaty. But, Ellie thought, that was much better than if it had been raining cats and dogs or howling a gale. And Jago and Arthur were together again, without any interference from her, even if their relationship still wasn't exactly harmonious.

'Faring well over there?' Arthur called from his side of the meadow, close to Ellie's solitary laburnum tree, its yellow waterfall blossoms just beginning to emerge.

'Yup,' Jago replied from the opposite side, where he was using Ellie's newest pair of secateurs to chop through a forest of brambles.

Ellie rolled her eyes. Maybe it was the heat making them terse. 'Just imagine if we discovered a rare species of butterfly,' she said, enthusiastically. Rose was in the kitchen making fresh lemonade which, Ellie knew from experience, was a messy but worthwhile process. She licked her lips.

'A rare butterfly?' Arthur scoffed. 'Why on earth would we?'

'Because this is the first time this patch of land has been touched in years,' she said. 'I haven't done anything with it since I moved in, and that was over two years ago. And before that, the old woman who lived here had Parkinson's disease. I don't think she was able to do much gardening at all, even before she ended up going into a home.'

There was a moment of silence, then Arthur said, 'How terrible for her, ending up in a home.'

The sarcasm wasn't lost on Ellie. Or Jago, it seemed. 'Dad, you chose to move into Seascape House.'

'I couldn't stay in the Falmouth house on my own, son. Not with those horrendously steep stairs, not after my operation. I needed care, and support. I'm not too proud to admit that.'

'You could have moved into a bungalow,' Jago said. 'Had carers come into visit until you were more mobile.'

'I considered it, but it would have been a lot of effort for what could well have been a temporary measure. I decided to do the whole thing in one fell swoop.'

'With that logic you should have just bought yourself a coffin and been done with it.'

Ellie sucked in a gasp at Jago's harsh words. She peered up from her patch of grass and watched him run an arm over his forehead, wiping away sweat. She couldn't see his expression.

'I know you think I gave up, Jago,' Arthur went on. 'Just

213

as you think that I need looking after; that you need to be here to keep an eye on me. But I am doing perfectly well at Seascape. If I were still living alone it would be a different matter, but I'm not. And you of all people should know I'm not one for giving up: I just did the most practical thing under the circumstances.'

Ellie was surprised by Arthur's candour. She waited, her breath held, for Jago's reply.

'I know it was hard after Mum died,' he said, eventually. 'And that I wasn't as . . . present as I should have been. I guess I dealt with it the wrong way.'

'You dealt with it in your own way, as did I. We just took very different approaches.'

'As with most things,' Jago replied. His voice was louder, closer, and Ellie looked up as he approached, clutching a tangle of brambles as if he'd vanquished a monster. He had an angry red scratch along his forearm, and Ellie chewed her cheek, resisting the urge to fuss over him. 'We don't often see eye to eye, Dad.' He crouched down, keeping his eyes trained on the ground.

'Which makes it hard to understand why you're back here, only a stone's throw away,' Arthur said. 'I've got my friends at the home, there's Mo and Rose. I don't need you spying on me.'

Jago's head shot up. 'I'm hardly spying. In case you hadn't noticed, this is where I'm living. If anything, you're spying on me.'

'It would hardly be worth it; as always you seem to have very little going on in your life.'

Ellie was torn. Part of her wanted to go and help Rose, to leave them to their awkward conversation, but she didn't want anything else resembling the lawnmower incident, so she stayed put. She wasn't interfering if she didn't get involved.

'That's not . . .' Jago sighed. 'I'm worried about you, OK? Isn't that my right, as your son? The last few times I phoned you from Plymouth, you sounded miserable. More mono-syllabic than usual.'

'Perhaps I didn't have anything to say,' Arthur said gruffly.

'Dad.' It came out as a groan. 'Other than your hip, which seems better since you've been here, moving more regularly, you're healthy as anything. Physically, anyway. It's your mental health I'm worried about.'

'Don't be ridiculous, Jago! There's far too much focus on all this hearts-and-minds nonsense these days. Everyone's gone soft. You just have to get on with things.'

Jago shot Ellie an exasperated look.

'But you love being here, don't you?' Ellie said tentatively. 'It lifts your mood?'

'It's being productive that does it,' Arthur replied. 'Sitting in those sagging armchairs all day does nobody any good, even if the view is pleasant.'

'Maybe that's what Jago's trying to say,' Ellie said. 'He was worried you weren't really *doing* anything. You had your garden at Seascape, but that was going to be taken away. Then what would you have done? Coming here wouldn't have been possible if Jago wasn't in the cottage. If I'd rented it out to somebody else, we wouldn't have been able to do this.'

Arthur waved a dismissive hand. 'There would have been other gardens, and Jago could have stayed where he was and not bothered with all this mollycoddling.'

'You haven't given me a chance to mollycoddle you!'

'Of course I haven't!' Arthur pushed himself up agonizingly slowly, and dusted down his trousers even though he'd been kneeling on Ellie's gardening stool. 'I've no need for it, which is what I've been trying to tell you from the beginning. This sometimes feels like an ambush.' He stalked down the garden, leaving Jago and Ellie and not even one butterfly – rare or otherwise – to lighten the mood.

'That went well,' Jago said, despondently. 'I spend most of my time thinking he's right; that I should never have come back. We're much better off living our own lives.'

Ellie went from crouching to sitting cross-legged on the grass. 'But he *is* your dad. And for what it's worth –' she rubbed at the dirt on her knee – 'I think you've done the right thing. From what Rose has told me, he hasn't been coping as well as he's making out, and the care-home manager, Mo, said he's been keeping entirely to himself, rejecting any attempts at friendship. At least here, he's in the fresh air and he's . . . talking.'

'Lecturing, do you mean?' Jago sighed. 'We should have done this about twenty years ago; lowered our boundaries, found some common ground. Even if we'd done it five years ago, while Mum was still alive, she could have been the referee – she was so good at that, placating us both – and we'd be in a much better position now. That's my fault, though. I moved away as soon as I could.' He flopped onto the grass alongside Ellie, and she caught a whiff of lime and spice overlaid with sweat and earth. Her pulse kicked up a gear.

'What do you want to achieve?' she asked. 'Why did you come back here?'

'I want Dad to be OK,' he said. 'More than that, I want him to be happy again.'

'Are *you* happy?' Ellie asked. 'After losing your mum, are you all right?'

He shrugged. 'I have no idea, really. I'm getting on with things, and after Sarah . . . I have no one to let me know how I'm doing. Does that sound crazy? That I can't be my own barometer? I need someone else to say, "You're getting this all wrong" or, "Stop being a dickhead". Since I've been on my own again, I've muddled through. But it feels important to me that Dad and I – that we try and work things out. I'm making a hash of it so far, though.'

'You're sticking with it,' Ellie said. 'And he's much more talkative than he was the first time I met him. Maybe it's not all sunshine and daisies, but at least it's happening. And he loves being here, I know that much.'

Jago's expression softened. 'I don't think I'd have got even this far without you,' he said. 'You and Rose. You're a buffer between us, not to mention that you're the one with the beautiful garden and the . . . uh, interesting meadow.'

Ellie laughed. 'Everyone knows that *interesting* isn't a compliment. Anyway, it's your garden right now. I'm trespassing.'

'You can't be trespassing if I want you to be here.'

Ellie didn't admit that she wanted to be here, too; more than anything. And not just in the garden, but here, in the meadow, with just her and Jago and the sunshine. She flopped down until she was lying on the grass, and Jago leaned back and lifted his face up to the sky. His stubble glinted in the sunlight, and Ellie wondered what it would feel like against the soft skin of her palm, or her lips.

It wasn't just the sun and Jago making Ellie feel so content. Pete had assured Charlie that Gertie would be back in business by the weekend, and Charlie was *almost* back to her old self with Ellie, which Ellie was supremely thankful for.

She and Daniel had chosen the flower garlands for the barn; a mix of roses, gerberas and alstroemeria in pastel shades that would give it a faded, almost sepia look, which fitted with the rustic style they had chosen. Orwell was delivering the glitter ball to Porthgolow Barn tomorrow; Ellie would oversee it, and at the same time talk to Jane and Pauline about her proposals for the courtyard and garden, and Hannah's menu was finalized bar a couple of last-minute tweaks.

Running it all through in her mind, checking for gaps or problems and finding none, Ellie closed her eyes and let the sun kiss her skin. Summer was on the way, and things were looking up.

They worked for a couple more hours in the lingering afternoon heat, Rose's lemonade giving them an extra burst of energy.

'I've got sweat in places I didn't know I had,' Ellie said to nobody in particular, stretching her arms towards a sky which had taken on the pearlized quality of late afternoon.

'You'll need to have a shower before we go to dinner,' Rose said from somewhere behind her.

'Dinner?' Ellie turned round. 'We're going out to dinner?'

'I've booked a table at the Seven Stars. For the four of us.'

'Why?' Jago asked. It came out as a tired huff.

'Because my goal in life is to torture you all,' Rose said. 'Don't you want the obligation of cooking to be taken out of your hands? After sweltering in a hot garden all day, the last thing I want to do is swelter in front of a hot stove. Even making a salad feels like too much effort, and I've spent enough time picking caterpillars off leaves today that I'm not sure I fancy one.' She gave Ellie a hard stare.

'If you don't pick them off, you may as well not bother growing any asters,' Ellie replied.

'I'm afraid I can't join you,' Arthur said. 'I need to get back for supper at the home.'

'Nonsense,' Rose scoffed. 'I've cleared it with Mo. You're coming – you all are. Honestly, I have never had this much resistance to the offer of a meal out. Right by the sea, with its delicious breeze, bottles of cold beer, the delicate flavour of smoked haddock and prawns in a creamy, rich sauce—'

'OK, OK!' Jago stood up. 'I'm in.' He held out his hand and Ellie took it, his skin hot as he pulled her up.

'Me too,' she said, quickly retrieving her hand and rubbing at her dirty shorts.

'I really must protest—'

'No, you mustn't, Arthur,' Rose cut in. 'Not tonight. Ellie and I will drop you at Seascape, we'll all have a chance to freshen up, and we'll be back around seven to collect you both. Any excuses you find in the meantime will not be believed.' She levelled an even finger at Arthur, then Jago, and when their silence seemed to indicate acquiescence, she beamed at them.

As Rose walked away, Ellie heard Arthur say to Jago, 'Son, if you ever wanted an idea of what it was like being in the Navy, then Rose isn't far off the mark.'

Jago's laugh was loud and unbridled, and Ellie hid her own smile as she headed towards the cottage.

They sat at a table outside the pub, with an unobstructed view of the bronzed sun sinking towards a turquoise sea, the crash of waves soothing, the breeze whispering softly around them. The beach was still busy with families and groups of teenagers making the most of the good weather, the hardiest swimmers still splashing in the waves. An elegant yacht, its sail silhouetted against the sun, cut through the water out towards the horizon.

The outdoor tables around them were buzzing with laughter and conversation, tea lights flickered in glass domes, and the smell of well-seasoned chips, of fried batter and fish and peppered steak, made Ellie's mouth water.

She had spent ages in the shower, washing off the mud and sweat under the pummelling water, and while she'd thought herself too tired to consider going out again, the promise of an evening with Jago, Arthur and her sister spurred her out of the door.

Both men looked equally refreshed, their earlier protests forgotten when Rose and Ellie picked them up. Ellie decided her sister was an evil genius. She'd waited until they were too exhausted to put up much of a fight and then invited them to socialize away from the garden. It made Ellie want to look back at her own interactions with Rose to see if – no, *when* – she'd been manipulated.

Rose sat back in her chair and sipped her apple and raspberry cordial. 'You must have seen a few things in your time out on the water, Arthur,' she said, gesturing to the yacht that was almost out of sight.

He nodded brusquely. 'I did, of course. Many of which I won't ever forget. So many people believe the sea to be a lonely place, especially when you're not in sight of land for days on end, but the truth is that it's teeming with life, and no two days are ever the same.'

'It must have been hard work,' Ellie said. 'That's probably an understatement.' She laughed and glanced at Jago. He was wearing a blue cotton shirt that made his eyes seem more intensely green. He was resting an elbow on the table, as interested as anyone in his dad's response. Ellie wondered whether Arthur had told him stories about his sea voyages, or if he'd been as reticent back then; Jago, a boy hoping for tales of adventure on the high seas from his hero of a dad, and being rebuffed.

'It was a career I am proud to have had,' Arthur said. 'Incredibly challenging at times, but worthwhile. Though it did mean I wasn't around much for Hetty or Jago. I provided financially, but I know that doesn't make up for being present. It was the only thing that Hetty and I argued about, though I was already in the Navy when we met, and we had Jago fairly late in life.'

'Do you miss it?' Rose asked.

He shook his head. 'Retirement was hard for me at first, and it was Hetty's suggestion that I work on the garden, go back to my parents' outdoor roots, as it were. She told me she'd read an article about all the health benefits, but that was only because she knew I would pay attention if there was some science behind it.' There was a pause as he sipped his wine. 'It wasn't until after her death that I realized she was the only one I should have listened to. She knew what I needed, far more than I did.'

'And me,' Jago said. 'She knew exactly what would motivate me, when not to push too hard. She accepted that I had to move away, even though it was the last thing she wanted.'

Arthur cleared his throat, and Ellie had the impression that he was annoyed with himself, possibly even embarrassed, for saying so much. Jago was looking at him as if expecting a response, perhaps wanting to find some shared ground over Hetty, at least. When Arthur stayed silent, Jago turned away, his gaze flitting to the beach.

'I'm going to Porthgolow Barn tomorrow,' Ellie said, a bit too loudly. 'The glitter ball's being delivered, and I've agreed to help Jane and Pauline with their outside space. They have a garden – well, it's more of a muddy patch of grass at the moment.'

'Is this another meadow scenario?' Jago asked. 'Call it something else, and hope nobody will notice what it actually looks like?'

'Hey.' Ellie swatted at his arm. 'They could do with the help. The barn is so beautiful. It's full of character, but with all the facilities you could ever need.'

'But the outside has a pig and some chickens and a whole load of mud,' Jago said.

'Exactly. And of course those things add *extra* character, but not the kind my clients are usually after.'

'You're doing all this for one of your weddings?' Arthur said. 'Is that really in your remit?'

'I'm doing it for the sake of many future weddings, hopefully. And for Jane and Pauline. They're so close to having the most incredible venue, it seems selfish not to use my expertise to help them get there.'

Rose chuckled, and Jago looked at her, his green eyes shining with amusement.

'What?' Ellie asked, a blush creeping up her cheeks.

'Is this your version of backing off on all the planning?' he asked lightly.

She shrugged. 'I have given up planning *some* things.' She didn't want to tell him that it was his and Arthur's relationship, because after their conversation in the meadow, he might not believe her. 'This, though. This job was made for me.'

'Don't forget you've got a team now,' Rose said. 'We're the Porthgolow gardening elite. You can draft us in whenever you need to.'

Jago laughed. 'Speak for yourself! Fixing things, woodwork, odd jobs – that's all I'm good for. I'll leave the green-fingered stuff to you lot.'

Ellie drummed her fingertips on the table. 'Thanks, Jago, I'll bear that in mind.'

'What?' His eyes widened. 'I just meant—'

Ellie shot him a grin, and he shook his head slowly, then gave an exasperated sigh.

'Right then,' Arthur said. 'Ellie, Rose, you come here frequently. What should we be looking at on this menu?'

They ordered fish platters and crunchy chips, and as the sun slipped below the horizon, the outside lamps and glowing heaters joined the candles, keeping them under a spotlight of warmth and light. Rose led the conversation, regaling them with outlandish stories of her time as a mental-health practitioner, years before she'd become a district nurse. Ellie knew she was embellishing her tales, and the care and respect with which she'd treated her patients was evident in the way she revealed herself to be the butt of every story. When she strayed towards family rather than work, it was Ellie who bore the brunt.

'Honestly,' Rose said, shaking her head, 'you think this business with Porthgolow Barn is bad. Ellie used to create homework tables in her notebooks. She drew vertical lines with her "Kings of England" ruler and wrote everything out meticulously: subject, teacher, task, duration, and then ticked them off when they were done. Our parents were worried something was wrong with her; she was silent for hours on end. Oh, and . . . and—'

'There is no need for any more "ands",' Ellie cut in, sipping her rosé. 'You're making me sound like such a lame child.'

'I was – and always will be – in awe of your planning gene, which skipped me entirely. And your love of a note-book. I saw how much of a wrench it was for you to move over to an iPad, though it's already revolutionized your life.'

'Goody Two-Shoes are never sexy,' Ellie protested. 'Other kids are only ever friends with them because they want help with their schoolwork. Or at least, that's how it was with me.'

Rose shook her head. 'Not true, Elowen. You had friends – of course you did. You're looking back on it with grey-tinted spectacles. But you did love a bit of homework.'

'When did you become interested in weddings?' Arthur asked.

Ellie opened her mouth to speak, but her sister got in first. 'It was Scott and Charlene's wedding on *Neighbours*.'

'It was *not*,' Ellie laughed. 'I just . . . weddings are a perfect combination of magic, reality and reward. If you put the effort in, plan it all out to the nth degree, then from the outside it's the most seamless, incredible thing.'

'Are you talking about weddings or marriages?' Jago chuckled.

Ellie rolled her eyes. 'Weddings. Marriages need a lot of work too, but planning doesn't always help. Too much of it, and you suck all the joy out. It requires a very fine balance.' She pictured Mark and then blinked him away, the evening too beautiful and fun to bring him into it.

But then Rose did. 'That's what happened with Mark and Ellie,' she said. 'Ellie was the more spontaneous of the two, if you can believe it.'

Jago's eyebrows flickered in surprise, and Rose picked up on it. 'Exactly, Jago. But he was suffocating her: it's hard to find any passion when every minute of every day is known in advance; when a person's opinions aren't even for bending, let alone breaking.'

'It wasn't that bad,' Ellie murmured. She felt scrutinized by Arthur, and the last thing she wanted from Jago was pity.

'Anyway,' Rose said briskly, perhaps realizing she had overstepped the mark, 'the next man you go for needs to be much more laid-back: someone with a chilled-out attitude to life. Now, does anyone want another drink? I'm popping to the Ladies.' She got up and went inside, the night-time beach sounds crowding into the silence she left in her wake.

Just after ten, Arthur announced that he was tired, and Rose said she'd run him home. They all got ready to leave, but Rose put a hand on Jago's shoulder. 'I'll take him and come back for the two of you in a bit.'

'That makes no sense,' Jago protested. 'The cottage is two minutes from Seascape House.'

'It's what's happening. Take time to finish your drinks.'

Ellie tried to meet her sister's eye, but Rose was too canny for that. They said goodnight to Arthur, then Rose led him to the car park and Ellie and Jago were alone at the table.

'I'm glad you—'

'Do you think—'

They both started at the same time.

'You go,' Ellie said.

Jago laughed uncomfortably. 'Do you think Rose did that on purpose? Took Arthur home and left us to it?'

'Of course she did,' Ellie said. 'Sometimes she's sneaky, sometimes she's as subtle as a sledgehammer, but either way, everything is calculated. She wanted us to get the hint.'

'The hint that I'm fairly laid-back and that's exactly the kind of man you need right now?'

Ellie felt herself blush. 'In *her* opinion.'

'And what's your opinion?'

She huffed out a laugh. 'My opinion is that I'm far too busy with work right now, which is the generic excuse, and then that you're not only my tenant, but you're my sister's patient's son, and now you're also involved in one of my weddings because you helped to fix Gertie. It's all very complicated.'

Jago shrugged. In the steady glow of the lamplight, his eyes held hers. 'Or maybe it's very simple.'

'How do you mean?'

'I mean that, even if you hoped to avoid me as my land-lady, then you've failed as my dad's nurse's sister, the owner of his therapy garden, an indirect colleague and, I'm hoping, as a friend. All this could be telling us something.' When she didn't reply, he went on. 'Or maybe the fact that I'm really attracted to you is telling me more; circumstance isn't as important as gut instinct.'

'Oh?' Ellie could barely hear him over the pounding in her ears. 'And your gut is saying . . .?'

'That next time we have dinner together, you should come to the cottage, and it should just be the two of us.'

She smiled while her stomach performed an aerobatics display. 'Jago, I—'

'And I would add that you should bring your toothbrush, but I'm worried that's both too presumptuous and far too organized. I need to uphold my reputation for casual spontaneity.'

Ellie's grin threatened to split her face. 'It's not too presumptuous, and I always have a spare toothbrush in my handbag, in case I have an important meeting after a lunch out or I get stuck away from home.'

'Of course you do,' Jago said, laughing. He leaned across the table and pushed a strand of hair off her forehead, his expression so intense that Ellie shuddered.

She pressed forwards, and had just enough time to realize that the table was too wide to reach him for a kiss, when a shadow fell across them.

'Arthur's safely back in his room,' Rose said. 'How are you two getting on? Want a nightcap before we head off? They've got toffee Baileys behind the bar.'

'Oh!' Ellie sat back with a jolt. 'That sounds nice.'

'A whisky would be good,' Jago said, 'but I'll get them. What do you want, Rose?'

'Hot chocolate, please, with all the toppings.'

'Great. One toffee Baileys and one loaded hot chocolate coming up.' As he got up from the table, he shot Ellie a wry, sexy smile that she felt all the way to her toes.

Ellie turned to her sister and resisted wailing in exasperation. She decided Rose wasn't as cunning as she had previously believed, unless her sole goal in life was to slowly torture Ellie to death.

Chapter Sixteen

After the perfection of the night before, the following day threatened to test Ellie's optimistic outlook from the very beginning. She was woken far too early by the buzz of a lazy bee that had flown in through the open bedroom window, and had to spend ten minutes coaxing it out, by which time she was too awake to go back to sleep. She met Rose in the kitchen, and proceeded to burn a piece of sourdough bread.

'Glad you spent all that extra money on the sourdough loaf now?' Rose asked smugly. 'Do you want me to poach you some eggs before I go?'

'You've got an early shift,' Ellie said, 'and I should be able to make *toast*.'

'That toaster has always been temperamental, but we've got a good relationship now, so I don't see the point of getting a new one.'

'Could you give me the key to your relationship, then?' Ellie scraped black bits off the toast to reveal more black bits, then cut herself another slice.

'What's got your goat? I would have thought you'd be floating on air after last night.'

'Why?' Ellie turned. 'Because you very generously offered to drive Arthur home, giving Jago and I some alone time, and then came back just at the wrong moment?'

'Ah, so it's frustration that I'm on the receiving end of, is it?' Rose didn't seem remotely perturbed by Ellie's accusations. 'Go round there this morning and jump his bones, then.'

'I'm not . . .' Ellie sighed. 'It's not like that.'

'What do you mean, *not like that?* There is an undeniable sizzle, and he is perfect for you right now, Elowen. I meant what I said last night.'

'Yes, but I don't want to just sleep with him and then say *see you later*.' She stared at the toaster, desperate for her second piece of bread not to burn, because it felt like a sign of her competency as an adult. She really had got out on the wrong side of the bed. It took her a few moments to realize that Rose hadn't replied. 'What?' she asked, popping the release button on the toaster. She was relieved to see that she had a piece of golden sourdough toast.

'You don't want to just sleep with him and then say *see you later*?' Rose repeated.

'No, of course not.' Ellie spread butter on her toast.

'Of *course* not?'

'Stop repeating everything I say. What is your problem?'

'But Ellie,' Rose said, 'that's all you've done since Mark. Not that you've done it very often, but when you've found a guy it's been no strings attached, a bit of fun and then move on. But now . . .' She shook her head. 'You really like Jago, don't you? It's more than just physical attraction.'

Ellie took a bite of her toast. 'It would make sense,' she said evenly, when she'd finished her mouthful. 'I've spent quite a bit of time with him. Of course we're going to build up some kind of rapport.'

Rose shook her head. 'No no no. You *really* like him. You think he might be a longer-term thing?'

'He's not going to be any kind of *thing*,' Ellie said. 'Because he's too caught up in all the areas of my life that I need to straighten out before I can even consider a relationship. The cottage, my wedding business, the . . .' At that moment, her brain flashed up an image of Jago leaning across the table outside the pub, his eyes burning into hers. She mentally shoved it away. 'It is unwise, and right now I need to be the most wise I've ever been.'

'Yet you're saying it through gritted teeth,' Rose pointed out. She downed the last of her coffee and patted Ellie on the shoulder. 'Even if you have no intention of pursuing whatever you and Jago have together – which I think is madness, by the way – you at least need to learn from him. Chill out, Elowen. You're never going to be happy if you're wound up as tightly as a two-bob watch.' She left Ellie standing in the kitchen, her toast dropping crumbs onto her cream silk shirt, thinking that was exactly what Jago had told her, albeit in a much less direct way.

She spent the morning focusing on the August wedding she had booked in: an older couple, both marrying for the second time, who were doing it at Porthcothan Bay. It was one of Cornwall's most beautiful, but secluded, beaches. It involved a walk over sand dunes, and Ellie was researching what types of matting would ensure the guests and their chairs had a firm enough base, but wouldn't be impossible to transport across a long stretch of sand. It couldn't look too utilitarian, but she didn't want Margot falling over in her dress, even if it was going to be blue rather than white.

After several hours researching beach weddings, she left the house and drove towards Porthgolow. The weather was blistering, and she sent up a silent prayer that it would continue in this vein for at least another month, and that Charlie and Daniel would have the perfect day. She hoped that Margot and Ivor would too, but in her experience August was a surer bet than June and therefore didn't require additional prayers.

Porthgolow Barn's courtyard was partly transformed. There were wicker hanging baskets strategically positioned along the brick walls, several glazed pottery pots in jewel tones of green, red and blue standing on the cobbles, and the wagon looked as if it had been dusted down. There was also a wooden arbour bridging the gap in the wall that led from the yard to the garden. Jane and Pauline had got everything ready for her; she just needed to plant the flowers, vines and shrubs that would bring the place to life. She flapped the front of her shirt to get some air circulating around her body, and opened the car door.

As she raised her arms in a stretch, she saw Millicent. The pig was shiny pink instead of mud-strewn, as if she'd been given a dusting down, too. She trotted over to her and lifted her snout up. She hadn't done that before, and Ellie wondered if the animal had become used to visitors.

'Ellie,' Jane called, coming out of the cottage, 'lovely to

see you! Orwell's on his way, apparently. I can't wait to get this glitter ball set up.'

'Jane, hi. This is looking great. I love the arbour.'

'We think it works,' Jane said, folding her arms over her narrow chest. 'The set-up, anyway. Obviously it's all a bit empty now, but that's where you come in.'

'Absolutely.' Ellie nodded. 'I've gathered up all my brochures too, and made lists of the caterers, photographers and DJs I use on a regular basis. I know you're already looking into landscape gardeners, but I've added the details of a couple I know, and I've done a bit of research on flood-proofing.'

'Flood-proofing?'

'When Charlie and Daniel came to see it, the courtyard was flooded, and it would be good to put some measures in place to stop it happening again; you can't leave it to chance and hope it never rains before a big event. It looks like there are several options.' Ellie waggled her iPad. 'As well as that—'

'As *well* as all that?' Jane laughed. 'I'm going to have to pay you a consultancy fee at this rate. At least come into the cottage, where it's cooler.'

Ellie nodded, hoping her blush wasn't visible. She did have a tendency to get carried away, but she felt that Porthgolow Barn, with all its bucolic charm, was worth getting carried away over.

Pauline was in the kitchen, squeezing oranges into an impressive-looking juicer. The cottage had been given the same attention as the barn; the beams and chunky fireplaces had been turned into focal points, but the Aga looked new, and there was a fancy coffee machine and a bread maker on the counter-tops. Country living made easy, Ellie thought, and wondered if Cornflower Cottage could do with a few upgrades. That thought inevitably led her back to Jago, and it took her a few seconds to realize Pauline had said something to her.

'I'm so sorry, Pauline, what was that?'

The older woman chuckled. 'Would you like a juice?'

'That would be lovely, thank you.'

They sat around the large pine table, and Pauline produced a tray of freshly made chocolates from the fridge and set them down without any fanfare.

'Help yourself,' she said, then added, 'they look hefty,' pointing to Ellie's stack of brochures.

'Just some of the businesses I use.' She reached over and selected a chocolate with a pistachio on top.

'You're giving away all your trade secrets,' Pauline said, chuckling again.

Ellie smiled. 'I'm sharing intel. You're new here, and it always takes such a long time to build up a network of clients and customers, people you can trust and join forces with. I want to give you a head start.'

'She's got some ideas for flood protection too, Mum,' Jane said.

Pauline's eyes hardened, and Ellie had a flash of the scared, angry woman she'd encountered on her first visit. 'Is that OK, Pauline? When we spoke before, you said you'd be happy for me to look into a couple of things for you.' She had explained this all at their last meeting, and had come away with the impression that they were delighted to have her assistance. Had she changed her mind in the meantime?

'You're doing all this out of the goodness of your heart?' Pauline asked.

'Not entirely,' she said carefully. 'This place is going to be big, I can tell. You've got a stunning venue with all the features and facilities anyone could hope for; it's a beautiful countryside setting, but close enough to Porthgolow that guests can stay at Crystal Waters or the B&B on the seafront, and there's the sea view for photographs. I want to help you get over the finish line, then I want us to work together. You're going to be one of my prime venues, so I'm really helping *myself*, as much as I am you.'

'It still seems overly generous,' Pauline said, but her expression had softened. 'You're giving us all this,' she gestured at the pile of brochures, '*and* you're going to fill all those hanging baskets, pretty up the courtyard yourself? Do you not believe in rest and relaxation?'

Ellie laughed. 'Gardening *is* relaxing for me.'

'Well, neither Jane nor I have a green finger between us, but if you tell us where to put things, I'm sure we can be of some use.'

'We'll be your worker bees, Ellie,' Jane added.

'Actually,' Ellie said, 'I might have someone else who can lend a hand with that side of things.' Musing on the idea that had just come to her, and remembering what Rose had said at the pub, she took another chocolate and popped it in her mouth.

In the end, Orwell called to say he and his glitter ball were running half an hour late, and Jane assured Ellie that it would go smoothly. Ellie should really have stayed: she should be on top of every single detail, but she had confidence in

Jane's no-nonsense approach, and wanted to leave them to mull over the information she had given them while she put the next part of her plan into action.

When she got to Seascape House, Mo was nowhere to be seen, but Della on reception greeted her warmly and told her that Arthur was outside. Ellie stepped back into the unwavering sunshine.

She walked round to his original garden, and felt a jolt of sadness when she saw him sitting on a bench close by, but facing away from it. He looked as smart as always, in a short-sleeved shirt and grey trousers. Ellie sat next to him and he glanced at her, his brows knitted in confusion.

'Elowen,' he said. 'Is something wrong?'

'You're not tending to your garden,' she pointed out. 'Though I suppose it isn't the ideal weather to be working away on a flower bed.'

'I don't shy away from hard work,' he said sharply.

'Sorry, I—'

'No need,' he replied quickly. 'I shouldn't have been so abrupt. But there's no point working on it now, when in a few weeks it will no longer exist.'

'They're starting the renovations soon?'

'According to the latest missive from the care home's parent company. Mo is apologetic, but there's nothing he can do, and at least I have been given fair warning and other opportunities. For which I'm very grateful, I hope you know.'

'I do, Arthur. I love having you at Cornflower Cottage, and I love having the opportunity to be back there myself. It's really Jago we should be thanking.'

He was silent for a while, and then said, 'You like him, don't you?'

'Jago?' Her laugh was shrill. 'Of course I do. He's a lovely man. Kind and generous, easy to be around.'

'His laissez-faire attitude doesn't bother you?'

Ellie glanced at Arthur, but he was staring resolutely towards the shimmering line of blue on the horizon, as if he was picturing a different time. 'I don't get that impression,' she said slowly. 'I think he cares deeply about a lot of things. He just chooses to live his life in a certain way. He's had a lot of time away – from Cornwall, from the UK, even, but now he's hoping to put down roots.'

'I can't see where he's coming from,' Arthur admitted, 'and that bothers me. I don't think I've understood a decision of his since he was eighteen. Moving away when he did, travelling around like that, his inability to settle down until he reached his forties. They're all alien to me.'

'But if you think about it,' she said tentatively, 'you were always travelling, too. It might have been a more structured career, but it wasn't *that* dissimilar to what Jago did. And what about him moving back here to be closer to you? Don't you appreciate that decision?' She leaned into him, nudging his arm with hers.

Arthur sighed. 'It seems to have no purpose, other than to throw a spotlight on how much time we spend at loggerheads.'

'I think he's trying very hard to overcome that,' Ellie said. 'It's not easy for either of you, but he hasn't given up.'

'And neither have I,' Arthur replied. 'But it's not as if I *need* him.'

Ellie wasn't sure about that. Arthur kept his loneliness hidden behind forthrightness, and it wasn't as if he'd forged strong bonds with his peers, despite realizing he needed the practical support of a care home. Jago was his family; the one link he had to Hetty. And as she'd got to know Jago, she'd seen more to him than an easy-going mechanic who was prepared to help anyone. There was loneliness there too, she thought; an uncertainty that *he* tried to keep hidden. She was sure it stemmed, in part, from his relationship with his dad.

'You might find that you need him more than you think,' she said. 'And vice versa.'

Arthur replied with what sounded like 'harrumph,' but Ellie was satisfied that he hadn't denied it outright. She felt as if father and son were slowly coming closer, working their way towards each other, even if the ground between them was still littered with potholes, gnarly roots and mole-hills. They would get there eventually.

'Anyway,' she added brightly, slapping her hands on her knees. 'I didn't come here to talk to you about Jago, though I will talk about him any time you want.'

'So you can take my words straight back to him?'

Ellie laughed. 'Nobody is spying on anyone else, OK? We're all on the same side. But I wanted to ask you what you thought about helping me at Porthgolow Barn?'

'This wedding place you mentioned before?'

'The very same. They've got hanging baskets, lots of attractive flowerpots, an arbour. Even an old-fashioned wagon. All of those need to be filled and decorated, and I *could* do it all on my own, but I thought you might like to give me a hand.'

'You're outsourcing me?' He sounded amused, which spurred Ellie on.

'I am offering you some variety, a break from my

meadow. If you want it?' She had also wondered, but only very briefly, how many people her own age Pauline got to see, working with Jane at the barn, perhaps still suffering from anxiety. But she wouldn't mention that to anyone. This was about doing what she'd promised, nothing else.

'I suppose it would be good not to be in Jago's home quite so much,' Arthur said, eventually.

Ellie held back her sigh. 'I thought you hadn't given up on Jago.'

'I'm not thinking of me,' Arthur said. 'He is perpetually laid-back, as we both know, but I do wonder if all your managing is going to send him over the edge one day.'

Despite the heat, a chill ran down Ellie's spine. 'What do you mean?'

'I mean that we've invaded his space, what with the gardening and Rose in the kitchen, cooking up lemonade, and all that bus business. He might continue to accept everything you throw at him, or he might decide enough is enough.'

'He's done that in the past, then?' Ellie asked in a small voice. She was alarmed by Arthur's observation.

'Only on a couple of occasions,' Arthur said, 'and, of course, not recently that I've seen. But you can organize me, Ellie, feel free. Take me to your barn, set me to work. We can still spend time on the meadow, but perhaps it's time to spread ourselves a little more thinly.'

'O-OK,' Ellie stuttered, feeling like a child who'd been told off. But she was also grateful for Arthur's frankness, because the last thing she wanted to do was upset Jago. He'd invited her to dinner; he'd given her clear signs that he liked her and wanted to get to know her better, but – as he'd told her himself – she needed to allow room for it to grow between them. It wouldn't happen if she was constantly in his periphery.

There was the small matter that they were all due to congregate at Cornflower Cottage that weekend; to make a day of it with a picnic, to soften the hard work of the meadow wrangling with lemonade and cold cuts and a distinctly summer party feel. Ellie had been looking forward to seeing Jago again after the previous night's invitation. If he thought she was meddling, he wouldn't have said all those things, would he?

'All right, Ellie?' Arthur asked. 'You're looking somewhat perturbed.'

'I'm fine,' she said. 'Just . . . thinking.'

Arthur stared at her with his clear green eyes, in some ways so like his son's and in others, completely different. Then, as if he could tell exactly what conundrum she was puzzling over – which might well be the case, considering he'd put it there – he patted her knee in a placatory gesture, and turned his attention to the view of yellowing fields and the blue sea beyond, glittering away without a care in the world.

Chapter Seventeen

Ellie felt conflicted as she dressed in a pair of denim shorts and a floral T-shirt that clung in all the right places. She couldn't help thinking of the toothbrush in her handbag – she did always have one, she hadn't been joking when she'd told Jago that – but after Arthur's intervention, she felt less confident, less sure of how she should behave around him. She twisted her hair up into a bun on top of her head, and examined herself in the mirror.

'My car or yours?' Rose called up the stairs. 'And what is taking you so long?'

'*Five minutes*,' Ellie shouted down. Sandals or trainers? Which said "spontaneous"? She pressed her palm against her forehead. Why was this so complicated? *Because you care about him*, a voice whispered back, and she shoved it aside, checked no strands of hair had escaped her bun, and went to join her sister.

Rose narrowed her eyes – she would have spotted in half

a second that Ellie had made an effort – but on this occasion didn't say anything.

'Shall we go, then?' Ellie said. 'In your car, if that's OK? Florence's air con is on the blink again.'

'Why don't you get Jago to look at it?' Rose asked as she locked the front door.

'He's helped us – *me* – out enough. He needs some areas of his life that don't revolve around the Moon sisters.'

'Does he? You've checked that out with him, have you?' This car's air conditioning worked perfectly, and yet Ellie's palms were sweaty.

'We've – *I've* – been rather overbearing since he moved in,' Ellie pointed out. 'And he's already fixed my car once. I feel like I should reduce his rent or something. He planned to move here, see his dad occasionally and get on with his life, and now he's buying lemons in anticipation of our visit so you can make lemonade. He texted to ask how many.'

Rose's face lit up. 'He is? Well, haven't you got him well trained?'

'*Rose*,' Ellie warned.

'Oh, did I mention?' Rose added. 'Mo is coming by today to have a look at the garden and see Arthur in his natural environment, as it were.'

'You didn't mention,' Ellie said, craning her neck so she could see the sea beyond the wall on the other side of the road. It was a blistering, glistening blue: no clouds causing shadows today. 'You should have, though. Jago is going to start feeling invaded.'

'Jago's a sweetie,' Rose said.

'All the more reason not to take advantage of him, then.'

242

But Ellie knew her words would fall on deaf ears, because this was Rose Moon, who always knew what was best and, even if other people didn't agree with her, would do it anyway.

They pulled into the driveway of Cornflower Cottage next to a dark-coloured Volvo.

'Mo's car,' Rose explained. 'He must be going on somewhere else, unless he and Arthur decided that the short walk up the hill would be too much in this heat.' She pulled her T-shirt away from her skin. 'Where's the sea breeze when you need it?'

'This *is* the sea breeze,' Ellie said, getting out of the car and holding out an arm to catch some tendrils of wind. There were hardly any. 'I dread to think how oppressive it is further inland. We're lucky.'

'Sunshine is overrated,' was Rose's reply. She picked up her handbag and went round to the side gate. It was their routine now; they never knocked on the front door, simply went through to the garden and got started. More often than not Jago was already there, and the few occasions he hadn't been, Ellie had wondered what he was doing inside. If it was early morning, those thoughts often strayed to the upstairs of the house: was he still in bed? Was he taking a shower? What did his tanned skin and chestnut hair look like against the fresh white bedsheets?

Instead of following Rose, Ellie went to inspect her rose bushes. They were in full bloom; a myriad of colours that wouldn't look out of place on a wedding cake. Candy pink and bright yellow, a soft, blush peach and gentle lilac. The soil at the base of every bush was dark. Jago must have come out early to water them, before the sun was on them.

Knowing that he'd been listening to her and Arthur talk about how to look after the garden in hot weather made her heart squeeze. He was the kindest man, but they *were* taking advantage of him.

Giving a quick shake of her head, Ellie went through to the back garden.

Mo, Arthur and Rose were sitting at the patio table. Jago was nowhere to be seen, but the kitchen door was open.

'Ellie.' Mo stood up to greet her. 'Good to see you again. I can see why Arthur's been spending so much time here. You have a beautiful garden.'

'It's much more beautiful since he's been here.' She gestured towards the meadow, which was a lot less shabby than it had been a few weeks ago. 'Where's Jago? Does he need any help?'

'Nope.' The man in question walked out of the kitchen carrying two mugs in each hand. 'I've made you a coffee, Ellie, if that's OK?'

'Lovely, thank you.' He was wearing grey shorts and an azure T-shirt, which perfectly matched today's sea. Ellie took her drink from him and leaned against the wall of the house. Jago's gaze held hers for a moment, then he handed out the other drinks. If there was any reluctance about having them all in his garden, he was hiding it well.

While Mo asked Arthur what he used to grow in his garden in Falmouth, Jago came to stand next to Ellie.

'Your soil turned up,' he said, gesturing to three large bags of compost lying against the side of the house. 'Do we need *more* soil here?'

'This is our job for today,' Ellie said. 'The plants suffer when the weather is this hot, but we don't want to over-water them, either. Spreading this around will give them extra nutrients to help them survive.'

Jago rubbed the back of his neck. 'So we need to get all this in a wheelbarrow, then take it round the garden and sprinkle it on all the beds? On the hottest day of the year so far?' He gave her a sideways look. 'I had hoped today would be a few bits of snipping and lots of long breaks in between.'

'It's those things as well,' she said, 'but you and I, Jago, we get to do this.' She tried to make it sound like they'd won a prize.

'Why us?'

'Because your dad can't lift these bags, Rose will point-blank refuse to do anything that might compromise her back – and I'm living in her house so I have to tread carefully – and I'm not sure we should ask Mo on his first visit. Besides, I'm the one setting the tasks so I can't shy away, and you have the best muscles.' Her gaze dropped to his biceps, visible below the short sleeves of his T-shirt and impressive even when he wasn't flexing them. When she returned her eyes to his face, he had an eyebrow raised.

'Is that so?' he said softly.

'It's just a fact.' She couldn't hide her smile. 'Don't read anything into it.'

'You're not flirting with me?' His voice was a low rumble that he must have known wasn't helping.

'Right now I am entirely focused on mulch.'

'Mulch,' he echoed. 'Right. Great word. Very sexy.'

'I like to think so,' she said. 'Come on, let's get the wheelbarrow.'

Ellie asked Arthur and Rose to focus on the meadow,

reminding them that everything they did, whether cutting or weeding, needed to be done delicately when it was so parched, and she and Jago set to work spreading the new soil around. Mo, she noticed, seemed content to stand on the sidelines and replenish their jugs of water. She also noticed how much of his time he spent watching Rose. Her sister, no-nonsense as usual, was fully involved with Arthur and their de-brambling, and didn't appear to be aware of the care-home manager's gaze. Ellie grinned, happy to have something to hold over *her* for a change.

'What are you smiling about?' Jago huffed and arched his back, his T-shirt already dark with sweat. 'This is bloody hard work. Are you sure it needs to be done *today*?'

'I thought you spent years helping build schools in Africa?'

'I was in my early twenties,' he said. 'My muscles didn't protest in the same way.'

Ellie shook her head, feigning disappointment. 'This is exactly when the flowers need the extra nutrients, but look – we're over halfway. And once it's done I'm calling it; we can't spend the whole day out here. I know the sensible among us have got hats on –' she gestured to her baseball cap, Arthur's panama and Rose's floppy, floral number – 'but even so, we're going to have to get out of the sun soon.'

'I don't suit hats, and I don't own one,' Jago said.

'Do you suit the peeling lobster look?'

'I don't burn, I tan.'

She used his reply as an opportunity to gaze at him, and had to admit that he was more golden than fuchsia. 'Heat stroke doesn't discriminate against the golden people.'

The side of his mouth kicked up in a smile. 'OK. How about ten more minutes, then we'll go inside for lunch and finish the rest afterwards?'

When they called time on their morning's efforts, Mo said goodbye and Ellie and Rose set to work in the kitchen. Ellie had insisted that Jago shouldn't have to cater their weekend on top of everything else, and Rose had stepped up and brought a feast for their picnic lunch. It included cold cuts of ham, chicken and roast beef, a selection of cheeses and pickles, cherry tomatoes and mini feta and spinach parcels, along with cucumber and celery sticks to dip in pots of hummus and tzatziki. There were gherkins, sweet Pepperdew peppers and artichoke hearts dripping in olive oil.

They laid everything out on the table in the living room, and with the windows wide open and a meagre breeze wafting in, Ellie felt comfortable for the first time in hours.

Lord Montague was lounging on the sofa behind where Ellie sat cross-legged on the floor. He reached out a lazy paw and swiped at the tendrils of hair that had come loose from her bun.

'Monty,' Jago admonished.

'He hates the heat.' Ellie rubbed the back of her neck. 'He gets unbearably grumpy.'

'Perhaps he'd like a bath,' Rose said from the other side of the room.

Ellie laughed. 'He would *not* like a bath. You can't resent him just because you're allergic.'

'I can and I do,' Rose said. 'And he resents me right back. Look at how he's glaring at me.'

'He wants your ham.' Arthur pointed at Rose's plate.

'He wants my slow, torturous death,' Rose countered. 'I know how cats' minds work.'

A bee batted against the window and drifted off again, and the sound of the gentle surf reached them, brought on the hot air. Ellie felt content, despite the sweat still running down her spine. She had that weary-limbed, satisfied exhaustion from knowing she'd done good things in her garden, and given her body a workout at the same time.

'I suggest another half an hour after lunch,' she said, 'because Jago and I have a couple more flower beds to cover, but then we should finish for the day. There's not much more we can do in this heat, anyway.'

'Are you crying off early because you have somewhere else to be?' Rose asked. 'You didn't say anything.'

'Nowhere else to be,' Ellie said.

'There's another picnic at Seascape House later,' Arthur muttered, staring at a beetroot as if it had mortally offended him. 'In the conservatory. I suppose I need to show my face for that.'

There was a moment of stunned silence, which Jago broke. 'That sounds great, Dad. It's good that you're getting involved.'

'There's no need to patronize me,' Arthur said, and Jago's smile fell. 'I know I'm not the world's most sociable person, but unless I stay here, cooking under the sun, I can't think how to get out of it.'

'You could just stay in your room like you always do,' Rose chimed in. 'Listen to everyone else having fun from there.'

Arthur shot her a cold look. 'Yes, thank you Rose. I am aware of what a stick-in-the-mud I can be. But not today.

Today, I will *mingle.*' He said the last word in a horrified tone, and despite the way he'd spoken to his son, when Jago and Ellie exchanged a glance, it was one of sheer delight.

After lunch, they reluctantly went back outside: Rose and Arthur with their hats and factor-50 suncream to the long grass of the meadow, to brambles, ivy and bindweed, and Ellie and Jago to their mulching. Lord Montague followed them and stood, nose raised skywards, as if he couldn't believe the day was so hot and cloudless. Then he decided to accompany Ellie and Jago, winding round their feet and the wheels of the wheelbarrow, and making the whole process ten times harder.

'What is it, Monty?' Ellie said with exasperation. 'You've had ham, you've got water, and there are loads of cool, shady spots *inside.*'

Monty glared at her and then stepped in front of her as she moved, almost tripping her up.

'For God's sake!'

'Monty?' Jago bent down and held out his hand, but the tabby turned away from him and sat next to a spray of wild oxeye daisies that had grown next to the aquilegia, and which Ellie was trying to cultivate. It was right where they needed to lay the mulch.

'He is being a royal pain in the ass today,' Ellie said, crouching down in front of him. 'Monty, you really need to move.' She reached a hand out, and the cat swiped his hefty paw forward and connected with the inside of Ellie's forearm. At first she just felt heat, and then the pain came, the white lines on her arm spilling crimson. Monty took off into the hydrangeas at a speed she wouldn't have expected from him.

'*Shit*, Ellie, are you OK?' Jago scrabbled over to her, wincing as he took in her bleeding arm. 'That looks nasty.'

Ellie was focused on the place where her cat had disappeared. 'Do you think he's OK? He's not usually *quite* so bad tempered.'

'We need to get inside and clean this.' Jago lifted her arm, his hand around her wrist as he examined the scratch. 'It's quite deep.'

She turned back to Jago. 'I'll be fine. I've had scratches before.'

'But we do need to clean it. Tetanus.'

'OK. Do you think Monty's all right?' she asked again, as Jago stood without loosening his grip, and she was forced to do the same.

'I think he's hot and pissed off, and he's taking it out on you because he knows you best. Once we've dealt with this, I'll look for him, if you want?'

'I can do that,' she said quickly. She had started to feel all manner of conflicting emotions at the way he was taking charge of the situation.

'Come on.' He led her into the kitchen, stared at the sink, where all the crockery from their lunch was stacked, and then toed off his soil-covered trainers. 'Upstairs,' he said, and Ellie slipped off her sandals.

Jago led the way up the stairs, holding Ellie's arm at a horizontal angle, presumably so it didn't drip blood on the carpet. He took her into the small bathroom she had designed so carefully, with white subway tiles and blue grout to match the mosaic-framed mirror above the sink.

She noticed the unfamiliar bottles in the shower; shower gel and shampoo in male scents that probably contributed to his enticing citrus smell. She wondered whether he did anything as unlikely as moisturize his skin.

'Here.' He led her to the sink, and they stood side by side while he ran the hot tap until a gentle steam rose. The space was so small they were pressed against each other, and despite the open window sending in tantalizing licks of air, with the hot water and their two overheated bodies, Ellie thought she might combust.

Jago gently brought Ellie's arm down, until it was under the stream. She winced as the scalding water hit her already tender skin.

'Sorry,' Jago murmured, 'but we need to clean it properly.' He squirted a generous amount of anti-bacterial soap onto his hand, and began rubbing it into the long scratches down Ellie's arm. His movements were slow and measured, but he kept up a steady pressure, making sure any grit from under Monty's claws was removed. It was unbearably intimate, and soon the sting of the scratches was the mildest thing Ellie was feeling.

'I could do this myself.' It came out as a whisper.

Jago glanced up at her. 'You were more concerned about checking on your cat than fixing this. I had to take charge.'

'Thank you.'

Jago nodded and dropped his head. When her skin was red-raw and shiny from the hot water and soap, he switched the temperature from hot to cold, and Ellie gasped at the change in sensation.

'Sorry, I . . .' Jago started.

'Sorry?' Ellie laughed. 'For what?'

He looked up, and this time his green eyes burned into hers. He was close enough that she could see a tiny patch of stubble that he'd missed, the pink sheen on his nose that was already turning to brown, a couple of barely there freckles.

She realized she was holding her breath, waiting for his answer; waiting for something. And when it came, she was both surprised and completely ready for it; desperate, in fact. Jago leaned in and kissed her, his lips grazing hers and then coming back stronger, with more purpose. His skin was hot but far from unwelcome, and Ellie kissed him back, gasping when his arm came around her waist and pulled her against him, crushing their chests together, deepening the kiss.

She brought her arms around his neck. The cold tap was still running and she sprayed them both with icy water, but it did nothing to reduce the heat between them. She gave a little jolt when her cut arm came into contact with his neck.

Jago looked down at her. 'OK?' he asked, his breathing heavy.

'Good,' she said, and reached up to kiss him again. Their actions became more fevered, and she couldn't resist sliding his T-shirt up, feeling his muscled torso while their kisses continued, her back against the glass shower partition. Jago groaned and shifted slightly, changing the angle of the kiss. When he slid his hand down the back of her leg, under her knee and then lifted it, Ellie faltered. 'We can't,' she whispered against his mouth.

His gaze was a mix of heat and frustration. 'I know.' He bent to kiss her neck and showed no signs of stopping.

Ellie let out a breathless giggle. 'It's your dad and my sister, Jago. What if one of them needs to come in here?' And then she bit her lip because he was kissing her earlobe, and it was sending sensation everywhere.

'I'll lock the door,' he murmured.

'Jago,' she said again, but her body was screaming at her to stop protesting. Rose and Arthur were both focused people, fully intent on their gardening task, and right now she was very much enjoying Jago's focus and intent. She didn't say anything else, but slipped a second hand under his T-shirt, bringing his torso flush with hers while he kissed her collarbone.

And then there was another kind of screaming, one that took a moment to reach her lust-filled brain but, when it did, made her feel as if she'd just stepped under a bucketful of icy water. It was Rose, more high-pitched than she'd ever heard her, and alongside that, she could hear Arthur shouting. They were calling for her and Jago, and he must have heard it too because he pulled back from her, his eyes wide.

'What the fuck?' he whispered, and then, as if to prove he wasn't leaving because he wanted to, he grabbed Ellie's hand and pulled her into the corridor.

Together they ran through the cottage, towards the back garden, Ellie's desire doused by fear and worry. If something had happened to Rose or Arthur while she'd been distracted with Jago, while she'd been doing the one thing she'd sworn she wouldn't do because it made life far too complicated, she would never forgive herself.

Chapter Eighteen

They burst into the back garden and Ellie had to squint against the bright sunshine, holding her hand like a visor against her forehead.

'Where?' she asked, frantically, and Jago pointed to Arthur and Rose, who were standing in the meadow. Rose beckoned when she saw them.

'Where have you been?' she called, as they hurried through the garden, Ellie's insides churning with a combination of panic and lingering desire.

'What's happened? Is Arthur OK?' Ellie kept pace with Jago, their fingers loosely intwined. She saw Rose's gaze flick down to their hands, then return to Ellie's face, her consternation softening to curiosity.

'We have something to show you,' Arthur said, taking off his hat and wiping his perspiring brow.

Jago stopped. 'Wait, you're both fine? You're not injured or dying or being attacked by a swarm of angry hornets?'

'Of course not,' Rose said. 'We have something very, *very*

exciting to show you. Why?' She narrowed her eyes. 'Did we interrupt something?'

Jago shook his head. 'Monty scratched Ellie, and I was cleaning it up.'

'Where?' Rose lifted Ellie's arm. 'Good lord, Ellie, that animal is a monster.'

'He's hot and grumpy,' Ellie countered, taking her arm back. It was still tingling from the hot water and the scratch, and the rest of her was tingling from Jago's kisses. 'Are you seriously both all right? You sounded like a banshee.'

Rose laughed. 'I did not. Now come here and see if you can tell me what this is.' She beckoned them forward, through the part of the meadow that had been cleared of weeds and brambles, to where the grass was still unruly. Ellie felt the sun beating down hotter than ever, the tickle of grass against her legs, and she could sense Jago at her side, could hear his breathing, still slightly elevated. She wondered whether her lips were swollen or her cheeks pink from his stubble. Was it obvious to Rose, who missed very little? And then she caught sight of something in the grass, and her head emptied of all other thoughts.

She crouched down, her mouth falling open.

'It is what I think it is, isn't it?' For the first time since she'd met him, Arthur sounded hesitant.

'I . . . I . . .' She crawled forwards on her hands and knees, barely feeling the prickle of nettles. It was a single stem, with three individual flowers coming off it. Each flower had three pointed petals in a shade of pinkish purple, their thin, intricate veins slightly darker, and then nestled in the middle of the petal trio was each flower's crowning glory:

a brown-and-yellow centre with a red tongue, mimicking the pollinators that buzzed through the garden in the spring and summer months. 'A bee orchid?' Her own voice sounded unsure.

'*Ophrys apifera*,' Arthur said. 'It is, isn't it?'

Ellie swallowed and nodded. 'It's early. And also extinct in Cornwall, so.' She shrugged and then laughed, the strangeness of the last half an hour working its way through her like a drug.

Jago knelt alongside her and peered at the orchid. 'This type of flower is extinct in Cornwall?'

'Since a couple of years ago,' Arthur confirmed. 'It's fairly rare throughout the country, and it had one solitary spot in Cornwall, at Hayle Causeway, but some ignorant blighter mowed it down when he was tidying the grass. It was a travesty; the plants themselves are uncommon enough, and the flowers sometimes take five or six years to bloom.'

'God,' Jago murmured. 'Good job you didn't let me loose with the mower up here, then.'

'I can't believe it.' Ellie reached out a hand, but didn't dare touch it. It was perfect; its centre so like a bee that she wondered at the machinations of nature, how it could come up with creations quite so magical. 'In our meadow.'

'It's obviously been here for years without anyone disturbing it,' Rose said. 'Which begs the question, what do we do about it?'

'Uhm.' Ellie felt a flutter of panic. Should they put some kind of cordon around it? Put it under a breathable glass jar, like the rose in *Beauty and the Beast?* But it had survived here, untouched, for who knew how long. 'I think we need to tell someone.'

Arthur scoffed. 'So they can come and destroy it, trampling their feet all over the place?'

Ellie sat back on her heels. 'There are a lot of people, organizations, who would be delighted to know there were still bee orchids in Cornwall. I don't think we can keep it to ourselves.'

'The Cornwall Wildlife Trust,' Rose said.

Ellie nodded. 'I think so. Goodness, I can't believe she's here. *Ophrys apifera.* Well done for finding it, you two.'

'It was Arthur,' Rose confirmed. 'He spotted it, and I think we should celebrate his discovery.'

'There's a bottle of Prosecco in the fridge,' Jago said absent-mindedly, looking at the miraculous flower.

'Really?' Rose lifted an eyebrow. 'I didn't peg you for a Prosecco drinker, Jago.'

He shrugged. 'I'm not the only one who's often at Cornflower Cottage though, am I?'

Rose stared at him, then her eyes flicked to Ellie. 'Indeed,' she said feelingly, and walked back down the garden.

'I need to step inside for a moment,' Arthur murmured. 'What Hetty would have given to see this.' He shook his head and stumbled past them, his joints obviously stiff from crouching. Jago got up and, after a second's hesitation, caught up with Arthur and put a hand under his elbow. Ellie held her breath, but the older man didn't shrug him off, and they walked slowly through the garden together. She watched until they reached the house, a lump in her throat.

Then she was alone, with the drone of insects and, if she closed her eyes and concentrated, the distant sound of waves crashing against the sand. She opened them again and looked at the flower, so beautiful but also somehow innocuous, nestled amongst the weeds and grasses, its petals gossamer-thin, the sunlight shining through them. This was in *her* garden. It was a moment she would never forget, for so many reasons.

As she sat there wondering what to do next, Monty sidled up and rubbed his head against her bare arm. 'Oh, so now you're choosing to be nice, are you? After doing this?' She held her arm out, as if he would be able to see the error of his ways. Instead, he narrowed his eyes and purred. 'Or did you plan the whole thing?' She lowered her voice. 'The scratch and Jago taking me inside? If so, then you're a clever and wicked cat, but I would have thought you could have come up with something that didn't cause me physical pain.'

She laughed as she realized she was admonishing her cat for orchestrating an ill-advised seduction. As if he was responsible; as if it hadn't been inevitable. She wondered about the bottle of Prosecco in Jago's fridge, whether it meant that – even before their heated moment in the bathroom – he'd been planning to ask her to stay after the others had gone home. Would he still ask? She was pondering this when Rose came to find her.

'You should come inside and have some lemonade,' she said, crouching a little way away and eyeing Monty warily. 'That orchid has survived for God knows how long without you sitting there keeping guard.'

Ellie laughed. 'I was just admiring it.'

'Oh? Is that all you've been admiring today? What were you and Jago up to when we called?'

'We told you, he was cleaning my cut.' She held her arm out like a schoolgirl proving she'd done her homework.

'I expect he was very tender,' Rose said. 'A muscular man like that, but with the care and dexterity to fix the fiddly parts of car engines. He must have nimble fingers.' Ellie shivered and Rose pointed an accusing finger. 'I saw that! Were you getting down to it? While we were *just out here?*' She burst out laughing. 'You *were!* I can see it all over your face. My God, Elowen. I think *that*, more than some rare flower, has made my day today.'

Ellie bristled. 'I'm a grown woman, Rose. Stop acting like I'm some lovesick teenager.'

'No need,' Rose said smugly. 'You're doing that perfectly well all by yourself. Now come and have some lemonade and we can plan who we need to call about this bee orchid.' She held her hand out and Ellie let her pull her to standing, and they went to join the others inside Cornflower Cottage.

Jago and Arthur were deep in conversation when Ellie walked into the living room, the bottle of Prosecco nestled in ice in her silver bucket, alongside four flutes and the jug of lemonade.

'Now,' Rose said, all authority, 'I suggest we start with lemonade. We're likely to be dehydrated enough without pouring alcohol straight down our gullets. I'll be mother.' She began pouring the pale yellow liquid into glasses, and Ellie caught Jago's eye, expecting to exchange a smile with him. Instead, he was frowning. She noticed that Arthur also looked pensive, his lips pressed into a tight line. Her happiness deflated.

'A toast . . .' Rose said, handing out glasses. 'To Arthur's discovery of the bee orchid in the Cornflower Cottage meadow, to Ellie's idea of setting up this motley crew of gardeners, and to Jago's kind acceptance of us trampling around on his property whenever we feel like it. Cheers!'

'Cheers!' they echoed, but it was a much less ebullient toast than it should have been, and Ellie was relieved when her phone rang.

She excused herself and stepped into the hallway. 'Ellie Moon.'

'Ellie, it's Charlie!' The bride-to-be sounded excited, and Ellie felt instantly relieved.

'Charlie, hi. How are you?'

'Good,' she said, 'really good. It's so great to have Gertie back, and Pete and Jago have done such an amazing job, it's as if the accident never happened. The bus is already busy again.'

'I'm so pleased, Charlie.'

'And I've arranged for Pete to collect her again a week before the wedding, so she can have the makeover you and Daniel had planned.'

'Really?'

'*Yes*! I was going to stop working then anyway, otherwise Lila was convinced I would stay busy until the day before and be stressed out for the wedding day. So the Cornish Cream Tea Bus will be having her own pampering session, which I did love the idea of, even if – by the time I found out – things were rather bleak.' She took a breath and then added, 'I'm sorry I was angry with you. The crash wasn't your fault, and I remembered that, the morning Liam drove it away, you were concerned. You've always been so thorough, and I shouldn't have blamed you.'

'Charlie, you honestly don't need to apologize. I *was* partly

260

responsible for what happened to Gertie, but I'm so glad everything's rosy again.'

'It is. But there's one other thing.'

'What's that?'

'My dress.' She cleared her throat. 'I hadn't settled on a design with Gina, and she's been looking at other options for me. But then yesterday, my mum and dad were going through some of my uncle Hal's things – Dad hadn't the heart until now – and they found my gran's wedding dress. Mum says it's a bit musty, understandably, but she showed me on FaceTime and, oh, Ellie, it's so beautiful! It's everything I've been imagining.'

'Vintage lace?' Ellie asked, laughing.

'Yes! It's very simple; a plain, strapless silk bodice with lace sleeves over the top, and some embroidery detailing on the skirt. I'm going to Cheltenham tomorrow, just for a couple of days, and Mum's going to make any adjustments I need.'

'It sounds amazing, Charlie. Will you send me photos?'

'Of course! And you don't mind about Gina? I'll obviously pay for the time she's put in.'

'Not at all.' Ellie leaned against the wall, relishing the feel of the cool plaster against her shoulders. 'You need to have the right dress, and from the excitement in your voice, it sounds like you've found it. Everything's coming together just as it should. All the creases are being ironed out.'

Charlie laughed. 'That's a perfect way of putting it – it really feels like things are smoothing out. I'm just so happy that it's going to be everything we hoped for. You can get so caught up in the details, can't you? Which is why I'm so grateful to you for taking those bits on, for making things simple for us. I just want to start my married life with Daniel in a positive way.'

'You will—' Ellie started, but Charlie kept going.

'Because I love him so much, Ellie. I am so glad that I found him, and that he feels the same way. I know some people would say that flowers and table decorations and glitter balls aren't important, and when you look at them individually they aren't, are they? But it's all the little parts that make up the whole, that turn it into something special. I know that from running the Cornish Cream Tea Bus. And I'm worried that if we start off on a bad footing, then it's somehow symbolic of our love. Even though, at the end of the day, all that matters is how you feel about someone.' She laughed. 'I'm not making sense, but I just – I wanted to thank you again.' She took a deep breath. 'Anyway, how are you?' The question was so unexpected after her monologue, that Ellie took a moment to answer.

'I'm fine,' she said. 'I'm at my cottage, the one I'm renting out, and we've . . . well, we've just found a bee orchid in the garden! As far as we know, they're extinct in Cornwall apart from this one plant.'

'Really?' Charlie sounded genuinely interested. 'Wow! What are you going to do?'

'Call the Wildlife Trust, and . . . I don't know who else. It's the kind of discovery that will be important to a select group of people, but it's also a bit of feel-good news we'd love to share.'

'I know someone who might like to cover it – a journalist for the local paper. Do you want me to talk to her?'

'That's a great idea. Let me just check with the others, to see if they're happy with that plan. Can I let you know?'

'No problem. Suddenly, my genuinely vintage wedding dress doesn't seem so noteworthy.'

'Of course it's noteworthy,' Ellie said. 'It's a serendipitous moment, as if it was waiting for you all along, and your mum and dad were always meant to find it just in time. You should see *that* as symbolic. I definitely am.'

Once they'd said goodbye, Ellie headed towards the living room, giddy with the news that a journalist might be interested in their discovery, but something about the tone in Arthur's voice brought her up short. 'Your duty is over, Jago,' she heard him say. 'I'm doing perfectly well at Seascape House, and I can continue to come here once you're back in Plymouth. Ellie's asked me to help with the wedding barn, too, so you don't need to worry about me mouldering away by myself. There's no need for you to be here.'

Ellie pressed back against the wall in the hallway, a lump lodging in her throat.

'It's not *duty*, Dad.' Jago sounded upset. 'I'm here because I want us to get past this rift, to make up for all the years when we didn't have much of a relationship. I'm not just here to see you settled.'

'I thought that was exactly why you were here,' Arthur said. 'And as for our relationship, we don't seem to have got very far. It's best if we cut our losses, get on with our own lives. You should go back to Plymouth, do whatever it is you do, and stop being suffocated by your misguided belief that I need looking after.'

The immediate response was a stunned silence, and Ellie stepped into the doorway just as Jago said, 'Hang on a minute—'

'I should be going to my picnic,' Arthur said, talking over

him. 'I don't want to be late for the others.' He gave Jago a pointed look and walked to the door, putting a hand on Ellie's arm. 'Please keep me up to date with the orchid, Ellie. I'd love to know who shows an interest.'

'Of course,' she murmured, and then, because she didn't want them to think she'd been listening, added, 'I've just spoken to Charlie, and she said she can mention it to a local journalist, see if she'd like to cover the story. Would you be happy with that?'

'Most definitely,' Arthur said.

'If she does, then you'll be front and centre – it's your discovery.'

'It's your garden, Ellie.'

'Jago's garden,' Ellie corrected. 'This is Jago's cottage.'

'We both know that's not really true.' He squeezed her arm and walked past, meeting Rose in the hallway.

'I'll be back in a bit,' Rose said, the look on her face suggesting she'd heard everything too. 'Arthur's keen to get going.'

Ellie nodded dumbly, waited until they'd closed the front door behind them, then went back to Jago. 'I'm so sorry,' she said.

He sighed heavily. 'How much did you hear?'

'Just the end, I think.'

He gave her a humourless smile. 'Apparently the discovery of the bee orchid means that Dad's fine and I'm no longer needed at Cornflower Cottage, or in Cornwall, for that matter.'

Ellie lowered herself onto the sofa opposite him. 'How are those two things connected?' she murmured. 'And how – how could he think that? I thought you two were starting to get to know each other again; to fix things.'

264

'Me too. Obviously, we were both wrong.'

'Jago, I—'

'You heard what he said. That we should cut our losses, get on with our own lives. And that this has never been my cottage.'

Ellie winced. 'If *anyone* thinks that, then it is entirely *my* fault. I should have left you alone as soon as you moved in, not come back here uninvited to see the garden whenever I fancied, or offered it as somewhere for Arthur to spend time. I've been treating it like this communal space, because you've been so generous, but I haven't been fair.'

Jago shrugged. 'You thought you were doing the right thing. And I can't blame you for missing this place.' A muscle was moving in his jaw, his posture tight.

'You don't need to be kind to me, Jago. You don't have to excuse anything, forgive everything, I—'

'All right then,' he said, and his voice suddenly sounded cold. 'I didn't want you here, or Dad or Rose or Mo. I wanted to come quietly back to Cornwall and see if, after a while, I could pluck up the courage to visit Dad. I didn't realize this property came with strings attached. None of this has gone how I wanted it to. Maybe if I'd been left to do it my way, this wouldn't have happened.' He flung an arm in the direction of the garden.

Dread settled in the pit of Ellie's stomach, even though she'd invited him to be honest. She stayed quiet, knowing there was more to come.

'There would have been no early morning interruptions where you were just . . . *there*,' he went on, his voice cracking. 'Outside the back door when I was barely awake; nobody forcing me to talk to Dad before I was ready. No

265

meals out or bloody homemade lemonade or rare flower discoveries, which are just going to bring more people here, to *your* garden, Ellie.' He levelled her with a look, and while there was definitely heat in it, it wasn't the same kind she'd seen in the bathroom. 'Because it *is* yours, isn't it? I've never belonged here. I should go back to Plymouth, like Dad said.'

'No, Jago, you can't mean that—'

'Why not? Because it's not like me? Because I'll put up with anything? Well not this time. I've had enough.'

Ellie swallowed, fighting the panic that was blossoming inside her. 'I am so sorry,' she said quietly. 'So, *so* sorry that this has happened; that I overstepped the mark and let my ideas run away with me. I just thought—'

'You thought you were doing the right thing,' Jago said again, some of the anger leaching from his voice. 'And it's not down to you that this hasn't worked. It's all down to me. I was fooling myself, not thinking things through, like always.'

'That's not true,' Ellie said. 'We can find a way to work this out. If you really want—'

'Could you just leave it, Ellie, for *once*?' His voice exploded into the cosy living room. 'Just try not to fix it, on this one occasion? It really isn't your place.' He wiped his hand over his face and turned to the window.

Ellie closed her eyes briefly and then got up, keeping her movements quiet and small, as if Jago was a wild animal she didn't want to disturb. At the doorway, she glanced back at him, but he hadn't moved. She went through the kitchen and into the sultry heat of the garden, picked up her gardening pouch and tiptoed out of the side gate. She walked down the driveway to where it joined Wilderness Lane.

Rose would be back in a moment, and then they could drive away together, without disturbing him any more.

She tried not to think of the sparkling possibility the day had started with; the hope and passion that had bloomed inside her when she was kissing Jago, letting him override her senses. She didn't understand Arthur's thinking, why he had suddenly dismissed Jago, as if he was an unruly butler rather than his only child, but she did get where Jago was coming from.

Ellie hadn't allowed him the space to breathe, to make his own decisions about how he lived or who came to visit him or how to handle the delicate, difficult situation with his dad. She had barrelled in, thinking she could solve all the problems and make everyone happy, the way she did with floral displays and white doves and vintage Rolls-Royces. But this wasn't a wedding; this was the lives of Arthur and Jago, and she'd treated them carelessly, like an item on one of her to-do lists. Arthur had even warned her this might happen, and still she hadn't been careful enough.

She stood on the path while the sun continued its slow descent towards the Cornish coast, and realized how much she cared about them. Arthur with all his properness and his flashes of humour, and Jago with his wide, generous smile and his kindness, and the way he had looked at her like she meant something to him.

She had known, when he'd kissed her, that this wasn't about a physical release, a hot guy she could spend time with and then send off into the sunset. She had been thinking about all the things she didn't know about him, all the ways she wanted to be with him; talking and walking, having meals and coffee together, exploring the parts of

Cornwall that they both loved, kissing and touching and doing all the things that her mind had run away with when he'd been pulling her against him while steam curled around them.

But he was right. She hadn't allowed him to do things his own way. She had crowded him, and so it made sense that he would push her away; that he would come to his senses and ask her to go and organize someone else's life in her do-gooding, over-zealous way, and leave him alone. And if he listened to what Arthur was telling him, he might not stay in Cornwall, let alone Cornflower Cottage. In the near future, she might find herself without a tenant and, more importantly, without Jago Carne in her life.

Everything was ruined, and she only had herself to blame.

Part Four

Breaded Bliss

Chapter Nineteen

It was widely known that Reenie Teague, matriarch of Porthgolow village and supposed recluse was, in fact, the best photographer for miles. It was something Elowen Moon might have challenged, because she knew a number of hugely talented wedding photographers, but for this purpose Reenie was exactly who she needed. The older woman had agreed to meet her on the beach, rather than at her precariously placed cottage on the cliff edge, or at the hotel where people – one person in particular – might start asking questions.

It was the end of May, Charlie Quilter and Daniel Harper were getting married in only a few weeks' time, and the weather was more like mid-August. In Texas. Ellie pulled her thin shirt away from her neck, relishing the sea breeze skating over her bare legs, and waved at the woman with long grey hair standing on the sand. The sea sparkled so brightly that she couldn't look at it for long, and while there were a few dog-walkers and a couple of families setting up their pitches, the brightly coloured windbreakers like fallen kites against the pale gold of the beach, it was too early for the crowds to have gathered.

'Elowen?' the older woman asked as she approached. 'You look like wedding planner material.'

'I do?' Ellie said. Reenie had sharp features and a knowing glint in her eye that made Ellie want to run away. Right now, she wanted nothing more than to do her job and not be appraised too closely; not when she'd found sleep almost impossible to come by for the last few nights.

'Your outfit, and that pink hair,' Reenie explained. 'Very wedding-ish. Those colours are all the rage at the moment, aren't they? Pink, violet and grey. Though why anyone would want to go grey before their time is beyond me.' She shook her head. 'Charlie said you wanted to talk to me about something.'

'If that's OK, Reenie?' They walked towards the water, the air fresher here than anywhere Ellie had been recently. Perhaps she should set up a makeshift office on the beach. 'She said you'd be the best person for the job.'

'And what job is that? I'm not wearing a flouncy bridesmaid's dress, if that's what she's asking. I'm at least fifty years too old for that.'

Ellie laughed. 'No, it's nothing like that. I'm after your photography skills.'

Reenie raised an eyebrow.

'Charlie told me that you run the Porthgolow Hideaway Instagram account. I follow it, and it's beautiful.' It was a grid full of well-composed photos of the seafront, sunsets and sunny beach shots, and the raging storms that hit the coastline in the winter months. Once Charlie had told her,

Ellie realized that Reenie's little yellow house, which was on the very edge of the cliff, gave her a unique viewpoint of the village.

'Thank you,' Reenie said. 'I love the shifting moods of this place, and it seemed churlish not to share them with others.'

'It always gives me such a longing for this beach.'

'Do you live in Porthgolow? Charlie said you were local.'

'I'm in St Eval, at the moment,' Ellie said, 'with my sister, but I've got a cottage on the outskirts of the village.'

Ellie kept her gaze trained on the sea, but she could feel Reenie watching her. Charlie had told her that the older woman was shrewd, and Ellie wanted to keep this meeting firmly work-focused.

'Anyway,' she went on briskly, 'Charlie wants to do something special for Daniel, as a wedding gift. Porthgolow is such an integral part of his life, of both their lives, so we've come up with the idea of an album. Photos of the village, places and people, any messages Daniel's friends want to add. Charlie's going to write captions for the pictures.'

'That's a lovely idea,' Reenie said. 'You'd like me to take the photographs?'

Ellie nodded. 'Nobody knows Porthgolow as well as you do, and Charlie said you and Daniel were close, so having you take the pictures would give it an extra-special touch. Obviously there's a budget; it'll take up a lot of your time, and the schedule's fairly tight, too.'

Reenie waved a dismissive hand. 'I wouldn't dream of asking for payment,' she said. 'That boy means the world to me; he and Charlie both do, and I would do anything for them. Do you have a list of the shots Charlie wants?'

'There are a few that she's keen to have in there,' Ellie explained, 'but she also said to use your creativity; that she trusts you to make Porthgolow sparkle.'

Reenie chuckled and gestured to the water. 'No need for me to do that. Porthgolow sparkles all by itself.'

With Reenie's full agreement, Ellie said she'd email over Charlie's list of photos that day, then left the woman strolling in the sunshine while she returned to her car.

She sat in Florence's driver's seat and stared out of the windscreen at the beautiful Cornish beach. Although it was late in the day to be arranging a gift that involved input from other people, Ellie wasn't worried. She'd organized far larger things at much shorter notice, including the venue for a hundred-guest wedding when the original hotel failed their hygiene certificate with ten days to go. Wedding pressure, she could handle. Besides, Porthgolow was such a tight-knit community, she had no doubt the residents would be more than happy to pose for photos and provide messages for Charlie's album.

Ellie looked at her to-do list for the week. She was seeing Daniel and Charlie later that afternoon – Charlie had returned from her parents' house and Ellie wanted to know how the dress fitting had gone; she had a meeting with Hannah to confirm the final dishes for the hot buffet so a menu could be drawn up, and one with the florists, Jamie and Dawn Fistrel, to finalize designs for the bouquet, buttonholes and flower garlands. She was seeing two prospective new couples looking to get married next year, and had already started compiling mood boards to show them. Everything in Ellie's professional life was going swimmingly; it was the rest that was fraying at the seams.

As if on cue, her phone rang.

'Rose,' she said warily, 'how's it going?'

'Josie, the journalist your friend Charlie spoke to, is going to be at the cottage in a few hours.'

'That's great.' Ellie tried to sound enthusiastic.

'And the local news station is coming later on this afternoon,' Rose added.

'Fabulous.'

'They want to interview Arthur about his discovery.'

'I expect he'll love that, though he'll pretend not to.'

Rose chuckled. 'He's already told me he's going to iron his favourite shirt and trousers.'

'Great,' Ellie said again.

The silence held between them, and Ellie chewed her lip and tried to think of a reason to get off the phone.

'The Cornwall Wildlife Trust are even talking about getting in touch with *Gardener's World*,' Rose went on, 'to ask them to come here and do a piece about Cornflower Cottage's found bee orchid, and how it's no longer extinct in Cornwall.'

Ellie rolled her eyes. 'They are not.'

'I promise you they are,' Rose said. 'And you would know I wasn't making it up if you'd been the one to call them. They said the orchid should bloom through the whole of June and into July. There's time for all sorts.'

'And I'm sure you, Arthur and Jago will be very happy to be the faces of it. I really need to—'

'Stop being such a stubborn wench!'

Ellie's mouth fell open in shock. 'A stubborn *wench*?'

'I'm not taking it back,' Rose said defiantly. 'You need to come to the cottage and make your peace with Jago. He's agreed to let Arthur come back, despite the words the two of them had, and they've been at cross-purposes for a lot longer than you two have been.'

'There's no peace to be made.' Ellie sat up straighter. The car was starting to feel like a sauna, and she rolled the window down. 'Jago was right. I've asked for far too much from him. He needed to make his own decisions, not have me controlling his every move. So I'm focusing on work, leaving him alone.'

Her sister sighed. 'He was understandably angry after what Arthur had said to him, and maybe he was too harsh with you, but you can come back from it, can't you? Don't forget that I know what was really going on when he was seeing to your cut in the house.'

Ellie was trying very hard not to think about how Jago had been planning to see to her, because it unearthed all kinds of emotions she didn't want to deal with right now. 'It was a mistake,' she said. 'He's got enough on his plate with his dad, and now, playing host to everyone who's interested in the orchid. God, he's never going to get a break, is he?'

'Which is why *you* don't need to stay away either,' Rose countered. 'Has he tried to get in touch with you directly?'

Ellie's phone had been hot with texts, calls and WhatsApps, but they'd all been wedding-related. She hadn't heard from Jago since she'd walked out of Cornflower Cottage on Saturday afternoon. And that, she had decided, was for the best. 'It's getting close to Charlie and Daniel's wedding,' Ellie said, not answering her sister's question. 'I need to put all my energy into that right now.'

'This rare little flower is in your garden, Ellie. It may have been growing there for years, but you're the one who's looked after that space so lovingly, suggested we go through the meadow with a fine-tooth comb instead of a combine harvester, otherwise it would have been mown down and nobody would be any the wiser.

'It's generous of you to share the spoils with Arthur, Jago and me, but you need to be part of it, too. It would be absolutely criminal if you weren't. And that is all I'm going to say on the matter, except that Josie's going to be at the cottage at two, and if Jago is prepared to keep trying with Arthur after all that's passed between them, then you need to get over your one tiny tiff with him and Stop. Being. So. Stubborn. See you later, sister of mine.' With that, the line went dead and Ellie's mouth was open once more, doing her best guppy expression.

Ellie did want to see Jago again, but whenever she thought about him, the overriding emotion was guilt over the way she'd behaved, muscling her way into relationships she had no business being involved in. And now they had discovered the orchid, and Jago's hopes of a quiet life were even further out of his reach. All because of her selfish desire to spend time in her garden, and her belief that meddling in other people's lives would make them better, not worse.

Should she go? She thought it was rather telling that he hadn't tried to get in touch with her. She was completely torn, and sitting in her sweltering car being indecisive wasn't going to help. She needed to take her thoughts off it all, and she knew just the place. Putting her car in gear, she drove in the direction of Penzance, and the Big Bonanza Warehouse.

An hour of strolling the aisles of the gargantuan warehouse, surrounded by all manner of celebratory items, from decorative candles to fake cherry-blossom trees to full-sized resin reindeers, calmed Ellie's soul.

The place was one big reminder that there were always things worth celebrating: you could have a party to celebrate discovering the sex of your child; you could celebrate a marathon run or sporting achievement with a fake gold cup, ready to be filled with beer or champagne or sweets. You could pick strings of fairy lights in almost every colour and shape, and hang them above your bed simply to celebrate each new day.

Ellie knew the style of decorations Charlie and Daniel wanted, and although much of what she was getting for them was bespoke, it was always worth coming to the Big Bonanza Warehouse to add to the haul. More than anything, it restored Ellie's faith in herself, in the happiness she helped bring to other people's lives. She may have made Jago's life harder – though not with *all* her actions, she reasoned, thinking back to the bathroom – but it had never been her intention.

Back in the car park, her boot full of simple glass vases and tins of copper, gold and silver spray paint, the view ahead of her an uninspiring road rather than sand and sea, Ellie knew she had run out of time. To go, or not to go? that was the question. What, she thought, drumming her fingers on the steering wheel, should her answer be?

'Arthur, what does this discovery mean for you? After the sad destruction of the bee orchid's one Cornish habitat two years ago, would you see the re-emergence of such a beautiful plant as a sign of hope?' The woman was tall and lithe and undoubtedly gorgeous, and as Ellie tiptoed through the side gate and along the wall of the cottage, she cursed herself for taking a detour back from Penzance that had turned out to be worse than the roadworks it was diverting people away from.

'That's a very good point, Josie,' Arthur said smoothly. 'We live in a world where hope is sometimes hard to find. And while the reoccurrence of a rare and beautiful flower in Cornwall won't seem important to everyone, for me and my son, Jago, Ellie and Rose Moon, and the local naturalists we've told, it feels like an event that is, somehow, bigger than itself. A sign that precious things are out there waiting, if you keep your eyes open and exercise a little patience. On this occasion one has found its way to this remote patch of Porthgolow.'

Ellie moved further along the wall. With the photographer no longer blocking her view, she could see Arthur standing near the back fence, close to but not crowding their prized flower, while Josie pointed a digital recorder at him. He looked smart in grey trousers and a short-sleeved, dusky blue shirt, his thin hair neatly combed.

Rose stood off to the side, and Ellie's breath caught at the sight of Jago, standing next to her, in a loose white linen shirt and jeans. It was the perfect outfit for him, and Ellie's body tingled to life. On the patio, jugs of iced, homemade lemonade stood next to a plate of fondant fancies that were as brightly coloured as the roses in the front garden. There was more air this afternoon, a stronger breeze coming in off the sea, and it felt less oppressive than it had done that morning. Much more *hopeful.*

When she looked back at the group, Jago was staring at her. He raised a hand in acknowledgement, but he didn't smile. And, just like that, Ellie's own hope shrivelled and died. She forced herself to concentrate on the interview. Josie had asked Arthur about the moment they'd made the discovery, and Arthur was explaining how he'd come to be at the cottage.

'It was an act of unfounded kindness,' he said. 'My son has recently moved back to the area, to this very cottage, and his landlady, that's Ellie – Elowen – Moon, has put so much effort into this garden. It was their combined generosity, along with my nurse, Rose's, in giving up her time, that allowed me to be here and, ultimately, to discover the bee orchid.'

'It sounds very serendipitous,' Josie said. 'A combination of circumstance and, as you say, kindness. What are your hopes for the flower now?'

'We have a botanist and a member of the Cornwall Wildlife Trust coming to document it. After that, I presume we will simply allow it to flourish. I believe Ellie has plans for this part of her garden, beyond the current . . . meadow, and I'd be very surprised if they didn't accommodate the new discovery.'

'Not planning on covering it in concrete, then?' Josie chuckled.

Arthur looked alarmed, her cheeky humour lost on him. 'Good Lord, no!' he said, and Josie's laughter stopped abruptly.

Once the interview was over, the photographer asked for some shots of them all with the garden behind them.

'Come on Ellie,' Rose called.

'Oh, are you the landlady?' Josie asked.

Ellie winced. She resisted the urge to look at Jago, and also the desire to tell the journalist that she was definitely *not* a Nora Batty landlady. 'I'm renting this cottage out to Jago,' she said instead.

'And you're also the gardener?'

'I was,' Ellie said. 'But now it's a joint effort. If I'd been working in the meadow on my own, it would have been months before I'd reached the place where Arthur and Rose discovered the orchid – well into the autumn – and it would have been long gone. The discovery is down to this unique set of circumstances.'

'There's a lot to be said for unconventionality,' Josie replied, her dark eyes flashing. Ellie could almost see the cogs working, as she ran through all the ways she could frame the article. Everybody loved a good news story, and this one had so many reader-friendly elements: a lonely old man having his beloved garden taken away from him, then given a second chance where he was not only reunited with his son, but also discovered a plant the county thought it had lost for good. Ellie wouldn't tell Josie that the bond between father and son was still, at best, fragile.

'Come on, Ellie,' Rose called, 'stop dawdling and join us. Did you have to wear that see-through blouse, today of all days?'

Ellie glanced down, horrified. 'It's my coolest shirt, and it is *not* see-through.' Her cheeks flamed, and when she stood between Rose and Jago, she resisted pinching her sister's arm, *hard*.

She felt the press of Jago's arm against hers as they posed for the photos, but there was a stiffness to his posture it was impossible to ignore.

'Lovely,' Josie said, shaking their hands in turn. 'Thank you so much. This will be a really good story to put in the midweek edition. Can you get your contact at the Wildlife Trust to give me a call when you've spoken to them?' She handed Arthur her card, and Ellie didn't miss the look of pride in his eyes.

Once Josie and the photographer had gone, Rose suggested that Arthur might like a final spruce-up before the TV crew arrived and, giving Ellie a pointed look, took him inside. Ellie noticed the brief nod that passed between father and son, could almost feel the hostility radiating off them, and realized that they hadn't smoothed things over, either.

She turned to Jago, drinking in his tanned complexion and his dark hair, and the way his shirt was open at the collar, showing a patch of tantalizing, kissable skin. His eyes met hers, and she saw so much more than anger in his expression; there was sadness and disappointment, too. The regret made her feel hollow. She had been the one to quash his almost permanent smile.

'I hope you didn't mind me coming,' she said. 'Rose told me about Josie, and she thought I should be here, but—'

'Of course not,' he said. 'This is your garden.'

Ellie squeezed her eyes closed. 'It's yours,' she said, opening them again. 'Whatever anyone else says. But I shouldn't . . .' She gestured lamely around her. 'I need to go. I have a meeting to get to.'

She gazed around the garden, thinking, now, that it might be a while before she saw it again. She needed to speak to Arthur about the barn, about getting the pots and baskets filled, the arbour decorated, in time for the wedding. When she turned back to Jago, his expression had softened.

'See you around, Jago. Good luck with the film crew later.'

'I won't be here,' he said. 'I have a job at the garage. Ellie, I—'

'I don't want to be late,' she said hurriedly, and before she could let the significance of this moment – of leaving Jago and her garden behind – overwhelm her, she turned and strode through the side gate, a blue tit watching her departure from the top of the hawthorn tree.

Chapter Twenty

Porthgolow beach, complete with the Cornish Cream Tea Bus standing proudly in its usual place, was a beautiful sight, and it lifted Ellie's heart marginally after her awkward, unhappy interaction with Jago. She parked in the car park and made her way across the sand, having to skip out of the way of a brightly coloured beach ball that came hurtling towards her. A young boy called out an apology as he chased after it, and Ellie waved a hand in acknowledgement.

Daniel stood up from one of Gertie's outdoor tables, his confident smile firmly in place.

'Great to see you, Ellie.'

'You too, Daniel. And it's lovely to see Gertie, too.'

Daniel rubbed the bus's red paintwork. 'She's good as new, and she's still going to get her makeover.'

'Charlie told me.' Ellie smiled, then looked down as something brushed her leg. A small, black and tan dog lifted up onto his hind legs and put his front paws on her knees.

'Marmite, *no*,' Daniel said sternly. The little dog cocked

his head, then turned his dark eyes on Ellie and yelped at her. She heard Daniel swear under his breath, and had to laugh.

'So this is Marmite.' She bent to stroke him.

'He's Charlie's,' Daniel said darkly. 'This,' he added, flourishing an arm towards a German shepherd that was lying sedately under the table, doing nothing more than blinking at her, 'is Jasper. He's mine.'

Ellie turned her affections towards the larger dog. She stroked his nose, even when Marmite bounded in front of her, not ready to relinquish her attention. 'One might say,' she said lightly, 'that in a few weeks' time, they'll both be your dogs. You'll be equally responsible.'

When she glanced up, Daniel was staring at her, his hands on his hips, and her laughter returned.

'I hadn't thought of it like that,' he murmured. 'Oh well. Marmite will steal your heart, just before he steals your sausage roll. It's hard to be angry with him for long.'

'I can see that,' Ellie replied, as the dog tried to crawl onto her lap even though she was only crouching.

'Have a seat if he'll let you,' Daniel said. 'I'll go and check where Charlie is.'

'No hurry.' Ellie gave each dog a final pat and settled in one of the chairs.

She would never get over this view; the gently curved bay busy with visitors, seagulls and the occasional cormorant swooping over the sea, which was glittering under the summer sun. If it hadn't been for the unwelcome lump in her chest that tightened whenever she thought about Jago – which was roughly every ten seconds – she would feel utterly content.

'Charlie will be out in a moment, she's just sorting through a few things with Juliette. She's going to cover the bus while we talk.'

Ellie nodded. She had met Charlie's friend – her other maid of honour alongside Lila – once before. She knew Juliette was the one who had invited Charlie to visit her in Porthgolow a few years ago; the event that had led to her setting up home, and the Cornish Cream Tea Bus, in the village.

'It looks like it's going to be a good summer,' Ellie said.

'Professionally, for both of us, I'm hoping so,' Daniel replied. 'Personally speaking, I don't have any doubts.' He sat down opposite Ellie, and bent to stroke the dogs under the table. 'You know,' he went on, 'when Gertie crashed I thought our wedding was doomed. I don't go in for that fatalistic attitude usually, but I honestly thought: that bus has been on so many journeys around Cornwall, and the one that we arranged as a surprise for Charlie, for the wedding, is when it crashes. Now, however, I think it was meant to be.'

'Meant to be?' Ellie asked with a laugh. 'Why?'

Daniel shrugged. 'Because it showed us that, even when the worst happens, it's not game over. With Pete and Jago on board, Gertie was brought back to life, and she's still getting her wedding makeover. It was a scare, but it reminded me that nothing's so bad it can't be overcome, and it also means that we must have had all our bad luck by now, so everything else will run like a dream.'

'Shhh!' Ellie couldn't help it. 'If there were ever words to tempt fate, it's those ones.'

Daniel grinned. 'I'm not worried any more.'

He looked up, and Ellie turned to see Charlie emerge from the bus carrying a tall cake stand, Juliette behind her with a tray.

'Ellie.' Charlie beamed at her. 'Thank you for coming.'

'What's all this?' Ellie asked, as Charlie put her cake stand on the table. 'Hi Juliette,' she added distractedly. 'How are you?'

'I'm really well, thanks,' Juliette said, her French accent just discernible. 'I can't wait for Charlie and Daniel to tie the knot.' She bumped her hip against her friend's, and Charlie laughed.

'It's getting close, now.' Ellie looked at the table, at the teapot and three mugs that Juliette had put down, and the tiny sandwiches, tarts and cakes on the cake stand. With her impromptu trip to the warehouse and all the traffic jams she'd encountered, she hadn't had any lunch. 'We're just going over the last few things, but . . .'

'This is an afternoon tea meeting,' Charlie said. 'Like a breakfast meeting, only better.'

'I'm going to get on.' Juliette gestured to the busy bus, and then hurried back inside with a wave of goodbye.

'It's to say thank you for everything you're doing,' Charlie said to Ellie. 'For keeping us sane throughout this whole thing, and it's also an apology for how I behaved after Gertie crashed. Oh, and say hello to Marmite and Jasper.'

'Little terror, large softie,' Daniel added.

'Those are not their nicknames,' Charlie said, glaring at her fiancé.

'Ellie's already been introduced,' Daniel said, 'and I think she'd agreed with me. Do you have any pets?' he asked, handing her a plate.

Ellie took in the delights in front of her, wondering which to choose: there were elegantly sliced finger sandwiches, their fillings spilling out of the sides in a way that was tantalizing but not too messy to eat; mini Bakewell tarts with glistening cherries on top; tiny chocolate mousses in bulbous glass dishes; gingerbread biscuits in the shape of suns, waves and buses with coloured icing details.

'This is . . . wow. You did all this for me?'

Charlie nodded. 'It's this summer's cream tea. I know I've got a few weeks off, but when I'm back it'll be all hands on deck, and I love revamping the cream tea for the new season.'

Marmite yelped as Ellie put a couple of sandwiches on her plate, and she remembered Daniel's question. 'I have a cat,' she said, then took a bite of the creamiest egg mayonnaise sandwich she'd ever eaten. 'He's called Lord Montague.'

Charlie laughed. 'Lord Montague?'

Ellie rolled her eyes. 'I got him as a kitten after my divorce, and I wanted to call him Monty. I did, in fact, call him Monty. But then my sister Rose, who's allergic to cats, said that he was clearly lording over the place, and me. She said he should be called Lord Monty, but that didn't seem quite right, so now his official name is Lord Montague. And he does live up to it.'

Charlie pointed at her arm. 'Did he do that?'

Ellie glanced at the scratch, her cheeks heating at the memories that came with it. 'Yup. He was hot and bothered, and I got in his way. But most of the time he's fairly well behaved.'

'I've always been a dog person,' Daniel said. 'They're less vicious than cats.'

'But they do chew shoes into oblivion and leave unwelcome presents on sofa cushions,' Charlie pointed out.

'Jasper's never done anything like that.' Daniel gave the German shepherd a fond look.

'Not even when he was a puppy?' Charlie raised an eyebrow and bit into a sandwich.

Daniel shifted in his chair. 'Well, maybe once or twice. But I soon trained him out of it.'

'Of course you did,' Charlie said. 'Daniel Harper, hotelier extraordinaire *and* dog whisperer. There is no end to your talents.'

'Glad you finally realize it.'

'It's because you keep them so well hidden beneath your carefully cultivated air of superiority.'

He gave a one-shouldered shrug. 'Just another of my many talents.'

Charlie laughed and turned to Ellie. 'It's good we're eating outside, because I'm pretty sure his head would be too big to fit through the bus door right now.'

'Why do you think I made all the hotel doors oversized? It's so I could saunter about without any risk to my inflated ego.'

'Did you design the hotel?' Ellie asked, surprised. 'You didn't just buy it?'

'Please don't encourage him,' Charlie said with mock despair. 'At this rate, he won't be able to fit inside the barn, and those doors are *massive*.' She rolled her eyes and Daniel grinned at her.

Ellie swallowed, her throat suddenly tight. There was so much love between them, their bickering undercut by deep affection, and she realized that she missed sparring with someone close enough to know all her foibles, who she'd learned about inside and out, who she could share private jokes with. She'd started to believe that she might have those moments with Jago, but that seemed impossible now.

'The barn doors *are* massive,' she agreed, pushing her thoughts aside. 'And we have a few decisions to make about that: about the placing of the decorations. I picked up a few things this morning, and after this,' she gestured at the delicious spread in front of her, 'we should go through them. Start working on the final touches.'

Charlie's smile was unabashed. 'I can't wait! All the foundations are rock solid, so we've earned our time on the fun, fiddly bits. It's just like when Gertie became the Cornish Cream Tea Bus and I added all the little details, the fairy lights and the bunting.'

'My life is plagued by bunting,' Daniel said. 'Sometimes I dream about zombie bunting chasing me across the beach.'

'You do not!' Charlie laughed. 'You love it really.'

'You keep telling yourself that, Charlie.'

'I could get some bunting if you wanted?' Ellie gave Daniel an innocent look.

He scowled at her, and Charlie's laugh got louder, until it competed with the waves crashing against the sand and the seagulls' cries. Charlie was a happy, excited bride approaching her wedding day, and Ellie had helped get her to this place. She realized that, bus crashes aside, she was proud of what she'd achieved. Their big day was close, and everything was looking as bright as the summer's day they were enjoying.

Once they had demolished the beautiful afternoon tea, including a round of crumbly, buttery fruit scones topped with strawberry jam and clotted cream, and the three of them had gone through the last few decisions, Ellie felt even more confident.

'Thank you for the gorgeous cream tea,' she said, letting Marmite clamber onto her lap now she'd finished eating. 'It was entirely unnecessary, but I'm very glad you did it.'

'It's our pleasure,' Charlie said. 'You've made the whole process so much easier. I keep trying to examine my feelings, to see if I have any worries about the big day, and all that's left is excitement. I've never felt less responsible about something that matters so much. It's a weird, but wonderful, feeling.'

'That's exactly as it should be,' Ellie said. 'It means I'm doing my job. Before I go, we need to send Daniel away so you can talk to me about the dress.'

'I'll go and see how Juliette's getting on.' Daniel stood up. 'But, once we're married, I want to talk to you about an arrangement with Crystal Waters. We already hold weddings there, but if you were on board, the sky would be the limit.'

'I knew you wouldn't be able to wait,' Charlie said, smiling. 'Leave the business side of things until afterwards.'

'I will – I am. But it doesn't hurt to get a meeting in the calendar.' He was his usual, smooth self but Ellie could see the determination in his eyes. If Daniel Harper was keen to partner with her for weddings at Crystal Waters after she'd arranged his own, then she was clearly doing something right. It was a bigger tick of approval than she could have hoped for.

'I would love that,' she said calmly.

Daniel grinned and took the empty cake stand back to the bus.

'How did it go?' Ellie asked, as soon as he was out of earshot. 'Is the dress everything you wanted?'

Charlie nodded, her eyes suddenly bright with unshed tears. 'It is *exactly* what I'd been imagining, *and* it's my gran's – Dad and Hal's mum. Look.' She scooted her chair round until she was next to Ellie, and swiped through photos on her phone. 'Here it is.' She handed the phone to Ellie.

Ellie only had to give the picture a quick glance to see that it was perfect, and that Charlie looked a million dollars in it. The lace detailing was delicate, the slender shape sat perfectly on her tall figure, and even with Charlie's face bare of make-up and her hair pulled into a scruffy ponytail, the effect was spellbinding.

'Wow, Charlie. It's stunning. Does it need a lot of work?'

'Not much at all,' she said, laughing. 'But Mum's doing it for me. I'm going to drive up to Cheltenham a couple of days before the wedding for a final fitting and to spend some time with them – have a last meal out before they hand me over to Daniel.' She rolled her eyes. 'Then we'll all travel here together – dress included.'

Ellie nodded, struggling to take her eyes off the photo of Charlie in the dress, the way her expression said, clearly, that this was the one. 'Perfect,' she murmured. 'This is perfect, Charlie.'

'I can't quite believe how close it is,' Charlie said. 'We just need Gertie to get her makeover and put the finishing touches to the barn, then Daniel and I will be getting married.'

Ellie grinned. 'I bet you can't wait.'

'No,' Charlie whispered, glancing at the bus, 'I can't.' She raised her hand in a wave, and Daniel gestured through the window. Charlie beckoned him outside, and Ellie handed her back her phone.

'I need to get going,' she said, when Daniel had rejoined them. 'But I have one last question for you both.' She stroked Marmite's silky ears, but her focus was on Charlie and Daniel. 'What makes the two of you work so well? Why are you meant to be together?' She watched the surprise on their faces, something she saw in all her clients when she asked them this question. 'It doesn't have to be an essay, I just want you to come up with one thing that makes your relationship, your love, so strong. There will be hundreds, but I just want one.'

Charlie and Daniel looked at each other, then Daniel took Charlie's hand and turned back to Ellie.

'I can't speak for Charlie,' he said, 'but for me, it's that we always have a great time together. I'm never happier than when I'm spending time with her. Even at the beginning, when we didn't always see eye to eye, I just wanted to be in her presence.' He gave a self-conscious smile, then added, 'Charlie is my happy place.'

Ellie looked at the woman in question, and saw that her eyes were glistening. 'I thought he was going to be flippant,' she said through a laugh. 'I thought he was going to say that I take his dog for a walk when the weather's shit, or that I keep him on his toes because Gertie's competition for the hotel restaurant, but . . .' she swallowed. 'I couldn't have put it better than that. Daniel is my happy place, too. Always.'

Ellie nodded. It was a check for herself, a reminder of how important her job was to the couples she worked for, and it was also a way of resetting things, taking them away from bouquet designs and seating charts and champagne orders for a moment. Reminding them what mattered. Though with Charlie and Daniel, she didn't think that had ever got lost: they'd always seemed anchored together, grounded in their love. They were each other's happy place.

'That's beautiful,' she said. 'Thank you for sharing it. I'll be in touch regularly from now on,' she went on, getting back to business. 'Keeping you updated with the big things and the little things. And I want you to do the same with me: consider me a twenty-four-hour hotline. Any queries or concerns, any worries or jitters, call me – together or separately. I'll be there.'

There were hugs goodbye, a lick on the cheek from Marmite and a gentle nudge from Jasper. Reluctantly, she walked back over the sand, away from the beach that was like something from a travel brochure, and away from Charlie and Daniel, and the best cream tea she'd ever had.

As she got into Florence and set her sights on home, Daniel's words were on a loop inside her head: *I'm never happier than when I'm spending time with her.*

Ellie had lost sight of how straightforward it was. She'd been clouded by pain and the disappointment of failure, the loss of the perfect life she thought she'd been building for herself and Mark. But those words were an arrow straight to her gut, making her think of how happy *she'd* been recently; the bubble of excitement she always felt when she was on her way to Cornflower Cottage, to see a certain mechanic with a warm smile and even warmer temperament. She was always happy when she was with Jago, but the same clearly wasn't true for him. Had she already blown it, or was there a chance for her to make it up to him?

Chapter Twenty-One

It must have rained in the night, because when Ellie woke up, the pavement outside her window was dark, and the silver birch tree opposite was spraying droplets into the light breeze. An hour later any signs of rainfall had gone, and by the time Ellie had climbed into Florence and started the engine, the heat was more sultry than ever. She couldn't remember the last time a summer, and *early* summer at that, had been so consistently hot.

Rose had told her the local news interview with Arthur had gone well, that he had been even more charming than he had been with Josie, and that she couldn't wait for Ellie and Jago to see it on the programme that evening. She had given her a knowing look over a breakfast of poached eggs and avocado on toast, which was Ellie's favourite and had immediately put her on high alert.

'What's this for?' she'd asked.

Rose had ignored the question. 'Did you speak to Jago yesterday?'

Ellie stared at her breakfast. 'He didn't want to talk to me.'

Rose's huff could have knocked over the table. 'Ellie, you *need* to sort this out. You should go round there, arrange to watch the news report with him.'

'He won't want me to,' Ellie protested, but a large part of her was on her sister's side, telling her to go and make it up to him, to at least *try* to apologize again. 'Anyway, I'm seeing Arthur this morning. We're decorating Porthgolow Barn.'

Rose frowned. 'But you won't still be there when the evening news is on, because Arthur and I are watching it at Seascape House with Mo and the other residents.'

Ellie took a bite of creamy avocado on crunchy toast. 'I could come and watch it with you,' she suggested.

Rose shook her head. 'If you turn up, I'll bar you.'

'What? You'll *bar me* from the care home? Why?'

'Because watching a load of octogenarians, several of whom no longer have their own teeth, is *not* an aphrodisiac. You and Jago have been dancing around each other for long enough, you need to get over your squashed toe and try that waltz again.'

'He could tell me he never wants to see me again, other than for bland landlady duties. We've had so many false starts. Maybe he was never destined to be on my dance card in the first place.'

Rose gave her an exasperated look. 'It's in your hands, Ellie. Take charge of your future. Honestly!'

It was hard not to replay her sister's words as she drove towards the coast. It was the prettiest route to Porthgolow, and she never missed the chance of a sea view. It was weird having her older sister egging her on like a bossy cheerleader to sleep with someone, and especially at their age. But Rose had always said what she thought, and Ellie had known that she was giving up a certain level of privacy by moving in with her. And Rose had welcomed her with open arms, not just given her space in her house: she had supported her, cooked for her, embraced everything about the less-than-ideal situation without a moment's hesitation. Ellie was lucky she'd had her to turn to when things were bad.

When she reached Porthgolow Barn, she saw that her delivery had already arrived. There was a van in the courtyard, its back doors wide open and the interior bursting with blooms – rose bushes in pastel shades of ivory, peach and dusky pink, bright geraniums, pots of London pride with its delicate, white-pink flowers. The smell was incredible, and she could see Arthur and Pauline poring over the contents, deep in conversation.

'Ellie,' Jane said, 'look at this! You've ordered enough for a whole fleet of barns.'

Ellie laughed. 'We want it to look celebratory.'

Arthur held up a plastic tub containing a honeysuckle growing up a stick. 'Is this for the arbour? It's a good specimen.'

'There should be two more of those,' Ellie said. 'And a climbing rose.'

'Arthur's been telling me about Cornflower Cottage.' Pauline took a container of White Sparkle begonias out of the van and clutched it to her chest. 'It sounds wonderful. And so close, too.' She gave Ellie a slightly accusatory look, as if she should have known about it beforehand.

'Arthur's made such a difference,' Ellie admitted. 'And he found the orchid.'

'We're going to watch the news piece later,' Jane said, lifting one of the hefty jewel-coloured pots and bringing it to the van's back doors.

'I wondered if Pauline and Jane might like to come and see it,' Arthur said, his gaze finding Ellie's. 'If I can smooth it over with my son.'

Ellie chewed the inside of her cheek. 'You could always ask him,' she said eventually. She would not, *could* not, make any more decisions when it came to Cornflower Cottage.

Arthur's tone softened when he said, 'Come and help me with the arbour. My hips are so stiff I'm not sure I can reach up to coax the honeysuckles round the top.'

'I'll get you a step,' Jane said, and hurried away.

Arthur took Ellie's arm and they strolled to the edge of the courtyard, where the very new-looking wooden arbour arched over the gap in the wall, and Ellie saw that Millicent was enjoying the mud puddles on the lawn. Jane had booked a landscaper, but the work wasn't happening until after Charlie and Daniel's wedding. Still, they could pose under the arbour, with the sea in the background, and at least the courtyard would be beautiful; flower-explosion beautiful, she thought with a wry grin.

'I understand that you and my son have had words,' Arthur said, bending to examine the climbing rose.

Ellie sighed. 'You were right. I managed him too much, and now he doesn't want anything to do with me.'

Arthur shook his head. 'I'm sure that's not true. The second part, anyway. And I hold myself partly to blame.

From what Rose told me, it was after *our* altercation that you and he spoke unkindly to each other. I shouldn't have spoken as I did,' he added, after a pause. 'I have had a chance to reflect on what I said to him.'

'Why did you tell him to go back to Plymouth?'

Arthur stuck his fingers into the soil surrounding the rose tree, loosening it. There were two more glazed blue pots at the base of the arbour, into which they would put the climbing rose and honeysuckles. 'Because I believed that was what he wanted to hear,' he said. 'He doesn't want to spend his life living in my shadow, even if he thinks he's duty-bound to. And my life, my outlook, has expanded significantly since meeting you and Rose.'

Ellie crouched alongside him. 'He wants to get to know you again. He's not in Cornwall purely out of obligation. And you do, I think, have some unfinished business.' She caught herself. 'But it's nothing to do with me. I've already done too much of . . . of everything. We should get on.' She went to get up so she could help Jane with the step, but Arthur gripped her arm.

'I hope that, after this evening, Jago will see that I'm sorry for what I said, for . . . well, for a lot of things.'

'What do you mean?'

He shook his head. 'What are *you* going to do?'

'About what?'

'To make things up with him,' Arthur said. 'He has a stubborn streak, as I'm sure you know, but I believe, where you're concerned, it's much weaker than usual. You just need to tap gently and that wall will come crumbling down.'

'You think so?'

Arthur nodded. 'Our wall has been thickening for a lot longer.' He pressed a hand to his chest. 'I haven't been the father he needed me to be, so I'm under no illusions that one tap will be all it takes. I've realized, possibly too late, that I'm prepared to put the work in if he is. But with you . . .' He sighed. 'Just talk to him, Ellie. Your intentions were good, and he knows it. Don't let him fall out of your life like I did. He's a good man.'

Ellie was too taken aback to speak, so she just put her hand over his, and smiled.

'Room for a little one?' Pauline said, bustling over with the step. She glanced between Ellie and Arthur, and Ellie saw her face change when Arthur looked up at her. She seemed ten years younger.

'I'll get started on the hanging baskets.' Ellie stood up. 'Arthur can show you what to do, Pauline.'

With Arthur's words playing through her mind, and a tiny shoot of hope in her chest, Ellie left them to it and went to find Jane. Perhaps, by the end of the day, it wouldn't just be Porthgolow Barn's prospects that had been improved; perhaps Ellie's would be, too.

It took Ellie two seconds to decide whether to call ahead or not. She decided not, because she didn't want an awkward conversation where he told her he didn't want to see her. This way it was significantly more like an ambush, but if that was what she needed to do, then so be it.

'I'm heading off,' she said to Jane, Arthur and Pauline.

Jane pushed herself upright, her hands on her knees, from where she'd been adjusting the leaves of one of the newly potted rose bushes. Ellie could see that she was already enamoured with the plants. She knew from experience that gardening and flower arranging were so rewarding it was easy to get hooked quickly. Especially when the transformation was so total.

'It looks wonderful already,' she added. 'We've done such a great job.'

'A true team effort,' Pauline said. 'I can't thank you enough for all this, Ellie. And for your help, Arthur.'

'It was my pleasure,' Arthur said sincerely. He tucked his chin in, his eyes cast to the floor as if he was embarrassed. If he was the type of person to blush, Ellie thought he would be doing it right now. 'Where are you heading off to, Ellie?' he asked gently, turning to her, and she was suddenly so grateful for him; for his quiet candour and his words of reassurance.

'I might nip up the hill for a bit,' she said nervously, and he nodded his approval. 'Do you want a lift to Seascape?'

'I thought Arthur could stay for a cool drink,' Pauline cut in. 'Perhaps some early dinner, if you'd like to? I can drop you at Seascape House in time for the local news.'

There was a surprised pause before he said, 'I'd like that very much; thank you, Pauline.'

Ellie said her goodbyes, assuring Jane and Pauline she'd be in touch in the next couple of days, and then left the three of them, along with the chickens and Millicent, and drove out of the courtyard.

She had a quick errand to run before she went to Cornflower Cottage, and she needed a few more minutes before she saw Jago, to calm her nerves and work out what she wanted to say to him. She drove into the village, stopped in the beach car park and walked across the road to the Pop-In on the seafront.

It was a busy, chaotic shop that had all manner of unusual things for sale. Ellie usually loved perusing its tall shelves, but she had her sights firmly fixed on the drinks chiller, and the small selection of wine they stocked. There was a single bottle of sparkling wine from a local vineyard – exactly what she was looking for. The woman behind the counter spent a few moments appraising her, and then the wine, as if it wasn't something she had purposely put in her fridge to sell; as if Ellie might be tricking her in some way.

'Off somewhere nice?' she asked in a broad Cornish accent.

'Just to see a friend,' Ellie said. 'I can't turn up empty-handed.'

'Course not,' the woman agreed. 'That would never do. I'm glad there's still folk who realize it.'

Ellie paid for the wine and picked it up.

'Have a good time,' the woman called after her as Ellie walked to the door. 'And take your time wi' it – that's not a cheap bottle of plonk to be guzzled in half an 'our.'

When Ellie got back to her car, she was grinning.

She parked in the driveway of Cornflower Cottage, the innocent presence of Jago's Golf suggesting he was at home, and giving her a moment of sheer terror. But she had to do this. Whatever happened, she would never forgive herself if she didn't at least try. She took her bottle of chilled wine, gripping the neck with a sweaty palm, and pressed the doorbell.

A few moments later, it swung open, revealing Jago in jeans and a grey T-shirt. He looked his usual, casually delicious self, and Ellie's mouth dried out.

'Ellie!' He sounded surprised rather than annoyed. 'Is everything OK?'

She took a deep breath, and decided honesty was best. 'No . . .' she said. 'No, it's not. Things aren't good between us, and I'm not OK with that.'

Something flickered in his eyes, and he stepped back. 'Come in.'

She followed him through the kitchen, where there was a tantalizing smell and something bubbling on the stove, and out to the back garden. A robin was singing, and a pair of cabbage whites fluttered between the lupins, cutting through the breezeless air.

'This is for you,' she said, when he turned to face her. 'I wanted to bring you something, even if this is going to be a short visit.'

'Why might it be a short visit?'

Ellie shrugged. 'Because you might listen to what I have to say, and then decide you want me to leave. I'm not here to pressure you, or manage you, or organize you in any way, but I do have a few things I need to say to you.' She realized that sounded quite forceful, so she added, 'If that's all right?'

Jago's eyes gleamed with amusement, which caught her off guard because he was supposed to be angry with her. He put the bottle on the patio table and crossed his arms over his chest. 'Go ahead.'

Ellie nodded and flexed her fingers. She couldn't remember the last time she'd been this nervous. 'I have behaved awfully to you,' she started, and Jago shook his head, so she held out a hand towards him. 'Please. Just let me say this.' He nodded, so she continued. 'My intentions were good, I promise, but I know that I . . . I took full advantage of your kindness. You let me come back here whenever I wanted, so then I pushed it further, asking if Arthur could come here, too. And then, once that happened, I tried to force the two of you together.

'I like you both, you see. In *very* different ways, obviously, but – I thought I could help. I thought how lovely it would be if you put your differences aside, and so I decided, in a spectacular lapse of judgement, that I could make it happen. But it was never my place, and even though you actually told me, indirectly, that I was overstepping – that I was too organized, that I didn't let things happen spontaneously – and then Arthur warned me, *specifically*, that you might only take so much and then break . . .' She saw him frown at that, but she ploughed on. '. . . I just kept going. I didn't get how much it was hurting you, until that day. Until you told me.' She swallowed. 'I am so sorry, Jago. I'm sorry I was so blinkered; that I took your generosity for granted and didn't properly consider how you might be feeling. It was horrible of me, and I want to make it up to you. If . . . if you'd like me to.' She chewed her lip, watching his face for any clues as to what his response would be.

'I should never have said those things,' Jago said softly. 'Or at least, I shouldn't have spoken to you in the way I did. I was mad with Dad, the way he just assumes whatever he says is a fact, rather than an opinion; his certainty about everything. He doesn't discuss, he dictates, and that really

305

pisses me off. But it's not your problem, and I shouldn't have taken it out on you.'

She wanted to ask if he'd spoken to his dad since Saturday, to tell him what Arthur had said to her a few hours ago, but she had just apologized for interfering. 'You had every right to say those things,' she said instead.

He shook his head. 'You say you've taken advantage of *my* kindness, Ellie, but what about yours? You've been nothing but welcoming since I got here; certainly beyond the duties of any normal, Nora Batty landlady.' The side of his mouth kicked up. 'You took me to the pub, you gave your garden over to Dad when, really, he could have been making up all that stuff about being green-fingered. He could have come in and trashed the place, for all you knew. But you trusted him with this.' He flung his arm out towards the flower beds. 'And I know what I said the other day, but honestly? I have never minded having you here, at Cornflower Cottage.' His voice lowered when he added, 'Not once.'

Ellie swallowed. 'Really? But I—'

'You pre-empted me,' he murmured, taking a step towards her.

'What does that mean?'

'I should have apologized yesterday, when you came to see Arthur being interviewed. I shouldn't have been cold with you. I hope that . . .' his eyes flickered to her mouth, 'that this will make up for it.' He lifted his hand, brushed his fingers across her cheek, then bent his head towards hers. He hesitated, looking into her eyes and then, when she managed a nod, he closed the gap and pressed his lips against hers. It was much more tender, more tentative

306

than it had been on Saturday, but it set her on fire all the same.

'Jago,' she murmured, when they pulled apart.

'I have been wanting to do that again ever since the bastard bee orchid was found.'

'Bastard bee orchid?' Ellie laughed softly.

He nodded. 'The most badly timed rare plant discovery ever. That was what sent everything downhill. But even when I was angry with you, I wanted to kiss you, which told me that I was being angry with the wrong person. I'm sorry, Ellie.'

'Stop saying sorry.'

'Will you stay for dinner?' he asked. 'Be here just for me, and not any other altruistic reasons, or flower-shaped reasons, but because you want to spend time with me.'

Happiness bubbled inside her like a spring. 'I would love to.'

'Good. It's just pasta, and it's probably gone to mush by now, but . . .' he grinned. 'Let me go and check on it.' He gave her a swift kiss, then took the bottle of sparkling wine inside, leaving Ellie dazed and a little bit ecstatic on the patio.

'All sorted,' he said, emerging a few minutes later with a bottle inside a metal ice bucket and two flutes. When Ellie looked, she saw it was champagne, and not her sparkling wine.

'What's this?'

'As I said before, you pre-empted me. I was going to call you, invite you over, apologize. Probably tomorrow. I was still working up the courage,' he added, looking suddenly sheepish.

'I got there first?'

'Your plan was more solid than mine, which isn't that surprising.' He popped the cork, then poured the champagne into the flutes. He handed her one, and held his out. 'We've got ten minutes until the local news. I think we should make a toast first, to us. Then we can do one for Arthur and Rose, and the bee orchid.'

'The bastard bee orchid,' Ellie said with a smile.

'Exactly. But for now, to you, Ellie, my very un-Nora Batty landlady. I'm glad that you're braver than me, and I'm very happy that you're here.' He went to clink her glass, but she pulled it back.

'I thought this was a toast to *us*?'

'I'm not going to toast myself.'

'OK, then.' She took a deep breath. 'Here's to you, Jago, my *very* welcome tenant, who has been far too generous in all sorts of ways, from fixing my car to fixing my clients' bus, to letting me sneak into the garden in the early mornings and hiring it out for the pleasure of others. For forgiving all of these impositions and more, and for bringing some added sunshine into my life, when I really needed it. To you,' she tacked onto the end, because of course she'd let it get too heavy. Jago's gaze had intensified, and he stepped towards her instead of stretching his arm out, so that when they clinked, they were inches apart.

'To us,' Jago said.

Ellie wondered whether she could take any more bubbles on top of the ones inside her.

'We should go and get set up,' he murmured. 'I put more pasta on and it needs to simmer for a bit, then it'll take moments to throw it all together, so we can watch the piece without any interruptions.' He led her into the living room, where Monty was lounging on a sofa, taking the prime telly-watching spot, as if he knew what was coming.

Ellie settled herself next to her cat, and Jago switched on the TV and sat beside her, his thigh brushing hers as he found the right channel and fiddled with the sound. Then he got up to adjust the blinds at the window. The sun was slanting through it, a shot of pure gold, and when Jago twisted the cord, the room was plunged into semi-darkness. The screen glowed and the TV announcer said something about a celebrity guest having a surprise on *The One Show* at seven. Jago settled beside her again, and they watched in silence as the credits for the news programme began.

The first item was about proposed cuts to the local council, and Ellie sighed, thinking of all the people who would be affected; thinking how she'd been struggling earlier in the year, had made the hard decision to give up her cottage, and what that had brought with it.

'OK?' Jago asked.

'Sure. It's just . . .' She hesitated.

'What?' He turned towards her.

'I'm just thinking about how lucky I am, with how things have been going the last few months.' She gave a tight shrug.

Jago nodded. 'You wouldn't have moved out of here if you hadn't needed to, would you?'

'No,' she admitted. 'At the time, it was a sad but necessary step, and I . . .' She swallowed. 'But I'm so pleased that I did. Because if I hadn't, I never would have met you.'

'You might have done,' he said lightly. 'I had made up my mind to come back to Cornwall and be closer to Dad, so if Cornflower Cottage hadn't been available, I would have been somewhere else nearby. Porthgolow isn't the biggest place, and I think we would have ended up meeting, regardless.'

Ellie raised an eyebrow. 'You're certain of that, are you?'

A smile flickered on his lips. 'Pretty sure. The way you hover in my thoughts for most of every day leads me to believe that this was meant to happen.' He tucked a tendril of hair behind her ear. His touch sent sensation zinging through her.

'Jago.' She wanted this so much, and there was always catch-up TV.

He leaned towards her, and she felt his breath against her lips, her whole body tensed in anticipation of another kiss. Then the announcer cut through the moment: *And now, to a discovery in Cornwall that has delighted experts and proved to be a real cause for celebration. Here's Sandy Wishaw to tell us more about the extraordinary comeback.*

Jago put his hand on Ellie's knee and turned towards the TV. Ellie nudged up, closing the space between them as a beautiful female reporter in a peach dress appeared on the screen, the garden of Cornflower Cottage behind her in its early summer splendour.

'In this quiet corner of West Cornwall, gardeners working in this stunning cottage garden at the weekend made a surprising, and very welcome, discovery.' She beamed her mega-watt smile, giving viewers a moment for that to sink in.

'She's made the garden sound more impressive than it is,' Ellie murmured.

'It *is* that impressive,' Jago countered.

'It's been two years since the last-known bee orchid in Cornwall was unfortunately and accidentally destroyed,' Sandy continued, 'and local experts had little hope that this wild flower would grow again. One of the most well-known orchid varieties due to its distinctive, bee-mimicking appearance, but also a rare sight outside wildlife books and websites – especially here in Cornwall – it's one of the treasures of the botanical world. And we're very lucky to have Arthur Carne, the man who found it, here with us today.' The camera panned sideways, and there was Arthur in his smart blue shirt.

'Hello Sandy,' he said, giving her a warm smile.

'Arthur, lovely to have you with us. Can you tell us a little more about your discovery?'

He nodded sharply. 'Of course,' he said. 'But first, I must tell you how I ended up being here, because it's a key part of the story. I'm a resident at Seascape House Care Home, a stone's throw from here, and it's only recently that my son, Jago, moved into this cottage in an attempt to rebuild a relationship that has, sadly, been on rocky ground in recent years.'

'Rocky ground,' Jago whispered, shaking his head. Ellie put her hand on top of his, where it still rested on her knee.

Sandy managed to look thoughtful, interested and empathetic all at once: the skills of a television presenter.

Arthur continued. 'Through a complicated set of circumstances, I was invited to come and help out here. Gardening is a hobby of mine, and there isn't much opportunity for that at Seascape House, though I do believe they're planning on bringing in a landscaper next month, so all that could change.'

'Very diplomatic,' Ellie said. 'He hasn't mentioned them destroying his garden.'

'That must have been a welcome opportunity,' Sandy said. 'It's a beautiful garden.' The screen showed a slideshow of the garden: close-ups of a bee on a lupin, wide shots taken from the side gate, encompassing the hydrangeas at both sides, the established beds in the middle, the blue sky framing it. It looked so pretty in the sunshine, and Ellie felt a swell of pride.

'It was,' Arthur replied. 'I wasn't as grateful as I should have been, but that was the offer that led me here, and to the discovery of the orchid, in the meadow we've been trying to tame.'

'He called it the meadow!' Ellie said with delight, and Jago nudged her shoulder.

'Tell me about the moment you found it.' Sandy gave Arthur an encouraging smile before the shot cut to a close-up of the bee orchid in all its striking glory, the cameraman catching it in just the right light to make its vivid colours glow.

Arthur, back on the screen, smiled. 'I knew what it was as soon as I saw it, and to be honest, Sandy, my heart kicked harder than it has done for a long time. When you're my age, it's not always easy to find things to engage and interest you.' He paused, and Jago's hand tightened on Ellie's thigh. 'Since my wife, Hetty, died, my life has felt particularly flat. I was resigned to that; I've lived a long time, and have some very happy memories. I was set to live out my days at the care home, but then Ellie and Rose Moon intervened. Rose is my wonderful nurse, and Ellie's her sister, and the owner of this cottage. They've brought colour and warmth back into my life, and I'm very grateful for that.'

'That's amazing,' Sandy said. 'So, Arthur—'

'I'd like to add one more thing if I may,' he went on, cutting her off. She nodded, her smile faltering slightly. 'It has also allowed me to see my son again, to realize that I've been treating him unfairly. I've seen him through eyes that have been narrowed for far too long; I've aimed some of my grief, my guilt, at him, when he hasn't deserved it. He's a good man, and I'm proud of him for living his life as he sees fit. If it hadn't been for this,' he spread his arm wide, 'for this garden and the kindness of people – strangers and friends and, most of all, family – I doubt I would have woken up to it. I know this is about our discovery of the bee orchid, and I hope that brings your viewers some pleasure. But for me, it's about another kind of discovery. I've still got a long way to go with my son, but I feel hopeful that a reconciliation isn't quite as far-fetched as I thought it was.'

Beside her, Jago went completely still. Ellie felt as if her heart was too big for her chest, and she realized that this was what Arthur had been talking about earlier.

On the screen, Sandy squeezed Arthur's arm. 'Arthur, that's wonderful. Do you have any final words for our viewers?'

'Get outside,' he said without hesitation. 'The weather is beautiful, Cornwall is a superior county to most, and whether it's your garden or the local park, a beach or cliff-top walk, there are always new things to be uncovered. Get outside and enjoy it.'

Sandy allowed her perfectly pink lips to curve into a grin

as she turned back to the camera. 'So there we have it. The bee orchid is flourishing again in a remote corner of Cornwall, and the kindness of others allowed Arthur to be here to discover it. I think you'll all agree that it's the story we need right now, and as Arthur says, why not get outside this evening, see what wonders are out there waiting for you? I'll leave you with some final shots of the orchid, and of this beautiful outdoor space.' Images of bright flowers and greenery filled the screen once more, the bee orchid taking centre stage.

Ellie risked a glance at Jago. He was staring at the screen as if a ghost had materialized in front of it.

'Jago?' She lifted her hand off his, and rubbed small circles on his back.

He cleared his throat. 'Why did they let him witter on like that? It was supposed to be about the orchid.'

'It didn't look like Sandy had much choice: Arthur's a confident speaker when he gets going, and clearly, once they'd got it on tape, they wanted to include it in the item. Aren't you pleased he said those things?'

'But on *TV*?'

'Maybe it was easier for him to say it to someone else the first time? And he knew you'd see it.'

Jago turned towards her, the weather map covered in yellow suns fading into the background as she saw how shocked he was.

'He said he was proud of me.'

Ellie swallowed past the lump in her throat. 'He did. He is. I know he's not the best at showing it, but—'

'I have waited *years* for that. Fuck.' He laughed and ran a hand through his hair, leaving it deliciously dishevelled.

'And if he'd said it to you directly, would you have believed it?' she asked tentatively. 'Or would you have questioned it?'

He shrugged. 'I don't know.'

'I think you should call him.'

He shook his head. 'This is our night.'

'Call him,' Ellie said again. 'Arrange to meet up with him. It's important, Jago. He's holding out an olive branch.'

He laughed again. 'It's more like he's hit me on the head with a whole tree. OK. I'll call him.' He tapped his palms against his knees and got up. At the door, he turned back. 'Go outside again, if you want? I'll be ten minutes, maximum.'

She nodded and smiled and, when she was alone, hugged a drowsy Lord Montague to her. He protested lazily, his yowl 50 per cent yawn. 'Oh, Monty, can you believe it? Arthur and Jago might work it out, after all. Maybe the bee orchid has magical powers?' The cat looked up at her with disdain, and Ellie patted him on the head and let him be. She didn't want to risk another scratch; she didn't think she'd need an excuse to get close to Jago tonight.

The garden was a couple of degrees cooler, the sun making its way over the front of the house towards the sea, intensifying in colour as it went. Ellie sipped her champagne and enjoyed the calm; the trilling of a warbler and the pip pip pip of a wren as it busied about in the bushes. She wondered whether to go and look at the orchid, but felt that, somehow, she should leave it to enjoy the evening peacefully, just as she was.

'I'm so sorry about that,' Jago said, appearing and refilling both their glasses. It could have been her imagination, but she thought he seemed lighter, as if a weight had been lifted off his shoulders.

'Do we have something else to toast?' she asked.

'I think we do. I'm seeing Dad the day after tomorrow. He's coming here, as usual, but then I'm taking him for a meal: I don't know where yet.'

'I'm so happy for you, Jago.' She was desperate to ask more, but she was trying very hard to learn her lesson. It was up to Jago how much he shared.

'I'm relieved, more than anything. So let's toast the bastard bee orchid after all,' he said with a laugh. 'It seems to have worked some kind of miracle.'

Ellie held her glass aloft. 'To the bee orchid! May it flourish in Cornwall for ever, and inspire a thousand other miracles along the way.'

'The bee orchid,' Jago echoed. They both drank, and then he said, 'Right. Food. Sit there.'

'Yessir,' Ellie replied, laughing at his command.

He returned carrying steaming bowls of tagliatelle that smelled creamy and peppery, and had her mouth watering instantly.

'It's salmon and asparagus in a cream sauce,' Jago said, sitting opposite her. 'I had the ingredients to make enough for two.'

'It smells amazing.' She twirled some pasta on her fork, and when she popped it in her mouth, the flavours and textures exploded on her tongue, creamy and rich, everything harmonizing. 'It's delicious,' she said. 'Really good. Wow, Jago.'

He laughed. 'You don't have to big it up.'

'I'm not. It's perfect. This is a perfect night.'

He raised an eyebrow. 'You might be throwing the word "perfect" around a bit too casually, there.'

'Nope. I really mean it.'

They ate and talked while the sun slipped out of sight and the sky darkened from azure to navy, and the stars shone as if they'd been polished. As the darkness fell over Ellie, so did a feeling of utter contentment, combined with a low bubble of anticipation like the base notes of some exotic perfume. Jago's harsh words seemed a distant memory, his forgiveness of her so complete that she felt refreshed; all her guilt and worry wiped clean. The outside light flicked on, and she was startled by how dark the world had grown around them.

'Shall we go inside?' Jago asked.

'Sure.'

Together, they cleared the plates and put them in the dishwasher, moving around each other with an easy intimacy. 'Dinner was wonderful,' she said again, when the silence felt too heavy.

'It was pretty great, even if I do say so myself.'

'Loving your modesty, Jago.'

'People are too modest,' he said. 'Nobody celebrates their own achievements; they wait for other people to do it, and then they act all humble and self-deprecating, dismissing the part they played. Then, after a while, they start to believe their own lack of importance, and it leads to a culture of nobody ever feeling good enough. For example.' He hung up the tea towel and turned to face her. 'Would you say you're a good kisser?'

She flushed. 'I don't—'

'There you go, you see. You're already deflecting.

Whereas I know you're a *very* good kisser, and I'm a good kisser, too. And together, I seem to remember we were phenomenal.'

'We were, were we?'

He hesitated, his breath catching in a way that Ellie found incredibly sexy. 'I *think* so, anyway. But I could do with a reminder. Earlier wasn't nearly long enough for me to be sure.' He stepped towards her, and before Ellie had a chance to speak or think or laugh, she was in his arms, feeling his strong, solid weight against her, and he was kissing her with more purpose than he'd done even on Saturday, when everything had been hot and frantic. This was more measured, but no less intense. A second of surprise, and then she was kissing him back, threading her fingers through his unkempt hair, melting against him.

'See?' he murmured, when he finally broke away. 'Phenomenal. It makes me wonder what else we'd be good at together. In fact, I've been wondering about it a lot recently.'

This time, Ellie didn't flush. She simply smiled and took his hand, pressed a kiss to the side of his mouth and then said, 'Let's see, shall we?'

Jago grinned his easy grin, his chest rising and falling as rapidly as hers was. 'Lead the way.'

Ellie led him out of the kitchen and up the stairs, then into the bedroom where, with the curtains open, moonlight fell across the bed in a bold white swathe. Jago traced the line of her jaw, slid his fingers to her neck and tipped her head up to meet his again, this kiss slower and deeper, vibrating through her in waves of sensation. As she slipped his T-shirt over his head, and he began working on the buttons of her blouse, laughing when his watch strap snagged on a button hole, she realized this wasn't just contentment. It wasn't just lust or desire, or answering a need for the intimacy she'd been missing.

Being with Jago like this, holding nothing back: it felt like coming home.

Chapter Twenty-Two

Despite all her self-directed pep talks, Ellie discovered it was much easier to be enthusiastic about making Charlie and Daniel's special day perfect when she was on cloud nine herself.

She didn't doubt that she would have done a good job even if things hadn't worked out with Jago, but since they had worked out, *were* working out really rather spectacularly well, she was fully engaged in all things romance-related.

It was, she considered, like trying to be 100 per cent committed to running a Santa grotto while knowing that he didn't exist, and that the guy you'd hired to play him had been out the back smoking a cigarette and swearing on the phone minutes before he'd put on the red suit. It was as if Ellie had taken a trip to the North Pole and discovered that Santa actually *was* hiding out there, with his elves making toys, letters from children piling up on the doormat, and no naughty-or-nice list because she'd always found that idea cruel when children were still learning how to be human beings.

Or maybe it was simply the glow of being in a new relationship, the way everything seemed covered in a layer of gold just like the sea had been in recent days.

Jago was as much fun under the sheets as he was out of them, though, to her delight and constant pleasure, she was discovering he wasn't always as laid-back. She had forgotten what it was like to be with someone she truly cared about; the difference between that and something purely physical was night and day, and Ellie was caught in a sunrise that never seemed to dim.

As Charlie and Daniel's wedding got closer, Ellie became a wedding-planning machine, ticking things off her to-do list with easy efficiency. Far from being distracted by Jago, Ellie thought her evenings and nights with him, her mornings sitting on the patio at Cornflower Cottage, sharing croissants and coffee and conversation in that ethereal, early light, had supercharged her.

The barn was looking beautiful, and the courtyard was transformed, with the vibrancy of all the new flowers and shrubs giving it a softer, summer edge, and perfectly complementing the rustic building. Whenever she went there – to adorn the inside with strings of lights; to put up the signs that would direct guests to the right entrance; to double-check something in the kitchen for Hannah – she found Arthur there, too. Sometimes he was having coffee with Pauline in the garden, sometimes he was feeding Millicent, talking to her like a beloved pet. He'd explained to Ellie, somewhat sheepishly she thought, that he had experience with pigs because of his parents' farm. And Millicent had clearly taken a liking to him, displaying none of the skittishness she'd shown on Ellie's earlier visits, often eating out of the palm of his hand.

And Ellie knew, mostly from Jago, that father and son were slowly growing closer. He told her about their lunches, and the time they spent in the garden of Cornflower Cottage, still working on the meadow, while Ellie tactfully excused herself. Sometimes Jago was frustrated and reluctant to share what they'd discussed, but most of the time he told her everything. The tension was easing between them, the taut springs slackening. It was a work in progress, but it was heading in the right direction.

So was everything for Charlie and Daniel's big day. Daniel's photo album was finished, bar the captions, which Charlie was adding in quiet moments when Daniel was busy at the hotel; the celebrant, Mary, would be visiting the barn the day before to make sure there were no surprises; Gertie was back in Pete's garage getting her wedding makeover; Hannah was on top of the catering; Lila had ensured Ellie that Sam had his speech prepared, and Hugh, the landlord of the Seven Stars, was bringing his band, the Cornwall Cornflowers, to do a set before the music moved to a prepared playlist.

Charlie would be driving up to Cheltenham to see her parents a couple of days before the wedding, then they would all travel back – dress included – on the Friday. In fact, the only thing that was giving Ellie any concern was the sun. It was a little on the oppressive side, but she hoped they would get a rain shower before the big day, to clear the air and lift some of the humidity.

In the week leading up to the wedding Ellie's to-do list got shorter, until she was left with only *Meet The Celebrant* and *Check everything is working* on her main list. Of course, there was a special wedding-day to-do list that was entirely separate, but those items couldn't be crossed off until the day itself.

While she had been counting down, the weather had been building up to something, and by Friday lunchtime the heat was so oppressive, the colour leached from the sun to leave it more white than yellow, that Ellie couldn't help feeling slightly dispirited.

'Everything's suffering,' Arthur called from the dahlia bed of Cornflower Cottage, where the flowers were almost ready to unfurl and produce the botanical equivalent of a firework display. Ellie had been looking forward to them blooming, the crimson, yellow and candy-pink buds like juicy boiled sweets.

'Everything?' she echoed, but she knew it was true. The garden was still colourful, but it had a limpness to it, too. She gave everything a thorough water in the evenings when she was here, and Jago had been doing the same when she was in St Eval, but no amount of careful watering could prevent the heat taking its toll. 'What about the dahlias?' She walked over to where he was crouched, in an olive-green T-shirt and navy shorts, as casual as she'd ever seen him. 'They look OK.'

Arthur nodded. 'They're doing better than the oxeye daisies. The marigolds are faring well, because they're partly in the shade of the hydrangeas, but as for the beds in the middle?' He shook his head. 'We just have to hope that the weather breaks, and does it gently.'

Ellie sighed. 'That might be a hope too far.' She turned in a slow circle, pushing her hair away from her forehead. 'Muggy is not the word. Anyway, I'm off to the barn now.'

'Oh?' Ellie hid her smile at the interest in his voice.

'Last-minute checks,' she explained. 'I'll tell Pauline you said hello.'

'That's fine, I . . .'

'What is it, Arthur?'

'I'm going over there later. Just to, uh . . .' He cleared his throat. 'I hope everything's as it should be. For the wedding, I mean.'

Ellie grinned. 'Me too, Arthur. Me too.' She slipped out of the side gate and set off down the hill.

It was strange to think that, in thirty-six hours' time, Charlie and Daniel's wedding would be drawing to a close. Months of planning, juggling and organizing would be over. For the happy couple it was the start of their new chapter, but for her it was the pressing of the reset button. New couples with their own fantasies, different occasions to schedule and plan.

She remembered the days of going home to Mark after a wedding, and how, towards the end of their marriage, he would barely look up from his documentary or book, forgetting to ask her how it had gone. She didn't think she would feel deflated this time. It was still early days, of course, and she had loved Mark once. But with Jago, it all felt so different.

The sea ahead of her was a deep, flat blue, its surface

like slate, and the sky above it was startlingly pale. Ellie wondered if the darker smudge to the north was cloud or a heat haze, a mirage tricking her eyes. She felt a slight prickle of disquiet. It was the humidity, she thought, the way the air hung low and heavy. The weather had a strong effect on everyone's moods, especially in Cornwall, where it was so much a part of the landscape and the lifestyle.

But the courtyard was sparkling, the cobbles clean and bright, the old-fashioned wagon filled with hay and strewn with trails of daisies, pansies and cornflowers that had come in a second delivery of cut flowers yesterday, the hanging baskets they'd planted fully bedded in and bursting with colour. Ellie's heart lifted: it looked magical.

Jane and Pauline came out to greet her, their faces beaming.

'What do you think?' Jane asked.

'It's magnificent,' Ellie said. 'Truly. There's space for Gertie, so she can be parked side-on and shown off in her full glory, and I love the wagon and the bunting.' The pastel pennants, which perfectly matched the wedding colours, ran the length of the barn, but Ellie hadn't bought them. 'This is everything Charlie and Daniel wanted.' Relief, happiness and gratitude flooded her chest. Their venue had started out being less than ideal, but now, with the dedication and hard work of the mother-and-daughter team, aided by Ellie and Arthur, it had exceeded her expectations. 'Do we have time to do a quick recce before the celebrant arrives?'

Ellie and Jane ran through the checks together. Everything was working seamlessly, the lights and sound system, the mics and the glitter ball. The room was arranged in theatre-style, ready for the ceremony, with tables waiting at the back for the switch to cabaret-style while photos were taken and champagne served outside, before the reception got going.

Ellie watched a car drive into the car park, Mary the celebrant behind the wheel, and let her last doubts flitter away like a butterfly. Everything was exactly as it should be.

She walked back up to Cornflower Cottage hot but satisfied, her pre-big-day to-do list cleared, her wedding-day list set to open on her iPad at the press of a finger. This evening she could relax with Jago, who had insisted she stay the night, so she was only minutes away from the venue in the morning. When she'd asked if it was only her business he was concerned about, he'd admitted there were some selfish reasons for wanting her there, too.

She found Lord Montague sitting on the stoop, keeping a watchful eye on the sea. Ellie turned to see what he was seeing, and gave a little start at the quality of the light. It was yellowish, the sky no longer white but grey, pale cloud above her but, out towards the horizon, darker and altogether more threatening. The sea had gone from deep blue to sullen green.

'Fucking hell,' she murmured, wishing she hadn't prayed quite so hard for rain to clear the air. This looked as though it was going to be a whopper. She hoped it came soon and cleared quickly. Nobody wanted to get married in a downpour.

She went inside, searching through the downstairs of the house until she found Jago sitting on the patio, wearing nothing but a pair of faded khaki shorts, a beer bottle resting on his knee. He turned at her voice, then stood up to greet her. His hair was damp, his skin shiny, and a bolt of lust went through her.

'Hey.' He kissed her. 'You look worn out.'

'I'm fine,' she said. 'Everything's set at the barn. It's just very, *very* hot.'

'Go and have a shower; you'll feel a hundred times better.'

'Is that where you've just been?' She ran a finger down his chest, and his gaze intensified. 'How was your day?'

'Gertie's ready,' he said. He had gone back to help Pete with the makeover, Pete deciding that, as he'd worked so hard on fixing her, he should also get the fun of dolling her up. 'She's going to shine tomorrow. Pete said he's picking Charlie and her folks up from her house, then bringing them to the barn?'

'That's right.' Ellie kept up the gentle caresses on his skin. 'Charlie's coming in the bus – she'll be back from Cheltenham with her parents sometime today – and Daniel's arriving in a vintage E-type.'

Jago raised an eyebrow. 'Nice.'

'What is? The car, or this?' she increased her pressure, hiding her smile in his neck when he wrapped an arm around her waist and pulled her against him.

'Let's get you in the shower,' he said, lifting her off the ground.

Ellie laughed. 'I thought you just had one?'

'I did, but I'm already too hot again, so it's probably best if I take another one. Besides, you've been working hard and tomorrow's going to be crazy, so I'm going to treat you to a relaxing evening.'

'Sounds great,' she whispered, kissing his earlobe.

Jago carried her up the stairs and into the bedroom, whistling as he went.

It was much later, when they were lying in bed, the window open wide on the darkness, the curtains pulled back to allow as much air in as possible, when the first raindrops began.

'How are you feeling about tomorrow?' Jago asked. She heard him turn and did the same, so they were facing each other, heads on pillows, eyes gleaming in the light from the digital alarm clock.

'I'm feeling good,' Ellie said. As if in answer, the rain picked up pace, the sound staccato as it hit the open window. 'And as long as this doesn't go on too long, we'll have a beautiful, fresh day.'

Jago shifted closer. He found her hand and took it. 'I can't wait to hear how it goes.'

'Charlie said you're welcome at the reception. Didn't I say that to you, the other day?'

'You did, but—'

'You worked so hard on Gertie,' Ellie cut in. 'They really want you there.'

'It doesn't feel like my place. Behind-the-scenes guys don't usually get an invite, and I was never expecting one.'

'I know that, but your invite is official, and I'd love to have you there. But if you don't feel comfortable, I'll see if I can bring you back a piece of cake.'

'Cake would be nice.'

'Good.'

'I would love to see you at work though,' he said. 'I bet you're sexy as hell when you're bossing people around.'

Ellie laughed. 'I don't boss people around. I just make sure everything goes to plan. With this one, I don't think there's going to be too much to worry about. As long as Millicent behaves herself, it should all be fine.'

Jago kissed her. 'I'd love to see you bossing that huge pig around.'

'Do you have any idea how weird that sounds?' Ellie asked. 'Is this some kind of fetish that you've kept hidden from me until now?'

'Hmmm?' His kisses trailed lower, and Ellie shivered.

'I need to get a good night's sleep, so I can be fresh as a daisy in the morning. Jago . . .' she gasped as his kisses went further south.

'You're always fresh as a daisy,' he murmured. 'Besides, this is exactly what you need to help you get a good night's sleep.'

'Jago Carne, you are insatiable.' Ellie closed her eyes and gave herself up to his touch, forgetting everything else, ignoring the sound of rain against the glass.

It wasn't until they were both asleep, breathing in sync, Jago's arm across Ellie's waist and her head nestled into the crook of his neck, that the pattering of raindrops turned to a torrent, and the sudden brisk wind carried the sounds of the crashing surf all the way up the hill, so that, if either of them had been awake, they would have realized that the heat wave had definitely broken, and in a rather more impressive fashion than Ellie would have liked.

Chapter Twenty-Three

She woke before the alarm clock. She wondered if she'd ever been fully asleep, because she was wide awake in seconds, hopping out of bed while Jago slumbered on. The sun was slipping in through the windows, but Ellie could sense the freshness, and knew that the cloak of humidity that had dogged them for days was gone. *Perfect*, she thought, and tiptoed to the window to look out. Her smile slipped.

The day was bright, the colours bold, the glossy greens, pinks and yellows of the rose bushes shining up at her. But that shine was enhanced by puddles. Her gravel driveway was half underwater. The distant sea was a churning mass of blue-grey, swelling and moving like a giant sea monster, the way it always looked when its natural flow had been disturbed by an influx of rainwater.

Maybe Ellie had been fully asleep, after all. She certainly hadn't heard a downpour and, judging by the size of the puddles, it must have gone on long and hard. She thought of delicate satin wedding shoes, long hemlines of fine, pale fabric, and her stomach clenched.

But there was time for it to burn off. The wedding wasn't until midday, the sky was already a clear blue, the storm clouds having moved on as swiftly as they'd arrived. It would all be fine.

She padded downstairs to put the coffee machine on, and went to check her phone. It wasn't unusual to have early messages from members of the wedding party, fretting or asking last-minute questions or simply checking it was all still going ahead. The coffee machine was gurgling when her phone, lying on the kitchen counter to charge, rang. She saw the name *Jane Porthgolow Barn* appear and, smiling, answered it.

'Hello,' she said. 'Happy big day!'

'Oh Ellie, thank god!' Jane sounded frantic, and the hairs stood up on Ellie's neck.

'What is it?' She kept her voice calm. She had to be the rock on her wedding days. No matter how many people ebbed and flowed, churned and harried around her, she would not get flustered.

'Ellie, it's . . . uh.' Jane choked out a sob, and Ellie leaned against the counter and counted to three.

'Just tell me,' she said gently. 'Whatever it is, we can work it out together.'

'I don't think we can,' Jane said in a rush. 'I really, *really* don't think we can. The barn's flooded. Not just the courtyard and the garden – which is like a mire – but the actual barn. I don't know how the water got in, but there's *so much of it*, Ellie. There's no way it's going to be dry by midday. Charlie and Daniel will be getting married in a lake.' Her voice cracked.

Ellie rubbed her forehead. 'Give me ten minutes, and I'll be there. We'll sort this out, Jane. Don't worry.'

'O-OK,' she stammered.

'Go and make yourself a hot drink, take some deep breaths, and I'll see you very soon.' Ellie said goodbye, and made herself wait until the coffee had filtered through so she could take a cup to Jago. She stayed calm because she had to. If she started flapping, everything would be lost.

Jago was awake, pulling himself up to lean against the pillows. He stopped when he saw her face. 'What's wrong?'

Ellie put his coffee on the bedside table, planted a kiss on his lips and took off the oversized T-shirt she'd been wearing, then pulled on her bra, and her skirt and T-shirt from the day before. 'Jane says the barn's completely flooded; that it's unusable.'

'*What? Fuck!* Ellie, what are you going to do?'

'I'm going to go and see how bad it is.'

'Do you want me to come?'

She shook her head. 'I'll only be half an hour, depending on what . . . happens. I'll be back for coffee in a bit.'

'You think it's going to be OK?'

She nodded tightly. 'It has to be.' She kissed him again, slipped on her sandals and hurried downstairs. She wouldn't allow herself to worry until she saw it, she told herself as she slipped out of the door and set off down the hill. Rain-spattered foliage glistened in the renewed sunshine, and while the road was still damp, it was a beautiful day. Ellie had coped with disasters before. This was just another one for her to deal with and tick off her list.

She turned onto the track that led from Wilderness Lane to Porthgolow Barn, and found that the further she walked, the muddier it became. Soon, her toes, exposed in her sandals, were sinking into the mud along with her hopes. She stepped onto the courtyard, and tried very hard not to wail.

It had none of the previous day's splendour. The rain had battered the hanging baskets, the perky flowers either flattened or dislodged completely, strewn over a floor that was unrecognizable as cobbles. It was a sea of mud, water and daisies, the puddles much more impressive than at Cornflower Cottage, where Ellie had ensured there were irrigation routes beneath the gravel. The bunting had become partly unsecured, and was hanging down, water-logged and forlorn, almost to the floor.

Jane appeared, dressed in wellies and a tatty jumper. She was wringing her hands.

'Jane,' Ellie said, and silently cursed the way her voice scratched out.

'This isn't even the worst of it,' Jane said, striding through the mud and detritus to the doors. Ellie followed, and when Jane flung them open, she was treated to a view of the barn's interior. The floral garlands and bottles filled with fairy lights, the shimmering glitter ball, all looked down on what could only be described as a swamp. It wasn't just that the floor was covered in water, but that the water also came with a generous dose of mixed-in soil. At the moment, the only person this place was fit for was Millicent.

'Oh, God,' Ellie said, unable to help it.

'I know!' Jane's voice was anguished. 'I should have sorted out the flood-proofing *before* Charlie and Daniel's wedding. I've got someone coming to look at it next week! *Next week!* I had no idea that it could get this bad. Ellie.' She turned towards her. 'I am so, *so* sorry.'

'But you'll have it fixed for next time,' Ellie heard herself say. 'At least this is only going to be a one-time thing, so while it isn't ideal for today, it's not going to ruin your venue for the future, and—'

'That's not going to help Charlie and Daniel, is it?'

Ellie let her shoulders drop. 'No,' she said, 'no, it's not.'

'So what's the answer?' Jane asked, and Ellie could see she was hanging on to her every word, that now was the time for her to step up and work a miracle. Troubleshooting was one of her main roles as a wedding planner, and this particular problem was a big one.

'I need ten minutes to think,' she said. 'I'm sure a solution will present itself.'

Jane nodded. 'But we can't have it here, can we? The wedding?'

Ellie looked again at the mud settling on the wooden floor, thought of the hours it would take a large team of people to clean it up, and felt herself go cold as shock gave way to undiluted panic. 'No,' she admitted. 'Charlie and Daniel can't get married here.'

Ellie strode back up the hill, her thoughts and her stomach churning, her hands clenched at her sides. This was a complete disaster. She pictured telling Charlie and Daniel, who would be waking up early, giddy with excitement and anticipation, looking out at the clear blue sky and thinking that nothing could go wrong. She couldn't do it: not yet. Not until she had a new plan.

She walked back along Cornflower Cottage's driveway, and noticed that the puddles were smaller than they had been first thing, the sun and sea breeze doing their job. It would take a lot more than that to clear up the barn, however. She pushed open the front door and, on autopilot, refilled the coffee machine. While it bubbled to life, she leant against the counter and stared, unseeing, out of the window.

Footsteps sounded on the stairs and then Jago was standing there, appraising her.

'Ellie?' he asked softly. 'How was it? What's happening?'

'The barn is a mud pit,' she said, turning to him and, under his steady gaze, allowing herself a moment of vulnerability. 'It's not going to be ready in time for the wedding, even if we get a whole team of volunteers to muck it out. It's . . .' She took a deep breath and looked away, but he put his arms around her, drawing her against him.

'Everything's going to be OK,' he said into her hair. 'You're brilliant at this, and there has to be some way round it. Some way of fixing the barn or moving the wedding; something to make this day happen.'

Ellie settled into his embrace, her head turned towards the window. 'But how?' she murmured. She watched as a robin danced purposefully along the grass and then, with a flutter of wings, landed on top of one of the patio chairs. The large flagstones were already partly dry, and she thought how ironic it was that her garden, only a short way up the hill from the barn, should be so much less waterlogged. Even though she loved this place more than anywhere else in the world, for today she would happily see their positions reversed. The robin let out a burst of song, and Ellie went still as a ludicrous idea popped into her head.

'You've thought of something,' Jago said, pulling back so

he could look at her. How could he already know her so well?

'It's ridiculous,' she replied. 'And a huge imposition. It's not . . . I can't—'

'Just tell me. If you haven't discarded it immediately, then it's worth hearing. What is it?'

She looked up at him and wondered if, despite their blossoming relationship, this was a step too far.

'We could have it here,' she said. 'In the back garden. We could bring some of the chairs and tables from the barn up the hill, clean them down. There's room for Gertie in the driveway, and there's the side gate so people wouldn't need to come through the house. The patio's big enough, and we could decorate the back of the house with some of the garlands and lights from the barn. It wouldn't be ideal, but—'

'It's a brilliant idea,' Jago said, and though his voice was soft, she saw the spark in his green eyes.

'Really? This is your cottage, and—'

'It's become more than that, though. And you know, now I've got used to it, that I couldn't be happier about what I've gained: it's brought me you *and* Dad. And if it saves Charlie and Daniel's wedding, then I'm all for adding one more good deed to the pot, and I'll do anything I can to help. *Anything*, Ellie.'

'Really?' Her heart was pounding again, but this time with excitement. 'Are you completely sure?'

He kissed her lips. 'Completely. Tell the happy couple, and then set me to work. Chair-carrier, patio-cleaner, general dogsbody – whatever you need. I'm here for you, and for them.'

She grinned and took her phone out into the garden. Her heart was beating double-time because of Jago's faith in her, and because she might just have come up with a solution that could, if she was really *really* lucky, and really clever about it, save Charlie and Daniel's wedding day.

Ellie tapped her foot nervously on the flagstone while Charlie's phone rang and rang and rang and, eventually, picked up.

'Hello?' Charlie's voice was shrill, and for a second Ellie thought that somehow she already knew. 'Ellie?'

'Charlie! Happy Wedding Day! Are you . . . is everything OK?'

There was a long pause, and then she said, 'No.' Except it came out more as a groan.

A chill ran down Ellie's spine. 'What is it? What's happened?'

'My car's broken down! It's really old and I think with all the rain, the storm, it's just . . . the electrical system just – it just went! I should have taken Daniel's BMW, but—'

'How far away are you?' Ellie cut in. 'I thought you were coming back yesterday?'

'We were driving down yesterday afternoon but the rain was so bad, and my car started making this funny noise, so Dad suggested we stop in Exeter overnight, get up early this morning to finish the journey. It was all going fine, but now . . .' She gasped in a breath. 'We're just outside Bodmin. I've called the AA, but they're so busy because of the storm.'

Ellie raised her eyes to the sky, then glanced at her watch. 'That's OK, we can come and get you.'

'You *can*? Who? Is . . . is everything OK there?'

It was Ellie's turn to sigh. 'The weather has also affected the barn,' she said carefully. 'I'm afraid that it's flooded.' Charlie listened in silence while Ellie explained what had happened, and what her plan was.

'In your garden?' Charlie said, her voice fraying at the edge.

'It's big enough for your guests, and I promise you I can make it look beautiful. I've checked with Hannah; she says there's no problem getting the food here, and everything else we can work round. It will mean some compromise, but not on the important things. If you're happy to go ahead, then I'll get it all sorted out, and I'll arrange for someone to come and pick you up. I just need your say-so.'

'You're sure about this?' Charlie asked. 'Your tenant is OK with us having it there?'

'Charlie,' Ellie said firmly, 'listen to me. Everything you wanted, *almost* everything, can happen at Cornflower Cottage. Are you happy for me to move the wedding? If so, then just make sure you, your mum and dad and the dress are all as safe and dry as possible. Get somewhere warm if you can. I'll phone you back as soon as I've sorted out your transport.'

'Yes, then,' she said quickly and then, much more clearly, 'Yes. Go for it, Ellie. Are you going to call Daniel?'

'He's next on my list. But I think I'll leave out the part that you're stranded. For now, anyway.'

'That's a good decision,' Charlie said, and for the first time that morning Ellie heard amusement in her voice. 'He'd come tearing up here in his BMW and . . . well, I really think that would be tempting fate.'

'Right. Leave it all to me. Stay safe, Charlie.'

She hung up, wondering how on earth she was supposed to move their wedding *and* rescue the stranded bride and her parents from the wilds of Bodmin Moor, and made the next important phone call.

Daniel was more laid-back than she thought he'd be – with the information she'd chosen to share, at least – but she understood when he said, 'I just want to marry Charlie today. I trust you to make it the day she wants.'

'And you,' she reminded him. 'You're just as important.'

He laughed. 'As long as she's there and she says "I do", I will be ecstatic.'

Ellie winced, but she assured him that there were no issues on that score.

'What about the fireworks?' she asked. Daniel had told her that he wanted fireworks, that they were symbolic for him and Charlie, but that he would arrange them himself. There was a professional company he'd used often enough, and who he trusted to run the display.

'I'll check with my guys,' he said, 'see if they can find somewhere on the barn site that's dry enough. I'm sure they can – they've worked in all sorts of conditions. We'll still see them from your place, won't we?'

'The barn's a little further down the hill,' Ellie explained. 'They'll appear over the sea, so it will probably look even better.'

'Great,' Daniel said. 'Everything's sorted, then. Nothing to worry about.'

She didn't entirely agree, so she simply said, 'Wonderful. See you later, Daniel.'

Her next call was to Jane, to explain their plan and how they could still use her and Pauline's help.

'You can use the chairs and tables?' Jane asked quietly.

'And we can decorate the outside of the cottage with the flower garlands and lights.'

'Mum and I will start getting them ready,' Jane told her, and Ellie smiled, pleased by her switch from forlorn to professional.

Ellie let Sam know the change of plan so he could tell the guests that they would need to come further up the hill, then she phoned Mary and the cake-maker, and the man who was bringing Daniel in the E-type. While she did that, she could hear Jago in the garden, clearing the furniture off the patio and taking a broom to it. She went out to join him.

'All going OK?' he asked, looking up.

Ellie had to laugh. 'Charlie and her parents are stranded near Bodmin.'

His mouth fell open. '*What?*'

'It's not just the barn that's been affected by this blasted storm. I need to arrange someone to go and get them, but there's not much time.'

Jago worried a hand through his hair. 'You could drive Gertie up to get her; that way you wouldn't have to detour back via Newquay, you could just come straight here.'

Ellie nodded. 'OK. But who? Pete's due to be driving the bus from his garage to Porthgolow just before noon, but he's on another job until then, and I don't want him to have to cancel for us.'

'I can do it,' Jago said.

'You can drive a bus?'

He shrugged. 'When you're a mechanic, it helps if you can drive all sorts of vehicles, otherwise you're limiting the jobs you can do.'

'You could get Charlie for me?' she asked. 'You'd need to pick up Lila and Juliette on the way.'

Jago shook his head. 'We have to go together. I'm going to be driving, and I don't know Charlie – I've only met her once – and if she's panicked or flustered, which would be understandable considering all that's happened, then I'll be no use at all.'

'Lila and Juliette will help calm Charlie down,' Ellie said, and then thought of how Lila was good at picking up on any kind of drama and running with it. But surely on Charlie's wedding day, and in her maid-of-honour role, she'd be the voice of reason?

Jago put his broom down and came to stand in front of her. 'You'll chew your whole lip off if you're not careful,' he said softly. 'You need to come with me. We can take Lila and Juliette, pick Charlie up and get her here in time for the wedding. Your main duty is to the bride and groom, and the bride is currently miles from her own wedding, probably distraught, and needs you there to make everything OK.'

Ellie's laugh sounded unhinged. 'What about all this?' She gestured at her garden, which was looking very beautiful but nothing at all like a wedding venue.

'Phone Jane and Pauline,' Jago said. 'I'm sure Dad would help, too, and he might be able to bring some of the other residents from Seascape with him. Mo, even. Also,' he added, his smile widening, 'you know someone who would have no trouble organizing this entire place, while you and I go and rescue Charlie.'

'Ah, yes,' Ellie said. 'I think I do.'

Rose answered the phone immediately.

'What's up, buttercup?'

'Porthgolow Barn is flooded and we're holding the wedding at Cornflower Cottage, and Jago and I need to go and get Charlie, because she's stranded near Bodmin with her parents and her dress.'

There was a moment of silence in which Ellie thought she might faint, waiting for her sister to tell her she was mad, or to laugh and ask for another joke. Instead, she said, 'Guests will need to park at the care home, because there isn't enough space in your driveway, so I'll talk to Mo. If you and Jago are picking up Charlie, who's organizing the garden?'

Ellie blinked, taken aback by her sister's response. 'I was wondering if you could? Hannah, the caterer, should be arriving soon, and she's bringing her boyfriend Noah. And Sam, the best man, could help too. Jago suggested Arthur, and there's Jane and Pauline at the barn, so—'

'A veritable army of helpers,' Rose said, sounding amused rather than stressed. 'It should take us no time at all.'

'Are you sure about this, Rose?'

'Of course! I could hardly desert you in your hour of need. I'll get on it right away. Oh, and Ellie? Whose idea was it to have it there? Yours or Jago's?'

'Mine,' Ellie admitted. 'But he had so much faith in me, and—'

'Oh, my God,' Rose cut in. 'This day is going to be awash with sentimentality as it is. Don't start now or we'll all be in floods before the ceremony. Get going, do what you have to do, and I'll rally the troops.' She hung up, leaving Ellie staring dumbfounded at her phone, until she remembered she had so much still to do, and hardly any time in which to do it.

It was time to swing into action.

As Ellie and Jago were preparing to leave, the pretty but unassuming cottage became a hub of activity. A procession of vans turned up in the driveway: Jane and Pauline bringing chairs, tables and decorations; Hannah arriving in a catering van; Ellie's favourite cake supplier, Lizzie Wilton, bringing the three-tiered lemon cake that Charlie and Daniel had decided on after numerous tastings.

Arthur, Mo and Iris, along with a couple of other Seascape House residents, appeared with Rose, and she led them through to the garden, setting them to work on the garlands and Mo to work on the grass. Ellie had time to be surprised that the usually managerial Mo got stuck in straight away, rolling up his sleeves and wheeling Ellie's compact lawn-mower around the lawns surrounding the flower beds.

Hannah brought trays of canapés through to the kitchen, her manner breezy and unflappable, wearing a gauzy, pale blue dress under her apron. Hugh from the Seven Stars was with her, and so was Noah.

'We've borrowed one of the trucks that's usually part of Charlie's food market,' Hannah said, 'so we can cook the hot food – the portions of fish and chips and the mini burgers – in that, rather than try and cater for everyone using your oven.'

'You're a marvel,' Ellie replied. 'Completely unfazed by such a huge change of plan.'

Noah walked to the back step and looked out. 'Your garden is incredible,' he said, turning back to her, his blue eyes wide. 'If I'd been given the choice of getting married here or in the barn, I would have picked this place.'

Ellie laughed. 'This is a one-off. I may be a wedding planner, but this isn't usually a wedding venue.'

Noah shrugged. 'It could be though.' His eyes slid to where Hannah was intent on her iPad screen, and Ellie wondered if the young chef might be getting her own proposal in the not too distant future.

'Let's take it one wedding at a time,' Ellie said. 'We have no idea how this will work out.'

'It's looking pretty good so far.' Noah pushed his glasses up his nose, then went back out to the van.

Ellie felt a hand on her shoulder.

'We should get going,' Jago said.

She took one final look at the garden, and the worry must have shown on her face because Rose glanced up from where she was unstacking chairs, caught her eye and gave her a double thumbs-up, followed by a shooing motion.

For once, Ellie was going to have to do exactly what she'd always feared, and leave the wedding-day arrangements up to other people. Jago was right, her main duty was to Charlie and Daniel, and Charlie was the one who needed her. She would have to let go, trust in her friends and family, and focus on what was most important. She had to rescue her bride.

Chapter Twenty-Four

Jago drove to Pete's garage in Newquay, which gave Ellie the opportunity to look out of the window, at the coastal landscape washed clean by the previous night's storm, the sun new and sparkling, the water a blistering blue. It was stunning, Cornwall at its best, and despite all that had happened, all the challenges they still had ahead of them, she was glad it was a beautiful day. Charlie and Daniel deserved nothing less.

'OK?' Jago asked, glancing over at her. They'd changed into smarter outfits, knowing they would have no time later, and Jago was wearing a pale blue shirt and dark trousers, looking effortlessly handsome. She was in a silk blouse and navy skirt, her lowest possible heels.

'I'm fine,' she said. 'As fine as it's possible to be under the current circumstances. I'm glad you're here.' She squeezed his knee.

'I'm glad I'm here, too. Glad I could help.'

'And you don't think I should have stayed at the cottage

to make sure it's all being set up properly? Sent someone else with . . .' She stopped herself, took a deep breath. 'No, this is right. Rose is entirely capable of turning the garden into a wedding venue. I need to look after the bride and groom, and Daniel won't be arriving until later anyway, so . . .' She glanced at Jago. She had expected him to interrupt her, but he was watching the road, and he was smiling. 'Sometimes,' she continued, 'things just need to happen as they happen.'

He nodded. 'You planned for pretty much every scenario, except the ones where the barn flooded and Charlie got stranded. There will always be something to outfox you, but now, this wedding is a team effort, and Charlie and Daniel will have this story to tell for the rest of their lives. A mad dash across Cornwall to make it on time, and a sublime, summer wedding in one of the most beautiful gardens the county has to offer.'

'If it all happens like that,' Ellie pointed out.

'Have faith, Ellie. Of course it will.' She went back to looking out of the window, but she could tell Jago's smile hadn't faded.

Lila and Juliette were waiting outside the garage for them, Juliette's face pensive, Lila's dark eyes gleaming with excitement. They were both in simple, elegant, slip dresses, Lila's violet and Juliette's light blue. With their long dark hair and slim figures, they could have been twins. They had tiny white flowers woven into their hair, and were wearing delicate diamanté necklaces.

'Ellie, oh, my God!' Lila rushed over and hugged her. 'I can't believe this is happening! Why did Charlie leave it until yesterday to come back, anyway? She should have got Bonnie and Vince last week!' She rolled her eyes and then grinned. 'Still, it's exciting, isn't it?'

'*If* we make it back in time,' Juliette said, giving Ellie a quick embrace. 'If not, then it's going to be disastrous.'

'It's going to be epic,' Jago said. 'The disasters have been the barn flooding and Charlie getting stuck. They've happened; we can't go back in time to change them, but the good thing is we get to save the day. Hi.' He held out his hand.

Lila shook it, laughing. 'Who is this voice of reason?'

'This is Jago,' Ellie said. 'He's going to drive Gertie. And he also happens to be my boyfriend,' she added, feeling her cheeks go pink. 'Jago, this is Juliette and Delilah.'

Jago grinned. 'Good to meet you both,' he said. 'Shall we go and get on the bus?' He jangled a set of keys. 'Pete isn't here this morning, but I have all the access we need.'

He unlocked the side door and Ellie ushered Lila and Juliette into the garage. She had called Pete and explained what had happened, and he had apologized for not being available to go and get Charlie, but assured them it was fine for them to take Gertie, and he would meet them at Cornflower Cottage in time for the ceremony.

'Let me open up.' Jago walked to a large button on the wall and pressed it, and the garage's main door slid slowly upwards, daylight flooding the space. Gertie, who had been in shadow, was suddenly bathed in a pool of bright summer sunshine. And she was, Ellie realized on a sharp inhale, magnificent.

'Wow,' Juliette murmured.

'Fucking hell,' Lila agreed.

Jago just grinned.

Where before the vintage Routemaster had been a bold, shining red, she was now antique gold, her pristine exterior glittering as the door rose higher and higher, like a curtain lifting on a theatre stage. She still had *The Cornish Cream Tea Bus* emblazoned on the side, but this was in pearl white, with dark shadows that made the text look 3D, and between *Tea* and *Bus* the word *Wedding* had been written in a swirly font above, as if it was a scribbled addition – a quirky design feature that Ellie loved.

Bunting was strewn around the upper windows and looped from the large wing-mirrors, the colourful pennants just starting to flap as the sea breeze drifted in through the opening.

Lila clapped a hand to her mouth, and Ellie could see her eyes were bright with tears.

'She's beautiful,' Ellie said to Jago. 'God. You and Pete have done an amazing job.'

'We should get going,' Jago said.

'Yes,' Lila agreed, snapping out of her daze. 'Charlie must be going insane by now.'

They all climbed on board, Jago into the cab to acquaint himself with the controls, and the others at the downstairs tables. Gertie puttered to life, her engine throaty and strong. Ellie thought how far the bus had come since Liam had driven her away from Porthgolow beach on that fateful day, and all that had happened for her since then, too. A couple of months, and so much had changed.

Jago drove the bus out onto the road, pausing while Ellie jumped out and locked the garage up, and then they travelled through Newquay, the sand still dark, the storm having pushed the water beyond the usual tideline. As they drove north and inland, there were more signs of the weather's force – side-roads flooded, a few fields resembling lakes, some stretches of the main A road where Jago had to slow to a crawl for fear of aquaplaning. Lila and Juliette chatted away, their voices lifting with the added excitement the day had brought, and Ellie took the time to call Charlie, then Sam, then Rose.

Charlie and her parents had walked to a roadside café close to where their car had broken down, and were warming up with coffee and bacon sandwiches. Sam, who knew about Charlie's predicament, assured her that Daniel, who was still oblivious, was fine. Rose sounded completely in her element, telling Ellie she had absolutely nothing to worry about, and that she would hardly recognize the garden when they returned.

Feeling slightly easier, Ellie went to stand up front next to Jago, passing through the bus's tiny but immaculate kitchen to get there.

'Enjoying it?' she asked Jago.

He laughed. 'She's a beast. I'd forgotten what it was like, but I'm not too rusty, I don't think. And then there's all this.' He gestured out of the window just as a car coming the other way honked, its passengers waving madly at the golden bus. 'This is a lot of fun.'

Ellie grinned, waving as a child in a passing Honda pressed his face and palms to his window, staring up at them as they passed on the other side of the road.

'Thank you so much for doing this, Jago.'

'You can thank me later,' he murmured, and took the exit that would lead them to their bride.

* * *

'*Ellie!*' Charlie raced across the café's car park, her eyes almost comically wide. 'Oh, my God! You came in Gertie! She looks . . . she's . . . she . . .' Her words finally ran out, and she bent double, hands on her knees, but never taking her eyes off the bus.

'Are you OK?' Lila asked, hugging her.

'Look at Gertie,' Charlie said. 'Look at . . .'

'I know!' Lila laughed.

'Breathe, Charlie,' Juliette said, a hand on her shoulder. 'Deep breaths: in through the nose, out through the mouth.' She demonstrated, and Ellie remembered Charlie telling her that Juliette was a serious yogi. She calmed them all down and then ruined it by saying, 'Oh, my God, Charlie, you're getting married today!' and then jumping up and down.

Ellie went to introduce herself to Charlie's parents, Vince and Bonnie. Bonnie had similar features to Charlie, her hair dyed an even bolder shade of red than her daughter's, and Vince was wirily thin, with a narrow face and a mischievous gleam in his eyes. Ellie warmed to them instantly; they didn't seem remotely put out by the stressful morning they'd had.

'Look at Hal's bus,' Vince said to Ellie, rubbing his cheek distractedly. 'It's bloody amazing! Hal would have been so proud. He *is* proud, wherever he's ended up.'

It took ten minutes for Ellie and Jago to corral the party onto the bus, check that they'd left nothing behind in the café or in Charlie's car, and make sure the stricken vehicle was secure and in a spot it could stay in until later that day when, Jago assured Charlie, he would arrange for it to be picked up by another mechanic he knew.

'See,' he whispered to Ellie as they followed the others on board Gertie, 'there's no way I would have managed this without you.'

Ellie grinned. She had to concede that he was probably right.

The drive back with their rescued quarry was much more jubilant.

Charlie showed Jago how the sound system worked and they soon had party music playing, while Charlie, Lila and Juliette went to the top deck, the maids of honour shielding Charlie as much as possible from other road users while she got changed into her dress. Ellie wondered whether she would be the only bride in history to have got ready for her wedding day aboard a moving double-decker bus.

Ellie talked to Vince and Bonnie, getting to know them, hearing the story of how they had discovered Charlie's gran's wedding dress, perfectly preserved in a vacuum-packed bag amongst Hal's things.

'He was always a lot more careful than me,' Vince explained. 'Very particular about things. I didn't even know Mum's dress still existed.'

'And it fits Charlie like a dream,' Bonnie added, dabbing at her eyes with a tissue. 'Oh dear, we're not even there yet and I'm leaking.'

'You've had a very stressful morning,' Ellie said. 'It's no wonder you're extra emotional. Still, there are no limits on wedding-day tears. Especially not for the mother and father of the bride.'

They drove back towards the coast, the blue strip of the

shimmering Atlantic ocean like a beacon calling them home. Charlie laughed and squealed with her friends, and Lila produced a bottle of champagne from somewhere and managed to open it and pour it with only a minimum amount of spilling, and by the time they drove into Porthgolow the sun was high in the sky, the seaside village looking prime for one of Reenie's ten-thousand-likes Instagram photos, and the atmosphere on board the bus was definitely celebratory.

'One final stop,' Lila announced, and as she directed Jago into the beach car park, Ellie saw a stocky blond man, dressed in a sharp grey suit, walk across the road with Marmite, Jasper, and a scruffy white and tan dog that she didn't recognize, on leads at his feet. Vince and Bonnie peered out of the window and made cooing sounds.

'Hey all,' the man said, climbing on board. He greeted Bonnie and Vince, hugged Charlie and Lila and, finally, gave Juliette a kiss. 'I'm Lawrence,' he said to Ellie, shaking her hand. 'Juliette's husband. I've been dog-sitting.'

'Oh, Marmite,' Charlie said, hurrying down the bus to ruffle his fur. 'Jasper, Spirit.' She gave the other two the same attention. 'You look amazing.'

Ellie smiled and said, 'So do you.'

Lila nodded. 'Daniel is going to have an actual heart attack.'

Charlie did a little twirl, her eyes wide. Despite her chaotic morning, she looked, Ellie realized, as happy as any bride should.

'These are my new, borrowed and blue,' she said, gesturing at the dogs.

'What do you mean?' Ellie asked, frowning.

Charlie gestured to her dress. 'This is old. Marmite is new,' she pointed to the purple lacy ribbon he had round his neck. 'Spirit is borrowed.' The little dog Ellie hadn't met before was also wearing a lacy bow, but this one looked more delicate, the lace a cream colour as if it, too, was old.

'I borrowed it from the *Estelle* costume department,' Lila said. 'It's one of the ghost's accessories. It's still technically borrowing it even if you don't tell them, right?' She gave a wicked grin.

'So old, new, stolen and blue, then?' Lawrence chuckled.

'I'm giving it back,' Lila protested.

Ellie laughed and shook her head. 'And Jasper is blue.' It was self-evident, because his ribbon bow tie was the same shade as Juliette's maid-of-honour dress. 'What a brilliant idea.' More and more, she was coming to realize that this wedding, above all the others she had – and would – organize, was one she would never forget.

'Right then,' she said, clapping her hands together, as much to bring herself to attention as the others. 'Are we all present and correct?'

There was a chorus of 'yes!'

'Do we have everything we need?'

Another resounding shout in the affirmative.

'Charlie,' she said, turning to her. 'Are you ready to get married to your man?'

Charlie grinned, her eyes already shining with emotion. 'I am,' she said. 'Let's do this.'

Chapter Twenty-Five

Jago drove Gertie up Wilderness Lane, the low, throaty put-put-put of her engine somehow reassuring as they passed the flooded-out Porthgolow Barn, then Seascape House, and finally reached the turning into Cornflower Cottage. Jago slowed and made the turn, and Ellie saw that the vans from earlier had gone – the only vehicle a gleaming red Jaguar E-type – and that there was a crowd of people waiting on the driveway.

She recognized Reenie, dressed in an elegant navy dress, and Chloe from the hotel. There was a man and woman holding tightly to two little girls, a boy of about fourteen hovering just behind them. A glamorous couple dressed like something out of a Hollywood film from the Forties– her blonde and pale skinned, him black and tall – were standing next to the woman who'd served Ellie the bottle of sparkling wine in the Pop-In shop. There was a hand-some older couple close to her rose bushes, the man with the same confident bearing as Daniel, the resemblance

354

striking. Standing in the front, alongside Hannah and Noah, was Sam, looking film-star attractive in his best man suit, his dark blond hair catching the sun. And then there was the groom.

Ellie could see Daniel's nervous energy shimmering just below the surface, his dark eyes glittering with something that went much deeper than his usual, laid-back charm. His suit was a dusky grey, the waistcoat beneath sky blue, and the buttonhole a perfect yellow rose. Dapper didn't even come close.

'Stay back there, Charlie,' she said, as Jago pulled the bus to a halt and she turned to face the small but expectant wedding party. 'We don't want anyone to see you until the last minute. Jago and I will get off first, then Lawrence, then Vince and Bonnie, and then you two, Lila and Juliette, in front of Charlie. Ready?'

'Ready,' they all replied, but it was only Charlie she was looking to for confirmation.

Ellie and Jago stepped off the bus, and Ellie went to check on the groom. 'Daniel,' she said, 'you look wonderful.'

He gave her a nervous smile. 'I understand your trouble-shooting's been in overdrive this morning.'

'You're not meant to know about *anything*,' she chided. 'Except, obviously, the change of venue. It has all gone swimmingly – though maybe that's not the best word to use,' she added, thinking of the barn.

He laughed and shook his head. 'Ellie, what you've pulled out of the bag here, and at impossibly short notice . . .' He gestured to the garden, partly visible through the open gate, and then the bus.

'All that matters is that you like it, that you're happy to

have your wedding here, and that Charlie has turned up –
which she most definitely has!'

'Thank God.' He took a deep breath. 'I am more than
happy to get married to Charlie here, and Sam's even
remembered the rings.'

As Daniel looked at him, Sam's smile turned into a horrified grimace, and he pressed a hand to his jacket pocket.

Daniel stiffened for a second, then smiled. 'You fucker.'

Sam grinned and clasped Daniel's shoulder. 'Ready for
this, old man?'

'One hundred per cent,' Daniel said, his eyes sliding back
to the bus. 'Charlie is all I want.'

'Then let's bring her out,' Ellie said softly.

Lawrence jumped off the bus, and went to stand next to
Reenie, and then Charlie's mum and dad stepped down.
Ellie had been surprised and delighted by their bold outfits:
Vince's suit was petrol blue, and Bonnie was in fuchsia
pink, which complemented her creamy skin and bold make-
up, and somehow worked against her bright red hair. They
were in charge of the canine trio, the dolled-up dogs drawing
laughter and murmurs of adoration from the crowd.

Lila and Juliette were next, walking elegantly off the bus
in their stylish dresses, and now carrying posies of tightly
budded roses in vintage pink. Ellie caught Sam's look of
pride when Lila emerged and gave him a cheeky wink, then
Charlie's two friends stood either side of the door.

Every pair of eyes was trained on the bus, the murmuring
falling away to nothing. Charlie appeared in the doorway,
and Ellie stifled a smile as she heard Daniel's unchecked
gasp.

Charlie Quilter was a princess on her wedding day; a

356

flawless princess with beauty and character and an air of happy confidence it was impossible to miss.

Her red hair was in tousled curls, pulled away from her face and secured with delicate rosebud clips, and her bouquet was a larger version of Lila and Juliette's, but with hot pink roses amongst the paler blooms. Her grandmother's wedding dress had a silk skirt that fell to her ankles, with delicate beading detail, and the ivory, heart-shaped bodice was overlaid with lace, which covered her shoulders and arms in three-quarter length sleeves. A diamanté choker sat daintily on her collarbone, and her earrings were tiny, sparkling hearts.

Ellie had seen hundreds of brides, and every one treated their wedding-day appearance – whether in the doorway of a church or register office, in a hotel entrance, on a beach or in a wooded glade – differently. Charlie looked poised standing in Gertie's doorway, but when she caught Daniel's eye, her face broke out into the biggest grin, and she laughed and waved, her whole body radiating delight.

'Charlie.' Daniel stepped forward, his voice choked when he said, 'You made it.'

'Just about,' she laughed.

He held her waist and lifted her gently to the ground, whispering something in her ear that was just for the two of them. His actions broke the spell, and there were cheers and wolf-whistles and exclamations, and an early smattering of some of the natural confetti Ellie had bought and which Rose must have already put out.

Mary, the celebrant, separated herself from the crowd and held out her arms. 'If you'd all like to take your seats in the garden,' she said, and as the guests filed through the gate, she went to greet Charlie and Daniel. Ellie hovered at the back, making sure everyone found their way, and as Jago walked past he squeezed her hand.

'We did it,' she whispered, leaning in close.

'We did,' he agreed, his green eyes dancing.

Ellie was the last through the gate, and she took a moment to absorb the transformation her garden had undertaken. Chairs were laid out on the patio in rows, facing the flower beds and with an aisle down the middle. At the head of it was the arbour from Porthgolow Barn. The honeysuckles and climbing rose were trailed around it, and someone had added a string of white fairy lights.

The back of her cottage was adorned with the flower garlands from the barn, and the bottles full of lights were standing against the wall: they would look like clusters of fireflies as soon as it got dark. There was one other, rather unexpected thing that had also made its way up the hill, standing off to the side of the garden, being chaperoned by a smiling Arthur and Pauline.

'*Millicent!*' Charlie squealed. 'You made it!' She let go of Daniel's hand and hurried – as much as she could in her floor-length dress – over to the pig, who was shiny pink and entirely mud-free. She bent and rubbed Millicent's forehead, and then tottered to the back of the chairs, where her dad was waiting for her.

All the guests had taken their seats, Mary was standing in front of the arbour, Daniel and Sam facing her, and Charlie and Vince, Juliette and Lila were waiting at the back.

Charlie had wanted no music for her walk up the aisle, even when they'd been planning for the barn, and so, with

358

Juliette and Lila ahead of her, and Vince at her side, she walked between the rows of guests to the sound of birdsong, and the gentle rustling of the breeze through the trees. She reached Daniel's side, and the two of them stood in front of Mary.

Ellie leaned against the wall of the cottage, Jago alongside her and close enough that she could feel the warmth of his body, as Mary welcomed the guests, and invited them to celebrate the union of Charlene Quilter and Daniel Harper.

When they turned to face each other, to say their vows, Charlie shot her friends and family an excited grin. There wasn't a hint of nerves or shadow of apprehension on her face. She seemed giddy with happiness.

'Charlie Quilter,' Daniel said, his confident voice carrying easily, 'from the very first day I met you, I wanted to say yes to everything you asked of me. It was an overwhelming feeling, one I wasn't used to, and so, being the contrary man I am, I decided to say no, instead. But I will never regret those early days, the times when I infuriated you – sometimes on purpose, sometimes not – because, in the end, they brought us closer: they brought us to today. And I am ready to make it up to you. I will try my best to say yes to you every day, in any way I can; to make you happy, to make you proud, and to fill our small corner of Cornwall with love and kindness. You have taught me to be that way, Charlie, and I will work constantly to get better at it. I love you, and I can't wait to spend the rest of my life with you.'

His vows were followed by silence, and then a sob. Ellie glanced at the guests, and saw that Lila was crying openly.

Her eyes weren't the only dry ones, but she wasn't even trying to hold back her emotion.

Charlie took a deep breath, her eyes glistening as she started to speak. 'Daniel Harper, you are my missing piece. You make my life complete, just by being by my side. I was attracted to your confidence, and the kindness and generosity you sometimes try to hide made me stay. We didn't have the easiest start, but every moment of adversity has made what we have now even sweeter. I promise that I will do all I can to be an equal partner in our marriage, not to interfere too much with your hotel, to walk the dogs at least half the time and to rescue you from cliff tops whenever you need it.' Daniel's smile turned wistful, and Ellie remembered the story Lila had told her about how the two of them had got together. 'I will even stroke your ego occasionally, though, to be honest, I don't think I'll need to do it too often.'

Daniel burst out laughing, the most uninhibited Ellie had ever seen him.

'I will spend every day from now until the end of time doing my best to make you happy,' Charlie continued. 'As happy as you make me. You are my happy place, Daniel, and this is the best day of my life.'

Now even Ellie was tearful, and she could see Rose – standing with Arthur, Mo, Iris, Pauline, Jane and Millicent – wiping her eyes with a tissue. Was this wedding more emotional because it had been such an effort to get here? Was it because it was taking place in the garden she loved so much, or was it simply that Charlie and Daniel were one of the loveliest couples she'd worked with? Ellie didn't know, but whatever it was, she was glad she was here, witnessing this moment.

When Mary announced that Daniel and Charlie were man and wife, and that they could kiss, the quaint garden of Cornflower Cottage erupted; everyone stood and cheered, their arms in the air, confetti raining down. Through the blur of petals, Daniel cupped Charlie's face and kissed her as if he never wanted to stop.

Photos followed the ceremony, one of Ellie's trusted wedding photographers, Sven Holden, setting up shots of the happy couple and various combinations of the bridal party – almost always including the dogs – in front of Ellie's blooming flower beds. The dahlias that Arthur had planted acted as a particularly beautiful backdrop, as did the front of the cottage, with its rose bushes, sea view and, of course, Gertie in all her celebratory pomp.

While that was happening, Ellie worked with Jago, Rose, Pauline and Jane to change the seating layout, arranging the tables on the patio. Jago had positioned Ellie's sound system on the kitchen windowsill and selected a party playlist, while Hannah, Hugh and Noah prepared the food.

The guests chatted and drank champagne, and the teenage boy, Jonah, swirled one of his younger sisters around in time to the music, her yellow fairy dress spinning in a circle around her. The smallest girl tiptoed over to Lord Montague, who was sitting imperiously at the edge of the grass, watching events unfold with a scowl.

'Oh, shit!' Ellie hurried towards her, but before she could get close the girl plonked her hand on Monty's head. She waited for the swipe to come, but her cat submitted to the rough handling, nudging his nose along the girl's arm and closing his eyes in ecstasy.

361

'Lord Montague loves children,' Jago said. 'Who knew?'

Ellie narrowed her eyes. 'Is it that? Or have you infected my grumpy cat with your extreme nonchalance?'

'What does it matter, as long as he's behaving himself?' Jago grinned, his eyes crinkling at the edges, and Ellie had to use all her willpower to resist kissing him. She was working, after all, even if romance was firmly on the agenda.

With the photos taken, the food was served, everyone tucking in to the dishes Hannah had created. There were mini cones of battered cod and triple-cooked chips; bite-sized beef, chicken, and mushroom burgers with a homemade onion relish, and individual portions of the famous Seven Stars' fish pie served in pastel ramekins.

The sky stayed steadfastly blue, while the breeze burned off what remained of the previous night's storm, as if there hadn't been a single drop of rain. Ellie helped Hannah and Noah serve, made subtle rounds checking that everyone – but mostly the bride and groom – had all they needed, and made sure the next steps – the speeches, the cake-cutting, the band and the first dance – were teed up.

She was in her element, keeping an eagle eye on proceedings while the guests laughed and joked, congratulated and hugged, ate and drank in the sun-soaked garden.

The speeches came next. Vince was candid and kind, and gave Charlie's uncle Hal a special mention. Hal and Charlie had been close, Gertie the legacy he left her in his will, and so he was still a huge part of her life and success. Charlie insisted Hal get his own toast, and everyone stood and raised their glasses, the moment punctuated by a chaffinch's song.

Sam followed, his acting skills coming to the fore as he

made a funny and generous speech about Daniel, his words light as a feather after the emotional tribute to Charlie's uncle. Daniel was last, his jacket discarded to fully show off the sky-blue waistcoat, his dark hair slightly ruffled. He treated the guests to a dramatic, self-deprecating retelling of the accident that had risked his life and secured his and Charlie's feelings for each other. He gave Sam a run for his money, adding tension in all the right places, and Ellie could tell the crash had been serious, even though he focused on Charlie and the bus, the way they had rescued him and the happy outcome.

The delicious food had filled their bellies, and the words of Charlie and Daniel's loved ones, and Daniel himself, filled their hearts. Everyone seemed fully sated, the mood in the garden softening, when Lila got to her feet and cleared her throat.

'And now,' she announced, 'we have a surprise! Another course before the cake. This is our present to you, Charlie and Daniel, from me, Hannah, Sam and Noah.'

'What is it?' Charlie turned to Daniel, but he shrugged.

'It's the Charlie and Daniel Harper Wedding Cream Tea,' Hannah said, carrying a vintage cake stand to the happy couple's table. It was only the sweet elements of the Cornish cream tea, Ellie knew, because she'd discussed it with Hannah in advance. There was a mini lemon tart designed to look like the sun, gingerbread biscuits in the shape of Marmite and Jasper, the biscuity dogs easily recognizable, and tiny Victoria sponges shaped like Gertie, as well as luxury fruit scones with candied fruit, served with a lemon clotted cream and strawberry jam. There was a cake stand for each table, enough for every guest to have one of each treat.

'I wanted to add some kind of ghost-shaped dessert,' Lila said, 'to recognize Crystal Waters' reputation as an officially haunted hotel, but Sam thought it would cut too close to the bone.'

Charlie laughed, and Daniel rolled his eyes. 'I would have relished eating it,' he said. 'Audrey's book came out on Thursday, with all the details of our Christmas ghost-hunting adventure, and so far we haven't had any complications at the hotel.' Charlie gave him a sharp look and he held his hands up. 'Not that I've been checking up on Crystal Waters. I mean, up until Wednesday, when I handed responsibility over to Chloe.'

Charlie narrowed her eyes at him, then planted a kiss on the end of his nose, seemingly satisfied.

Ellie knew this story too; about how a researcher had investigated the hotel over Christmas, discovered that it was still occupied by the ghosts of previous guests, and was publishing a book with a whole chapter dedicated to the Porthgolow hauntings. She had secretly been looking forward to reading it, but hadn't admitted it to Charlie and Daniel.

'But this . . .' Daniel went on, gesturing to the beautiful cake displays. 'You've gone to so much effort.'

'It's delicious, too.' Charlie broke a Marmite gingerbread in half and popped it in her mouth. 'So delicious. Wow, Hannah, Lila. And you two,' she added, pointing at Sam and Noah. 'I can't believe you did this for us, so we could have a cream tea at our wedding.'

'And *not* have to make it,' Lila added. 'That's the important thing.'

'After this, I'm not feeling quite so worried about the

honeymoon.' Daniel leaned back in his chair and gave Lila an easy grin.

'Where are you going, Mr and Mrs Harper?' Ellie asked, and Charlie flushed with pleasure.

'That's the thing,' she said, 'we don't know. Lila told us we weren't allowed to organize it, because she didn't think we'd actually ever leave, so she's booked us somewhere for two weeks, and we have no idea what we're doing.'

'Wow!' Ellie raised her eyebrows. 'That is some trust.'

'Especially in Lila,' Daniel said, and Lila hit his arm.

'It's OK.' Sam grinned. 'I was involved too, so it isn't *completely* barmy.'

'Very reassuring,' Charlie said, and blew a kiss at her cousin.

Ellie left them to their cream teas and their easy conversation, to their post-anxiety bliss now that most of the logistics were done with, nobody had abandoned anyone else at the altar, and they were happier than they had believed they could be. Ellie had put Daniel's photo album in the living room, had let Charlie know it was there, and wondered if she would give it to him publicly, or wait until they were alone.

The sun began its descent towards the sea, and Charlie and Daniel cut the lemon cake strewn with delicate icing-daisies, while everyone stood and cheered, and Jonah prevented his younger sister Flora from throwing more confetti and making the light, delicious sponge decidedly less palatable.

While Jago, Rose and Mo moved the chairs and tables to the side of the patio and Hugh and his Cornwall Cornflowers set up their band, Ellie went into the kitchen and switched on the extension cable that connected the trails and bottles of fairy lights. They were lost in the afternoon sun, but as dusk crept over the garden, they would turn the patio into a rustic, twinkling ballroom. Not as hi-tech as the barn's panelled disco floor, or the glitter ball, but at least it was something.

She stepped outside and saw a swirling pattern of coloured lights dancing across the flagstones. The two young girls, Jem and Flora, jumped up and down, chasing the beams. Confused, Ellie looked up and saw a small glitter ball secured to the edge of the roof.

'Oh, my goodness!' Charlie pressed her hands to her chest. 'We've actually got a glitter ball? Ellie, thank you! How did you manage this?'

'I didn't,' she admitted. 'It isn't me you need to thank.' She spotted who she thought must be the culprit standing at the edge of the lawn, talking to Arthur, his expression unguarded.

'Well, whoever is responsible, you've worked miracles. I can't thank you enough for today.' Charlie pulled Ellie into a hug. 'Not only did you come to my rescue, but your garden is magical, and in lots of ways it's even better than the barn. It means so much that you let us get married here.'

'It was my pleasure,' Ellie said. 'I'm so happy it's all worked out.'

'Worked out is an understatement.' Daniel followed his new wife's example and gave Ellie a quick embrace. 'It's been better than I hoped.'

'There's a lot of it left to go,' Ellie pointed out. 'Including your first dance. Ready?'

Charlie and Daniel looked at each other, and then back at her, and nodded.

The Cornwall Cornflowers played the first bars of 'Loving You' by Seafret as the sky began to fade from bright to dusky blue, and the lights dotted around the garden shimmered to life. Daniel and Charlie stood in the centre of the patio, their arms wrapped around each other, the glitter ball dusting them with twinkling confetti. They began moving in time to the music, gazing at each other as if they were the only two people in the whole of Porthgolow.

At that moment, Ellie knew the wedding had been a success. If the bride and groom were comfortable enough to act like they were already on their honeymoon, then she'd created a day they would remember for all the right reasons.

Slowly, other people joined them on the makeshift dance floor. Sam and Lila, Juliette and Lawrence, Hannah and Noah. Ellie watched, her surprise far outweighed by her happiness, as Mo led Rose onto the patio, her sister looking like the cat who'd got the cream, and then Pauline and Arthur joined them, Arthur more at ease than Ellie had ever seen him.

She was content to watch, the adrenaline that had kept her going through problem after problem, fix after fix, fading to weariness. Was it really the same day she'd walked down the hill and found a swamp inside the barn? She knew the venue would recover, that once they had their flood-proofing in place they had a real chance of being successful. She would check in with Jane and Pauline on

Monday, make sure they were both OK after the upheaval and disappointment of today. She got her phone out to add a reminder to it, but a warm hand clamped over hers, then took her phone away.

'Do you *still* need to be working?' Jago said softly. 'You can relax now; it's been the perfect day.'

'Mainly because Charlie got her glitter ball, after all. Where did you find it?'

He grinned at her, his green eyes bright under the twinkling lights. 'In one of the boxes I hadn't unpacked. I remembered that a friend had bought it for me when I settled in Plymouth. I'd told him that nothing could match the stars in Africa, and he said he'd got it to make me feel more at home. Completely tongue in cheek, of course – I'm not exactly the target market for a glitter ball. I just never got around to getting rid of it.'

'Well, it looks beautiful, and Charlie's so happy.'

Jago squeezed her hand. 'Come with me.' He led her away from the patio, further into the garden.

'Where are we going?' she asked, her hand brushing the delicate petals of a dahlia as she passed it.

'There's something that's been forgotten in all the magic of today.'

'Ah,' Ellie said, as they wove between flower beds towards the meadow, the pale grass almost glowing in the inky twilight.

'What do you mean, "ah"?'

'The bastard bee orchid.' She pointed to where it stood, tall and proud, still easy to spot despite the fading light.

'I did think we needed to pay it a visit,' he said, 'because of what it represents. But that wasn't what I was talking about.'

'Oh? How's your dad? I saw you chatting to him earlier.'

'He's good,' Jago said. Ellie expected him to keep his gaze averted, so she couldn't read his expression, but he turned to face her, his smile uninhibited. 'We've decided to go back to some of our old haunts together; some of the places we used to go as a family. Falmouth, Trebah Garden, a couple of places near Tintagel. Sort of revisit the past, talk about Mum but also . . . I don't know. Create new memories.' He shrugged. 'Anyway, you're getting me off topic. I wasn't talking about Dad, either.'

'Who were you talking about, then?' Ellie stepped towards him. The band had moved onto a jauntier song, and she wanted to hear him properly.

'Who do you think?' Jago cupped her chin, and tilted her head up.

'You?' Ellie murmured, her lips inches from his.

'Wrong again,' he said. 'It's you, Ellie. The way we are together, the way you make me feel, I think it always was. You've been my destiny from the very beginning, I just had to come and find you, waiting on the side of the road, with your car overheated and that slightly cool, professional attitude, and your insistence that you were nothing like Nora Batty. I can say it again if you want. You are *nothing* like Nora Batty.'

'That's a very impressive speech,' she whispered. 'Almost the best one I've heard today.'

'Not quite the best, then?' Jago raised an eyebrow, and Ellie bit her lip, holding in her laughter. 'OK then,' he continued, when she didn't reply. 'Let's see if I can move it into first place.' And with that, he brought his lips down onto hers, kissing her with so much purpose that Ellie wondered how she'd ever thought of him as laid-back.

As Charlie and Daniel's wedding continued in the garden of Cornflower Cottage, as they danced and laughed and drank, and the Porthgolow sunset came into its own, competing with the glitter ball and the twinkling lights twisted around the arbour, Elowen Moon realized that this was, in fact, the perfect day. And she hadn't created it all by herself; it had been a collective effort of guests and helpers, the newly married couple and their friends and family, Hannah and Noah, Mo and Rose, Pauline, Jane, Arthur and Jago.

Ellie had spent the last few years trying her best to be independent, to find her own, solitary space in the world, but it turned out that happiness was a family affair, and it didn't matter if that family was one you'd been born into, or one you'd hand-picked for yourself: what mattered was that it was yours.

She leant into Jago and kissed him back, while the bee orchid danced in the whispering breeze and the stars above them flickered on one by one. It was at that moment that the first of the fireworks brightened the night sky; a pop and rush, followed by an umbrella of golden glitter that, when she raised her eyes and looked out towards the sea, was drifting down to the horizon like fairy dust.

Ellie decided that, as Cornish weddings went, this one might be her favourite yet.

Acknowledgements

I loved escaping from the real world to write this book, but – as always – it wasn't just a one-woman job. If I was renewing my vows, then all the following people would be on the guest list.

Kate Bradley, my wonderful editor and friend, for her constant encouragement and humour. She always knows exactly what my story and characters need to take them to the next level of romantic, escapist happiness.

Agent extraordinaire, Hannah Ferguson, for supporting me, being a voice of reason, and for always championing me and my books. I feel on such solid ground having her in my corner and ditto with the whole Hardman and Swainson team.

I am so lucky to have the HarperFiction team working on my books. Thank you for turning my words into beautiful, enticing paperbacks and making sure, even in these challenging times, that they find readers. Thank you to Lara Stevenson for all her help – for being so quick, efficient, and kind. Thank you to Penny Isaac for her brilliant copyediting skills, for her ability to both zoom in and see the wider picture, and for her generous words. Thank you to designer, Holly MacDonald, and illustrator, May Van Millingen, for the stunning covers which are a large part of the reason my books get picked up from shelves or clicked on online.

There would be a special table for writer friends at the vow renewal ceremony. Even from afar, I have had so much support and laughter from writer pals, and I'm not sure what I would do without any of them. All the BookCampers – I cannot wait to see you again in person – and Shelia Crighton and Penny Thorpe, who have been the best virtual cheerleaders.

To friends and family who have filled the gaps in-between, especially Kate and Tim, Kate G, Katy C and Kelly.

Obviously, David would be at the ceremony. The whole thing would be pointless without him, and that's how I feel about life in general. He is the original and best romantic hero inspiration, who has made the last, strange year not just bearable but fun. I am the luckiest person in the world to have him as my Mr McLaughlin.

To Mum, Dad and Lee, who I have spent a lot of the last year missing terribly, but who are always there on the phone or FaceTime, and let me ramble on for hours about books – mine and other people's. They don't just support me, they inspire me, and I am so lucky to have them.

Last but not least, thanks to the readers and bloggers who contact me on social media and through my website. There is nothing better than getting a message from someone who loves your books – especially when you're stuck in a plot hole or nothing seems to be working – reminding you that you can actually do this. To hear that my books have given readers some much-needed escape in these difficult times is the biggest compliment I could ever get. Thank you for reading my books, and please keep getting in touch. I really hope The Cornish Cream Tea Wedding brings you some joy.

Discover more delightful fiction
from Cressida McLaughlin.
All available now.

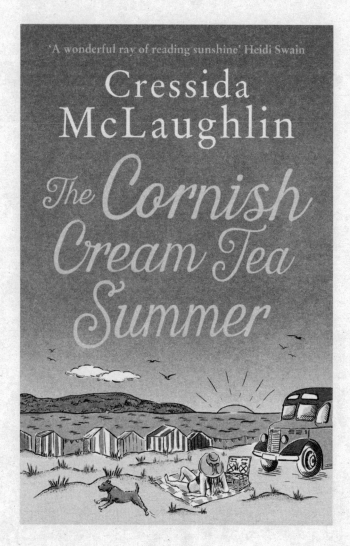

Cressida McLaughlin

The Cornish Cream Tea Summer

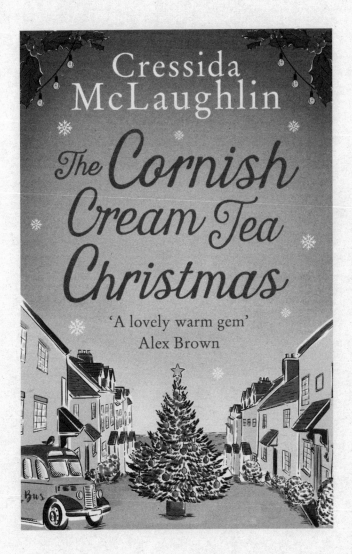

Cressida
McLaughlin

The Cornish
Cream Tea
Christmas

'A lovely warm gem'
Alex Brown